Also by

MINDY KLASKY

and Red Dress Ink

Sorcery and the Single Girl
Girl's Guide to Witchcraft

Magic and the Modern Girl

MINDY KLASKY

RED
DRESS
INK
TM

MAGIC AND THE MODERN GIRL

A Red Dress Ink novel

ISBN-13: 978-0-373-89577-9
ISBN-10:   0-373-89577-1

www.RedDressInk.com

Printed in U.S.A.

To Joan Craft and Melissa Jurgens—
every witch should have
friends like you to stand beside her

ACKNOWLEDGMENTS

In the end, colleagues, friends and family are responsible for the continued existence of Jane Madison—my crazy witch-librarian would not live inside these pages if not for the support and guidance of many wonderful people.

Countless thanks to all of the "book" people who not only kept Jane alive, but who made her experiences richer and more complete. Richard Curtis continues to win the award for most supportive agent ever; I could not write without his frequent and generous gifts of time, career guidance and moral support. The Red Dress Ink crew has been phenomenal as always. Mary-Theresa Hussey, Margaret Marbury, Elizabeth Mazer, Adam Wilson, everyone who works so hard behind the scenes— I cannot thank you enough!

As always, I owe thanks to the "library" people who worked beside me throughout this book's creation—the library staff at SNR are some of the finest professionals I've ever had the privilege to work with. Thank you for welcoming me into your lives and for supporting me through Writing Marathons, National Library Week and hosts of other evils.

My family has been there every step of the way as well—Klaskys and Timmins and Maddreys and Fallons, who always are ready with a phone call or a recipe or a letter to let me know that they support me on this crazy road.

Mark continues to be my anchor, day in and day out, as I plot my way through sometimes stormy writing seas. I could never play this writing game without his constant, unquestioning support. I simply cannot thank him enough.

To correspond with me and keep track of my writing life, please visit my Web site at www.mindyklasky.com.

1

Computers are the modern world's way of controlling witches.

No need for burning at the stake. No need for hanging. No need for crosses and prayers and good citizens of Salem driving elderly women from their midst because butter won't set. Just give a witch a computer, and watch her magical abilities come to naught.

I stared at the blue screen of death on my library computer and swore softly under my breath. This could not be happening to me. Not now. Not when I had spent the past six hours composing a brilliant—if I do say so myself—presentation about the James River plantations and their impact on the growth of colonial America. Without saving the file. Even once.

I should have known better.

After all, I'd been a reference librarian at the Peabridge Library for long enough that I knew my ancient computer couldn't be trusted. In the past year, we'd only had the budget to upgrade three of our machines—the sleek new ones used by our patrons at the public access desk.

I knew better. I should have saved every single word. Only a fool would have gone on for more than a page without protecting herself. I had just gotten so wrapped up in my work—for the first time in weeks—that I'd forgotten. Now, the mouse was dead. The keyboard was dead. The entire computer was locked up.

And the worst part was, I knew what I had to do. I knew that I had to press the power button, turn off the damn machine and lose whatever brilliance lurked inside what passed for its silicon mind. I'd be lucky if it kept my title page: Jane Madison, Reference Librarian, Peabridge Library, Washington, D.C.

I felt as stupid and as frustrated as when my ancient laptop froze, six months before. At least the laptop was at home, in the cottage that I enjoyed as a rent-free perk from my under-paying library job. I could rant and rave there, threatening to throw the metal-and-silicon doorstop out the window, knowing that I had the privacy of colonial gardens to spare me from disapproving neighbors' delicate ears.

And to think, I'd hesitated to accept living in the cottage two years before. Of course, at the time, I hadn't known that there was a treasure trove of books on witchcraft lurking in the basement. And, of course, I'd had no idea that *I* was actually a witch, capable of using those books. I would certainly have embraced the idea of the cottage a lot sooner if I'd known those little details.

Even if I'd known the heartbreak my laptop would cause when my entire, carefully constructed catalog of witch's books disappeared into the electronic ether with one computer-based blue screen of death a few months ago.

Yeah, I should have learned to be wary of computers on that deceptively mild spring day. But I'd told myself that the catalog disaster had been inevitable. I'd created the listing on my ex-fiancé's computer, and the stupid machine was cluttered with bad memories and no-one-knew-how-many electronic viruses.

At least I'd found a silver lining in that catalog destruction. I'd needed a break from my witchcraft studies. After taking a year to figure out that I actually *was* a witch, and another year to discover that I never, ever wanted to be a member of the snooty local coven, I'd spent six months totally immersed in my esoteric supplies.

I had organized bags of runes. I had stacked boxes of crystals. I had refined my original book catalog, not once, not twice, but three times, creating a system that was so carefully cross-referenced, I could find any one of my possessions in a heartbeat.

Losing that catalog on the laptop, though, had brought me back to my senses. I mean, witchcraft didn't pay the bills. I needed to devote some energy to my day job, to the Peabridge, if I ever wanted to get ahead in the fiscal world. Even if the library was less and less my dream job and more and more the place where I showed up to work, so that I got a paycheck every two weeks.

The weeks had slid together, clumped into months. How much time had gone by? Could it actually be six months since I'd worked a spell? Was it really already August? I shook my head and felt my mobcap shift on my humidity-challenged hair.

Yeah. A mobcap. You know, those muslin caps that milk-maids wore in the eighteenth century? Deporting me to the cottage had not been my boss's only cost-savings measure. All of us librarians wore colonial costume to help bring in patrons (and with patrons, hopefully, dollars). And I was lucky enough to serve as the library's barista as well, mixing overpriced coffee drinks for our eager researchers.

At least I'd managed to eliminate the frothy cappuccinos and time-consuming lattes from our caffeine repertoire. We'd reduced our offerings to hot tea, hot coffee, and—for a few select patrons—a shot of chocolate syrup, to make a mocha. We compensated for the change in beverage service by offering up baked goods—delicious cookies, brownies and cakes created by my best friend, Melissa White.

Melissa, in fact, was number one on my speed dial. She would understand my disappointment about my library pre-sentation computer disaster. Still glaring at my peacock-blue monitor, I picked up my phone. One ring. Two. Three. She must be helping some customer in her increasingly popular bakery. "Cake Walk," she finally answered, just as I was considering hanging up.

"Mojito therapy," I said.

"I am already there," she replied, and I remembered that the bakery had to be hotter than the library, even more uncomfortable in the middle of Washington's August humidity. I could picture her blowing her honey-colored bangs out of her eyes as she asked, "Your air conditioner or mine?"

I looked at my watch. It was already a quarter to five. Melissa's underpowered window unit would take hours to cool down her second-story apartment. "Mine. I'm off work in fifteen minutes."

"See you there."

We hung up our phones simultaneously. And then, there was nothing left for me to do but turn off the power. Lose the entire afternoon's work. I sighed. Monday would be another day, and I could write about the James River plantations then. Maybe even faster than I had today. With more brilliant observations. Or at least a better flow of thought.

I made short work of straightening my desk, then ran a clean rag over the coffee bar. The Peabridge had been quiet as a tomb all afternoon—most of Washington took vacation during the late summer. I waved at my boss but did not take time to poke my head into her office; Evelyn could snare me into chatting for hours.

At least my commute was short. One brick path through the colonial garden, and I was slipping my key into the lock, opening the cottage's door onto my living room of hunter-green sofas and a braided rug. I kicked off my shoes and loosened the ties on my dress, easing my whalebone stays as I made a beeline for the freezer.

A pint of New York Super Fudge Chunk waited for me. Ben and Jerry were calling my name, promising to ease my frustration, to soothe my savage brow. They were whispering sweet comforts about my computer woes, offering up smooth, creamy sympathy.

Except the freezer was empty.

Oh, a few partly evaporated ice cubes sat forlorn in their trays. And a couple of chicken breasts were camouflaged beneath coats of ice crystals. But Ben and Jerry were nowhere to be found.

Until I checked the trash can.

The pint container was licked clean.

"Neko!"

I don't know why I even bothered to say my familiar's name. Ever since I had awakened him, releasing him from his magical form as a huge statue of a black cat, he had plagued me with his saucy attitude. Nothing was private in my cottage—nothing was secret in my life. And my kitchen was most violated of all.

It was a wonder I still spoke to the guy. Actually, truth be told, we'd spent a good part of the past two months *not* speaking to each other. Even our Post-it notes had gotten shorter, more terse:

Neko, if you're going to drink the last of the milk, please leave a note on the fridge so that I can buy more. Love, Jane.

Jane, I wouldn't drink that blue water if it was the last dairy item on earth. I poured it down the drain to spare you the horror. Buy a gallon of whole milk. Love, Neko.

N—Don't touch the leftover chicken; it's my lunch for tomorrow. J.

J—So sorry. Only saw the "don't" after Jacques and I had a little post-romp sustenance. Kisses. N.

Do NOT eat the caramel ice cream.

Jacques ate it, not me.

NO!!!!!

Whoops!

It was that *whoops* that got me. I mean, anyone could have seen the *NO* note I'd attached to the plate of Melissa's cream puffs. She'd brought them as a special treat one morning, when she'd carried in the library's standing order of sweets. I'd written my warning with letters three inches high, underlined them three times, and added five exclamation marks for entirely unnecessary emphasis. But obviously, I should have added a French translation, just for security. Just so that my nervy familiar could not (again) place the blame on his French lover, on poor, besotted Jacques.

Those cream puffs had been the last straw. I couldn't share my little cottage with Neko and Jacques any longer. It was time that I sent my familiar out into the world—at least while we weren't working magic together. He could find his own milk and chicken and—God save the fish market— tuna.

He would still be bound to me magically. He'd still come when I summoned him to work a spell. He'd just be free to pursue his own entertainment the rest of the time. Win-win, right? Especially since I hadn't found the time to cast a spell in ages.

So, rather than mourn my missing New York Super Fudge Chunk, I told myself to celebrate. After all, that was the last time Neko would raid my freezer. Ever. I'd almost convinced myself of that rationale when Melissa sailed through my front door, swinging a net bag of limes and a carefully wrapped forest of mint, freshly cut from her extensive herb garden. She balanced a plate in her other hand, carefully covered with tin foil.

"What's this?" I asked, relieving her of the burden.

"Lemon Pillows." Citrus-flavored whipped cream cheese, cradled in crunchy meringue. Perfect for the beastly hot weather.

"Thank God you're here," I said.

"Go change out of those clothes, and then we can talk."

I took her up on the offer, stripping off my colonial attire in short order. One black T-shirt and a pair of well-worn shorts later, I was almost feeling human again. Almost.

"You are a goddess," I said, returning to the kitchen, where cocktail construction was already well under way. I wolfed down a Pillow, moaning a little as the sweet-tart lemon flavor melted across my tongue.

Melissa shrugged. "I couldn't find our usual pitcher, but I figured this would work." She held up a glass bottle that had formerly held orange juice. She'd already managed to pour fresh-squeezed lime juice from a measuring cup into the narrow neck, and she was coaxing cut mint leaves in, as well.

"Oh, the pitcher should be right—" I cut myself off as I opened up the cupboard to the right of the sink. No pitcher. No clear glass with brightly colored fish on the side. "Neko," I said.

"Today's the day?" Melissa asked.

"And not a moment too soon. He was supposed to get all his stuff out of the basement this morning. Jacques helped him while I was at work."

"It'll be strange around here for a while. No roommate, after two straight years?"

"I welcome the strangeness," I said. I squatted in front of the sink, reaching to the very back of the storage space for my bottle of rum. After a certain episode of *The Not-So-Mystery of the Disappearing Vodka* around Independence Day, I'd taken to hiding all of my alcohol behind my cleaning supplies. I flattered myself that my strategy had worked. In reality, I think that Neko and Jacques just hadn't had a taste for hard liquor in the past month.

"You're going to be lonely. You should plan on getting out. Doing stuff."

I recognized that note in my best friend's voice. I watched as she glugged rum into the glass bottle. "What did you have in mind?" I asked dryly.

"Nothing much." I'd recognize that air of breezy manipulation anywhere.

"Just—" I prompted, before turning to the fridge for soda water. Fortunately, my stock had not been touched. Jacques would not let anything as common as generic soda water touch his Gallic lips. He required Perrier at the very least.

"Just-a-weekend-seminar-on-yoga, focusing-on-the-animal-poses-to-bring-you-into-greater-harmony-with-the-natural-world."

"Melissa…." I sighed. My best friend, in addition to being a stellar baker and a shrewd businesswoman, was more flexible than anyone I'd ever met, and she had the best sense of balance this side of an Olympic gymnastics team.

"It'll be fun!"

"For you, maybe." I pouted and took down two glasses.

"Come on, Jane. The class will focus on inner balance. Peace. All the tools you need to live in harmony with your fellow man."

"My fellow man is moving out." I gestured toward the basement and Neko's now former lair. "I'm not living with anyone. In harmony or otherwise."

"Rock-paper-scissors," Melissa said.

Melissa and I had cast rock-paper-scissors over disputed matters for years, ever since we were little girls. I'm pretty sure that I won half the time, but it seemed like she always got the upper hand when it mattered. Not that there was any way to cheat. Unless… No, if there'd been a way to harness my witchy powers to win at the childish game, I would have figured that out long ago.

"Melissa—"

"Am I going to have to Friendship Test this?"

Wow. She was really serious. A Friendship Test was the ultimate power play in our relationship. We could Friendship Test the last bite of chocolate cheesecake—the person who called the test got to spear the final perfect morsel (although even then, we usually ended up splitting dessert). We could Friendship Test an evening, dragging each other out in a rainstorm or on a slippery winter night.

But we didn't call Friendship Test lightly, Melissa and I. She really wanted me to go to yoga class. She must be certain that it would be good for me. Or good for her. Or good for both of us together.

No reason to make her waste a Friendship Test. I sighed and held out my palms, curling my right fingers into a fist. "One," we said together, and I couldn't help but let a smile twist my lips. "Two. Three."

I cast paper.

At the precise same instant, Melissa cast scissors.

I shrugged in resignation. At least I owned a heating pad. I'd certainly need it after the class. "When's the torture?"

Melissa beamed. "A week from Sunday."

"Great," I said, without the slightest hint of enthusiasm.

Melissa filled two glasses, taking the time to set a whole-leaf mint garnish on the edge of mine. "To animal yoga!" she exclaimed, raising her glass high.

"To animal yoga," I echoed. At least the mojitos were perfect—icy and crisp, the lime balancing the sweetness of the rum. I swallowed again and felt a little of the tension ease from my shoulders. I complemented the mojito therapy with another Lemon Pillow. Then, I glanced at the calendar on my wall. "Wait! I can't make it! I have mother-daughter brunch!"

"That's *this* Sunday, isn't it?"

Why did I share so much of my life with my best friend? It was ridiculous that she should know my schedule better than I did. But she was right. I had brunch with my mother and grandmother the first Sunday of every month—we'd started the get-togethers almost two years before, as my grandmother attempted to build ties between her "two favorite girls," as she described Clara and me. I loved my grandmother without question—she had raised me, after all, taking in a scared and lonely four-year-old whose parents had died in a tragic car crash.

Except that my parents hadn't died. They'd just split up. And neither of them had wanted the responsibility of caring for the daughter they'd brought into the world. My mother had scampered off to a series of New Age havens, seeking spiritual purity without looking back at me.

Until two years ago, when she had finally decided that she was ready to come back into my life. Our relationship was rocky at best—even if she carried the same witchy blood that pumped in my veins. She and my grandmother both.

In fact, Clara—I still wasn't used to calling her *Mother*—had always had an affinity for crystals and stones; that's probably what had drawn her to her previous home in Sedona. And she loved the coded magic of runes, the secret messages that were revealed when the symbols were cast.

"Oh," I said to Melissa, and there was a tangled skein of recognition in the single word. "You're right."

Melissa laughed at my depressed tone. "Come on," she said. "You'll have a great time with them. Wasn't Clara going to cast your star chart?"

I grimaced. Both my mother and grandmother possessed limited witchcraft skills; their powers had been substantially magnified in me, for reasons that weren't at all clear to any of us. Clara, though, had an annoying tendency to embrace anything that sparkled with New Age hocus-pocus and she had taken to star charts with an astonishing vehemence. "That reminds me," I said. "I told her I would give her my set of jade runes. She managed to mislay her Tyr and Nyd."

Melissa eyed me over the edge of her own glass. "Tyr and Nyd?"

"The runes that stand for war and loss. I almost accused

her of throwing them out on purpose. You know how she is about accepting grim reality." Conforming to the expectations of the real world was *not* my mother's strongest suit. "Anyway, I told her I'd give her my set, so that she can do complete castings. It's not like I use them much, anyway."

"When was the last time you used them at all?"

Melissa just sounded curious, but I felt a flash of guilt. My answer was defensive. "They're just some stupid jade runes."

"Hey, don't get upset." She sipped from her mojito, reminding me to take a therapeutic swallow of my own. "I know that you've been busy. It's just that I don't even remember the last time I saw David around here."

David. David Montrose. My warder. He was my astral bodyguard, the man appointed to protect me in my witchy workings. Over the past two years, we'd had our ups (a couple of shared kisses) and our downs (his hidden past with a witch who had challenged me before the Coven).

"Did you guys have another fight or something?" Melissa asked, widening her eyes with mock innocence. She'd always liked David, and she thought that I should appreciate his guidance more than I did.

"No." Blessed mojito lubricated my thoughts. "Not a fight. Just a sort of…drifting. I haven't found time for witchcraft stuff for a while, with Evelyn on the warpath about the James River presentation, and mentoring the reference intern, and—"

"And a hundred and one other excuses." Melissa's tone

brooked no protest. "You shouldn't cut him out of your life like that."

"I'm not cutting him out!" I heard the shrill note behind my words and eyed a third Lemon Pillow as a way to sweeten my tone. "Well, not exactly."

I could still remember the compassion in his eyes, when he'd seen what a wreck I'd made of my dating life the year before. David's sympathy unnerved me. Not that I liked his supercilious instruction any better.

I washed away my discomfort with yet another swallow of mojito. "I better run downstairs to get the runes now. If I wait till Sunday morning, I know that I'll forget them."

Melissa held out her hand for my glass, silently offering a refill. I thought about taking the freshened glass down to the basement, but then I pictured sweet, sticky cocktail spilling over my witchcraft treasures. Better to brave the secret stash alone. Grinning, I handed over my glass and said, "'I drink the air before me, and return or ere your pulse twice beat.'"

She faked a yawn. "*Tempest*," she said, continuing our long-standing game of trading Shakespeare quotations. "Ariel. Hey! Have you seen the posters around town for that production?"

"Of *The Tempest?*"

"Yeah. They're putting it on at Duke Ellington."

"The high school?"

"It's part of some outreach program. They're updating the language and performing it in street clothes, making it 'accessible.'" She made quotation marks in the air with her fingers.

"Sounds horrible."

"But they've got a picture of the guy playing Prospero on the poster. He's really cute. Looks a lot like David." I didn't say anything as I tried to reconcile the notion of my warder and the magician Prospero, not even trying to apply the adjective *cute* to David's sometimes-severe demeanor. "David Montrose?" she said, as if I knew a dozen Davids we might be talking about.

"I knew who you meant."

"I let them put up a poster at the bakery," Melissa said, refusing to take offense at my dry tone. "Anything I can do to help preserve the arts," she added piously.

"Even if preserving them destroys them? I hate that modern update stuff."

"You're just feeling superior because you've got the entire play memorized."

I stuck my tongue out and quoted Prospero himself, "'Now does my project gather to a head.' Maybe I just feel superior because I'm right."

"Or because you're stubborn! Drink some more." Melissa toasted me with her full glass and recited part of a line from later in the play. "'If all the wine in my bottle will recover him…'" She laughed.

It was wonderful to have a friend who didn't mind that I was a total, utter geek. I hurried downstairs to get my runes, before I forgot them again.

If I'd expected the basement to look different now that Neko was gone, I was sorely disappointed. I'd been consistently shocked that a man as fashion-conscious as my familiar had so few personal possessions. Of course, he *did* have a seemingly limitless supply of black T-shirts. And black trousers made out of leather, denim, linen and a couple of other fabrics that I couldn't name. And an omnipresent pair of sleek shoes, vaguely European in their leather perfection.

But that was it. And now, even those meager possessions were gone.

I sighed and shook my head. Melissa was wrong. I wasn't going to miss my housemate at all. I was going to revel in his absence.

I turned to the mahogany bookshelves that lined the walls. Clearly visible dust had settled over the nearest books. So, I wasn't going to win any *Good Housekeeping* Seals of Approval for my housework. Who really cared?

When I had first classified my newfound books, I had sequestered all of the other witchy paraphernalia to one set of shelves. I had collected all of my crystals there, and delicate glass jars containing ingredients for potions. I had carefully laid out the wand that David made me use when I read from some of the oldest texts, the rowan pointer that made the words come into focus in a way that had more to do with magic and less to do with my itchy contact lenses or my often-smudged eyeglasses.

And there, on the bottom shelf, were the bags of runes. The jade ones that I had promised Clara, but other sets, as well—one carved out of wood, another cast in sturdy clay. The jade runes were held in a silk bag, its delicate embroidery hinting at some Chinese ancestry.

I found the bag exactly where I'd left it months before. The brilliant red stitches were a bit dulled with dust but that would be easy enough to brush away. Clara would never know the difference.

I clutched the sack. I expected to feel the runes shift inside. I expected to hear the jade squares click against each other, a familiar clacking sound like oversized mahjong tiles. I expected to see the faintest hard-lined bulges against the delicate silk fabric.

But something was wrong.

The bag was heavy in my hand, shapeless and sodden, like a sack of flour on the bottom shelf in the supermarket. Catching my lower lip between my teeth, I pulled open the laces that cinched the bag shut.

Inside, where I should have seen bright, green squares, I found nothing but dust. A sickly dust, like heavy, dried moss. I shifted the bag in my hands, wondering if my lousy housekeeping had somehow buried the runes in dirt. But there were no runes inside the bag.

My heart started pounding, and I reached for the next item on the shelf, the leather bag that held my wooden runes. I knew that there was something wrong before I opened the sack, before I found the sawdust that clumped in the bottom of the container. My clay runes were in a burlap sack. When I tugged it open, though, I found nothing but grit.

My runes, all of them. Destroyed.

I glanced toward the stairs, fighting the impulse to call for Melissa's help. After all, what could she do? She'd never worked a lick of magic in her life.

Struggling against a rising snake of panic in my gut, I wrestled my box of crystals off another shelf. The wooden container was familiar to my fingertips; I had handled it every single day for months, when I'd worked regularly with David and Neko to hone my powers. I slid the hasp from its lock, threw back its lid to reveal the treasured crystals inside.

Amethyst. Spiritual uplifting.

Obsidian. Grounding.

Kunzite. Emotional balance.

Onyx. Changing bad habits.

All ruined. All faded, shrouded in gray webs, in dull destruction that seemed to have eaten the stones from within.

I bit back a cry and reached for the nearest book. *On the Healing of the Sick.* I tore open its cover, only to find my hand covered with red-brown dust, the detritus of dry, cracked leather. The parchment pages themselves remained unharmed, but the words danced and wavered as I flipped through the volume. As soon as I flipped the pages, the ink faded away, drifting to nothingness in the time it took for me to catch my breath.

I stormed across the room, reaching for a volume at random on another shelf. *The Role of Familiars in American Witchcraft.* Cloth binding. Faded as if it had been left for weeks in the heat of summer sun. And when I opened the covers, the rag-cotton pages blurred, then were bare.

I started to reach for another volume, and then a chilly finger stroked the nape of my neck. If I opened another book, I would destroy it, as well. If I so much as touched a cover, I might wipe away forever the words of wisdom contained inside.

My witchcraft resources were crumbling around me, and I didn't have the first idea of what I could do to stop the destruction.

2

David! I thought my summons without voicing my warder's name out loud. *Neko!* Even as I reached out with my powers, calling the men toward me, I realized how strange it felt to be using my magic. How long *had* it been since I'd worked a spell? Hurrying back upstairs, I wondered if this magic stuff was like training for a marathon. Was I going to be achy and sore tomorrow because I was overexerting myself right now?

I couldn't worry about that—I needed to get to the heart of whatever was happening in my basement. *David!* I mentally shouted again. *Neko! Now!*

As I walked into the kitchen, Melissa must have read something on my face. She set down her glass and stared at me. "What?" she asked, and her eyes drifted toward the silk sack in my hand. "You decided not to give Clara the runes?"

"They aren't there."

"What?"

"They're ruined. Crumbled to dust. I don't know what happened."

"What do you mean, crumbled? They're made out of jade, right? Out of hard stone?"

The cottage's front door opened before I could answer her. "We're in here," I called out, trying desperately to sound nonchalant. Hoping that I *could* be nonchalant. Hoping that I was worrying for no good reason, that nothing was truly wrong, that there were dozens of benign explanations for how magical translucent stone could crumble away to useless green dust.

David Montrose swept into my kitchen. I could still remember the first time that I'd seen him, appearing on my doorstep like *Jane Eyre*'s Edward Rochester in the dark of a stormy night. He'd been furious with me then, enraged that I had released Neko from his form as a statue. Now, I recognized the power that had frightened me that night, the strength—both physical and astral—that coursed through his body, down his arms, into his fine-fingered hands. But I wasn't afraid of him. He was my ally. My friend.

"What's wrong?" he asked, and we might have been picking up a conversation after a separation of a few minutes, not several weeks. Months, I thought, with a curious flip of my belly. It had been at least three months since I'd seen David. Um. Four. Could it really be five? Where did time go?

Wordlessly, I offered him the silk bag.

His dark eyebrows nearly met as his lips pursed into a frown. Silver glinted at his temples—more silver than I remembered. All of a sudden, I wondered what he'd been doing in his spare time, without needing to ride herd on me and my sometimes wayward witchcraft. There was a hardness to his eyes, a wariness, that made me think that he hadn't spent the time catching up on back seasons of *American Idol.*

Before I could ask him what was new, though, before I could say anything to direct his study of the green dust in the bag, the cottage door flew open again.

"Let me guess, girlfriend. You just couldn't stand the thought of an evening without— Oh."

If I hadn't been so worried about the destruction of my witchy paraphernalia, I might have laughed at my familiar. Neko stopped just inside the door to my kitchen. With perfect timing, he absorbed the presence of my warder, immediately twitching to an alert status that made me wonder if all the rest of his existence—the late-night party hound, the fashion guru, the man-man lover extraordinaire—were all some elaborate acting gig, all artfully created to misdirect the world from his true purpose as a channel of magic power.

Neko's nostrils flared as he edged into the kitchen, and his gaze remained glued to the silk bag. I could almost see the hair rise on the back of his neck, and a low growl hummed deep in his throat. He moved like a ballet dancer, stepping sideways with a dangerous caution, and when he reached a single finger toward the sack, he glanced first at David's face, then at mine, as if seeking approval. Permission.

I nodded. "Go ahead. Either one of you. Both."

Poor Melissa was leaning against the counter, and I could see that Neko's intensity frightened her. Hell, Neko's intensity frightened *me*, and that was before I let myself wonder what David was thinking.

My warder nodded slowly and loosened the ties on the bag. He peered inside like a chemist examining unexpected results in an experimental test tube. As his thin lips twisted into a frown, I forced myself to say, "There's more." My voice came out thin and broken, and I cleared my throat, wishing that I could toss back another mojito or two before continuing. "There's more," I repeated, and this time my words were too loud, but I brazened through. "My other runes, and my crystals. My books."

David passed the sack to Neko, who quivered daintily. I half expected him to hiss as he accepted the green dust, to offer up one of those terrifying feline sounds of disapproval, displaying fangs like a snake as he stretched his lips into a snarl. Instead, he weighed the evidence of destruction in his palm, shaking his head and setting it on the table with a moue of distaste.

"What?" I asked, and this time some of my fear came out as anger. "What is it? Is the Coven back? Are they ruining my collection because I wouldn't share it with them?"

David shook his head slowly. "No," he said. "Nothing quite that simple."

Simple! I wanted to shout. There was nothing simple about this! Someone had bespelled my cottage, my collection. Someone was attacking me, and I didn't have the first idea who. Or why. Or how. I didn't know anything at all.

"What, then?" I asked. "If it isn't the Coven, what is it?" I heard the panic rising in my voice. I'd had a difficult enough time holding my own against my fellow witches last year. If David had the nerve to say now that that confrontation had been *simple*…. I was afraid I wouldn't have the fortitude to face whatever he said next.

But David didn't answer. My faithful warder didn't give me a simple response, easy words that would still the pounding of my heart, that would make the metallic taste fade away at the back of my throat.

Instead, he shook his head and sat down at my kitchen table. The scrape of the metal-legged chair against my linoleum floor echoed the irritation in my brain. What was it? What was he not telling me? This must be something truly terrible, if he had to sit to tell me the news. I searched for a sign on his face, for any hint of meaning, but I could read nothing there. His smooth features formed a mask, like the blue cotton a surgeon hides behind before he tells exhausted, anxious loved ones that the worst has happened in the operating room.

That was it. David was going to say that my magic was killing me. He was going to tell me that I must stop practicing, that I had to give up all the arcane goods in my basement. He was going to explain that the collection was dangerous to me, that there was nothing to do but cut it out, destroy it, make one final brave effort to save my tragically shortened life.

"Do you have another glass?" he asked, looking meaningfully at the pitcher by Melissa's hand.

Okay. Maybe he wasn't going to give me dire medical-magical news.

Melissa, clearly unaware that I was halfway down the road to writing my last—and first—will and testament, shook herself back to life and poured, both for David and for Neko. My familiar, apparently taking his cue from David's bemused approach, busied himself with excavating the darkest reaches of my refrigerator. So much for the bare-larder advantages of having Neko move out.

As if he could sense my blossoming disapproval, he moved quickly, pouncing on a brick of cheddar cheese and half a wheel of Gouda that I had hidden behind some ancient whole-wheat tortillas. "What?" he asked, when he caught my accusing glance. "You're going to hold back food at a time like this?"

"A time like this?" I repeated dryly. "I don't have the faintest idea what this time is like." Of course, Neko refused to recognize the warning in my glare. Instead, he actually whistled as he placed the cheese on a plate, and then he began to ransack my cupboards for Triscuits and water biscuits.

"David!" I exclaimed, as my warder cut a substantial slice of cheddar and covered two crackers. "Stop!"

"What?" He shrugged. "You know that he'll eat all of it, if we don't help ourselves."

"I'm not talking about cheese!" I looked at Melissa, waiting for her to back me up. She didn't throw herself into my corner, though. Instead, she cocked her head to one side, studied the snacks arrayed before her, and helped herself to a handful of crackers. When I harrumphed my disbelief, she merely quirked one eyebrow, in that annoying way that she could, as if to say, "What do you want from *me?*"

I pounded the table hard enough that a dollop of mojito sloshed out of my glass. "What is happening to me, David? What's going on in that basement?"

"Nothing," he said, and then he crunched away.

I barely resisted the urge to sweep the cheese plate onto the floor. Instead, I pointed at the silk bag. "That doesn't look like nothing to me!"

"Relax, Jane," he said.

I'd heard that tone from him before. It was the Superior Warden tone. The I-Know-More-Than-You-Do tone. The You-Just-Don't-Know-Very-Much-About-Being-A-Witch-Do-You tone.

And it drove me crazy every time he used it. It drove me to practice my spells a dozen more times before making them public, to work on feeling the vibrations in my crystals until I could sense them in the middle of a moonless night, to concentrate on my runes until I truly *did* understand the meaning of the marks incised in them, felt the designs with an inner chord, infinitely deeper, infinitely more detailed than strict memorization of their supposed symbolism would have created.

Er, not that I'd engaged in any actual witchcraft study for ages.

But that was how he'd always made me feel, when he'd used that tone in the past.

At least Melissa understood the tension that David's patronizing words raised in me. Silently, she set the plate of Lemon Pillows on the kitchen table, centering them like a peace offering. Neko's hand snaked out to grab four, but he caught my glare and returned two to the edge of the plate.

I forced myself to sit down next to David, making my body relax into the unyielding chair. If my warder wasn't concerned, if the man charged with maintaining my physical and astral well-being wasn't worried, then I wouldn't be either. At least that's what I told myself.

I sipped from my glass, but I couldn't taste the lime or the rum, couldn't remember the sharp bite of mint, even a moment later. I spread my fingers on the table in front of me, willing my tension to flow away. One steadying breath. Another. A third.

I met my warder, eye to eye and asked, "What is going on here?"

Despite my desperate question, he took his time to finish chewing. He swallowed. He cleared his throat with a sip of mojito. And then he said, in a deceptively mild tone, "Your runes crumbled because you stopped using them."

"What?" His words didn't make any sense.

"Your crystals clouded because there wasn't any magic to keep them clear. The text in your books faded because you don't need them any longer, because the magic is unnecessary. Dead."

"Dead?" I swallowed hard. "What do you mean?"

All of a sudden, I thought about how I'd used my powers in the past. I'd wasted them. What had I been thinking, working a love spell or two? Worrying about the sorority sisters of the Coven? I'd turned away from making a real difference in the world; I hadn't even tried to use my powers for good instead of for evil. Why hadn't I worked on changing the world in permanent ways, in ways that would last long after I slipped this mortal coil?

"To be or not to be," I almost said out loud. Hamlet's soliloquy went on, "For in that sleep of death what dreams may come when we have shuffled off this mortal coil, must give us pause."

Melissa would certainly get the allusion, and David might, as well. But melodrama wasn't going to solve the problem of the day. Instead, I needed to get to the heart of the matter. Why had I given up the chance to use some really cool magical tools, just because a laptop crash had cost me a catalog of my collection? What had I been doing for the past six months?

When David didn't immediately answer my question, I looked at the silk bag of dust and repeated, "Dead?"

He shook his head. "Maybe that's too strong. I should have said 'Dying.'"

Great. Like that made it all better.

"But I love my powers!" I found myself saying. Melissa had the good grace not to contradict me, although Neko managed a delicate snort into yet another Lemon Pillow. When had he stolen that from the serving plate? "I do!" I nearly shrieked.

"Not enough to have kept them in proper form," David said, ignoring the edge in my voice that sounded suspiciously close to hysteria.

"I don't understand," I protested. "Magic isn't like yoga. It's not like I'm going to lose my powers just because I don't work out every day." Even as I protested, I wondered where I'd come up with that argument. One quick glance at my beloved best friend showed that she didn't think I knew the first thing about yoga, much less about my magic abilities.

And, truth be told, what *did* I really know about my powers? I mean, I'd learned to use the tools in my basement. David had been a harsh taskmaster as I studied for my confrontation with the Coven, and he'd forced me to become an expert at crystals and spells, herbs and potions.

But the whys and wherefores of being a witch? The actual history of magic? Functioning as a witch separate and apart from her Coven?

We hadn't had the luxury to study all of that last autumn. I'd been scrambling too hard to learn enough of the basics, enough that I could keep my familiar, my newfound, new-loved life as a witch. And after I'd finished my dealings with the Coven, issued my little Declaration of Magical Independence, I'd hardly been interested in learning more. The laptop crash had only cemented my lassitude in my mind.

As if saluting my spring and summer of indolence, David helped himself to his own Lemon Pillow, and then he leaned back in my kitchen chair, acting like he didn't have a care in the world. Which, if I truly was no longer a witch, and he truly was no longer my warder, might very well be the case.

"These," he said to Melissa, gesturing to the plate of pastries, "are excellent."

"Thank you," she said. "I use lemon rind, along with a little fresh lemon juice, when I beat the cream cheese for the filling—"

"Excuse me!" I interjected. Neko jumped at the harshness of my tone. Melissa and David turned to me in surprise. "I am in the middle of a witchcraft emergency! I don't care about the recipe for Lemon Pillows! I don't care about baking or yoga or any of the rest of this. Help me!"

"Jane, you don't know what you're in the middle of," David said maddeningly, and then he took another bite of Pillow. "Besides, witchcraft is actually a lot more like yoga than you might think. Discipline is the key to both."

I flashed a glance at Melissa, but she managed to look innocent as she sipped her mojito. I toyed with the idea that this was all some elaborate game she and David had devised, some grand ruse to get me to go to the animal yoga class without any additional sulking.

But Melissa had already won that battle. And she'd had no way of reaching David for the past five months. And

David didn't joke. Especially not about magic. And the tools in my basement were being destroyed.

"So," I said, forcing myself to play along until I understood the rules of the game. "I just have to master the magical version of Downward-Facing Dog, and everything will be all right? Stretch those hamstrings, and my runes will be back in no time?"

David sighed. "The runes are gone. You can acquire another set, of course. They'll stay stable for a while—a year or two, anyway—even if you never practice magic again. But if you don't go back to using your power regularly, any new runes attuned to you will crumble, as well."

"But that doesn't make any sense! Those jade runes sat in my basement for years, for *decades* before I ever used them! Why would a few months of sitting around make them disintegrate now?"

David grimaced and helped himself to some cheddar. The slice that he cut was large enough that Neko whined in dissatisfaction, but my warder did not seem at all concerned. "Your magical tools were put into stasis by Hannah Osgood when she hid them downstairs. Once you found the materials, once you started using them, you broke the seal. Power could leak out."

His matter-of-fact explanation angered me, broke some sort of seal in *me*. Frustration seeped into my words. "Then why didn't they all just crumble to dust two years ago? Why didn't the books erase themselves when we were working together last year?"

"That's just it. We *were* working."

David sounded utterly uncaring, as if he had no interest in the endless hours we'd spent together, in the countless magical details that he'd taught me. The dispassion in his voice made my heart beat faster. My cheeks flushed, and I wanted to tell him that he should speak more respectfully, that he should sound as if he *meant* what he was saying.

But that was stupid. He was just telling the truth. Cold, historic facts. We *had* been working together. Intensely. For over a year. And then we hadn't been.

"I don't get it," I said, and I was surprised by just how miserable I sounded. Even Neko cocked his head to one side, as if he recognized a hidden story beneath my words.

"You're not trying, Jane." There. That was my old warder talking—remonstrating with me when all I wanted was a sympathetic ally. I started to protest, but David raised a hand, palm outward. The gesture might have connoted peacemaking in another context, but now it felt combative. Absolute. Controlling. "You don't want to understand what I'm saying."

He reached for the crumbled runes and tossed the silk bag up and down, like a tennis player reminding himself of the weight of a ball before an important serve. "When we worked together, your magic kept the goods charged. The power within you spread to everything in the basement, kept it…fresh. Active. Once you decided to abandon your witchcraft, the tools deteriorated. The destruction was expedited because of how much power you had, how strong the charge was that jolted them out of quiescence. Your magic was strong, and Hannah's items immediately became accustomed to a very high base level of power around them."

"But I haven't abandoned my magic!" I protested.

David looked at Neko, and his silent glance wrote volumes. What sort of witch let her familiar move out of the house? The only words David said, though, were, "You haven't seemed to need me very much lately."

"I thought you'd be pleased by that," I groused. "Have a little time away."

His eyes flashed like quicksilver as he stared me down. For the first time in ages, I remembered that he was a warrior. A fighter. A man trained to get what he wanted by whatever means necessary.

But in the past, he'd always wanted to protect me. I had a sudden, sickening feeling that everything had changed. When he spoke, his voice was so low that I had to lean forward to tease apart his words. "I was your warder. I never asked for time away."

Was. I heard the warning in that word, in that tense. Something had gone wrong. Very, very wrong. Still, I stumbled ahead. "You may not have asked for it, but I'm sure you managed to use it, all the same."

Neko winced. He'd never become accustomed to the sparring that seemed normal to me where David was concerned. At David's impassive stare, I felt forced to add, "What have you been doing, anyway? Taking the Arcane Grand Tour? Whiling away the hours on the Witchy Riviera?"

Even as I needled him, I thought back to when we had first met, when David had first commandeered my sanity and my rogue witch powers. Then, he had told me about his life when he wasn't serving as my warder, when he was working to redeem himself for past sins before the sisterhood of witches. "The Court of Hecate," I said, and I could read the truth in the iron line that stiffened his jaw. "They busted you back to a file clerk!"

"I was never a file clerk!" he protested.

But he had been. He'd been responsible for organizing papers. Or scrolls. Or whatever. And he'd hated it.

"Why didn't you come here?" I asked. "Why didn't you come get me?"

"What was I going to do, Jane? Beg you to use your powers? Plead to serve as your warder?"

I heard the questions that he didn't ask. Why hadn't *I* summoned *him?* Why had I been content to let my powers go unused for so long? Why hadn't I thought—even once— to reach out to the warder who had stood by me, through physical and emotional battles, for well over a year?

"I've been busy," I said, even though no one had asked me to explain myself. "Work has been crazy, with the program I'm putting together on the James River plantations. I'm mentoring an intern. I've been trying to be a good librarian. And a good daughter—Clara can exhaust *anyone*, you know. And a good granddaughter, too. Gran isn't as healthy as she was—even though my crystals got her through pneumonia a couple of years ago, that illness really took a toll."

I heard the crazed note behind my words, the pressure I was putting on myself to explain. To justify. To make excuses.

I should apologize, but I didn't know how. I couldn't make myself say the words. But when David didn't bother to respond, I forced myself to take a deep breath. "All right, then," I said, and I made myself meet his eyes. "What do I do now? How do I make this right?"

Melissa and Neko might have disappeared from my kitchen, drifted away as thoroughly as the ink lines in my books, for all the attention that David gave them. Instead, he stared at me, pierced me with his gaze. I longed to reach for my chilled glass, to ease the sudden ache in my throat with a tangy sip of mint and lime. I was frightened. That must have been it. He frightened me, and so I said, "I'm your witch. You're my warder. You have to help me. Now."

I had never ordered him to do anything before.

Oh, I'd asked for his help countless times. I'd whined. I'd protested his requirements. But I had never stated our relationship as a bald fact, never mandated his compliance with such an air of authority. I watched his Adam's apple bob as he swallowed, and then he said, "Work a spell."

"That's it?"

"Not just any spell," he said, cutting short the laugh that bubbled up in my throat. His tone was sharp. Brutal. Like the ceremonial sword that I'd seen him carry in my defense the year before. Goose bumps rose on my arms. "Something special. Something strong. Something that pulls and twists your powers, that makes you use everything you have at your disposal, all of your abilities."

He sounded like he would enjoy watching me drained of my power. "Like what?" I asked.

"Jane, there are some things you're just going to have to learn for yourself."

"Something like awakening a familiar? Is that enough?"

"You can't think in terms of 'enough'!" His shout made me jump. I glanced at Melissa, and she had curled her fingers around the edge of the kitchen counter, as if she were seeking strength in the ordinary, in the mundane. Neko cringed and turned his head away from both of us. David went on. "This isn't about 'enough.' This is serious. You need to grow. Build your powers. Become a better witch. Or you won't be one at all. And if you aren't a witch, then Neko won't be your familiar. I won't be your warder. We'll both be gone, assigned to the next witch who claims us."

Fear beat in my chest, smothering me with its fluttering wings. "But how can I come up with options, if I can't even read the books downstairs?"

"Build a buffer, Jane." He shrugged as if any idiot could have figured that out. "Work some minor spells. Store the effect and build up a reserve."

"Like what? Do the dishes with a water spell?"

"That could be a good beginning," he said, with a dismissive glance toward my kitchen counter. My counter, and my morning cereal bowl. And last night's tea mug. And a plate with toast crumbs from I couldn't remember when.

I blushed, and my embarrassment about my housekeeping made me even more terse with him. "But when should I do the real working? The one that will save my collection?"

"You're the witch," he said. "You decide."

The raw anger in his voice made Neko squeak with discomfort. I could practically see my familiar offer up his soft underbelly as he interceded between us. "What about a week from Sunday?" Neko said, hopeful as a child begging for a sundae. "That would be a good day, wouldn't it? Dark of moon?"

"A week from—" I glanced at Melissa, who remained completely silent. Sunday was the day that she and I were going to be yoga goddesses.

David spoke to me, following up on Neko's suggestion without a hint of emotion. "Whatever you work under the dark of moon will be bound to you. Not free to wander, like full-moon creatures." He glanced at Neko. "I assume that your familiar can make himself available?"

My familiar scratched at his ear nonchalantly, his momentary bravery in entering our battlefield nearly forgotten. "She said that I could leave here, you know. I didn't just walk out."

But now I wondered about that. Sure, Neko had the right to roam the city; that was the result of my having awakened him on a full-moon night. But there'd been something different over these past months. We'd grown apart from each other. Sure, I said it was because of stolen food and pilfered drink, but there was something more at play. My magical bond to Neko was as damaged and frayed as my connection to my other magical paraphernalia.

"Well," David said, silently passing judgment, even if his words stayed noncommittal. "Whatever magic you work this time will have to be explicitly bound to you. To your collection. Right?"

Out of the corner of my eye, I saw Neko nod, and Melissa blinked. I realized that David was staring at me, a question haunting his somber eyes. The weight of the moment settled over my shoulders like a wet wool coat, and I resisted the urge to shrug. Instead, I said, "Yes. The magic will stay. This time."

"Fine, then," David said. "I'll see you a week from Sunday."

And he left. He turned on his heel, and he stalked out of my kitchen, leaving behind a nearly full glass of mojito and a plate with a few cracker crumbs.

I started to go after him. I started to open the door, to call him back. I started to explain that I *had* missed him. I'd missed *us*. I'd missed being witch and warder, but I really, truly had been busy.

But I couldn't make myself move. Not to apologize. Not with Neko watching, and Melissa. Not when I hadn't been wrong. Had I?

When the silence became so heavy that I thought I might never be able to speak again, I noticed Melissa moving. Shooing Neko forward. Mouthing to him to *do something*.

My familiar took a moment to shake himself back to awareness. Then, he sprang over to my cupboards and stretched for the top shelf, for a half-dozen tumblers of cobalt-blue. I'd placed them out of his reach months ago, when I'd realized that every glass he brought down to the basement never made it back to the kitchen.

"Jane, as long as you're using a spell to wash dishes tonight, could you clean these up, too? Jacques and I broke our last highball this afternoon, and these will be perfect replacements!"

I contemplated priming my magic with a spell to shatter all my glasses, just to spite him, but I settled for a sigh. "Sure, Neko. Whatever."

He beamed. "Great! They'll look great with the fish pitcher! Bottoms up!" He drained the last of Melissa's concoction into one of the blue glasses.

I drank with both of them, but I wondered what the dark moon would bring. And whether David would truly stand by my side when I faced it.

3

I settled into the booth at Whitlow's On Wilson, trying to squelch my unease at traveling to the Washington suburb of Arlington, Virginia. I didn't venture out of the city often, and the last time I'd come to Arlington had been a disaster. I thought that I'd been visiting my one true love, but I'd discovered that he was a lying, cheating scoundrel. He now went by the name of the Coven Eunuch, when I brought myself to talk about him at all.

Live and learn, I told myself. Live and learn.

And eat.

A lot.

The waitress had just brought mountains of food to our table. I had asked for Eggs Nova Scotia—essentially, Eggs Benedict, with lox standing in for the Canadian bacon. I began ordering brunches centered around English muffins when I started spending the first Sunday of every month with my mother and grandmother. When the family tension got a little too thick, I could saw away at the hearty bread, imagine my frustration flowing away to fill the tasty nooks and crannies. After more than a year of our distaff gatherings, I'd made a fine art of Benedicts.

This morning, Clara had splurged on the bacon and cheddar omelet—her most recent vegetarian phase seemed to have died a quiet death. Gran, though, was going for the gusto; she had chosen Whitlow's because she'd heard they had an expansive buffet. While Gran ventured over to the sprawling tables of food, Clara and I busied ourselves with our tea.

I was hoping that tea would help to settle me down. Following David's instructions on Friday night, I had worked a minor spell in the kitchen, gathering together soap and water to cleanse the dishes that had collected in my sink. I'd managed to keep everything under control, but the astral exertion had left me light-headed and dizzy. I felt as if I'd run a mile after being bedridden for a week.

Still, I had done what the doctor had ordered. Slow and steady won the witchcraft race. Or so I had to believe.

And a combination of Eggs Nova Scotia and tea was bound to make me feel better, more grounded. Besides, tea was one of the few things that Clara and I had in common. (The others were our hazel eyes and our stubborn personalities.) We both preferred tea over coffee. The restaurant obliged us in our still-awkward mother-daughter dance; the waitress presented us both with a wooden chest, and we got to study a scramble of tea bags to determine the perfect one for the morning. I began to dunk my Lemon Lift in a clear mug, moving the bag with a vengeance as I tried to think of something to say.

"I wish they had Raspberry Royale," Clara said, obligingly filling the silence.

"That one always smells like Jell-O to me," I said. "Every time I drink it, I feel like I should be back in Gran's kitchen, laying out rounds of canned pineapple in the bottom of her ramekins, just before she helps me pour in boiling water."

Clara winced.

Damn. I hadn't even *intended* to attack her for abandoning me when I was a child. I really, truly, positively, certainly—well, possibly—was ready to forgive her for that. I'd just meant to fill the silence.

Bravely, she said, "I remember those ramekins. The brown ones? That always look like they should be filled with gingerbread?"

I seized the peace offering gratefully. "Those are the ones!"

Fortunately, Gran returned before Clara and I could tumble down the cliff of some other conversational chasm. My delicate, octogenarian grandmother had created quite a sculpture, piling a forest of steamed crab legs on top of a neat little village of scrambled eggs, hash browns, bacon and sausage. I thought that the foundation of her building was a raft of French toast, but I couldn't be sure.

My stomach growled, and I attacked my eggs, crafting a bite perfectly balanced with English muffin, poached egg, lox and hollandaise. I chewed carefully, relishing the simultaneous salt and tang, and then I placed my silverware on the edge of my plate. It was time to fill Gran and Clara in on the witchy developments in my basement. "I have news," I said.

"I have news," Gran said at the same time.

"I have news," Clara said, perfecting our triad.

We laughed—a simple, unburdened sharing of amusement—and each of us gestured for the other to go first.

"Go ahead, Gran," I said expansively. "You're the matriarch. Your news leads the day."

She looked pleased, even as she finished tearing apart a crab's leg. She took a moment to suck on the sweet white meat, watching our anticipation grow. At last, she smiled demurely and settled her hands in her lap.

"Uncle George and I are getting married."

"You're what?" I choked out the words past a bite of lox. I couldn't help myself—Gran? Getting married? At her age?

"Best wishes," Clara said wryly.

"Oh." I remembered my manners. "Best wishes," I said, my mouth still full. Gran sat up primly and nodded her thanks.

Gran and Uncle George. He wasn't really my uncle. They had been friends for decades, after her husband—her *first* husband?—died. George had escorted her to countless galas, to endless plays and dinners and parties. She had attended innumerable operas just to be with him, just to keep him happy, even though she had admitted to Clara and me in a rare family bonding moment that she found the caterwauling boring.

"What took you so long?" I asked, when I had finally chewed and swallowed.

"For years," she said, "it just seemed silly to go through the whole thing. Why bother, when our friends all know that we're together, when our families don't really care?" She caught the look on my face, and she reached across the table to pat my hand. "I don't mean that as a bad thing, dear. Really, I don't."

"Then what changed?" Clara asked, quite reasonably.

"I decided that there are times in life when people should make a statement. When they should stand up for what they believe in. When they should announce to all the world their goals. Their priorities. The things that are important to them. Besides, I never got to plan a real wedding before." She glanced at Clara. "You eloped, of course. And your father and I got married in the backyard at his parents' house. I just want to do something grand. Something exciting. Throw a party like no party has ever been thrown before."

Suddenly, I felt as if I was sitting on a roller coaster, as if I had just crested a gigantic rise, and I was swooping into a panorama of disaster. "Gran," I said, forcing my words past the block of ice that was rapidly congealing in my belly. "Are you sick?"

She blinked and set down the rasher of bacon that she had been lifting to her mouth. "Sick?"

"Do you think you need to marry Uncle George?" I asked. "To guarantee that someone will be there for you? To take care of you?"

"Of course not, dear. He's a man. His idea of taking care of me is bringing me two aspirins and a cup of tea, no matter what's wrong. For anything serious, I'll always call on you." She took a sip of coffee and then added, "And you, too, Clara, dear." She almost made it sound as if she had intended to include my mother all along. At least she got close enough that Clara did not react visibly. "But, I have to be realistic. Neither George nor I will last forever. I think we both want to make it official—the 'till death do us part' side of things." Contentedly, she forked an entire coopful of eggs into her mouth. She chewed, took a swallow of coffee, and said, "*We* know that we'll be there for each other. But we want everyone else to know that, as well."

"Well, Mother," Clara said, "I think it's wonderful. I'll call him 'Dad' the next time I see him."

The absurdity of that statement made me return to my own breakfast, to a steaming bite of home fries. Uncle George would never be "Grandpa" to me. He was…Uncle George. He'd been there my entire life, and if Gran wanted an official document and a little party to say so, who was I to begrudge her?

Sometimes, Clara tried too hard. (And other times, I immediately thought, she didn't try anywhere near hard enough.)

Gran patted Clara's hand and said, "That won't be necessary, dear, but thank you for the thought. And what was your news?"

Clara set her fork down amid the rubble of her omelet and beamed at both of us. "I'm leaving."

This time, it was Gran who exclaimed, "What?"

As for me? I just sat there, staring at my plate, suddenly unable to swallow.

Clara. Leaving again. I'd always known that she was going to do that. I'd always known that she was going to wait until I'd gotten used to her, until I'd grown comfortable with the notion of my mother being around, day in and day out. She'd lulled me into a false sense of security and now she was going to walk out of my life, the same way that she had when I was a child, when I was four years old and too naive to recognize how feckless she was.

Don't get me wrong. I didn't *like* having Clara around. I always felt as if I needed to be on my guard with her, as if I might say the wrong thing, that I might make her angry, make her…leave me. But I couldn't help myself. I said the things that I was thinking. I let my suspicions show on my face. I displayed my heart for all to see.

For Clara to see, even now.

"Oh, Jeanette," she said. Jeanette. The name that she had given me, before she walked out of my life the first time. "Don't look at me like that."

"My name is Jane," I said automatically, retreating into the comfortable, the familiar, the *me* that Gran had raised.

"It's been great," Clara said, "my visiting, and all. But it's time for me to move on. It's time for me to head back to Sedona. To the Vortex."

The Vortex. And all the other New Age crap that Clara had sought, to find balance in her life. She, like Gran, bore strains of the witchcraft that was expressed full strength in me. But she had never learned about her powers, never discovered how to harness them. The astral energy had led her to wander, to wonder, to seek out new experiences her entire adult life.

I searched for a neutral question. "When are you going?"

Clara puffed out her cheeks and exhaled slowly, as if recognizing the battle we'd apparently decided not to fight. "Not right away, of course. I'd been thinking of wrapping things up in the next month or so. Now, I guess I'll wait till after Mother's wedding." We both looked at Gran, as if we were surprised to find her still sitting there.

Gran looked up from another crab claw. "Well, George and I haven't set a date yet. We were thinking that we should wait until after the Concert Opera Gala. We'll be too busy to do anything before then—the Gala takes so much planning, you know."

"I know," Clara said companionably, and I fought the impulse to flash daggers at her with my eyes. What did she know? She had never helped plan the Gala. She had never attended the meetings in Gran's apartment, serving coffee and cake to the assembled operaphiles, putting up with their endless prying questions, inquiries they meant as a sign of affection, but which felt like an invasion of privacy.

Clara merely shrugged and spread her fingers. "Or so I hear. Well, an October wedding should be lovely."

"An autumn wedding for two people in the autumn of their lives," Gran said, pushing back her plate.

"Don't say it that way!" I said.

"Now, dear, it's true. There's nothing wrong with acknowledging the truth. Besides I've always liked fall colors. Crimson and gold and orange. Orange is George's favorite color."

I didn't like it.

Not orange. Well, I'd never liked the color much, but that wasn't what I was thinking about now. I didn't like any reminder that Gran was old, that she was ever going to leave me. But she seemed so perfectly content, chatting about shades of fall, that I could only force a smile and nod.

Clara set her palms on the table, as if we had just concluded some grand business meeting. "It's settled, then. I'll leave on November 1. Winter in Sedona should be beautiful."

Of course. This entire conversation *was* about Clara, wasn't it? I bit my tongue to keep from saying the spiteful things I thought. In a flash, I thought of old King Lear, before the madness overtook him, asking his daughters how much they loved him. Goneril and Regan lied through their teeth, piling on false compliments, even as they plotted to destroy their father. Only the youngest daughter, Cordelia, spoke the truth, saying, "I love your majesty according to my bond; nor more nor less."

Of course, Lear learned all about lies and betrayal by the end of the play, and honest Cordelia died a pretty pitiful death. So maybe I should have lied to Clara there in Whitlow's. Maybe I should have told her how much I would miss her, how much her departure panged me. Melissa would have been able to quote all of *Lear*, lay out a perfect argument about why I must make peace with my mother.

But Melissa wasn't there. I was. And I wasn't promising any love to the woman who had borne me.

Clara, that was, and Gran, who were both looking at me expectantly. "Now, dear," Gran prompted. "What is *your* news?"

I pushed my egg-soaked lox around on my plate. "I'm losing my powers," I muttered.

"What?" Clara asked. "I can't hear you, Jeanette. It sounded like you said that you're using your powers."

"Losing!" I said, and I probably spoke a little too loudly. Definitely spoke a little too loudly, I amended, when a dozen people at nearby tables turned to stare. "Losing," I repeated in a softer voice, and then I told them about my search for runes, about the gift I truly had intended to make to Clara, about the cleaning spell that had left me dizzy and dull in my kitchen.

Gran reached out and patted my hand, the eternal picture of loving concern. "Don't you worry, dear. I'm sure that you just need a rest. And Clara can get new runes elsewhere. I'm sure…" She trailed off, obviously uncertain about just *where* a witch went to acquire the basic tools of her trade. Witch★Mart, maybe?

I shook my head. "That's just it," I said. "I've had too much of a rest. David says that abandoning my magic is what put me into this ridiculous situation."

"Ah, David," Gran said. I recognized the fondness in her voice. She had always liked my warder, always trusted him. He, for his part, treated her with the exquisite courtesy of an ambassador addressing a dowager empress. That respect, along with the occasional well-chosen basket of sweets, had made him a great favorite in Gran's household. "How *is* David these days? I never hear you talk about him."

"He's fine, Gran." I answered automatically, the same pro- grammed response that I'd used as a sullen teenager, when my grandmother wanted to know who I was hanging out with, where we were going. But then, I forced myself to stop, to think about my answer. "I haven't seen a lot of him lately. I *think* that he's fine."

And yet, even then I knew I was telling something of a lie. Physically, of course, my warder was as well as ever; I had seen that on Friday night. But what exactly *had* my slacking off meant to him? Why, precisely, had he been so angry with me? So abrupt? What *had* he been doing during the past five months? And how had he felt, being rejected by his witch, being forced back into the mundane work of Hecate's Court?

I'd been too wrapped up in my own drama to ask him.

Gran, never a fool, pounced on my nonresponsive response. "Make me a promise, Jane."

"Oh, no." I pushed my plate back with authority, casting

an immediate appeal to Clara. *Please*, I asked her silently. *Get me out of this*. It was almost worth it to harness my magic, to face another wave of dizziness and confusion, if only I could get my mother to read my mind.

Clara said, "Oh, a promise! You always have been one for promises, Mother. That's one of the many things I love about you."

I gave Clara a dirty look. Maybe Goneril and Regan just had bad publicists. Maybe they had been right to gang up on their stupid, insensitive, uncaring parent. "Gran," I said, dismissing vengeance on Clara from my thoughts. "I am not making any promises today."

"This one is easy to keep, Jane. And it's right. It's good. You should do it."

Of course, Gran would think that she was right and good. Gran *always* thought that she was right and good.

And, truth be told, she was.

Oh, she might have gotten a little carried away with some of her promises. She'd made me swear that I wouldn't lick any *toads*, for heaven's sake. But I had to admit, I'd come across the situation—or one close to it—given the requirements of witchcraft and a certain potion that Neko had coached me on brewing. And sure enough, I'd stuck by my oath. A vow was a vow, no matter how silly it sounded when Gran got me to say it out loud.

She was staring at me across the table, her eyes sharp and curious, like a bird's. I knew from past experience that she had all the patience in the world. She would simply sit there and wait until I agreed to whatever promise she was going to demand. I might as well give in to the inevitable and wrap this thing up quickly. "Fine, Gran. I promise."

Her smile was so quick that I almost missed it. "Talk to David about this witchcraft problem of yours."

"Gran, I already did that! David was the first person I called when I realized what was happening."

"And how did that conversation go?"

I took a sip of cold tea, manufacturing a break to think some more. Gran knew me so well. She had clearly discerned that things had not gone well when I summoned David. Exactly how much had she read between the lines? Did she know how dismissive David had been? Did she believe that I had actually hurt his feelings by ignoring him for so long? I thought back to my mandate that he answer me, my pulling rank on him. Maybe, just possibly, in a teensy, tiny way, I had overstepped my bounds as his witch. Or at least as his friend.

"Jane," Gran said. "Do you remember last year? When you promised that you'd speak with Melissa after you two had your disagreement?"

Of course I remembered last year. I remembered how things had spun out of control for a long time, before they'd come back to normal. I remembered how much I had missed my best friend, how much I had needed her. I'd promised Gran that I'd reach out to Melissa, and it had taken me weeks to swallow my pride.

But as soon as I had done it, I'd felt infinitely better.

Melissa and I had slipped back into our old friendship patterns with barely a hiccup. I sighed. "Okay, Gran," I said. "I promise. I'll work this out with David."

Gran nodded, as if she'd been certain I would see the wisdom of her ways. "Go to him, Jane," she said. "Don't make him come to you."

I hesitated. Before I could say anything, Clara said, "You do know where he lives, don't you?"

"Of course, I know where my warder lives!" I snapped.

Gran merely nodded, as if she hadn't heard the roughness of my tone. "Perfect, dear. Now, how about ordering some dessert?"

"Dessert sounds good," I said. "But I want to heat up my tea." Gran started to turn around, to seek out our waitress. "No," I interrupted. "Using magic."

My mother and grandmother cast twin skeptical glances toward me. Clara spoke first. "Jeanette, it's really not a problem, to get another cup of hot water."

I shook my head. "David said that I should use my powers. That I should get back into the habit of working magic."

Gran looked doubtful, but she equivocated, "Well, if David says…"

That fired me up. My own grandmother didn't trust me to make decisions about my magical powers, but if my *warder* said to… If my absent, judgmental warder said to… If the warder I had just promised to reach out to said to… I'd show her. I could do magic any time and any place. Of my own volition.

I folded my fingers around the clear glass mug, closing my eyes to concentrate better. As soon as I decided to work magic, I became aware of the noise surrounding us in the restaurant. A small child was screaming at a table across the room. A man was trying to get a waitress's attention by bellowing, "Miss! Miss!" over and over again. A fire engine drove by outside, siren wailing.

I took a few deep breaths, trying to center myself for the working. Hurriedly, afraid that I would call embarrassing attention to what I was doing, I touched my fingers to my forehead, offering up the power of my thoughts. I brushed my palm against my throat, offering up the power of my voice. I fluttered my fingers over my heart, offering up the power of my spirit.

I remembered the words from one of my first spell books. They were originally meant to be used by a nursemaid, to raise the temperature of a healing draft or a poultice. My Lemon Lift was nearly as medicinal, I justified to myself.

"Fire and water, water and fire,
Combine now in gentle heat.
Hear this witch who does inquire
After an easy healing feat."

The mug trembled in my fingers. My eyes flew open, and I caught a shudder in the air, like a shimmering reflection on a sunbaked summer road. My mind told me that my fingers should be burning, that my tea should have risen to the boiling point.

My body, though, told me something else. The tea *was* hotter, that was true. But my magic was nowhere near as powerful as I'd expected, as it should have been. My fingers tingled as I set the mug back onto the table, as if I'd fallen asleep in an odd position. I sighed and took a sip from the mug, faking a grin in response to Gran and Clara's concerned smiles.

"There we go," I said, anxious to shift their focus. "Well, which dessert were we going to order?"

It came down to the brownie sundae or the apple cobbler. Clara turned the conversation back to Gran's impending nuptials, and no one was surprised when we ended up with both desserts, along with three spoons. We spent the rest of the morning talking about appropriate colors for an autumn wedding. I tried to let the distinctions between crimson and scarlet, between tangerine and orange carry me away from my worry about my warder—my warder, my witchcraft, and a promise that I might have made a little too rashly for my own good.

4

I'd lied to Clara.

I had absolutely no idea where David lived. In fact, when she asked me in Whitlow's, I'd been so surprised that I hadn't been able to answer for a moment. He and I had worked together for two years, and it had simply never occurred to me to wonder about where he lived.

I knew that must sound strange. After all that we had been through together, all the times that he had swooped in to my rescue....

But that was it. *He* had swooped in. He had come to me. Besides, we *worked* together. I didn't waste my time worrying about where my library boss, Evelyn, lived. I didn't waste a spare moment thinking about the respective abodes of my intern, the circulation clerk, the cataloger.

Now, boyfriends—I had a long history of caring about *their* houses. Deep in my heart, I think I had always been the teensiest bit suspicious of the I.B. (that used to stand for Imaginary Boyfriend, before everything went south, and I started making up brilliant new pet names for the lying, cheating scum of an Infuriating Boob). I had wondered about his home, pictured myself in his kitchen, his living room—okay, in his bedroom. I should have read a lot more into his never taking me to see his home.

And last year's romantic debacle of the Coven Eunuch? In retrospect, everything had gone wrong just after I visited his house. Well, it had gone wrong from the moment we'd met, if I wanted to be brutally honest, but I'd become aware of the wrongness after I visited his home. All the clues were laid out for me there, everything that I should have known, should have recognized.

So why hadn't I ever given any thought to where David lived?

Not that it really mattered now. I was a reference librarian. I could find one person's home in a major metropolitan area, without even breaking a sweat.

Except, David wasn't listed in any of the phone books I had at my fingertips—print or electronic. I needed to resort to more obscure databases. If I crossed my fingers and clicked on the box that said I had a legitimate legal reason to be searching credit records…. Well, no one would be the wiser.

Unless David decided to prosecute me for tracking him down.

Not that he would do that, I reminded myself for the thousandth time. It wasn't as if we had fought. I had just hurt his feelings a little. He would be pleased to see me, I whispered inside my head. He would be thrilled that I had taken the initiative, come to him for a change.

Yeah. Right.

I'd always pictured David living in a D.C. rowhouse, maybe on the third and fourth floors of some nineteenth-century socialite's converted city manse. I imagined him walking down a long block, shaded by oak trees. He was anonymous, lost in the city as he let himself in the security door on the street, as he climbed the flights of stairs to his own pied-à-terre. The house itself was filled with odd-shaped rooms, accented by dark corners where generations of dust defied good housekeeping.

David walked to little neighborhood restaurants, supplementing his empty refrigerator with leftovers from meals eaten at family-owned dives. He haunted used bookstores, trying to scare up a witchy title or two. And he rarely drove his gorgeous Lexus, the night-black car that I had seen only a handful of times, the luxury automobile with such sensuous leather that goose bumps rose on my arms whenever I thought of it.

Well, I was right about the car.

According to my rather illegal databases, David didn't actually live downtown. He didn't live in Washington at all. Instead, his home was out in the Maryland suburbs. The exurbs. Who was I kidding? He lived in the country. I pulled a map from the Internet, but I still checked one of the road atlases that we keep in the Peabridge reference collection, because I had never driven out that far from civilization.

On Saturday morning, I sent a quick e-mail to Gran before I swung by her apartment building. I used my own set of keys to borrow her Lincoln Town Car, not even stopping upstairs to say hello. She'd never miss the car—she only took it out once a month or so. Besides, she was the one who had made me promise to take this trip.

I worked my way through the city and headed into Maryland. I passed the infamous Beltway and watched the scenery change from freeway to small town America to open farmland. When I'd traveled almost to the Pennsylvania border, I knew that I was getting close. I double-checked the map a couple of times, but even using the odometer as a gauge, I missed the final turn and had to backtrack. Twice.

David lived at the end of a winding unpaved road. The countryside swelled in gentle hills to either side of the twisting drive, waist-high grass rippling like a living creature's pelt. A clutch of trees ended the meandering path, and I pulled Gran's car into a gravel-strewn turnout, parking next to a dusty white pick-up truck.

The house that nestled in the trees looked like a farmer's dream from a generation or two past. A porch wrapped around the two sides of the building that I could see, and a glider invited me to settle onto its thick striped cushions. The clapboard walls were crisp with white paint, their hunter-green shutters beckoning like an advertisement for peaceful country life. From the front seat of the Lincoln, I couldn't see inside the curtained windows.

As the car's engine ticked into silence, a huge Labrador retriever stirred on the porch. I'd missed him at first; he'd been in the shadows from the eaves. Before I could worry about opening my door, about approaching the possibly hostile hound, the dog began to pound his tail against the porch in a steady, welcoming rhythm. My warder might be forbidding, but his dog had failed to get the memo.

I wiped my hands against the skirt of my cotton dress. I'd dressed carefully for this meeting. I didn't want David to think that I took this intrusion lightly. I'd thought about shorts; they were appealing, given the humid blanket that smothered the summer air. But shorts were too casual, too flippant. I'd tried on jeans, but they were too hot for the journey. I'd slipped into khakis, but I knew that they'd be wrinkled by the time I completed the drive.

At last, I'd settled on a sea-green sundress. Its halter neck left my shoulders bare, so it was cool enough for the weather. Neko had picked it out for me at the beginning of the summer. He and Jacques had somehow scored tickets for an afternoon tea at the British embassy, and the guys had invited Melissa and me to join them, on condition that Neko could dictate our wardrobe. So that we wouldn't embarrass them. We, Melissa and I, not embarrass them, Neko and Jacques. As if Neko's downing an entire pot of clotted cream hadn't set our British hosts on edge….

Enough. I wasn't accomplishing anything sitting in the

car. Besides, with the air conditioner turned off, the heat was rapidly becoming oppressive. I could feel my hair curling against the back of my neck, rebelling against the simple French twist I'd accomplished before I'd left the cottage.

When I opened the car door, I became aware of a noise—rhythmic, constant. There was a sharp chop, followed by a sweeping sound, a pause, and then a repeat of the sequence. Over and over and over.

Curling my toes against the soles of my sandals, I followed a path around the edge of the house. The walkway was paved with shattered oyster shells, following the finest tradition of our colonial forefathers. I knew of a dozen books that discussed the layout of eighteenth-century footpaths. Perhaps I should get one for David, provide him with original source support for his landscaping. That would surely sweeten my appearance on his proverbial doorstep. I could just head home, find the perfect volume, and then I'd return. I promised.

I turned back toward the car, but the dog blocked my way. I'd been so intent on keeping shards of shell from slipping beneath my feet that I had not heard the animal trailing along behind me. He stopped when I did, his heavy tail lashing back and forth. It was a friendly motion, not threatening, but it was enough to remind me that I had a mission. I had a reason for being here. I couldn't retreat into the Peabridge's collection as an excuse from confronting my warder.

Chunk, came the sound again. Swish. Pause. Chunk. Swish. Pause.

I took a fortifying breath and a few more steps, moving forward until I could peer around the corner of the house. The dog moved up to my side.

Chunk. Swish. Pause.

And there stood my warder, in the shade of a massive oak tree, dressed in faded blue jeans and a tattered plaid shirt. He wore a pair of protective goggles that would have been geeky, if they hadn't made me realize just how hard he was working.

Working. Splitting wood. Coolly. Methodically. With a precision that sent a chill up my spine, despite the heavy August heat.

Chunk. His wedge-shaped maul bit deep into the edge of a round. Swish. He swept the cut wood off the block. Pause. He shifted the round, readying himself to make another Paul Bunyan stroke.

Chunk. Swish. Pause. Chunk. Swish. Pause. Chunk.

Silence.

I'm not sure what made him notice me at last. Maybe it was something about the witchy bond between us, the warder ties that stretched taut, even though we hadn't worked together for months. Maybe it was the dog's wagging tail. Maybe he just happened to glance up.

But he took his time setting down the maul, removing his goggles. He raised the tattered tails of his shirt and wiped his face dry. I became intensely aware of the sounds around us—the breeze cresting through the long grass in the field beyond the oak tree, the birds that called to each other from their hidden retreats.

"Jane," David said, and he might have been greeting me at some formal party.

The dog started to whine deep in his throat, as if he wanted to go to his master, but knew that he was forbidden from approaching the work area. "Stay, Spot," David said, enforcing the verbal command with a firm hand gesture.

"Spot?" I asked. My laugh sounded a little giddy, somehow relieved. I looked from the jet-black animal to his inscrutable master.

David shrugged. "It seemed like a good idea at the time."

"I know the way that feels." Now, why had I said that? What had seemed like a good idea at what time? And why was I admitting any of that to my warder, who could be one of the bossiest, most controlling men on the planet?

He swallowed, and I could just make out the pulse beating at the base of his throat. "What are you doing here, Jane?"

Busted. I hadn't expected him to ask me so directly. Or so soon.

And what was I going to answer? That I'd made a promise to Gran? That I had woken up filled with insatiable curiosity? That the spells I'd been working had made me twitch for the time we used to spend training together?

"Can't a witch visit her warder when the spirit grips her?"

"Not usually. No." I looked at him, sudden panic sprinting across my brain. Had I really bucked some long-standing witch-and-warder rule? He sighed and amended, "At least, not usually. Most witches summon their warders *to* them."

"I'm not most witches."

"So I noticed." The dryness in his voice ratcheted up the heat beneath the oak tree. Once again, I felt the tingle in my fingertips, the spark of energy that had been growing since I'd worked my dish-washing spell a week before. I couldn't tell if he read something in my face, but he suddenly seemed to remember his manners. "Do you want something to drink?"

"A glass of water would be great."

For just a second, I thought that he was going to leave me standing there, set Spot to guard me while he went into the house. But he waved the dog to his side as he stalked away, making for a side door that I quickly learned opened onto the kitchen. He gestured for me to enter first, and the black lab followed behind me, his nails clicking softly on the Mexican tile floor.

As my eyes adjusted to the lack of full sunlight, I saw just how wrong my made-up vision of David's home had been. My warder wasn't living in dust and shadows. Instead, he was living in the heart of a Crate and Barrel catalog.

The farmhouse kitchen was huge and airy, flooded with sunlight that streamed through tall windows. Through a doorway, I glimpsed a dining room, and beyond it a living room with a single austere couch, matched by two chairs that seemed comfortable enough to settle into for a rainy afternoon of book reading. There were a couple of wooden end tables and a lamp or two. Everything looked neat. Calm. Ordinary.

The kitchen was picture-perfect, as well, in the same well laid-out, highly functioning way. Somehow, I'd never pictured David as a cook, but now I could clearly see him standing over his Viking stove, anodized aluminum pans heavy in his strong hands as he whipped up some sustaining dish.

Unerringly, he went to the cupboard beside the sink and retrieved two simple clear glasses. Ice cubes clanked against each other as he excavated them from the freezer, and he tossed one to Spot, who caught it in midair. He poured water from a sleek filtered pitcher in the fridge.

As he handed my glass to me, I blushed unexpectedly. I had to be reacting to the precise perfection of his movements. If I had served a guest in my own kitchen, I would have searched for a clean glass for at least a minute, and then I would have needed to crack a stubborn ice-cube tray. My kitchen faucet had never even seen a filter, and the water ran warm in the middle of the summer.

"Your home is beautiful," I said, trying to distract myself.

"It's been in my family for decades."

"I was surprised to find you out here," I said, desperately attempting to make this conversation a normal one, between two ordinary people, not between a witch and her warder. "I expected you to live in the city."

"There are too many eyes in the city."

"What do you mean?"

He flexed his hands, as if he could pull the right words from the air around him. "As a warder, I lead a rather unconventional life, wouldn't you say? I keep strange hours. I can come and go from here in the blink of an eye. No one notices when I translocate from here."

I thought of him, appearing on my doorstep in full Mr. Rochester ire. I'd never asked him about his strange arrivals. "How *do* you do that?"

He started to answer, then thought better of his words. "We warders have to keep some of our tricks secret." The words stung. I heard the rebuke behind them, the wall that he erected between us. There'd been a time when he would have answered any question I posed about magic, when he had believed that my arcane education was more important than any trivial matter of personal privacy. Before I'd walked away from spellcraft. Before I'd set him aside for nearly half a year.

I could order him to tell me. Demand, as witch to warder.

But I wasn't going to do that. Not today. Not when I was trying to reach out, to rebuild the surprisingly fragile bond that we had shared.

"But your Lexus? It doesn't fit into this life at all."

"It's in the garage." He nodded toward the window, and I could see the detached building, door shuttered like the entrance to a secret cave. "I usually use the truck when I'm out here."

"And the wood?" I thought again about the streamlined action I had watched, the perfect ballet of exercise and practicality. "Do you usually split wood in the summer?"

"I split wood when I have time. I go through two cords

every winter. And the exercise is good, when I'm not busy
with anything else. When I'm tired of sitting at a desk."

At a desk. Where he'd been working as a clerk for Hecate's
Court, wherever that was located. What did it matter? He
could apparently commute anywhere with the power of his
warder's thoughts. Had commuted to my cottage, on a
regular enough basis, before I'd decided to stop being a witch.

I swallowed, making more noise in my throat than I'd
intended.

David's voice was in perfect equilibrium as he asked, "And
to what do I owe this visit?"

"Gran," I said, and the single word echoed strangely in the
kitchen. I sipped some water and remembered to keep my
voice down. "Gran made me promise."

He sighed and leaned back against the counter.
"Promise what?"

"Promise that I'd talk to you. Promise that I'd try to make
things right between us."

There. Faster than a blink, but I was certain that I'd seen
him flinch.

"There's nothing wrong between us." Spot stood up from
his guard spot at the center of the kitchen floor, a soft whine
coming from deep in his ebony throat. David flashed a hand
signal to the animal, waiting just a moment before the dog
settled back onto his haunches. Then, my warder cleared his
throat and repeated, "There's nothing wrong."

"But there is," I said. "I've been working spells. Little
ones. Just enough to…prime the pump, as you said."

"And?" he asked when I stopped.

"And it's strange! It's different from how it used to be, from before I took a break. I *feel* what I'm doing. It's like an energy, a force field." I closed my eyes for a moment, trying to figure out words for what I'd been sensing all week long. "My fingers tingle, and my heart jumps faster than it should. If I didn't think that I'd sound like some matron in a Regency romance, I'd say that I'm getting palpitations." I blinked and stared at him, like a patient waiting for a diagnosis from her trusted doctor.

David's lips twisted into a tight smile. "I doubt that anyone would ever say you're a matron, in any romance whatsoever."

I tugged at the skirt of my dress, suddenly aware of the heat outside, of the wood chips that dusted the front of David's shirt, of the dampness at his temples that darkened the familiar silver glints. "I wasn't fishing for compliments."

"And I wasn't biting a lure." He set his glass down on the polished granite counter. "Jane, you're feeling the strength of your magic. I keep telling you, but you don't listen to me. You have a lot of power. A lot of magical energy. You can bottle it up, contain it, but if you start to let it seep out— like you've been doing to recharge your collection—you're going to feel the pressure. There's nothing that you've felt in the past week that was wrong or bad or dangerous."

"How can you be sure?" Even as I asked the question, I knew the answer. He was my warder. He could feel my witchy powers. He knew when I used them. He felt everything I did with my magic.

I couldn't meet his eyes. There was something incredibly intimate about my realization. It was as if he'd found my high-school diary, read about the silly crushes I'd had on utterly unattainable football quarterbacks. No. This was more than that. It was as if he'd read about the silly crushes I'd had on *him*.

I looked around the kitchen, at the precise placement of every last detail. I saw the dish towel, folded into perfect thirds over the handle on the oven door. I saw the morning newspaper, squared up, reassembled into its hot-off-the-presses precision, even though I was willing to bet my best prefogged rhodosite crystal that he'd completed the crossword puzzle inside. In ink.

I glanced out the window at the chopping block, and I imagined the countless hours that he'd spent splitting wood. The controlled physical grace of the maneuver. The inevitable bodily exhaustion.

"David—" I started to explain that I had never meant to hurt him. I'd never meant to alienate him. I'd never meant to cut *him* out of my life, when I left my witchcraft sitting by the side of the road.

"Jane," he interrupted, shaking his head. "Don't go there."

And for once, my warder refused to meet my eyes.

I was so accustomed to his challenging stare, to the unforgiving truth of his chocolate-brown gaze. But David had suddenly become fascinated with the rim of his glass, with the melded ice cubes that clanked against the sides. Before I could say anything, before I could try to find the path back to what was right and normal between us, he said, "This isn't right. You shouldn't have come out here. Let me take a quick shower, and I'll drive you home."

"I can drive myself home."

"I'm your warder. Chauffeuring is part of the job." He smiled tightly. "I'll only be a minute." He walked past me to get to the hallway, to the stairs that led to the farmhouse's second floor. I stepped to the left, and he matched my movement, then we both shifted to the right. I laughed nervously as he shook his head and edged past me. "Make yourself at home," he said from the foot of the stairs.

I listened to the steps creak, and then I heard the water begin to run above my head.

He was my warder. He knew everything about me. He certainly should have known better than to leave me free to explore his house. "Stay," I said to Spot, as I hurried out the kitchen door. I wasn't about to pass up what might be my only chance to see how David Montrose truly lived.

The stairs seemed louder under my feet than when David had trod on them. At the top landing, I could see one closed door—clearly the master bedroom suite. Another room was laid out as a guestroom, queen-sized bed covered by a simple navy comforter, a white dresser left bare, except for a simple arrangement of crimson blown-glass bowls.

The third room was an office. An office that showed the only hint that a real human being lived in the house. An office that was half-filled by an enormous desk, a horizontal surface that seemed ready to buckle under the combined weight of a gigantic plasma computer monitor and several reams of paper.

I recognized the Torch on most of those pages, even across the room. Hecate's Torch, the symbol of witches everywhere. Its art deco lines swooped in simple authority, announcing to the world that the papers dealt with witch-craft.

I heard a whuffling noise behind me, and I wasn't surprised to find that Spot had followed me up the stairs. His nails clicked as he shadowed me over to the desk, and he leaned close against my side as I picked up the first document.

"The party of the first part doth give, bequeath and bequest to the party of the second part…"

Great. An arcane deed.

I picked up another paper, from another pile. "Comes now respondent, who demurs before this august body…"

Another pile. "I, Roberta Inglewood, being of sound mind and body…"

There were hundreds of papers on the desk. I glanced toward the closet, where an ancient steamer trunk hulked, more documents cascading from its sides. So many pages. So much to sort through, to organize. Of course, I could sense the lines of magical power, jumping between papers. I could see connections, recognize materials that belonged together, envision the order that should control everything in the office.

Spot whined as I stepped toward the tangled mess, and I

obliged him by stopping. I set my fingers on his broad black head, trying to soothe him. The motion reminded me of my own calming ritual, before I worked my spells. I took deep breaths and offered up the power of my thoughts, my speech, my spirit.

The magic potential gathered inside of me, shimmering like dust on butterfly wings. As I breathed in a fourth time, my lungs trembled; I felt like I was sitting at the top of a Ferris wheel, poised in that inevitable moment before the car swoops down into its disorienting arc. I stretched my hands over the piles of papers, toward the mess in the trunk.

I could feel the individual strains of magic in the papers. I could sense the separate witches who had drafted the pages, who had set quills to paper. I could measure the energy, the power; I could feel what belonged where.

The knowledge came to me so firmly, so thoroughly, that I didn't even need a spell to manipulate the pages. I didn't need a charm. The magical energy came from the materials them-selves; they were endowed with the force of Hecate's Court.

Spot moved in front of me, his whine now constant at the back of his throat. I touched his head again, but I couldn't feel his fur past the tingling in my fingers. I raised my hands high, relishing the rustle of my sundress against my body, of the crisp cotton halter sliding against my neck.

I spread my fingers wide, and I reached out for the first piece of paper with my mind. Clearly, it belonged *there* with the other documents written by one Susan Albright, a witch of some renown from the Boston family of Albrights. I knew that. I could see it. I could feel it, with the zip of power that sparked through me.

Spot barked once, a short sharp sound, made even louder because the house was utterly silent.

Utterly silent. Not even the sound of a shower running behind a closed door.

And then, before I could move the papers, I heard David. "Jane," he said. "No." His voice was low, even. He coiled his urgency into those two words.

Urgency, yes. But meaningless drivel. The power had risen in me. I needed to use it. I needed to ground the energy, the thrum, the drive. I needed to channel my powers into the Court's documents.

"No," David said again, and then he moved between me and the desk. I felt his presence like a stone cast into the pool of my magic. He rippled out toward me, a liquid presence, soothing, smoothing. I was barely aware of the gray bath sheet that was tucked around his waist, gray the same color as the faded ink on a stack of astral deeds.

Still, I jangled with the energy I had gathered. "I need to," I said, and my words caught against the back of my throat in a harsh whisper.

"You can't. There is magic in those documents. Power that is not rightly yours. Witchery that the Court would punish you for taking." The papers called to me, though, tugged at me, echoing and amplifying my own considerable magic, increasing the longer I delayed. I tried to step around David. "Jane," he said. "I can't let you do it."

I closed my eyes, and I could see the golden arcs of power that I had raised. I knew them, recognized them as the basic web of magic that I wove before I worked any spell. But the strands were thicker than I expected, brighter than I'd had any reason to predict. The palpitations that I'd felt earlier in the week came back, so strong that I swayed in sudden dizziness. My magical energy surged higher, bounced off the skeins of power spun out from the papers. I needed to plant my powers somewhere, needed to sink them into something.

"Jane," David said, and his voice was so urgent that I was forced to look at him. "They'll destroy you. The Court would never let you work alone, without a Coven to control you. Not if they knew you had touched all of this, manipulated all these records." He set his hands on my shoulders. "Stop."

And I understood what he was saying. I knew that he was right. I knew that I only stood to hurt myself—and him.

But I didn't know how to tamp down the magic that was still rising in me. I didn't know how to bleed off the energy, how to bring it back to a level that I could control. "David," I said, and his name was filled with all of my fear, all of my frustration.

He moved his hands down to my arms, setting off a storm of magical sparks. "Stop," he said again.

My jangling madness responded to the grip of his fingers, spinning out, beyond my control. He absorbed the first glinting needles as if they were nothing. After all, he'd been caught in the midst of my spells for two years. He knew me. He protected me. He kept me safe.

Before I was fully aware of what I was doing, I stepped into the circle of his arms. His chest was broad against my sundress; I felt the heat of his body, smelled the woodsy soap from his shower. He folded his arms around me, pulling me closer, absorbing the energy that I could not control.

I was astonished by how much strength I had summoned, by how much witchery pulsed through my body. He took it, though, absorbed it all.

At some point, I realized that my arms had clutched at him. I pulled him as close as I could. I curved my fingers against the back of his neck, brought his face down to mine. Just before I kissed him, I could *see* the magic leap between us.

I don't know if he moved us out of the office or if I did. I don't know if he pushed me onto the king-sized bed of the master suite, or if I pulled him down beside me. I don't know if he slipped off my sandals, or if I made the buckles come undone magically, made them fall to the floor.

He was the one who looked up, though, who saw that Spot had followed us into the room. "Out," he said hoarsely, but the dog only wagged his tail. "Out!" he said again. "Dammit, Spot!"

The command sounded so much like the famous line from *Macbeth* that I started to giggle. Maybe the proud lab took offense at my laughter, or maybe he just decided to obey his master, but he sighed like an old man and padded down the stairs to the floor below.

And then David was poised over me, brushing my hair

from my face. I thought of the times when we'd been close before, when he'd kissed me, when he'd undressed me after magical workouts that left me too tired to move. I thought about him sleeping beside me—once—with the chastity of a brother.

"I don't—" he said, but I put a finger against his lips. The motion made the sparks rise in me again, like a new log tossed onto a fire.

"I do," I said. And then I turned my magic inward for just a moment, wrapped my body in a protective blanket. I used my powers to manage my cells, to guarantee that there would be no lasting repercussions from this long-fated encounter. I'd never thought that I would use that particular magic, harness that particular knowledge from one delicately illustrated volume in my library.

When I felt a perfect understanding, recognized the *snick* that told me that my spell had set, I turned back to my warder. My fingers fumbled at the towel still—incredibly— tucked around his waist. I tore it loose with a rioting tumble of magical energy. And then I collapsed back on the bed and let David Montrose build another, even more ancient type of magic between us.

5

"It was a mistake."

"He said *what?*" Melissa came just short of executing a spit-take with her iced coffee. We were huddled at the local Starbucks, killing time until the torture chamber, er yoga studio, opened up.

"He said that it was all a mistake. That he never should have let it happen."

"What sort of patronizing, misogynist—"

I had to cut her off. I'd already run through the entire roster of name-calling a dozen times since my overprotective, straitjacketing, strong-willed pig of a warder had sent me packing the night before. "I really don't think that he meant it that way."

"What other way *is* there to mean it?"

"The witch way."

"The which way?"

"Witch. You know. Magic." I tried to drown the word in a dip of shaken iced tea and lemonade.

"Shouldn't he have thought of that *before* he took you to bed?"

"That's the thing. I'm not certain that *he* took *me*. I think that I might have been the one doing the taking." I grimaced, shoving aside memories of the second spell I'd ever worked, a love spell that had gone ridiculously astray. "I'm the one whose powers were sparking out of control. I'm the one who was working magic when I had absolutely no right to do so. Those were his papers. It was his job I was interfering with."

"And the only thing he could think to do was rip your clothes off, to distract you?" Melissa's scorn was palpable.

I shrugged. I'd run out of arguments the day before. After a mutually satisfying afternoon in David's bed, I'd treated myself to a cool shower. When I came out of the bathroom, I'd expected to see him still tangled in the 400-count cotton sheets, but the room had been empty. I'd pulled on my sundress and stepped into my sandals, humming to myself as I pinned up my hair. I didn't realize just how badly things had gone until I came down the stairs, until I found David in the kitchen, surrounding himself with pots and pans, dishes and glasses, anything he could use to put up a domestic wall between us.

He wasted no time announcing his edict: we'd been

wrong to give in to the power sparking between us, and he would never let such a mistake happen again. I might have felt better if he'd let me be responsible, if he'd let me step up and say that I had done what I had wanted to do.

Instead, he talked to me as if I was a student, as if I was the naive young witch he had first encountered two summers before. He should have shown more restraint, he explained. He should have set the boundaries. He should have sharpened his concentration, kept his eye on the warding prize. He was at fault, and he was sorry. It was, quite simply and unalterably, a mistake.

At first, I was embarrassed. Then, I was angry. Then, I was deeply, almost unbearably sad.

And the stew of emotions only continued to boil in the hot August night as he insisted on driving me home. He sat behind the wheel of Gran's Lincoln while I huddled against the opposite door.

I thought about asking him if his rejection was really about us—about him and me. I wanted to tell him that I wasn't Haylee; I wasn't his former witch (that was witch with a capital B). I wasn't the woman he had sworn to protect and fallen in love with and then been hurt by when she found another warder, a man who could help her climb the Coven's social ladder faster.

I was me, and I was utterly, completely confused.

At least he didn't try to make small talk. And he dropped me off at the Peabridge before taking the car back to Gran's by himself. He did say, though, that he'd be back the next night, Sunday night. Tonight. The night that I was supposed to complete my big power-recharging working.

Yea. Rah.

The ironic thing was, I could feel power stirring inside me, more power than I had felt since recognizing my dire witchy straits. The palpitations or power arcs or whatever they were had become almost constant, and my fingers tingled as if I had rubbed them repeatedly with sandpaper. Energy sparked inside me, rounded up by the contraceptive spell that I had worked, by the arcane energy that I had passed to David. That he had passed back to me.

I felt sick to my stomach.

I glanced to the side, eager to find something to distract me from the jangle of magical energy that was keeping me off center. A bulletin board hung on the wall, featuring notices about apartments for rent and dogs to adopt. The bottom half was covered by the poster that Melissa had mentioned the week before, the ad for the high-school production of *The Tempest*. Empower The Arts proclaimed bold white letters, printed on a diagonal.

Prospero's face peered out at me above the slogan. Melissa was right. The actor did look like David. It was something about his eyes, combined with the line of his jaw. And his lips….

I forced myself to look at Melissa, to twist my own lips into some sorry third cousin twice-removed of a smile. "Enough about my life of witchy glamour. How are you?" She grimaced and stirred the ice cubes in her milky coffee.

That look could only mean another collision on her own personal dating highway to Hell. "That good?" I asked. "Who was he?"

Melissa's love life read like the *Rand McNally Atlas of Dating Disasters.* She was determined to find the Perfect Man by the day that she turned thirty, a deadline that was all too rapidly approaching. No one could accuse her of sitting back and letting the world move around her, though, of her passively waiting for action without trying.

She had worked through a pantheon of dating rejects over the years, tallying up more first dates than any girl should suffer in a lifetime. She fit in at least one a week, selecting her endless string of hopefuls from a variety of sources: FranticDate.com was a favorite (although I kept telling her that she was bound to end up with an axe murderer if she kept that up), *Washington Today Magazine* (where there were more married men looking for a bit of spice on the side than there were good, solid candidates for marriage), Dedicated Metropolitan Singles (a constant source of earnest young men who weren't quite ready for a prime-time dating experience). Then there was the great catchall, the collection of "independents" who came recommended by friends and family (where "friends" was a loose category, elastic enough to include such shrewd judges of character as the clerk at the local monolith bookstore who had recommended his cousin one evening when Melissa had taken an inordinately long time to find her discount card in the bottom of her purse. The cousin had turned out to be a Nietzsche freak with a lisp. Man and Thuperman became a tagline for months).

"Which one was this?" I asked, bracing myself for my best friend's tale of woe. Okay, who was I kidding? I loved her stories—each and every one of them. They made the shambles of my own nondating life seem a little less dire. What was the word? *Schadenfreude?* I had to admit it—I took pleasure in her misfortune. What else were best friends for?

"An independent." Even in my emotionally frazzled state, I barely suppressed a grin. The independents were the best. Or at least the weirdest.

"Where'd you meet him?"

"At the wholesale flower mart. I went down there yesterday to buy some herbs."

"Oooohhh… A man who knows flowers!" I put all my energy into being fake-impressed.

"Yeah. But I'd never seen him there before. He pulled up in a dusty Chevy truck—one hundred percent baseball, mom and apple pie. Big guy—he looked like Grizzly Adams's more athletic brother."

At the mention of the pickup, my heart twinged, but I continued gamely, "So you fell for his outdoorsman's soul?"

"Looks can be deceiving."

"Can they now?" I tried not to sound too pitiful, thinking of the deception I'd experienced the day before.

Unaware of my momentary mental retreat to my own dating disaster, Melissa shuddered and plucked at the loose shirt she had donned for our yoga class. "At first, I didn't think anything was strange. He left his truck at the flower mart, and we took the subway over to Chinatown. When we got up above ground, he whipped out a bottle of gel, you know, that antiseptic stuff?"

I nodded, wondering where this was headed. Melissa had a very low tolerance for kink, and I didn't think Purell was going to make any great hits with her. She went on. "He said, 'Gel up?' and I thought, why not? I mean, we had just been pawing over all the greenery at the market, and the subway is, well, the subway."

I nodded and said in as careful a voice as I could manage, "So you're rejecting this guy because he offered you hand gel?"

Melissa glared at me and swirled her coffee before saying, "I didn't mind the gel after the subway."

"But?" I prompted.

"But the subway wasn't the end of the story. We decided to eat at Tony Cheng's. You know, Mongolian barbecue? The restaurant that has those heavy glass doors?"

"I love that place! It's got those giant fu dogs outside, protecting the world from disaster."

Melissa sighed. "Those fu dogs apparently aren't enough to protect the doors from infection. Kevin had to gel up after opening the outer doors."

"Well," I said, perversely forced to carve out some explanation. "Hundreds of hands touch them every day."

"And the inner doors," Melissa deadpanned. "The ones that actually go into the dining room."

"Gel up after those, too?" I asked, trying not to laugh.

"And after unrolling his silverware from his napkin. And after collecting his barbecue ingredients in a bowl. And after the chef handed back his cooked food."

"You have got to be kidding," I said.

"Do I look like a woman telling a joke?" Melissa grimaced and drained her iced coffee.

"That gel stuff is nasty," I said. "It's got to be ninety percent alcohol. Murder on the cuticles." Neko had told me that once.

Melissa rattled the ice cubes in her cup then stretched her hands out in front of her, studying her nail beds as if they held the secret to the universe. "Yep," she confirmed. "Murder on the cuticles."

"You didn't," I said, staring at her hands with a queasy twist of horror rippling through my belly.

"I did," she confirmed grimly.

"You gelled up every time?"

"What was I supposed to do?" Melissa yelped. "He kept offering me the bottle, with that same little smile each time. 'Gel up?' I mean, I could see the concern in his face. If I'd passed on the offer, he would have thought that I was some sort of heathen. Or worse—he might have called the CDC and announced that he had found the vector for every disease in North America."

"But what was that?" I asked, still grappling with disbelief. "Five doses of gel, in less than fifteen minutes?"

"I won't even mention his paying the bill. Do you have

any idea what they do when they take your credit card to that back room?" She shook her head. "I grabbed a cab as soon as I could—I figured it was worth it to pay the fare, just to escape with some of the skin on my palms still intact!"

"Let me guess—Loverboy didn't give you a kiss goodbye."

"I wasn't about to test the waters. I'm sure he would have made me brush, floss *and* rinse with Listerine first!"

"Another one bites the dust," I said, draining my tea-and-lemonade in a sisterly affirmation of our sorrowful tossing on the dating seas. "I don't know how you do it," I said, shaking my head.

"Hey," Melissa said, as if she'd just thought of something brilliant. "I've been meaning to ask you…"

"What?"

"What would you think of…" She caught herself and looked away.

"What?" I asked again.

"It's a stupid idea." She was blushing. Melissa White was blushing. My strong-willed, straight-shooting best friend in all the world was blushing.

"*What?*" I asked again, with enough force that the tattooed hipsters at the next table turned to stare.

Melissa fiddled with the empty sugar packet she had used in preparing her coffee. "What would you think if I dated…" She swallowed hard, and I tried to imagine what she was thinking, what could be so terrible that she could not even complete her sentence. A prisoner from the local penitentiary? A married millionaire who wanted to trade his fortune for sexual favors? An admitted pervert who wanted her to dress up like Minnie Mouse but promised a ring on her finger and a wedding that she could invite her great-aunt Gertrude to attend?

"What!" I exclaimed, pounding a fist on the table with enough force that the hipsters gave *me* dirty looks and moved to a different table.

"A customer."

"A customer? Like from Cake Walk?"

She nodded her head, but she refused to meet my eye.

"You mean a paying patron? Someone who comes into your place of business and conducts a retail transaction like a totally normal human being? A man who has the good taste to recognize the best bakery in all of Washington, D.C., and who thinks to pay you the compliment of asking you out to dinner or a movie? That sort of customer?"

"Well, when you say it like that…"

"Is there some other way to say it?"

"It's just that it feels scummy. Sly. Like I met him under false pretenses or something. I hate to think that the only reason he's been coming in for the past year is because he thinks he'll get something on the side."

"For the past year! Melissa, you're practically engaged to this guy already!"

"I hardly know him."

"What's his favorite coffee?"

"Anything with caramel. He gets one every morning."

"What's his favorite cookie?"

"The Almond Brick Roads. He gets them in the after-noons."

"What's his favorite cake?"

"My grandmother's Apple Cinnamon Cream. But he only gets that on special occasions."

"Where does he work?"

"Down in the Harbor. He's a lawyer."

"Well, that's a major strike against him, I'll admit," I said dryly.

"Do you think so?"

"Hello! Melissa! You just described a dream man! What's his name, and why didn't you say yes, the instant he asked you out?"

"Rob Peterson. And I just couldn't. I don't want to mix work with play. It seems cheap. Besides, if things don't go well, I'll lose a customer."

I gaped at her. All of her years of shopping around, all those First Dates from Hell, they'd melted her brain. Or maybe it was the fumes from all the hand gel she had absorbed the day before. "Melissa White, if you lose a single customer, the world will continue rotating on its axis. But if you pass up this chance—this chance to go out on a date with a perfectly normal guy, who has stopped by to see you at least twice a day for God knows how long…" I trailed off, running out of enough words, enough threats to make her see sense. I finally settled on "Please, Melissa. Just this once. Date a customer. Say yes."

She squared her shoulders. "Okay," she said. "I can sort of see that you're right."

"Sort of—"

"I'll say yes. If he asks me again."

"You'll ask him! You'll say that you've reconsidered!"

"I—"

"Friendship Test!" She looked flustered, but she raised her chin as I went on. "I Friendship Test this. You have to go out with him. At least once."

"Friendship Test," she finally conceded. And then she glanced at her watch. "Oh! We're going to be late!"

No such luck.

We got to the yoga studio in plenty of time. Everyone was still rolling out their spongy mats, finding the perfect pied-à-terre for the torture session that was to follow. After a winsome smile at me, Melissa laid out her own mat in the front row, closest to the instructor. I nodded in approval, being perfectly content to set up in the second row, slacker heaven, away from the direct oversight of the Vinyasa dominatrix who masterminded these classes.

I settled into a Half Lotus position in the center of my mat, familiar enough with the drill to know that I was supposed to be centering myself, finding my core, understanding the peace and harmony and balance in my body. Instead, I used the time to replay the horrific embarrassment of the day before, the instant that I realized just how wrong everything had gone between David and me.

Maybe he was right. Maybe it was all a mistake. If I felt this terrible just *thinking* about what had happened, this uncomfortable just remembering how his lips had…

I forced myself to take a trio of deep yogic breaths. Everyone around me was settling on their mats. To my left, a spry woman who looked as if she was made for the arched backbend of the Wheel Pose settled into Full Lotus and breathed herself into apparent nirvana. I felt chastened, as if I shouldn't be thinking about David but should instead be focusing on all the peace and harmony that ancient Indian contortion techniques could bring to my life.

I tried to settle back into my own centering, but I couldn't keep my attention from wandering to the other students. On the far side of the room was a man who had to be seventy, if he was a day. He spread out his mat and flowed through a loud but precise sun salutation, his breath coming in staccato snorts as he showed off perfect physical form before settling into his own Full Lotus. A pair of teenagers sat behind the old guy, giggling behind their hands to each other.

Next to me, another man tossed out his yoga mat, trying to make the rectangle lie flat on the studio's wooden floor. The ends kept curling up, though, despite his best efforts at pressing them to the ground. I watched his struggles for a minute before my librarian instinct to help kicked in. "If you turn it upside-down, it'll lie flat."

He looked surprised that anyone had noticed his dilemma, but then he flashed me a smile. His brown eyes were large behind round black glasses that made him a total ringer for an adult Harry Potter. His grin was crooked as he followed my instructions. "First day with the new mat," he said self-deprecatingly. His smile was an invitation to chat.

I wasn't ready for that. Not ready for the flirtation, not ready for the getting-to-know-you dance. I noted the guy's eyes, and I thought about other brown eyes, familiar ones, flecked with green, brown eyes that had drawn me in only the afternoon before. I saw unruly chestnut curls, and I thought of straight black hair, of silver glinting at temples that I wanted to reach out and touch…. I shook myself back to the studio.

Fortunately, I was saved by the bell. Literally. As the instructor flowed into the room, she carried a tray with her, a lacquered surface filled with cones of incense, a tiny vial of lavender oil and a palm-sized brass bell. She set the tray on the ground in front of her own impeccably flat mat, and then she pressed her palms together. She raised her joined hands chest high, letting her fingers point toward the ceiling. "*Namaste*," she said, inclining her head in a graceful greeting.

Namaste. I honor that place in you where the whole universe resides. The traditional Indian greeting that started every one of the twisting, turning torture sessions that Melissa dragged me to. At the instructor's urging, I struggled for a deep breath, honestly trying to reach out for the universe inside me.

The universe of confusion, that was. The universe of what-had-I-done. The universe of what-had-I-been-thinking-going-to-bed-with-my-warder.

But I soon ran out of time for thinking about my stupid actions of the day before. I needed all my energy to focus on my stupid actions there and then, in the yoga studio.

The instructor started us off with easy poses. She led us through a half-dozen sun salutations, designed to get our hearts pumping, our minds and bodies primed. I kept up well enough, hopping back into a perfectly serviceable Plank, lunging into Downward-Facing Dog. The round of exercises certainly served its purpose. I was breathing like a warrior by the time we finished, furiously trying to manage my gasps for air, breathing in through my nose on a not-quite-steady count of five.

The instructor became my own personal hero when she ordered us into the breath-saving all-fours pose of Cow. I tugged at my yoga pants a couple of times, trying to keep them from riding up on me, and then I gave in to the series of interlocking exercises—Cow, with my spine curving in, my belly sagging toward the floor and Cat, my spine arching up like a Halloween icon.

The movement felt good—my back actually enjoyed the contrast from sitting in my chair at the Peabridge. I was even able to get my breathing under control, to find some semblance of the peace and inner strength that Melissa and the instructor always rambled on about. I flashed a smile at my best friend as we rose to our feet for the next round. She had been right after all. The yoga class was precisely what I needed; it was just the ticket to get past my crazy schedule at work, the turmoil that was my twisted family life, the shambles I'd left things with David.

And then the instructor told us to move into Eagle Pose. I'd done it before. Once. A lifetime ago, when my bones were still made out of Silly Putty, and I'd believed in the power of concentration. And balance.

I stood as straight and tall as I could. I told myself not to be aware of the perfect bodies all around me, the women who looked like they had been sculpted into their yoga pants and body-hugging T-shirts. I raised my hands, bending my elbows and executing a complicated pretzel twist that tugged at my shoulders. I reminded myself we were all beginners at something, that we all needed to strive toward perfection. I picked a point on the wall ahead of me, staring as if my concentration on this pose in this studio at this moment was the most important thing in my entire life. I reassured myself that we all worked at things, that we all struggled to find balance and peace and harmony.

I raised my right leg, knee turned out, my foot gliding along the inside of my left calf, my left knee, my left thigh.

And I stumbled out of Eagle, staggering forward two full steps to end up on Melissa's mat.

"Sorry," I said, hopping back onto my own spongy rectangle. She barely acknowledged my presence, perfectly relaxed as she was in her own flawless Eagle.

Embarrassed, I tried again. Back straight. Arms twisted. Eyes focused. Leg up.

Graceless tumble—but at least I stayed on my own mat. That was the good news. The bad news was that I was the only student who fell out of the pose. Even the new guy, the guy who had his mat set up next to mine, managed to sway and keep his balance.

Gritting my teeth, I rallied one more time. Back. Arms. Eyes. Leg.

Collapse. Collapse and stagger and tumble and—

"Easy there," the guy said, hopping out of his Eagle Pose just in time to keep me from knocking him halfway across the room. Melissa turned to look at me. The entire classroom turned to look at me. I felt as if I was some sort of circus freak show.

The instructor said, in her calm, soothing voice, "If you ever find a pose too difficult, remember that you can assume Child's Pose. Find your center. Start again."

I'd be damned if I was going to collapse into Child's Pose. In fact, I'd be damned if I stayed in the room for another two hours of contortionist torment. Catching Melissa's eye, I mouthed, "I'll call you later," and waggled my fingers beside my ear in the universal sign for a phone. I snatched up my mat and headed for the door before the surprised instructor could say anything else, before she could suggest another pose to the entire room full of perfect yogis.

I stood in the hallway, gasping for breath. I couldn't tell if I was more winded by my awkward Eagle Poses, or by my embarrassment at having given up. I forced myself to walk up and down the hallway outside the classroom. Now, the deep breaths were easy to come by. Now, I could feel the tension draining out of my shoulders.

The classroom door opened, and the guy who had broken my fall came out of the studio. My sandals dangled from his hand, and he had slipped my handbag under his arm. "I'm sorry—" I started to say.

"Don't be," he said, handing over my things. "Your friend was going to bring these to you, but I offered. I've had enough of the Peaceable Kingdom in there."

"You were doing fine," I said automatically.

"I was making a fool out of myself," he said. "I only signed up for the class because my girlfriend wanted me to."

"Then you should get back in there!"

He winced. "Um, that would be *ex*-girlfriend. We broke up three months ago. Right after we paid for the session, actually."

"You should have gotten a refund," I said, shaking my right sandal into place. I reached out for my purse.

"Ah…" he said, handing it over. "Pride goeth before a fall. If you hadn't given up on Eagle Pose, I'm sure the next position would have taken me out." I couldn't believe that he was highlighting my awkwardness, that he was teasing me for falling into him. He apparently couldn't believe it, either. He winced and said, "That didn't come out right. *I* would have fallen in the next pose. I was barely managing Eagle."

I made a wry smile but accepted his explanation, glancing at my watch. "Thanks for bringing me my stuff. I'm sorry to be rude, but I really should be going."

"Can I buy you a cup of coffee?"

"I have to be somewhere," I said automatically.

"You were supposed to be *here* for two more hours," he pointed out. "Come on," he said. "Just a cup of coffee. And you can explain to me about the peace and centering and holistic healing that you women find in there." He nodded back toward the studio.

"I absolutely cannot do that," I said. "The only thing *I* find in there is a best friend who's a whole lot better at this than I am. Not that we're supposed to compare ourselves to others." I mimicked the instructor's saintly tone. "We're here to grow our own spirit, not measure ourselves against the rest of the class."

"Maybe that's why most guys can't get into this stuff," he said. "We men should start our own studio. Extreme yoga. Competition for our modern age."

He pulled his face into a horrifying grimace and struck a fake body-builder pose that was so incongruous to his Everyday Joe build that I couldn't help but laugh. "There," he said. "One cup of coffee? Make me feel like I didn't totally waste my afternoon."

"One cup," I finally said, deciding to choose companion-ship over an afternoon of nursing a bruised ego. Some more. I held out my hand. "Jane Madison," I said.

"Will," he countered. "Will Becker."

He held the door for me as we stepped out onto the street. I imagined Melissa in the studio, gliding into Camel Pose or Cobra Pose or something even more exotic. I was never going to make it as a yoga goddess. But I was excelling at living the life of a caffeine queen.

6

"**W**hat's up, girlfriend?"

I pushed my hair back behind my right ear for the thousandth time. "What do you mean?"

"I mean that you're more nervous than a cat," Neko said, arching one eyebrow. "And believe me, I know what I'm talking about."

"Why shouldn't I be nervous?" I countered, catching myself chewing at my lip. "This is the biggest working I've undertaken in months."

But not the only magic I had done, a part of my mind nagged. No, I had used my powers only the day before. I could still feel the little twist in my belly, the spark that told me my magic had worked. The spark that—supposedly—reminded me that there would be no lasting impact from my indiscretion with David. For the thousandth time, I panicked that I had misperformed my contraceptive spell, that I was misreading the magical record in my body. But no. I was enough of a witch that I could tell it had worked. I was safe from that worry, at least.

Even if I had to keep racking my brain, trying to figure out how I was going to act natural, act normal, when my warder walked through my front door.

Matters weren't helped any when Neko sniffed the air, his nose twitching with all the delicacy of a calico scenting rotten salmon. I was suddenly horrified by the thought that he knew what had happened between David and me. I had showered—twice—since then. And I was wearing completely different clothes. But my familiar had strange abilities when it came to knowing that I'd made a fool out of myself.

There was a knock at the front door, and Neko nodded. "There," he said. "I knew he was out there."

So, that was all that he had sensed. David's arrival. Nothing more secret. More embarrassing. Neko waited for me to wave a purposely languorous hand, freeing him to answer the door as I descended to my basement lair. I sneaked in a half-dozen deep breaths before my partners in magical crime joined me in front of all my books.

Neko was quivering with excitement, each muscle stretched taut beneath his revealing black T-shirt. He was wearing the leather pants he'd sported when I first awakened him from his statue form, over two years before. His feet looked small and neat in his European-styled shoes, and I might have described his walk as delicate, if I hadn't known the power that lurked just beneath his flesh. He could mirror my own magic back to me, magnify my spells into things of true arcane spectacle. Without Neko, I was a powerful witch. With him—if David was to be believed—I was almost unstoppable.

And David was someone to believe.

He stopped at the foot of the stairs, as if awaiting formal permission to enter my witchy domain. He was wearing charcoal-colored slacks, as neat as if he'd just retrieved them from his tailor. A flawless cotton shirt blazed white against the gloom of the staircase, crisp without the stiffness of starch. I glanced at his face, fearing what I might see there, but his features were smooth. Implacable.

We might have been presidents of our very own Fortune 500 companies, meeting to collude on prices in the most illegal antitrust scheme in the history of capitalism. We might have been spies sent to assassinate each other for shadowy government agencies that claimed to keep peace in the world. We might have been strangers meeting in the hallway of some luxury hotel.

"Good evening," he said.

Or we might have been awkward former lovers, trying to figure out how we could continue working together.

Strike that. *I* might have been an awkward former lover. David seemed utterly unaffected by what had happened.

Neko looked at me, and I realized that my familiar truly was going to figure out what was going on if I didn't pull myself together and start acting normally. "Hi!" I said, and I realized that my voice was a dozen shades too bright. I cleared my throat and said, "Thank you for coming."

Ouch. Wrong word choice.

David didn't react, though. Instead, he glanced at the rows of books behind me. "Have you thought about the ritual? About what you're going to do?"

Fine. If he was going to act as if nothing had happened, I could be every bit as blasé.

I nodded, with the aplomb I harnessed every day as a reference librarian. Hardening my voice, I made myself sound like the trained professional I knew I could be. "Yes." There. I almost kept my voice from quaking. "I'm going to create an anima."

Neko sucked in his breath, and I took a perverse pleasure in knowing that I'd surprised him. I smiled sweetly and found the strength to go on. "I'll vivify it tonight and then task it to straighten things up around here. It can use its powers, its focus of *my* powers, to work through the crystals and the books, to get everything back in order. Each task it completes will build my reservoir of power."

David's eyes narrowed, and I watched his Adam's apple bob as he swallowed. I remembered kissing his throat, and a sudden breathlessness crushed my heart like a ton of featherbeds. *Concentrate*, I told myself. *This is important.*

"Have you reviewed the spell?" he asked, and he might have been inquiring if I'd had a chance to check the weather forecast, for all the emotion he loaded into the question.

"Three times," I said. "At least, my memory of it. I studied it in depth last winter." And I really had. At the time, I'd still been smarting from my encounter with the Coven. I'd contemplated creating an anima, a creature to do my own arcane bidding, just to prove that I was not magically alone. I'd memorized the spell, but I had not worked it before the laptop crashed. Before the laptop crashed, and my interest in my witchy abilities had faded.

I had winged things often enough when I'd worked with David and Neko, but I couldn't take that risk this time. I could sense the truth: we were approaching a true transition. Either I saved my powers now, or I lost them forever. The anima working was the strongest spell I knew by heart, the most elaborate working I could accomplish without benefit of the spell books that would fade away at my touch.

I glanced at Neko, wondering how he felt about tonight's magic. Last year, when I had done battle with the Coven, Neko's independence was on the line. David had warned me numerous times that I needed to perfect my skills as a witch or the Coven would reject me and take Neko away. Take all of my accoutrements away.

I sighed. As a librarian and a scholar of Elizabethan literature, I understood the meaning of irony. Alanis Morissette and her song aside, I knew it would be ironic if I'd fought the Coven, gained my witchy independence, only to lose Neko and my arcane collection now, through lack of use.

David nodded, accepting my determination as if I'd

always been a star pupil. Yeah, sure. "All right, then. Shall we get started?"

And that was it. No great debate. No long discussion. No back and forth about whether I had chosen the correct ritual, the proper symbols, the perfect expression of my magical intentions. Momentarily speechless, I nodded.

David reached inside the pocket of his trousers and pulled out a small silver flask. It was the sort of vessel that might hold holy water, if he'd belonged to a different esoteric school. "What's that?" I asked.

"Rainwater, collected under a full moon."

Of course. "So you knew, all along, what I was going to try?"

He shrugged. "I knew that you'd likely be calling on the elements for whatever you work. I can take it back, if it bothers you. If you have your own that you want to use."

"No!" My voice still sounded too shrill to me. I glanced at Neko, only to find that he was staring at me curiously.

Well, everyone knew what curiosity had done to the cat. I made a silent vow that he would learn the full meaning of that adage if he tried to question me directly.

I reached out for the flask, automatically twisting my fingers to avoid touching David's. That motion made my wrist bend at a strange angle; he rotated his own grasp on the flask to keep it from falling. Like an awkward fool dancing sideways to pass someone in a narrow hallway, I contorted my own fingers, only to end up grasping his with full force.

I sucked in my breath, as if I expected an electric charge to pass between us, but there was nothing. No residual glimmer of magic. No lingering sparkle of my contraceptive spell. No hint that anything had happened the afternoon before.

My belly twisted and, for just a moment, I thought I might be ill.

"Ready?" David asked, and his voice was calm and smooth, the steady baritone that had always anchored my magical workings.

I closed my eyes and took a deep breath, beyond caring if Neko suspected anything. "Ready," I said.

I set the flask of water on the high bookstand that occupied the center of the basement. A burlap sack sat in the center of the mahogany surface, the same sack that I had explored a week and a half before, with Melissa obliviously drinking mojitos in my kitchen. I tried not to think about the clay runes that I had enjoyed using, the smooth tiles that had clicked in my fingers as I shuffled through their smooth, glazed surfaces.

Dust, now. Nothing but dust.

I shook my head. "Let's go," I said to David.

He eyed me for a long moment, and I wondered what he was thinking. Was he questioning my witchy ability? Was he wondering about our little diversion the day before? Was he doubting my dedication to my arcane arts?

I'd never know.

Without a spoken word, he ducked down. It took me a

moment to figure out why he made the graceful motion, but when he stood, he clutched a silver dagger. I glanced at his ankle, unable to make out any sort of hidden sheath. Not for the first time, I wondered what other secrets my warder kept from me.

So. David was going to treat this working as high ritual. He was moving beyond the ordinary spellcraft that he and I had practiced so many times here, in the comfort of my basement. He was elevating this magic to the limits of my witchy ability, making sure that we had the utmost astral protection.

My throat was suddenly too dry for me to swallow. I had known this spell was important. I had understood that a lot rode on what we were doing. I had believed that my future as a witch would be determined by my ability to create an anima.

But I had not truly grasped the seriousness of my endeavor.

Or the danger. David rarely used his warder's powers this blatantly. I had to assume that he sensed some very real threat to what we were doing.

Or else, he was being his usual, paranoid, controlling self.

Before I could decide if that last thought made me feel more or less safe, David inclined his head over the dagger and muttered a few words, too softly for me to hear. At the same time, Neko glided to my side.

I felt my familiar magically as much as physically. He was like a highly polished bronze mirror, reflecting my own power back at me with a deep, steady glow. Neko might be a fashion king, and he might chide me far more than was fair about the makeup that I should or should not wear, but when arcane push came to magical shove, I could not imagine having a better resource at my side. I'd missed his astral companionship as we'd squabbled over milk and ice cream.

David nodded when he saw that we were poised for spell-work, and then he extended his arms in front of him, holding the dagger steady before his eyes. "May Hecate watch over our working here and keep us safe from evil."

Neko and I responded as if we had rehearsed. "May Hecate keep us safe."

David walked a quarter circle, continuing to hold the silver blade high, like a dowsing rod searching for magical potential. I knew from past work in this basement chamber that he was facing due north. He bowed slightly, like a courtier acknowledging the presence of another haughty lord. "May the Lady of the North, the Lady of Water, watch over us during this working."

Once before, I had called upon the compass coordinates, the ancient elements, for protection. As my body folded into an automatic bow of respect, I remembered that other circle of power that David had trod with me, the night that I had rejected membership in the Washington Coven. The words rose to my lips without conscious recollection. "Lady of Water! We ask that you protect our workings and bless them in the name of our mother Hecate."

If David was proud of me for remembering the incantation, he gave no sign. I shoved down a nibble of annoyance. We had more important things to attend to than his pig-headed refusal to acknowledge my accomplishments. Or his stubborn determination to accept that we *had* slept together whatever his warder's code of ethics might demand. Oops. I'd promised myself not to go there.

As if to pull my mind back to the matter at hand, David strode another arc of the circle, planting his feet at due west. "May the Lord of Earth watch over us during this working."

"Lord of Earth," I replied, "we ask that you protect our workings and bless them in the name of our mother Hecate."

South came next, with the Lady of Air, and then east, with the Lord of Fire. When David strode back to the northern start of the circle, a faint glow shimmered in the air, a silver curtain that separated us from ghosties and ghoulies and long-legged beasties. I swallowed hard, sensing the tremendous power my warder had raised, even as my paranoid hindbrain whispered, "And things that go bump in the night."

Enough with childhood fears. I had woman's work to do. Witching work.

As Neko and David drew closer to the bookstand, I lifted the bag of clay dust. It felt heavier in my hands now than it had when I'd first picked it up, as if the destroyed runes could sense how I was planning to use them. Taking a deep breath to slow my pounding heart, I pulled the rope ties loose at the neck of the burlap sack.

I started to shove my hand into the bag, but then I thought of the clay dust settling under my fingernails. I wasn't the most fastidious of women, by any means, but I imagined those grains of clay, once they were animated, and my belly flipped at the thought of living flesh underneath my nails. Grateful that—for once—I'd thought of consequences, I tilted a generous pile of the dust into my open palm.

"Earth," I intoned. "For earth doth make us all."

"For earth doth make us all," David repeated, and I was surprised; I had not expected any sort of call and response. Apparently, my warder thought otherwise, because he cast a sharp glance at Neko, who squeaked a belated, "For earth doth make us all."

All right, then.

A giddy thought rose in my mind, that I could manipulate the pair of them, saying whatever I wanted to hear them say. Jane Madison is a powerful witch. I will do whatever Jane tells me to do. I will never, ever question Jane Madison again for as long as I shall live.

Yeah. I was their witch, not their goddess. If I led them down such ridiculous paths, they'd snort themselves silly with laughter, however grave the atmosphere that David had created with his warding spell. I recognized my thoughts for what they were—my own mind's attempts to keep me from focusing on the magic I was about to work. To keep me from focusing on the magic that frightened me. Terrified me.

Because, if the anima spell failed, then I was through being a witch.

Before I could dwell on that possibility, I clutched the flask of rainwater that David had brought. "Water," I said, in a voice that was overloud. "For water doth bind us all."

"For water doth bind us all," my minions repeated, and I forced myself to set aside my momentary pleasure at the thought that I had minions.

I poured about a tablespoon of water into my palm, into the middle of the clay ruins. At first, the water floated on top of the red granules, sliding like a giant bead of clear mercury. But then, I poked at it with a finger that wanted to tremble, and the water's surface tension broke. It seeped into the clay, staining it, turning it the color of blood.

Quickly, before I could frighten myself with that image, I kneaded the earth and water into thick clay. Drawing on kindergarten skills that I'd thought long forgotten, I shaped a very rough human form, pinched here for legs, there for arms, rolling a rough ball onto the top to form a head. My tongue caught between my teeth as I concentrated, but even that pressure wasn't enough to keep my memory from straying to some contorted clay monstrosity I had made for Gran, as a Halloween treat long ago. I could still remember rolling my careful ball of clay, pinching a bit at the top for a pumpkin stem, and then stabbing eyes into my Play-Doh jack-o'-lantern, using a sharpened pencil to make perfect conical indentations. Gran probably still had the thing somewhere in her apartment.

Again, I identified my wandering thoughts for the avoidance that they were and pulled my concentration back to the matter at hand. Body, arms, legs, head. I had done all that was necessary.

Glancing quickly at David and Neko, who wore matching implacable expressions, I raised the little figurine toward my mouth. Pursing my lips, I breathed onto it gently. "Air," I whispered, as if I were afraid to upset the balance I was building. "For air doth lift us all."

"For air doth lift us all."

I cradled the clay form on one palm and touched one free finger to my head, my throat and my heart, completing the familiar offering of my thoughts, my words and my spirit to the powers of the arcane universe. Before I could wonder if I'd built up enough of a magic reservoir, before I could ask myself whether I had the power to work the spell I'd chosen, I whispered:

"From the darkness, light will spring
Out of nothing, something bring.
Gather power, dark take wing,
Flames will crackle, fire sing."

I breathed a silent prayer to some unnamed entity that I had enough magic stored. I prayed that I could empower my anima.

Empower The Arts. The phrase came to me unbidden, yet another attempt by my deceitful mind to shy away from the working at hand, from the arcane and sexual tension that filled my basement. In a flash, I could see the

Tempest poster hanging in Starbucks, picture the commanding Prospero's face. That face, which was so much like David's.

That was the wrong thought. Suddenly, I pictured David and me together, sprawled across the bed in his Pottery Barn perfect room. I remembered how he had brushed my hair back from my face, how he had looked at me with eyes that seemed to see me *truly*, differently than he had ever looked at me before.

I shuddered and forced my mind back to the present, to the now. Energy was flowing across the bookstand, pooling in the center of its mahogany surface. I spread the fingers of my empty hand and closed my eyes, summoning the full power of the spell, even as I pushed down the memory of the illicit time I had spent with my warder, pushed away my hurt and shame and confusion. *Empower The Arts,* I thought again, then pushed away the words. This was more than art I was empowering. This was magic.

A tiny bud of fire burst from the surface of the bookstand, burning without consuming the wood.

It was nothing to be proud of. Nothing that the most powerful witch on the eastern seaboard—if my warder was to be believed—should boast about. Nothing that any sister of the Washington Coven couldn't do with her eyes closed and one well-manicured hand tied behind her back.

But it worked. And it was mine.

The rosebud of fire spread across the wooden bookstand, no larger than the span of my fingers. It flickered—crimson and magenta and sunshine-orange—miniature flames that gave off heat but consumed nothing. Nothing but magic.

Not knowing how long I could maintain the bewitching, I settled my clay doll in the middle of the flames. "Fire," I said, and I was surprised to find that my breath was raspy. I had drawn more power from my dwindling stock than I'd thought. "For fire doth enliven us all."

"For fire doth enliven us all."

I stared at the figurine, saw that the magical flames were already baking it into a solid, permanently misshapen form. As I watched, I suddenly feared that I did not have the strength to continue, that I could not awaken the spirit of my creation. I had already poured so much into her—*too* much into her. I did not have the power to complete what I had begun.

Before I could step back, though, before I could surrender, before I could collapse on the cracked leather couch and beg David to let me try again, try with something simpler, something easier, something that I was capable of finishing, Neko glided to my side. He leaned against my shoulder, or I leaned against him. He tilted his head toward mine.

I sensed my fragile witching strength multiplied by his physical presence. Like a car windshield that magnifies the heat of the sun on a summer day, Neko was collecting the final strands of my power, beaming them back toward me. I wasted a moment, basking in the energy that he gathered together.

There I was, in a magical space, outside the normal flow of time, of energy. My Georgetown basement was separate and apart, like an island lost in a tropical sea. The books that lined my shelves had belonged to famous witches, to powerful women. I was like Miranda in *The Tempest*, awed by the secret volumes, by the library on her enchanted isle. I was Miranda. Separate and apart from Prospero. From David. Miranda. Alone.

And that thought gave me the focus to continue.

I had already done the hard part, summoning the elements, combining them into a form. Now all that was left was the naming. Well, the naming, and the final transformation.

Thinking of Shakespeare's spirit, I extended my hand over my baking clay creature. Empower The Arts, I distracted myself one last time. "Ariel," I said. "I name thee Ariel."

I closed my eyes and gathered together the four strands of power that I had raised—earth and air, fire and water. I wove them into a garment, into a skin, into living, breathing flesh. I reached down to the very bottom of my arcane reservoir, reached through the remnants of magical strength that I had fed with cleansing and heating spells. With the magic of sex. I drew on the memory of all the spells that I had ever worked, crystals I had ever charmed, potions I had ever brewed beneath the power of a full and silver moon.

"Ariel," I whispered again, and there was finally the familiar flash of darkness, the all-absorbing expansion of complete and utter lack of sight, followed by a gradual clearing, and a return of all my normal faculties.

And when I peered at the bookstand, the figurine was gone.

In its place, crouching at the bottom of the mahogany structure, was a fine-boned woman. Her skin was so fair, it looked carved from ice. Delicate rivers of veins branched just beneath the surface. Her hair was as dark as a farmer's fresh-turned field. She was covered by a gauzy length of silk, as if she had converted the fire of her birth into a garment.

I had created an anima.

I nearly staggered—as much at the thought of what I had accomplished as by the feeling that I was empty, bare, stripped of all my magical power. The anima spell had taken more than I had thought I had to give; it had excavated deeper into my scant store of power than I had thought possible.

This must be how I had felt every day, before I awakened Neko. Before I knew I was a witch. Hollow. Hungry. Alone. Desperate for a solution that I scarcely believed existed.

I glanced at David and caught a pleased look on his face, a prideful smile that reminded me of how much he had invested in my witchy education. Neko, on the other hand, was clearly nervous about the newcomer. The newcomer I had made. The newcomer crafted from the last of my arcane ability.

She stirred, stretching out one foot from beneath her delicate blanket. Neko leaped away from my side, shuddering like a cat caught in a sudden rainstorm. Once we were no longer touching, I could only feel his presence like a memory, like a phantom of an amputated limb.

My Ariel sat up, clutching her silk with a grace that I could only imagine possessing. She turned around the room slowly, scarcely registering the presence of Neko and David. Instead, she focused on me, taking a single, tottering step toward me before she inclined her head. *Witch*, she said.

Except she didn't say it.

She thought it.

She thought it directly inside my mind.

I looked quickly at my warder and familiar, but they seemed completely unaware of the communication. I let myself fall back into the snare of my creation's sky-blue eyes. *Anima*, I thought. *Ariel*.

What would you have me do, Witch?

Her words oozed the smallest drop of power—a hint, a whisper. A memory of the magic that had once been mine dropped into the very core of my magical self.

It was something.

And she was talking to me. She was asking me for direction. This must be the way the spell was supposed to work. This must be the way that I was supposed to rebuild my strength. Pour it into my anima, then have her leverage it. Multiply it. Feed it back to me, purified and increased beyond recognition.

Clean, I thought to Ariel. *Those crystals, first. Each one in the box*. I gestured toward my stash in the corner.

I can do that, Witch. I will call their earth to me. I will cleanse them with my water.

Just be careful with your fire, I thought, trying to make a joke, to lighten the formality of her speech. I sensed her confusion, her perplexity. *Call their earth,* I thought quickly. *Water is fine.*

Yes, Witch. As you command.

Another pure drop of power coalesced inside my mind, the product of our exchange. I wanted her to speak to me again. I wanted her to return my power faster. I wanted her to fill me with the astral energy that was mine. But I knew that I needed to practice patience. I knew that my aching loss was part of a larger plan.

Ariel crossed the room on legs so graceful that she seemed never to touch the ground. She knelt beside the wooden box that held my crystals, opened the complicated hasp with smooth and confident fingers.

She lifted the first stone she saw, a highly polished aventurine. Seemingly unaware of the three of us humans (or whatever Neko was), she raised the crystal to her lips, breathed on it once, with a breath that seemed scented with apples, even this far, across the room. Then, she folded the foggy stone inside her perfect hand, closed her fingers around it. Her brow furrowed with the sort of intense concentration I usually saw devoted to Samurai Sudoku puzzles spread in front of time-wasting library patrons.

When she opened her palm and raised the aventurine to her lips again, I almost cried out loud. The crystal's fog was gone. The spider cracks that had spread across its surface were healed. In their place was a placid glow, a subtle beacon of arcane power. Healing, the aventurine broadcast. Health.

I waited to feel another drop of power fall into my reservoir of magical strength. I gathered myself for a deposit in the bank of my depleted witchy energy. But there was nothing.

Maybe one stone wasn't enough. Maybe one crystal didn't register. I made a sound at the back of my throat, and Ariel immediately lifted her eyes to mine. *"Yes, Witch?"*

"Nothing," I thought, resenting my craven gratitude when her question fed me another drop of power. *"Just keep doing what you're doing."*

She inclined her head and reached for the next stone.

And suddenly, I was overwhelmed with everything that had happened. I tried to step back, tried to turn around, to explain to David and Neko the communication that had passed between my anima and me.

David was staring at me. His brow was creased, as if he was worried, as if he was disturbed by Ariel, or by the thoughts we had shared, or by something else in the strange working. I knew that I should ask him what was wrong, ask him why he was looking at me that way.

My lips were too tired to form words, though. My feet were too tired to move me toward the men, to take me close enough to whisper. My arms were too tired to raise up, to gesture toward the crystals, even as I hoped that another drop of magical power would appear in the depths of my witchy powers.

My anima might have fed me three drops of magical ability, but my physical power was utterly depleted.

I barely kept my eyes open long enough to watch David disperse his protective wards. He reached out for me, concern in his eyes, but I could not let him touch me. Not after what had passed between us. Not after he had tossed me out of his bed the day before.

He read my rejection through my exhaustion, and he said something to Neko, something I could no longer hear. My familiar eased an arm around my waist and helped me up the stairs. He guided me into my bedroom, onto my inviting mattress. He swung my legs onto the bed, settled a cotton throw across my body. I barely heard him tiptoe out of the room, and I might have only imagined a conversation that he muttered with David in the living room.

As I fell asleep, I longed for another magical drop to return to the well of my powers. I knew that Ariel would work long into the night.

7

By morning, I had fully recovered.

I quickly tested my reservoir of power, hoping to find it filled with anima-inspired magic. Nothing. Well, the three drops, contributed by Ariel the night before. But nothing else.

I tried to drown my disappointment in the shower, and then I dressed for work quickly, pulling on my eighteenth-century garb. I couldn't quite say when I'd become accustomed to settling wicker frames over my hips, to tweaking tiered skirts into place over those curving strips of wood, to flicking a patch of soft lace across my chest. I'd even mastered a couple of quick twists for my unruly auburn hair, securing my muslin cap with a couple of near-invisible bobby pins, as if I were—as Hamlet said—to the manner born.

Of course, the melancholy Dane's next line was "More honour'd in the breach than the observance," and I didn't have the luxury of breaching the Peabridge's dress code. I made a face at myself in the mirror.

Even though I was running late—as usual—I had to tiptoe down to the basement to see how my anima was faring. I had to make sure that there wasn't a giant puddle of misdirected magical potential, soaking into the basement's intricate silk rug.

Ariel crouched beside my box of crystals, as if she had not moved all night long. I could make out a small pile beside her, a tumble of reinvigorated stones. From across the room, I could see that the minerals were shiny and clear, all hint of fog and striation washed away by the magical touch of my astral housekeeper.

I edged another mental fingertip toward my powers, wondering why my strength had not been built up by the operation. After all, David had been quite clear about the advantages of this working. The more I used my powers, the more I'd regain my strength. Ariel was a simple extension of myself; I should be reaping the benefits of her work.

Except I wasn't.

I hadn't lost the few drops of power that she'd fed me the night before; those still glistened like lonely quarts of milk in a grocery store cooler the night of a Washington snowstorm. But there'd been no growth. No additional power.

Something was wrong. David had sensed something. He had been ready to tell me that what we had done was broken.

Unless he wasn't. Unless I'd imagined it all, as I fought to keep my feet, exhausted beyond all reason.

Who was I fooling? I had no idea how this anima thing was really supposed to work. I'd studied the spell during the winter because I'd wanted to create an animate being, a creature that I could use to thumb my nose at the Coven. I hadn't been concerned about regaining my witchy strength, about building any sort of astral boomerang.

I would just ask David what was going on.

But I had no desire to do that. I closed my eyes and sucked a sharp breath between my teeth. I could still picture the calm understanding in his eyes when he'd summoned Neko to assist me. Was there pity there, too?

It had been bad enough that I'd thought of David while I was awakening Ariel, that I'd let that silly promotional poster for *The Tempest* steal away my attention. I wasn't going to run crying to him now, when he'd likely tell me that I'd just have to be patient. That sometimes magic didn't come easily. That some things took time to work. Especially when I'd been so irresponsible for so long, ignoring my powers for days, weeks, months. This was like a diet. I couldn't lose a lifetime of Ben & Jerry's fat by completing a single morning of treadmill miles.

I would just have to give Ariel time to work. After all, the magical potential she must be generating had to go *somewhere*. I could reclaim what was mine later. After I'd grown accustomed to my anima's eerie ways.

And they were eerie. She worked in total silence, reaching

for the next crystal with the uncanny accuracy of a blind man in a familiar space. She plucked a tiny apatite from its compartment. Ugly gray faded to clear blue as she worked, and I wondered if she felt a corresponding boost in her own mind. "Good work, Ariel," I said, hoping that encouragement might turn the tide.

She turned to me slowly, as if she were walking in her sleep. *Witch*, she said, and the word was toneless in my mind.

"Um," I said, speaking out loud because that felt more natural to me. "Keep doing what you're doing."

Witch, she repeated, and I decided to believe that she was acknowledging my instructions.

"Great! The crystals should take you the rest of today, at least."

Witch, was my anima's only reply.

That third repetition of my title was enough to slide a single drop of power into my mind. Well, that was better than nothing. And at least she didn't offer sartorial advice, like Neko constantly did. I thought of my familiar's presence, made comfortable over nearly two years of togetherness. Even when he wasn't in the cottage, I'd always had a faint tie to him, the bond that I could use to summon him in an emergency. I reached out for that connection now, to comfort myself.

It was gone.

I could feel where it used to be, like a gulley carved deep by runoff water. There might have been a glimmer there, a reflection of the old tie. But my power was well and truly missing, invested in the creation of the strange creature who toiled silently in front of me.

Was this what David had meant, when he had said that losing my power would set Neko free? Was this how another witch could find my familiar, could steal him as her own?

Neko! I thought. But there was no answer, no magical reply.

I scrambled upstairs, grabbing my cell phone off the coffee table, where I'd left it the night before. It was faster to punch in Neko's number from my stored list than to press ten separate buttons on my home phone. It rang and rang and rang. I finally snapped the cell closed and tried to tell myself that the radio silence meant nothing. Neko had left my cottage late last night. He and Jacques were probably still tangled in their sheets, lost inside their lovers' bower.

I needed to call David.

I couldn't call David.

I had to.

His number rang unanswered, as well. At least he had voice mail. "David, it's me. I can't feel Neko. It's not working, this whole Ariel thing. Call me."

I'd tried to sound calm. Collected. Dispassionate.

My heart was pounding so hard that I could barely breathe, but I still needed to get to work. In fact, Evelyn was standing guard at the front door of the Peabridge. She nodded to greet me as I sailed in with less than a minute to spare. "How was your weekend, Jane?" she asked, her face even more heavily powdered than usual, as if she were trying to tone down any hint of florid expression against the shock of her magenta-and-peach suit.

"Fine," I said, thinking that I'd better keep things simple. No need for Evelyn to hear about my mistake with David. Or my failure at yoga class. Or the arcane creature who crouched in the basement of the Peabridge gardener's cottage.

Simple was going to be my watchword for the workday. I was going to be a good reference librarian, a solid worker. There was nothing I could do about my magical problems until David called me back.

Before I could elaborate a harmless lie about my weekend adventures, there was a flurry of activity on the library steps, and a flash of muslin and indigo-dyed trousers. "Kit!" Evelyn exclaimed.

"I'm here," my intern said. "I'm on time!" She brandished a large paperboard box. "And I have the pastries from Cake Walk!"

Evelyn glanced at the giant clock on the wall over the coffee bar. "Well, it *is* just nine." I could see that she wanted to argue about something, wanted to launch into yet another explanation that Katherine Elizabeth Montague—Kit—should be wearing a dress instead of a boy's outfit.

But Kit was too valuable to me to lose. I clutched her arm and said, "We'd better get ready for the first coffee wave, before Colonial Story Hour begins."

Kit flashed me a grateful smile and followed me across the large reference room. She started to set up the coffee bar with swift, automatic motions. Kit had graduated from Georgetown University in May. She'd spent her summer in town to avoid heading home to a horrendously large family in horrendously crowded New York.

Kit had been accepted into graduate level public policy programs at Harvard and Brown; she was such an attractive candidate that both schools had offered her full scholarships. She knew that she wanted to change the world, that she wanted to focus on schools and teaching and where the collective we were failing the children of America.

But she also knew that the rest of her life hung on the decision she had to make. Harvard, Brown. Harvard. Brown. She couldn't go wrong. But she wanted to go right. So she had begged extensions from both programs and committed herself to working for a year to decide.

Working without pay. Working as an intern at the Peabridge Library because we were close to Georgetown University, and because we were familiar, and because she just happened to wander by the day that we posted a notice in our front window announcing our internship (my little brainchild, when I'd realized that I would likely murder the next children who came in for story hour, if I had to continue doing the activity unassisted). I didn't know how she supported herself; I was afraid to ask, for fear that she would admit she couldn't make ends meet, that she would announce that she had to leave.

And Kit was perfect for the job. She had the academic knowledge that Evelyn craved and an enthusiasm for working with small children that left me truly awed. The only catch was that Kit flat-out refused to wear a colonial woman's clothes. She said, "What am I going to do, chase after kids with eight layers of petticoats tripping me up?"

My point exactly. That was why I had sought an intern in the first place. I was tired of kid-chasing.

Kit was the one who hit on a compromise. She would wear colonial costume—but the far more forgiving attire of an eighteenth-century young man. Evelyn had wanted to protest the first day, but she found herself swayed by our shrewd college graduate's justifications: (1) the kids should see more than just women's costumes, (2) there was a surplus of men's clothing that had been donated to the Peabridge by Colonial Williamsburg, (3) (and the killer argument, in my humble opinion) Kit might be more successful in bringing more boys into our summer program, expanding the library's demographic in the Georgetown community.

Kit had a future as a public policy maker. She won her argument handily, and I gained an intern who freed me from the worst of my job responsibilities. My savior even lived a block away from Cake Walk, so she brought over our morning pastries, along with gossip from Melissa.

As if on cue, Kit exclaimed as we set out the display of baked goods, "Oh, Melissa wanted me to give you a message!"

"She's won the lottery, and we're on our own for baked goods for the rest of the year?"

Kit made a face and shook her head. "At least I'd understand what she meant by *that*. No, I'm supposed to tell you that she made a special pot of Caramel Caravel, and now she's sailing to *The Tempest* on Friday night. Does that make any sense to you?"

I winced at the mention of the damned play, but I nodded. Caramel Caravel… Melissa had said that her would-be beau preferred caramel flavors for his coffee. Melissa must have kept her obligation under our Friendship Test. She had spoken to Rob-Peterson-the-Lawyer. Why they were going to the Shakespeare play, though, I really couldn't say.

With Ariel returned to the front of my consciousness, I reached out with another tentative mental finger, gauging again the accumulation of cleared-crystal energy. Nothing added. Nothing new. I glanced at the phone on my desk and willed David to call. At least I wasn't foolish enough to be disappointed when it stayed silent.

He'd call me when he got my message. David was responsible that way. David was responsible *every* way. Before I could dwell more on my warder-inspired peccadillo, the library doors opened and a half-dozen mothers swarmed in, surrounded by their whining, crying brats. I watched a smile bloom on Kit's face, and I shook my head at her crazed enthusiasm. "Divide and conquer?" I asked.

"Come on, kids!" she called out, not even bothering to nod. "Down to the basement!"

In exchange for Kit's cheerful herding of the masses, I twisted my lips into a smile and ducked behind the coffee bar. When Evelyn had first instituted our beverage service,

I had resented the time that I spent as a barista—after all, I hadn't attended library school to learn how to pour the perfect latte.

Now, though, with our new and improved simplified menu, I found that I was nowhere near as down on the notion of library-cum-coffee bar. It would seem practically churlish to begrudge the poor mothers of Georgetown a simple cup of coffee. Although, I still thought they overstepped their bounds when they asked me to pour their caffeinated brew over ice.

It only took a couple of minutes to get them all served and to settle them at a table in the reference room, where they pretended to whisper to each other about the house-and-garden show down at the Convention Center. The grand display of stage whispers lasted for about thirty seconds, and then they were chattering away in normal voices. My reference librarian nerves were on edge, but I knew that Evelyn wanted the local community to feel at home around us, so I pasted a smile on my lips and headed back to my desk to get some real library work done.

I straightened my mobcap and fired up my old computer. I had half a dozen e-mails waiting for me, and I quickly settled into a series of short research projects. I could still remember when I'd started at the Peabridge, how every new request sent me delving into incredible specialized resources. I'd loved learning new things, exploring new intellectual opportunities.

Now, it seemed as if I knew my subject matter a little too

well. There was one person asking about colonial customs for Thanksgiving. Again. (Our founding fathers did not observe the holiday.) Two more patrons were planning even further ahead, asking about Christmas. Again. (I had a little more to tell them. I already knew they weren't going to be pleased when they learned there was no Santa Claus, no Christmas Tree and gifts were minimal.)

I enjoyed helping patrons—I still got a thrill out of locating the occasional rare and obscure resource. But these days, there was too much same old, same old about my job.

I got my first interesting question of the day when I opened an e-mail from a woman who lived a few blocks away from the library. She wanted me to track down some finer points of colonial garden layouts, designs that were intended to maximize vegetable yield in poor soil. I wondered whether she really wanted to serve a family of four through the dog days of summer, all on the plantings of her quarter acre lot.

I muttered the research librarian's motto: Ours not to wonder why. Remembering a specialized treatise that I had shelved a few weeks before, I pushed back my chair and wandered into the stacks, taking along my very own cup of coffee (with a half shot of cinnamon syrup for good measure, and a white plastic lid snapped on top for good stewardship of the library's collection).

Mindful of past disasters involving my colonial skirts and awkward library shelves, I pushed a step stool over to the stacks with my toe. I set my cup of coffee in a conveniently book-free space on a shelf just below eye level, and then I stepped onto the round step stool as gracefully as I could manage. I stretched for the volume that I recalled, certain that it was hiding beside the ragged leather-bound farm accounts from one of the signers of the Declaration of Independence.

Victory! The planting treatise was exactly where I had remembered!

Still balanced on the stool, I opened the book and paged through the chapter headings, wondering if I had recalled the contents as thoroughly as I'd mastered their location. By force of habit, I started to gnaw on my lower lip. That was a substantial improvement on my past expression of studious nerves—there was a time when I would have chewed on my fingernails as I worked, wearing them down to ragged nibs. Becoming aware of my lip-chewing, though, I reached for my coffee cup, determined to distract myself from all bad habits.

"Ah! There you are!"

I started at the voice, smothering a little cry at the back of my throat. Apparently, I had been more engrossed by colonial gardening techniques than I'd believed; I had totally wrapped myself into the text I was reading. Even as I recognized the speaker, even as I felt an odd, lazy swoop at the pit of my stomach, I tried to step down off the awkward stool, juggling my book and coffee cup. Just to make matters a bit more challenging, my mobcap chose that moment to slip free from its bobby pins (a break for freedom that it practiced at least a dozen times a day).

Well, I rescued the book.

My librarian instincts were strong, even in the most dire of circumstances. I was able to thrust the treatise forward, settling it onto a top shelf without ruffling a single page. Unfortunately, my sartorial instincts were substantially weaker. The coffee cup splashed against my chest, plastic lid bursting open with an embarrassing *pop* that seemed to echo in the stacks, only to be drowned out by the sound of a splash as lukewarm liquid cascaded across the black-and-white tiled floor. Even the splash, though, was drowned out by the noise of my curse as I stared at the ecru stain that soaked my bodice. My lacy bodice. My white, flimsy, now-see-through, lacy bodice.

I turned to face the owner of the hale and hearty voice. "Will," I said weakly, fumbling to retrieve my traitorous mobcap from my wide skirts, so that I could cover my over-exposed décolletage.

"I am so sorry!" Will Becker said, and the look of chagrin on his face chased away any angry words I might have been inclined to deliver. "Oh, God, let me help you with that." His hand on my elbow was steady as he helped me down from the stool, and he kept his eyes averted from the muslin headpiece that was incompetently masquerading as a camisole. As soon as I was steady on terra firma, he reached down to scoop up my now-empty coffee cup.

He fished a handkerchief out of his pocket and spread the snowy cotton across the milky puddle on the tiled floor. At least there was one advantage to my soaked lace—*most* of the library had been spared a caffeinated bath. He wiped up the rest of the offending coffee with an efficiency that would have made Gran proud—she had always despaired of teaching me the finer points of mopping. I took advantage of his face being averted to pluck the wet cloth from my chest, wishing I had stored enough magical power to mutter a quick spell to dry the fabric.

"I'm sorry," Will repeated as he straightened, and I reluctantly folded my mobcap-enhanced arms back across my chest. "I should have cleared my throat or something, so that you knew I was there."

I pictured him standing earnestly at the end of the row of books, clearing his throat like a character in a sitcom. Something about the image made me smile, despite my sodden discomfort. "What brings you here?" I asked, trying to make my question casual.

After a year of lusting after the Infantile Baby, I was leery of any man who came into my library and made casual conversation with me. Particularly any man who had watched me make a fool of myself in public, as I had in Melissa's yoga class. Especially any man who had bought me coffee and entertained me for two hours with self-deprecating stories about his own social failures, after he had witnessed my yogic disaster.

"I had research to do," he said, as if that was the most normal response in the world. Which it might even have been, given the fact that we were standing in a research library.

"About what?" I was still suspicious.

"Colonial outbuildings," he said promptly. "I need them for that Harrison project I told you about."

The Harrison project. He had mentioned it while we talked. He'd been hired by some dot-com billionaire who had gotten tired of living the high life in a San Francisco loft. The rich guy had decided to return home to Virginia, and he wanted a replica of James Monroe's home, Ash Lawn-Highland. Will had earned the commission to convert a colonial country home into a twenty-first-century living space suitable for a man as wealthy as the Sultan of Brunei.

Well, colonial outbuildings might be enough to warrant Will's presence at the Peabridge, but I couldn't help but bristle. The Ingrate Bastard had routinely come to the Peabridge for his professorial advancement; he had secretly reveled in making me his private research assistant, without offering even a footnote of thanks.

What was it about men and me—men who exploited my good nature and my research skills for their own good? I set my teeth and tested my tone until I could be certain it would be civil—even if it was cold as stone. "Well, let's go back to my desk. I can check the catalog for appropriate resources."

"Oh, I already looked up what I need." He gestured with the hand that wasn't holding his sopping handkerchief, and I saw that he was indeed clutching a slip of paper. Numbers and letters angled across it in a peculiar style that I'd only seen etched into blueprints before.

"If I read the call number right, books about outbuildings should be here?"

He nodded with his chin to the books behind me, to the shelf immediately across from my own specialized gardening treatise. To the shelf that, indeed, held a couple dozen books on outbuildings on colonial estates.

Will had not been looking for me to complete his research. He'd been doing his own work.

I couldn't help but grin. "Yeah," I said, edging past him. I needed to get out of my soaked clothes, the sooner, the better. "They're all there."

"I just need some basics," he said. Apparently, the overwhelming aroma of cinnamon-tinged coffee did not offend him because he went on in a conversational tone. "I'm just trying to get some feel for the design elements. I know that a lot of the original buildings had carved wooden clapboards, so that they looked like stone from a distance. Vanity of vanities, and all that."

"Just like my cottage," I said without thinking.

"Your cottage? Where is that?" His smile was easy, interested, and I found my own lips curving again, in response to his good nature.

"Here, at the Peabridge. I live in an old caretaker's cottage, at the back of the garden."

"How did *that* happen?"

"It's a long story," I said, wondering what he would think if I told him all of it—including the bit about the books hidden in my basement. Another time, maybe. A time when I wasn't drenched in Eau de Café. "The short version is they let me move into the cottage so that they could cut my salary."

I could see the question that he wanted to ask. I could even hear his voice forming the words. I could feel my own face flushing, reddening at the thought of this man inviting himself into my home, under the guise of studying the design. And yet I heard myself say, "Would you like to see it? Would it help your research?"

"I don't want to impose," he said, not quite smothering his eagerness with reluctance.

I started to sigh but stopped when I realized that motion stretched my clinging bodice tighter. "Well, I'm going to have to go home and change anyway."

He winced. "I really am sorry. I insist on paying to have that cleaned."

"No worries," I said. Maybe by tonight I'd have a little spell ready. One that would make laundry a breeze. No reason for him to know all my secrets, though, within twenty-four hours of meeting me. (Had it really only been twenty-four hours? A lot had happened to me since then.)

After all, it was one thing to have a clumsy woman body-check you in a yoga class. It was another to learn that the clumsy woman was a rogue member of the local Coven, capable of weaving spells with a single word. At least in theory. I thought about reaching out for Ariel, to see if I could bolster my powers yet, but I wasn't sure I could do that without some strange expression crossing my face. I didn't want to look any more bizarre in front of Will than I already did.

Apparently, I was entirely successful in hiding my unusual

train of thought, because Will was shrugging and saying, "At least let me buy you lunch, then."

I should have heard the jangle of warning bells.

No man ever just asked me out to lunch. At least, no man who wasn't enthralled to me in a spell. Or attempting to commit adultery with my all-too-eager assistance. Or intending to discipline me for setting aside my witchy studies.

And yet, I didn't feel a single thrum of warning. No tingle of imminent danger. No threat of disaster, looming, if I said yes.

There was always the possibility that my relationship radar had gone on the blink along with my magical powers. Okay, okay, there was the possibility that my so-called relationship radar had never *actually* functioned—that would explain my horrific mistakes with my Imaginary Boyfriend. And the Coven Eunuch. And David.

I wasn't going to think about David.

Instead, I'd cross my fingers and hope—pray to whatever dating gods might be listening—that going to lunch with Will wouldn't be a complete disaster.

It couldn't be, right? I mean, I wasn't expecting anything to come of it. I wasn't pinning every girlish hope that had ever crossed my heart on what we'd discuss over platefuls of food. I could even picture myself ordering spaghetti at the little Italian place down the block—a first date culinary and sartorial violation that would have sent Melissa into conniption fits.

But this wasn't a first date.

And my lace bodice was already soaked with milky coffee.

A drop or two of red sauce added to whatever fresh clothes I collected from the cottage couldn't make me look any worse than I did now. Besides, I honestly, truly had no goal or intention to impress this guy.

"Lunch then," I said. "Yes. I'd like that." I led the way out of the stacks, back toward the front of the library. "Let me just leave this book on my desk, and then we can go."

Kit was behind the coffee bar, serving up the last of Melissa's baked treats for the day. She raised an eyebrow as Will hurried off to collect his own books, and I managed to quirk an unobtrusive smile. There wasn't any need for that "conspiratorial girlfriend" look on her face. There was nothing going on between Will and me. Nothing at all. He was a patron in my library, and he just happened to be interested in the false stone siding of my cottage.

And if I had believed that there was anything else at stake, my illusions would have been destroyed as we approached my home, walking side by side on the Peabridge path. "Hollyhocks!" he exclaimed. "Pennyroyal and sweetbriar! You've planted a complete colonial garden!"

"Well, not me personally," I said, feeling strangely proud of my employer's efforts at verisimilitude.

"The Peabridge, though. I've always known that the library was here, but I never thought about checking it out in person until I met you."

"I guess you should thank the yoga nazis, then, who got us both into that class." We laughed together as we reached my front door.

For just a minute, I hesitated. It was one thing to invite a man out to inspect the walls of my home. A plumber or electrician could do as much, and there wouldn't be any hidden meaning in his presence. It was another thing entirely, though, to invite a man inside while I slipped into something a little more comfortable (or at least a little more dry).

As if he possessed his own magic skills, Will seemed to sense my discomfort. He stepped off the marble doorstep, demonstrating tremendous interest in the wooden facing that was routed to resemble stone. "This is it? This is the way they created the false facade?"

"Just like Mount Vernon," I confirmed.

"If you don't mind, I'll just take a moment to study it. While you change."

"That would be great," I said, trying not to let my gratitude color my words too much.

I darted inside and made short work of stripping off my colonial finery. Truth be told, I wasn't the least bit sorry to be out of the heavy dress. I could not imagine how my eighteenth-century foremothers had managed August heat and heavy skirts, without the comfort of central air-conditioning.

I was just going to have to wear street clothes for the afternoon. Evelyn would not be pleased, but she could hardly expect me to spend the day parading around like the Milk Queen of Georgetown. I opened my closet and grabbed the first outfit that came to hand—black slacks and a silk blouse, cut to show off my minimal, coffee-free décolletage. The outfit used to be one of my favorites, but it had been a long time since I'd worn street clothes to the office. I slipped on a pair of kitten heels and started to cross the living room, ready to head out to lunch with my visiting architect.

As I walked by the stairs to the basement, though, I felt a twinge of guilt. Ariel. I should at least check on her, make sure that she was having no trouble working through my collection of crystals. It was so strange to have an anima to do my bidding. This must be what it was like to have a maid, or a cook—someone to take care of all those details of daily life that I just couldn't be bothered to do.

I flipped on the overhead light before I descended the stairs. It was quiet in the basement, absolutely silent. "Ariel?" I called.

Nothing.

"Ariel? Are you okay?"

Nothing.

Nothing at all. I spun around my stark basement, eyes automatically darting to the nooks and crannies where a full-sized woman-spirit-magic-creature-thing could hide. Couch—bare leather, not a hint of occupation. Wardrobe—door ajar, ditto. Trunk—lid leaning against the wall, ditto yet again.

I tugged at my slacks, as if straightening the fabric could restore order to my life. With a sickening swoop in my belly, I realized that I was going to have to reach out to David and Neko again—easygoing colonial architect and lunch date be damned.

My anima had utterly and completely disappeared.

8

As it turned out, I didn't reach David until the next day, when I called to leave my ninth voice mail message. My relief at finally talking to him was almost drowned out by my rage at his inaccessibility. When I demanded to know what he'd been doing, he merely said, "Working." He refused to elaborate.

I explained what had happened, told him that Ariel had gone missing. I didn't bother to say that I'd needed to make excuses to Will, babbling that I couldn't go to lunch, that I'd only just remembered an important library meeting, complete with an imaginary board of trustees, so that he wouldn't think I was blowing him off for nothing.

"Something must have gone wrong with the spell," David said, stating the obvious.

"You knew something was wrong that night, didn't you?"

He started to reply but then caught himself, hesitating just long enough that I was certain he was crafting an evasive response. For a split second, I thought about offering to drive up to his place, to talk to him in person. But then I realized that the absolute last thing I wanted to do was stand in that kitchen, to sit stiffly in that perfect living room. And there wasn't a chance in hell that I'd be walking up those farmhouse stairs for anything else, anytime, ever. Better to soldier on over the phone.

"I saw it in your eyes," I insisted. "After I worked the spell."

He sighed. "I should have been able to feel her. To feel the anima."

"What?" I was so surprised that he was admitting something, I couldn't structure a coherent response. David was saying the same thing that I was. He should have felt Ariel after the working, the same way that I should have felt Neko.

"You know that I can feel you," he continued to explain. "I can feel your magic. I know when you're working a spell." I made a wordless sound of agreement. I'd chafed often enough under his warder ability. "I should be able to feel the results of your spell, as well. Especially an anima that you created, an embodiment of your essential magic."

"What happened?"

"I don't know." I could picture him running his hand through his hair. He'd completed the action in front of me often enough. "It's almost as if a bond was cut. A tie was severed."

I thought about the spell I had worked, the way that I had thought of David. I remembered the embarrassment of reliving those moments in his kitchen, the shame as I realized he was pushing me back, setting us—whatever "us" we were—aside. I had pushed David away from my thoughts as I awakened Ariel. I had skewed my magic to keep him from being part of my working.

Even as I closed my eyes, trying to will away my confusion, the chaos my magical mis-working had created, David said, "You know the parameters of magic, Jane. You offered up your thoughts, your voice, your spirit. Were those all true offerings? Were you absolutely focused on your working?"

"Of course!"

But I hadn't been. I'd been distracted by my warder. My attention had wandered, to our indiscretion, and then to the stupid play that Melissa had told me about, to the damned poster. Empower The Arts. Well that was just stupid. "Of course," I repeated, but I was a little less certain.

"I don't know what to say, then. Have you tried to summon her?"

I had. I'd tried thinking her name, in the loudest silent voice I could manage. I'd tried ordering her to come home. I'd tried commanding her to serve as my spirit, as she was intended to do, from the moment I'd poured rune dust into my palm. And I'd been met with complete and utter silence. "Of course I've tried to summon her. There's nothing there. Nothing at all."

"What about Neko?"

"What *about* Neko? I can't feel him, either. And he doesn't even have the decency to keep voice mail on his phone. What sort of idiot doesn't have voice mail?"

"You can't feel him?" David asked, ignoring my question. For the first time, he sounded truly concerned. He might finally be through playing the dispassionate instructor, the cold analyst.

"I told you that, in the first dozen messages I left for you."

"You didn't leave a dozen messages."

"Might as well have," I muttered. But complaining wasn't going to get me any closer to a solution. I tried to clarify, "I can feel that I *used* to feel him, if that makes any sense. I can feel that we used to be able to talk to each other, that I used to be able to reach out to him. But there isn't anything there now. I don't have any power!" The more I explained what was happening to me, the more frustrated I became, until my voice cracked on the last word. I cleared my throat and said, "You said creating the anima would make it all better. You have to do something!"

David paused for so long that I wondered if the phone had cut off. When he finally replied, his voice was grave. "There isn't anything I can do. Not until we find Ariel."

"Then look for her!"

"I will. I have contacts, obviously. I'll let you know what turns up."

"That's all?"

He sighed, and I could picture him running his hand through his hair in familiar exasperation. "I don't know what else I can do, Jane. I'll reach out again to Neko. I'll let him know what's going on."

"And in the meantime? I'm just supposed to go to work and act like nothing's wrong?"

"Do you have a better idea?"

And that's what it came down to. I didn't have a better idea. I had no ideas at all.

So, for four straight days, I went in to work. An entire week of being a librarian, of sitting at my desk, of mentoring Kit and answering questions, and pretending that I was a totally ordinary woman, leading a totally ordinary life.

On Wednesday, I called Melissa to book mojito therapy for Friday night, but she begged off, reminding me, "Rob and I are going to *The Tempest*."

"Don't even mention that play to me."

"Still no word, huh?" I'd told Melissa everything on Tuesday evening, over platefuls of Key Lime Locks and Cinnamon Smiles. It was a miracle that she didn't need to roll me out the Cake Walk door.

"Nothing."

"There's an all-afternoon yoga session at the studio on Saturday. Way of the Warrior. You'll find it really restful."

"I'd find it really maddening, but thanks anyway."

Friday night, I sat by the phone, waiting for it to ring. I actually used my cell to call my land-line twice, to make sure that the connection was working. How could everyone abandon me at the same time? No Neko. No David. And definitely no Will.

Not that Will had any real reason to call me. I'd given him my number when I made up my lie about the library board meeting, but he'd probably read through my storytelling. He probably felt utterly and completely snubbed, and I'd never hear from him again.

I went to bed at eight o'clock, pulling the pillow over my head to block out the last of the summer sunlight that peeked in my window.

I was sound asleep by nine o'clock, buried in one of those foggy, dream-bound places, where you can't move, can't see, can't talk. I came to the surface slowly, opening my eyes to peer at my clock. The green numbers glowed patiently, but it took a long time for me to realize that it was still Friday night, that I'd only been asleep for an hour. It took me even longer to realize that I had been awakened by someone pounding on my front door.

"I'm coming!" I called as I shuffled across the living-room floor.

The racket didn't make sense. Neko or David would have just come into the cottage; they both had full rights to disrupt my privacy, by the nature of our arcane commitment. I couldn't imagine Ariel making so much noise, even if she had decided to come home.

My heart pounded as I thought of Gran—I hadn't seen her in nearly a week. What if her excitement about the wedding had proven too much for her aged heart? What if she had collapsed at home, giving in to the lungs that had been weakened by pneumonia two autumns ago? What if she was lying in an emergency room even now, if police had been dispatched to bring me running, to let me kneel beside her bed, grab her hand, listen to her dying words?

I flung the door open and saw Melissa standing on my doorstep.

"Oh," I said, letting the door frame bear my weight as relief crashed against me. "It's you."

"Yes, it's me! Who did you think it was?"

"I thought that Gran—I mean, I thought that you weren't Neko. Or David. I mean…" I rubbed at my face, muzzier than I should have been.

"Were you asleep?" Melissa sounded shocked.

"Yeah," I admitted, looking down at my nightshirt and feeling vaguely ashamed. As if in surprise, Melissa sneezed. "Bless you," I said. "Come on in. Every mosquito in D.C. is going to attack me if we leave the door open."

Melissa closed the door behind her, and I led the way across the living room. "Jane!" she said, her voice raw with urgency. By now, my mind was working a little better. Melissa was supposed to be on her date with Rob Peterson. It must have self-destructed in a truly spectacular way, for her to report the disaster in person. "Jane!" she repeated, as I flipped on the kitchen light. "I found her! I found Ariel!"

"You what?" The words didn't make any sense. Melissa wasn't supposed to be looking for Ariel. Melissa was my mundane friend. She was ordinary. She was normal. She didn't have any confusing witchcraft flowing through her blood. I told her my arcane problems, over and over and over again, but she didn't have the ability to fix them. Still, any port in a storm. "Where?"

"Duke Ellington High School."

"Duke— She was at the *play?*"

Melissa nodded, her smile so wide I thought she might burst out laughing. "On stage, front and center."

"What happened?" I grabbed for a chair and sat down heavily. I was still having trouble waking up; the world felt blurry, smeared.

"Well, you know it was opening night tonight, right?"

"Not really," I said.

"That's why we went," Melissa said, with a certain exasperation. "Rob's on the board for the D.C. Arts Council." She blushed. "He was the one who brought the poster into the shop in the first place. That's why I knew about the show, when I asked him out."

Rob was the one I could blame for all this. If he hadn't brought the poster to Melissa, she never would have mentioned it. I wouldn't have noticed the actor who looked like David, and I never would have strayed from my magical summoning when I created Ariel. Great. Just great.

Melissa tumbled on, apparently oblivious to the fact that there was any blame to spread around. "Well, we were sitting there watching the opening scene. You know, the shipwreck, with all the shouting and confusion?"

I nodded. I hadn't seen the play in years, but the first scene was one of those classic Shakespeare moments—a shipwreck! Live! On stage! I could only imagine what an Elizabethan audience must have felt. Certainly they would have been more enthralled than my impatient twenty-first-century self.

"Well, that's when it happened."

"When *what* happened?"

"When the play was interrupted. Miranda was talking about how the only thing she could remember from her childhood were the women who used to take care of her. It was weird—the language of the production was all updated, so she sounded like a whiny suburban reject from *High School Musical*. I half expected her to break into a song about how Prospero had never understood her."

"But what *happened?*"

"All of a sudden, in the middle of one of Miranda's lines, this woman walked on stage."

"This woman?"

"Your Ariel."

"What?"

"She looked just like you described her. She was really tall—like she could be a model or something. Her skin was so white it glowed in the theater. All I could think of was marble. And her hair was black. It almost disappeared in the stage lights."

My heart pounded as Melissa completed her recitation. Tall, thin, pale. Black hair. "What was she wearing?"

"This strange gauzy dress. It flowed when she moved, sort of floated all around her. It was woven from different colors, red and orange and yellow."

I knew that dress. I'd seen it in my basement. I'd made it with the last of my magic. I forced myself to ask, "And she walked on stage?"

"She just stood up in the audience and walked down the aisle, like she was part of the show. She climbed onto the stage and looked out at all of us. About half the audience thought that she was part of the production, that she was supposed to be some sort of dream scene or something."

"And the other half?" I asked, a queasy feeling turning my belly.

"The other half thought something was wrong. The guy playing Prospero pretty much confirmed it. I mean, he tried to ad-lib and everything, to pretend like he was summoning servants to clear a ghost. He actually did a decent job— at least with all the modern talk, he didn't have to make up lines in iambic pentameter. But the stagehands who came out weren't anything like island servants."

"What did they do?" I tried to picture what she was describing, tried to imagine the entire production stalled by this strange woman. By my anima.

"Only one guy came out at first. He tried to walk her off the stage, but she refused to move. It was creepy. She didn't say anything, just stood there, like a statue."

Didn't say anything. Like a statue.

Or like an anima.

"So what happened next?"

"The entire crew came out on stage. They were all

wearing black, and a few of them had headsets. They gathered around her like she was some sort of wild animal."

Wild animal… That wasn't too far from the truth. "And then?" I asked.

"She held up a sign."

"A sign?"

"A poster. Like something we might have made in school for a pep rally. I didn't see where she'd been hiding it, it was like she just produced it out of nowhere. She held it up above her head so everyone could see. It said 'Empower The Arts.'"

Empower The Arts. The slogan that had been on the play's promotional poster. The slogan that I'd thought of when I created Ariel. The slogan that had apparently taken the last of my magic and twisted it into something I could no longer recognize, something that was utterly foreign to me, something that had been stolen from me.

"Empower The Arts," I echoed.

"She held up her sign, and she pivoted around, making sure that everyone in the audience saw it. People started clapping—it was like she was Norma Rae or something. And then the stage crew got serious. They closed in around her, trying to herd her into the wings. Before they could make her move, though, she just jumped off the front of the stage. Jumped off and ran away."

"Did she take her sign with her?"

"That was the strange thing. That's why I'm here." Melissa looked at me with eyes that were half-afraid. "The sign totally disappeared, Jane. It was like she'd never been there. Like she was totally a figment of our imagination. Everyone was talking. They thought it must be some theatrical trick. But I was pretty sure it was something else. Something you needed to know about."

I felt sick to my stomach. "What happened next?"

"The stage manager came out. She said that they'd start the show over from the top, that it would take them fifteen minutes or so to reset the shipwreck, and there was coffee in the lobby for anyone who wanted it. I told Rob that I had to leave, and I came over here as fast as I could."

"Without Rob?"

"Your witchcraft stuff is strange enough to *me*, and I've known about it for two years. I couldn't figure out a way to tell him what was really going on."

"What did you say?"

"I said that I knew a reporter, someone who was going to be thrilled to get the scoop. Rob was still going to come with me, but he couldn't because he had to do the whole glad-hand thing with the rest of the Arts Council people, after the play." She shook her head and sneezed again.

"Bless you," I said automatically. "Melissa—" Even as my mind was racing, even as I was trying to process everything that she'd said, I felt terrible that I'd ruined her date.

"Don't worry about it," she said, reading my mind with the ease of years of friendship. "I mean, there'll be other dates. Another one tomorrow, as a matter of fact."

"You go, girl!" I said, climbing to my feet.

"What are you going to do?"

"Put on clothes. I've got to get over to the high school. I have to see if it was actually Ariel."

"Do you really think it was?" Now she sounded doubtful.

"A tall, black-haired woman who makes an albino look tan, wearing a gauze silk dress? Naw. Couldn't have anything in common with my anima."

I strode into my bedroom, palming on the light and tearing open my closet door. What did one wear for anima-hunting on a Friday night in Georgetown? I settled on a pair of jeans and a green blouse. I carried my tennis shoes into the living room and tugged them on as Melissa watched. "Aren't you going to call David?" she asked.

I'd been hoping to avoid that. Still, Melissa was right. I'd be an idiot not to bring my warder into the hunt. I reached for him with my mind reflexively.

Nothing.

The bond between us shimmered with the faintest reflection of memory, taunting me with the fact that it had been there, that I *had* relied on it. But there was nothing now. I sighed and picked up the phone. And cursed when I got his outgoing message. "David, Ariel was here in Georgetown. At the high school. I'm going to try to find her. Call me on my cell when you get this."

I didn't even bother trying to reach Neko, certain that he'd be at some unbearably fashionable nightspot, surrounded by music too loud to hear his phone ring, by activity too vigorous for him to feel the vibration in his pocket.

In the end, Melissa and I shouldn't have bothered. We got over to the school while the play was still going on; we had a chance to rattle a bunch of locked doors, to peer into night-dark classrooms. We decided to comb the nearby streets before the crowd let out, but our gesture was meaningless. Ariel could have been anywhere, hiding in any shadow, lurking behind any tree or car or house. My efforts to think a command to her were utterly unsuccessful.

After an hour, we headed back to Cake Walk. Melissa turned on the working light below the cabinets on the back counter, but she purposely left off the overhead so that we wouldn't be disturbed by late-night patrons with the munchies. She excavated a platter from beneath the serving counter, peeling back tin foil to reveal an almond-and-chocolate confection. "Lust After Dark?" she asked.

I giggled, letting off some of the pressure that had gathered while we searched unsuccessfully for my magical creation. Almond Lust was one of Melissa's signature creations. The addition of chocolate had been my idea, long ago, and the new name always made me laugh. I sighed in appreciation as Melissa poured a tall glass of milk to accompany the toothsome sweet.

We sat in companionable silence for a while, before Melissa asked, "Notice anything different?" She waved a hand toward the wall.

There was the spotless sink. A clean dishrag. A wall-mounted telephone. A little white board for writing down emergency messages. A calendar.

Melissa's dating calendar.

Melissa's dating calendar with each day for the past week shining through with unadulterated white squares. Not a single red *X* for a week—no First Dates.

"Melissa?" I asked. "Are you feeling all right?"

"What?" She grinned.

"Did you lose your red pen?"

She laughed again. An open and friendly laugh. An honestly cheerful, not sulking at all, enjoying-herself-like-an-ordinary-person open and friendly laugh that was so contagious I almost forgot the misery of my missing anima. "I decided I was being a bit obsessive."

Obsessive? Melissa? The woman who had counted off her First Dates for the past dozen years? My best friend, who had alternated her evenings out with all the precision of a professional stocking the dairy shelves at the most exclusive grocery store on the eastern seaboard?

"Do you think?" I asked, not bothering to disguise my mocking tone.

"I was just marking off the disasters in red to give myself the feeling that I was doing *something*. That I was trying to make myself happy."

"And now?"

She blushed. She blushed the color of the red ink that used to reconfirm her spinster status on a painfully regular basis. "And now, I really *have* done something to make myself happy. Asking Rob out was the best thing I ever could have done. We flirted all week long. He helped me close up on

Wednesday." She blushed even deeper. "He stuck around for…dinner. By the time we got to tonight, it was like we'd been dating forever."

"Where'd you eat tonight?"

"Don Lobos."

The little Mexican restaurant was one of our favorites. More to keep her talking happily than because I had any real interest, I said, "What did you have?"

"We shared the garlic shrimp, and then I had—"

Okay. Worried about Ariel or not, I had to call her on that one. "*You* ate the garlic shrimp? You? The queen of appropriate First Date foods?" Ariel be damned, there were some announcements so earthshaking that they needed to be given their full, unstinted due.

"We *both* ate the garlic. Besides, I don't think First Date foods apply when you've been talking to a guy every day for a year."

"What about your Five Conversational Topics?" For years, Melissa had prepared for potentially awkward dates, queuing up discussions to drop into any uncomfortably long pauses.

"I forgot to pull them together."

"You *forgot?*" My world was spinning out of order. Mountains were crashing into oceans. The sun was hurtling into the abyss. Every truth that I had ever known had just been dashed to smithereens on Cake Walk's tiled floor. I barely managed to repeat, "You forgot to set five Conversational Topics?"

"I guess I didn't need them. I mean, I've known Rob

forever. We could talk about real things—his work at the firm, the Arts Council, my work at the bakery."

"I don't believe it," I said. "You. The queen of Conversational Topics. Going cold turkey."

Melissa shrugged, and the motion seemed to trigger another sneeze.

"Not again!" she said. "I must be coming down with a cold." She turned to her stainless steel sink and soaped up her hands with the thoroughness of a surgeon going in for some lifesaving procedure. As she scrubbed beneath her fingernails, she blushed a spectacular shade of crimson.

"What?" I asked, like any prying best friend.

"Nothing."

"What!" I repeated.

"It's just that Rob had a cold. He said that he was almost over it, but…" Melissa giggled.

My cool as a cucumber best friend giggled. Like a schoolgirl. Like a schoolgirl with a wicked crush.

"You really like this guy, huh?" I couldn't help but grin, myself, even as a corner of my mind still tried to figure out the best way to lay a snare for my wayward anima. What had drawn Ariel to the theater? Was it her namesake play? Or the actor who looked like David? What *had* I planted in whatever passed for her psyche, when I thought about *The Tempest*, about the Empower The Arts campaign at the precise moment that I summoned her to life?

Melissa just looked down at her hand towel, suddenly bashful.

I felt a rush of warmth for her. Even if this didn't turn out to be the real thing, it beat her usual stream of dating disasters. "Well, let me see if I can do anything to help you with the cold."

"Like what?"

"Like a little magical potion." I glanced around the bakery and bit my lip, trying to remember my herbal spell books. "Have you got any white water lily?"

"Sure," Melissa said airily. "I keep it right here in the fridge. Behind the snakeweed and the lotus pods." She laughed at my grimace. "I run a bakery, Jane, not a greenhouse. Of course I don't have any white water lily."

"Look, I'm just trying to help you," I said. "If you don't have any water lily, then we can probably work something with ginger."

"Ginger, I've got. But I can make ginger tea on my own."

"Do you know the right words to say over it, to make it really work?"

"Um, with that tone in your voice, I'm guessing the answer is no."

"Get the ginger."

Melissa cast me a doubting glance, but she turned back to her cavernous refrigerator and excavated a gnarled root of ginger. It branched a half-dozen times, almost breaking itself into walnut-sized nodules. "Will this do?"

"Perfect," I said.

"What comes next? 'Get with child a mandrake root'?"

"That depends," I answered with a wicked grin. "Do you

want to get rid of the cold that Rob gave you? Or do you want to snare him by having his baby?" I saw the nervous glance that Melissa cast on the ginger, and I laughed. "Come on," I said. "I don't even know any baby-making spells."

"You don't know nothin' about spellin' no babies?" But there was a nervous quality to her laugh. She handed over the root.

I hefted it in my hand, as if I were trying to estimate how much it would cost me, checking out at a magical grocery store. Closing my left fingers loosely around the ginger, I raised my right hand to touch my forehead, my throat and my heart. I exhaled each time, centering myself for my working. I shut my eyes and tried to remember the herbal spell book that I had studied, one of the first volumes in my collection that I had thoroughly committed to memory. After all, with a best friend like Melissa, with her herbal garden just outside her back door, I would have been a fool not to focus on such nearby riches.

Still holding the image of the spell book in my mind, I took one more deep breath and started chanting in a low voice, keeping the words between Melissa, the ginger root and I.

"Wild ginger, fire and earth—"

Nothing. I felt a gaping hole of nothing. There should have been a tingle gathering in my fingertips, a frisson of energy threatening to spark and spill over into the knobby root.

I cleared my throat and started again:

"Wild ginger, fire and earth,
Unveil power, show your worth—"

Absolutely nothing. I felt as if I was reciting a nursery rhyme, a silly little poem that was never intended to have the faintest hint of arcane power and force. I could just as easily sing a rhyme from *Sesame Street* or mutter the words of a Christmas carol.

Melissa, accustomed to my moods, accurately read disappointment on my face. "The magic thing still isn't working?"

"Not so much," I said. I set down the ginger root, trying to act nonchalant. "This has never happened to me before."

"You know," Melissa said, "you sound exactly like one of my first dates from last year."

I laughed along with her, but my heart wasn't in it. I'd tried to work one of the simplest herbal spells I knew. If I couldn't charm away a cold, how did I expect to catch up with my anima?

And where else was that creature going to end up in D.C., before I managed to track her down?

9

I rested my forearms against the lectern in the Peabridge basement, watching the last of my lecture attendees leave the room. I was pleased with the crowd—they'd asked shrewd questions about the relationship between our colonial fathers and the Spanish adventurers who had controlled Florida at the time. I'd pulled together the lecture on a whim over the weekend, using my nervous energy about Ariel to replace a tired presentation on colonial economy. I'd alternated research with waiting for my phone to ring.

Evelyn stood at the back of the room, chatting with Mr. Potter, one of the library's trustees and our greatest benefactor. In fact, Mr. Potter's generous donation had funded the cataloging project that had led to our finding the book on colonial gardens, the one that I'd been reading when Will startled me into spilling my coffee.

Will…. I caught myself daydreaming about him for the thousandth time in the past three days. What had he thought when I stammered out my excuses, ducking out of our impromptu lunch date? Had he been so turned off by my pretended scatterbrained calendar-keeping that he'd vowed never to speak to me again? Since he hadn't called over the weekend was it time for me to write him off altogether?

"Jane!" Mr. Potter exclaimed, cutting short my reverie. "Excellent job! I never realized that the Spanish influence was so strong in the early colonies!"

"Mr. Potter," I said warmly. "May I get you a cup of coffee?"

"Do you have any chocolate syrup to add?"

"And whipped cream?" I smiled, knowing the answer before I'd even finished the question. Mr. Potter would have been content with a mug of whipped cream, a dash of chocolate and a spoon. Evelyn beamed as I escorted our favorite trustee upstairs.

We indulged in small talk as I made the man his drink. I asked about Beijing, his shih tzu, and he asked about my various research projects. Then, he smiled. "Great news, isn't it, about Sarah and George? Weddings are such happy times!" Mentally, I kicked myself. I'd somehow managed to forget all about Gran, about Uncle George's proposal.

Mr. Potter's pleasure transported me back to brunch, to Gran's announcement about her impending nuptials, and to

Clara's imminent departure. I truly *had* been neglectful—and my little anima disaster would only buy me so much forgiveness. I sternly told myself to phone both Gran and Clara that night.

But I said to Mr. Potter, "I was so pleased when she told me."

"We're really going to miss her at the Autumn Gala."

"What about the Gala?" I had no idea what he was talking about. The Concert Opera event was the most important part of Gran's social year. She'd even said that she was going to plan the wedding date around it.

Mr. Potter shook his head. "Sarah realized she just couldn't organize both things at once. With only two months till Halloween…."

"Halloween?"

"That's the date they chose." Mr. Potter obviously read my confusion. "I'm sure Sarah just forgot to tell you. She and George have decided to host a costume ball for their wedding, and Halloween just made sense." Made sense to a lunatic, perhaps. A costume ball? Was Gran slipping into some sort of second childhood? Mr. Potter nodded as if every octogenarian wedding was a dress-up game. "It'll be a lot of work getting everything ready. At least she has your friend to help her."

"My friend?" Melissa hadn't said anything about helping Gran. And I would have thought that Melissa would mention something as basic as Gran setting a specific date for her wedding.

"What's his name?" Mr. Potter mused. "Neko?"

"Neko is helping Gran plan the wedding?"

That little bastard! He couldn't be bothered to phone me back about Ariel running around the city, but he could help Gran pick out flower arrangements? I guess he had no use for me, now that my freezer was empty, my cupboards were bare and I could not bind him as his witch.

Mr. Potter mistook my exclamation for concern about Gran. "I'm sure Sarah just didn't want to worry you about the details. She told me that your friend has been charming, helping her pick out colors and everything."

"Picking out colors?" I asked, morbidly fascinated by the notion of my down-to-earth grandmother poring over fabric swatches. "What did she choose?"

"Orange and silver."

"What!"

Mr. Potter had to be teasing me. Neko would *never* aid and abet the pairing of orange and silver, not in a hundred years. Not in a thousand weddings.

"I was surprised, too, especially when Sarah brought the samples to our last Opera Guild meeting, the night she handed over the account books. The orange is really quite, er, bright. But I know you'll be lovely as the maid of honor."

"Maid of honor?" I asked automatically. What other secrets were floating around out there about the Wedding of the Century? But then it made perfect sense. Who else was Gran going to dress up in an orange-and-silver frou-frou dress? Clara would certainly stand up for her right to wear a normal outfit. Even if it meant that she had to light out for Sedona early.

And maybe that wasn't a half-bad idea. Flee the scene of the fashion crime.

I glanced over Mr. Potter's shoulder, half expecting to see Neko chortling in the doorway. This conversation was precisely his idea of a practical joke. No Neko, though. But there was another person standing there, someone who made my heart leap against my rib cage. "Will!" I exclaimed.

My architect friend smiled and shrugged at the same time, as if to apologize for startling me. "Do you have another cup of coffee there?" He reached for his wallet.

I looked at the dregs in the brewing carafe. "Um, let me make another pot," I said, as I handed Mr. Potter his whipped cream-laden treat.

Will glanced at the clock. "Don't bother. It's too late in the day. You'd end up tossing most of it." I flashed him an appreciative smile. "Instead, why don't you let me buy you dinner? It's the least you can do, after that trustee meeting pulled you away from lunch on Friday."

"Trustee meeting?" Mr. Potter asked, and I could read the confusion on his face.

"Yes," I said quickly. "Last Friday. The emergency one? About funding the special exhibits downstairs? The one they called without any notice at all?" I could hear my voice ratcheting higher. "Mr. Potter, let me introduce one of the Peabridge's newest patrons, Will Becker. Will's an architect." I turned back to Will, hoping that Mr. Potter would be so impressed by Will's credentials that he would let the phantom trustee meeting drop. "Will, Mr. Potter is one of the library's greatest benefactors, and a close personal friend of my grandmother."

I longed to reach out to Mr. Potter's mind, to flick some magical switch in his memory so that he would accept my offhand introduction without questioning my lie about the trustee meeting. I didn't have the power, though. And if my familiar was heading toward a second career as a wedding planner, I might never regain my ability….

I almost collapsed against the coffee bar when Mr. Potter gave me the slightest wink and asked Will about his interest in colonial construction. The old guy came through yet again—an ally in my lonely-hearts battles, despite his utter ignorance about the never-ending complications of my love life. Before I knew it, Mr. Potter and Will were chatting like old friends.

I glanced at the clock. My lecture had made the afternoon fly by; the question and answer session alone had eaten up nearly an hour. I sighed disconsolately, though, not wanting to take time to clean up the coffee bar. As if summoned by my disappointment, Kit materialized from the stacks. "My turn to shut things down, isn't it?"

I could have thrown my arms around her muslin-clad shoulders, but I settled for a grateful smile instead. "Thank you!"

"At your service, madam," she said, sweeping her tricorn hat off her braided head before she started to fill the little sink with soapy water.

"Well, Jane, dear," Mr. Potter said. "Beijing calls. I really must be going. Enjoy Don Lobos."

"Don Lobos?" I said, as if I'd never heard of the place before.

"Er, I just thought…" Will started. "I just mentioned it to Mr. Potter…. That is…"

Mr. Potter only winked at me again. "Have a wonderful time, both of you," he said, and then he shook Will's hand before heading to the door.

"Don Lobos would be wonderful," I said quickly, smiling after the dapper old meddler. And it would be. Melissa had certainly enjoyed her dinner there.

I glanced at the clock. It was still only ten minutes to five. Ten minutes to freedom.

"Go ahead," Kit said.

"Evelyn" was the only reply I needed to make.

"She's on a phone call with Colonial Williamsburg. She wants to get barrels from their cooper, to replace all our trash cans." She rolled her eyes, even as she smiled. "It'll take half an hour to sort out the delivery. I'll cover for you."

"Thanks," I said. "There's a pastry in it for you, tomorrow morning."

"Yeah, yeah," Kit said. "Bribe me with baked goods. Just don't torture me with one of those Blond Brunettes, whatever you do."

I laughed, knowing that the swirled butterscotch brownies were Kit's favorite. I turned back to Will. "Let me just run back to the cottage and change. Give me five minutes?"

"They're yours," he said with a smile. "I'll meet you at the garden gate?"

Even in ordinary street clothes, the September evening was warm, but the worst of the late summer humidity had baked away during the day. I settled for a pair of black jeans and a sleeveless turquoise blouse that Neko had given me as a birthday present the year before. He remained determined to diversify the portfolio of my black-on-black wardrobe. Who was I to complain? His taste was better than mine.

And at least this garment wasn't orange-and-silver. Orange? Was Neko playing some demented joke on Gran?

I glanced at my answering machine as I closed the cottage door. Its red light glowed solid; there were no waiting messages. What had I done to be ignored so thoroughly by my familiar and my warder? Why weren't they helping me with Ariel? Did they think it was *my* fault that I'd lost my powers, as if I'd left them behind on the subway?

"What's wrong?" Will asked, as I caught up to him at the gate.

"Nothing," I said, consciously wiping away the frown that had settled on my face. "I was just thinking about some work I have to do."

"There's always tomorrow for work."

"Spoken like a true hedonist," I said.

"Nope. Just a realist." He held the gate for me, the perfect gentleman. "Is Don Lobos really okay? I just mentioned it to Mr. Potter in passing. We could go anywhere."

"Don Lobos is perfect," I said.

And it was. Taking a cue from my best friend's sudden romantic success, I ordered the garlic shrimp, splitting it with Will. I embraced the cheese and onion enchiladas, not worrying about stringy cheddar ruining my date-ly grace or red sauce destroying my silk blouse. I savored sangria, fishing out a slice of orange without thinking that the red wine might discolor my fingertips, that I might look awkward as I poked at the festive drink.

Throughout the entire meal, we talked. Will told me about growing up in Rockville, a Maryland suburb, about going to William and Mary for college, about falling in love with architecture. I told him about pursuing a master's degree in English literature, only to realize that Shakespeare was never going to pay the rent, then discovering that library science and the Peabridge didn't do a great job on the practicality front, either.

He asked about Gran, and I told him about the upcoming wedding. I told him about Clara, as well, about her return to my life two years before, and her determination to leave me again. Somehow, when I was talking to him, the story was simple, truthful, not fraught with emotional peril. It was balanced by his tale of being a middle child with divorced and remarried parents—two older brothers, two younger sisters, all living in suburban harmony like a mini-Brady Bunch.

Just before we dug our spoons into a shared caramel flan, I thought about Five Conversational Topics. No wonder Melissa had abandoned the notion when she went out with

Rob. Who could ever need five scripted ideas, just to keep an evening's chat going? Will and I could have talked forever about anything. In fact, we ordered coffee after we finished the flan. Both of us seemed eager to extend our rental of the Don Lobos table, to maximize our evening together. Everything was right. Everything was easy.

When we had finally run out of excuses to sit around the Mexican restaurant, Will paid the bill. I reached for my purse, like any self-respecting woman of the twenty-first century, but he waved off my offer of payment. "You'll get the next one," he said with a smile, and a slow fire rose beneath my belly, as I imagined another perfect evening with this man who was so very easy to spend time with. Not that this evening was over yet….

The early September night was heavy as Will walked me back to the Peabridge. We left the busy commercial district quickly, picking our way along quiet residential side streets. Will took my hand as we walked. His fingers were strong and firm; I could imagine the tight creativity curled inside them. I could picture him making firm lines on some architectural drawing. On another walk, in another time, I would have stammered when I felt his touch, but everything seemed simple about this companionship, everything was comfortable. Everything was right.

Until I saw the black Lexus parked directly in front of the Peabridge.

There were a lot of black luxury sedans in Georgetown. Many of them had onyx leather that whispered of old money. Some even had walnut trim that glinted under street-lamps. But none of them had my warder, folded into the front seat, sitting perfectly still in a white shirt that glowed faintly in the ambient light.

"Damn," I said, suddenly fighting to draw a complete breath.

Will stopped with me, smiling easily into the night. "What's wrong?"

"I've got a visitor." I slipped my hand from Will's, suddenly feeling like a sixteen-year-old caught out after curfew.

"Who's that?" Will asked, the faintest note of concern dusting his words.

Even as my mind scrambled for a lie, David opened his car door. As he unfolded himself from the front seat, Neko glided forward from the shadows of the garden wall, looking for all the world like a cat returning from a midnight hunting expedition.

I wondered if Ariel had come home. Or, worse. If she hadn't.

"Will Becker," I said, taking a deep breath. "I'd like to introduce David Montrose and, um, Neko. They're…business associates." The men all shook hands, and there was a sudden tension in the air, a jagged energy of unease that I hadn't felt all evening. I sloped my hands down my side, reaching for the pockets of my jeans, but the angle was all wrong, and I felt stupid with my arms akimbo. I started to raise my right hand to my lips, to chew on my well-shaped fingernails, but I stopped myself just in time.

David completed a thorough appraisal of Will and nodded his head minutely. "I'm afraid I'm going to have to interrupt your evening, Jane. We've got a bookkeeping problem."

Bookkeeping. As in, the keeping of the books in my basement. I understood exactly what David was saying, even if I wanted to ignore his message. I could also read the set to his shoulders, his dangerous politeness as he prepared to argue with me. I was going to have to deal with my warder; there was no way that I could simply send him away, return to my evening of carefree dating.

I turned to Will and shrugged helplessly. "I'm so sorry," I said. "I'm really going to have to take care of this."

He frowned. "You're all right, though?"

"Yeah," I said, and I sighed. "I'm fine."

For just a moment, I worried about what he would say, how he would take his leave. There was a part of me that wanted to send David and Neko off to the cottage, order them around the corner of the library so that I could capture the kiss I was dying to take from Will.

There was another part of me, though, that didn't want to start down that road. There was no way to follow that one kiss to its logical destination, to the end point that I'd realized—sometime between the garlic shrimp and the coffee—that I definitely wanted to reach. I wasn't going to go any further with Will, though. Not tonight. Not with my warder prowling like a frustrated lion in the zoo.

And Will seemed to sense my indecision. He stepped between David and me, turning his back to my warder with a grace that belied his alleged incompetence in the yoga studio. He settled one hand against my throat and then leaned in to kiss my cheek. "Call me tomorrow," he whispered, and then he stepped back.

"Nice meeting you," he said evenly to David, nodding.

My warder nodded back, apparently out of reflex. I stared after Will's back as he walked to the corner. I longed for him to turn back, to sneak another glance at me before he turned away, but he did not look in our direction again.

I closed my eyes, breathed deeply, and then centered myself with a long, slow exhale.

"It took you long enough," I said, forcing myself to meet David's eyes.

"I was away for the weekend."

"And you couldn't check messages?" My tone was sharp, mixed from my frustration at letting Will walk away and my worry about Ariel.

"I didn't," he said evenly.

"And what's your excuse?" I said, turning to Neko.

He shrugged, shoulders slim and elegant in his tight black T-shirt. "I didn't realize that I needed one. You weren't working magic, so I wasn't bound to come."

His insouciance angered me.

Here, I'd been worrying about Ariel. I'd been trying to track down my anima. I'd been chasing after her, trying to corner her, trying to bring her home. Trying to find out what had happened to my power.

And Neko had been enjoying some party-hearty weekend

with Jacques, free from responsibility, free from any care in the world, safe from my witchy summons.

"You managed to find time to choose colors with Gran," I accused.

He shrugged. "A boy's got to do what a boy's got to do."

Something about his devil-may-care flamboyance set me off, touched a match to my scarce-restrained frustration, about Ariel, about watching Will walk away. I spoke before I even thought about the impact of my words. "I'm not sure I want to do this anymore."

I was as surprised as David and Neko—maybe even more so. But as soon as I said it, I knew that was the truth. If I weren't a witch, I would be a free woman. I could spend a Friday night sacked out at home, catching up on well-warranted sleep. I could listen to my best friend's story of her perfect date without feeling guilty that I'd pulled her away from the man of her apparent dreams, forced her into a fruitless hunt for a disappearing magical creature. I could create solid presentations for the Peabridge without spending half my time listening for my phone to ring, for my astral colleagues to join in on the hunt.

I could invite Will Becker into my home.

That was the heart of it. I'd shared more with Will in one evening than I had with any man since…. Than any man ever. And yet, I hadn't told him the full truth. I hadn't told him about the real me. I hadn't told him I was a witch. And I wasn't sure I wanted to. I wasn't sure I could. Every other man who'd found out about my powers had left me. Left me, or turned traitor on me.

Maybe losing my powers wasn't the end of the world. Maybe I was ready to go back to what I'd been, to how I'd lived for all those years before I discovered the books in the Peabridge basement. Maybe I was ready to be normal.

"You don't mean that." David's voice was gentler than I expected. Softer. Kinder.

It was the voice I'd heard in his kitchen. The voice he'd used when he'd told me we'd made a mistake. The voice that had embarrassed me and angered me and made me realize that I didn't have the first clue about who he was, who I was, who we were together. For one moment, I thought about challenging him, about forcing him to talk about what had happened in his home, in his bedroom. I glanced at Neko, though, and I knew that I couldn't do that. Not now. Not with an audience. Not with the memory of my nearly perfect evening with Will so fresh in my mind.

I took a deep breath and forced myself to say the words that frightened me. "I think I do."

Neko arched his back. "Don't we get a vote, Jane?"

"You cast yours!" I protested. "You both voted by not answering my calls. You voted by not being there when I tried to track down Ariel!" Every word I said made me angrier. I'd felt like a social reject, calling David and Neko, over and over, the girl who could never get a date. Their refusal to pick up their phones was like the confirmation of every hopeless crush I'd ever had.

"And you!" I went on, actually putting the flat of my palm against Neko's shoulder and shoving. "What the hell do you think you're doing with Gran? Wedding planner? Don't you think *I* should have a vote in that?"

"If you called your grandmother once in a while, you'd know that I was helping her! I was trying to reach out to *you*, Jane! I was trying to tell you I was still around, that I was there for you, even if you couldn't tug my familiar leash." He was really angry at me.

"You make it sound like it's my fault! I didn't mean to lose my powers. I thought that they'd get *stronger* when I poured them into Ariel."

"It may not be your fault, but I'm the one who suffers if you just give up. Me, and Jacques, too! If I'm transferred to another witch, what happens to us? What happens to him?"

"You're not being fair! I tried to reach you. I called a dozen times! You were just too busy with your stupid love life!" I couldn't keep the words from tumbling out of my mouth. Without my bidding, my mind flashed back to Will, to our perfect dinner, our effortless conversation. That wasn't my *love* life, I told myself. That was my life life. That was my future. That was what I could be, if I weren't constantly mired in perpetual drama, in the bizarre world of witchcraft.

Neko stared at me with unblinking eyes, his ravenous black pupils making him more catlike than ever. "Yes," he said, and disdain dripped from the single word. "This is all about my stupid love life." He turned to David, who had watched our exchange in dangerous silence. "Will you be working tonight? Do you need me?"

David shook his head. "Go." I started to protest, but he

cut me off, even more abruptly than Neko had. "She doesn't have the power to work. I'll call you if we need you."

Neko started to stalk away, but before he reached the edge of the Peabridge property, he stopped. His hand glided into the pocket of his sleek leather slacks, and then he pounced back to me. "Here," he said, thrusting something into my hand.

I took it automatically. "What?"

"Breath mints," he said, with a breeziness that was so false I almost choked on his tone.

"I don't—"

"Yes," he said. "You do. After garlic shrimp, you most certainly do."

And then my familiar was gone, stalking into the shadows of the hot September night. I stared after him, waiting for him to turn around, to laugh, to admit that he was merely joking, that he was tweaking me, yet again, with his endlessly wry sense of humor.

No such luck.

"Shall we?" David finally asked, with deceptive mildness.

"Shall we what?" I said, barely biting back my frustration.

"Shall we head downstairs to your basement? See what we can figure out about this missing anima of yours."

I started to protest. I started to say that I had no desire to touch the books. That I couldn't open them, couldn't read them, not without wreaking even greater havoc on my collection. Besides, I'd been serious. I really wasn't sure I wanted to be a witch anymore.

But David wouldn't take no for an answer. He was stubborn. Driven. Bullheaded. I'd come up against his determination before, and I'd always yielded. Besides, *he* could read the books down there, even if I couldn't. He might be able to find a way out of this mess yet.

Silently, I turned from the darkness and headed toward my cottage.

David opened the front door, working the lock with some remnant of the warder's magic that he continued to hold as his right—his obligation—to keep me safe. I glanced down at my fingers, curled into a loose fist, hiding the mints that Neko had given me. I knew that David had heard my familiar's snarky comment, and I felt my cheeks flush. "Do you want a cup of tea?" I asked, saying the first thing that came to mind as I scrambled for a way to escape David's nearness.

"Sure," he said. "I'll get started downstairs."

He crossed the living room with the ease of a man comfortable in his own home. I stared as he palmed on the light switch, listened as he loped down the steps. I felt more uncomfortable than he, walking around my own cottage, heading into my own kitchen.

I put on the kettle and rummaged around in the cabinets for my teapot and mugs. I automatically set aside the peppermint tea that sat at the front of the cupboard; David didn't care for mint. Too bad, I thought, popping one of Neko's parting gifts into my mouth.

I hunted around for the lemon chamomile, finally finding

it at the back of the shelf. I fished out two bags and added them to the pot. Excavating a tray, I put a couple of spoons beside the mugs, adding some brightly colored cocktail napkins that I'd scavenged from some gift basket too long ago to remember the specifics. All in all, I kept myself incredibly busy for a woman whose life appeared to be on the edge of some massive transition.

As I waited for the water to boil, I looked around the kitchen. I could still remember how it had appeared when Melissa and I entered the cottage for the first time. The spiderwebs had hosted spiderwebs of their own; dust had been thick on every horizontal surface. We had cleaned and scrubbed like madwomen, and I'd repaid her with a plain hamburger, loads of fries and an endless debt of friendship. Everything had been normal then. I'd been happy, content with my friends and my job and my life.

The kettle whistled, and I poured out the boiling water with smooth, automatic motions. It had taken me forever to learn where I stored things in the kitchen; for months, I'd opened the wrong cupboards, searched in the wrong cabinets. Somewhere along the way, though, this place had come to be home. I could pour myself a drink by moonlight. I could grab emergency Oreos from the very back of the second shelf, even in the midst of an on-phone crisis. I could locate every one of my serving dishes, my mismatched pieces of silverware, my chipped but serviceable plates.

The Peabridge cottage was my home.

The Peabridge cottage, complete with its books, its crystals and its witchy accouterments. Complete with the warder who waited for me downstairs. What the hell was I going to say to him? How was I going to carry on a conversation, alone, with David Montrose? Especially a conversation about leaving my powers behind forever?

I chewed the remnant of my breath mint and took a deep breath before heading toward the basement.

David took the tray from me when I got to the bottom step. He had already starting browsing through the books, stacking ones with likely titles on the bookstand. He'd be a valuable addition to a research library, I thought. Despite myself, I smiled wryly.

"What?" he said, lifting a questioning eyebrow to ask if I wanted him to pour.

I shrugged, and he raised the teapot. The grassy fragrance of chamomile washed over the basement. "Nothing," I said. "I was just thinking about the books. About how much knowledge is in them."

We drank our tea in uncomfortable silence. Uncomfortable on my part, anyway. I kept wanting to ask him questions. I wanted to know what he was thinking. What had changed his mind? Why he had been content to sleep with me, but then decided that we'd been wrong?

Was I that lousy in bed?

"Do you really want to give it up?" he asked, as if we'd been chatting away for the past five minutes.

"I'm not sure. I think so. I don't know if I can."

"It's not an easy life, being a witch. You know that. But you don't have to do it alone."

"It sure seems like I do. I tried to reach you and Neko for two days." There. That was apparently what had me upset. I wouldn't have been sure, if tears hadn't broken into my voice on the final word.

David sipped from his mug before answering. When he did speak, it felt as if he was plucking individual words from a tree, searching out the perfect ones that were ripe. "I unplugged my phone. I didn't want to call you, just because *I* thought it was a good idea. I wanted to give you space, time alone. I hadn't thought through the loss of your power. I assumed that you could reach me, that you could call me as your warder if you really, truly needed me."

"I did need you!"

"I know. I was wrong."

The simplicity of his confession stunned me. He wasn't trying to make excuses. He wasn't trying to shift the burden. He wasn't trying to make me doubt myself, question what was what, who was who. He was accepting responsibility.

All of my arguments fled, tumbling into the dark basement corners like dust bunnies fleeing under the sofa.

He stared at me, his gaze painfully direct through the swirling chamomile steam. "We need to find her, Jane. We need to get Ariel back. Once you have your powers restored, then you can make a decision, an informed decision, about what you want to do. Whether you want to be a witch."

"I don't know what else I can do to track her down."

"Whether you want to be one or not, you're still a witch for now, Jane. Witches are meant to work in covens."

"No," I said flatly. "I won't go back to the Washington Coven." The thought of approaching that clique of gossiping manipulators made my stomach turn. They were exactly why I wanted out of this magic business; they were the sort of knotted complication that I could avoid completely if I lived as a normal human woman.

"Do you have a better idea?" David said.

I thought of all the better ideas I'd had. I had thought I would be a librarian. I had thought I would be Will's girlfriend. I had thought I would be Gran's granddaughter. I had thought I would squabble with Clara forever, begrudging her the poor decisions that she'd made in her youth. I had thought I would live a totally normal life, in a totally normal city, with totally normal friends.

Without a warder to confuse me with a simple six-word question.

I shook my head. "Not yet. But I will. Give me a little more time, and I will."

"Mabon is in three weeks. The Autumn Equinox. You have to find Ariel by then."

"Mabon," I said, and it sounded like a promise.

"Now, let's see what we can learn here. Maybe one of these books can help us out after all."

I set aside my tea mug and took a deep breath. I knew how to do this. I knew how to be a librarian. I knew how to track down resources and bring them to an interested patron. Even if my catalog had been destroyed six months before. Even if I couldn't read the texts on my own. Even if I wasn't sure that I wanted to be part of the solution.

"David," I said. "I'm scared."

"I know," he replied. "I know you are. We'll get through this together."

And then we worked side by side in companionable silence, until long after our chamomile tea grew cold.

10

So, it took a week. A week of careful thought. A week of tossing and turning at night. A week of wondering if I had done the right thing, letting Will leave after our dinner at Don Lobos, driving off Neko, working with David. A week—well, every other day—of getting a voice mail message from Will at work, and calling him back, fingers crossed, hoping to get his own voice mail, hoping not to, trembling with relief when I heard his recorded message. A week of telling Kit that I'd be the one to pick up the daily sweets at Cake Walk, so that I could rehash things, each and every morning, with Melissa.

"Jane," she finally told me. "I don't have anything left to say. You acted. Now live with it. Or change it. But don't just keep telling me about it. Call Will when you know he'll be there, and ask him out. What's the worst that can happen? He'll say that you hurt his feelings, and he'll refuse? From everything you've said, it sounds like he's fine with what happened."

I wanted to protest. I wanted to tell her that she was making things too simple. I wanted to huddle on a stool at her counter, drinking endless cups of Apricot Pekoe and ignoring the Peabridge, and its reference desk and its cottage.

But I wasn't a complete idiot.

"Can I use your phone?"

She nodded toward the wall.

I glanced at my watch. 8:40. Maybe he wouldn't be there. Maybe I could leave another witty and entertaining nonreply. Maybe I could get all the "cool girl" points, without worrying about the real world penalties. Ring. My heart started pounding. Ring. My lungs constricted, making me gasp for breath. Ring. My knees started to buckle in relief; I knew that his answering machine picked up after the fourth ring.

"Will Becker."

That was it. That was my cue. That was the trigger that was supposed to make me reply, make me say something out loud. "Hi," I finally managed. "It's Jane."

"Jane!" He honestly sounded pleased. "I'm so glad that you kept trying to end the phone tag."

"Yeah," I said, hoping that he couldn't hear any silent confession, any whisper of just how hard I had hoped that I'd get his answering machine. Again. "Look, I'm sure that you're busy. I just wanted to know if we could maybe go out to dinner next week. You know, we agreed that it was my treat next time. After dinner. At Don Lobos. Before you walked me home. Before—" Melissa made a slicing motion across her throat, reminding me that I needed to shut my babbling mouth. I stammered, "W-w-well, you know…" And then I trailed off, tucking the phone against my shoulder and grabbing for my mug of tea like a drowning woman clutching a life vest.

"That would be great," he said.

"It would?"

He actually chuckled. Chuckled. Like a comfortable, easygoing guy who had no idea that he was dealing with a madwoman. "Did you have anything particular in mind?"

Something particular. That's right. If I was going to be a liberated woman asking a guy out on a date, I should have something specific planned. Something intentional. Some-thing thought through *before* I asked out the first totally normal guy that I'd met in a million years. I looked at Melissa, panicked, but she shrugged her incomprehension. *What*, I mouthed at her. She screwed up her face, but she clearly had no idea what I was asking.

"Um…" I said, knowing that I'd sound like an idiot, but I was afraid that I'd never breathe again, if I didn't say *some-thing*. "I thought…" Yeah, right. I thought about nothing. I thought that I'd hated Sadie Hawkins dances when I was in middle school, and obviously nothing had changed since then. I thought that my face was probably about ten different shades of crimson. I thought that I might as well just hang up the phone. I thought that it was absolutely, utterly, completely impossible that teenaged boys were expected to carry on this sort of conversation on a regular basis, if they were going to have any sort of love-life whatsoever.

And somehow, miraculously, magically, I don't know how, Will stepped into the breach. "Maybe we can go to a lecture at the Smithsonian? It's on Thursday night, six o'clock. It's about Greek temples and contemporary architecture—one of my friends is the speaker. She's going to talk about classic architecture and then lead a quick tour of the Mall. I've got a couple of free tickets."

"Perfect!" I said, and the vise that had constricted my chest suddenly sprang loose. "That would be wonderful! We could go out for Greek food afterward. Stick with a theme," I said in a flash of sudden inspiration.

"One of my favorites," Will said, and I was pretty sure I could hear him smiling down the phone line. "Should I swing by the Peabridge to get you? You get off at five o'clock?"

"Yes. But give me fifteen minutes to change."

"Five-fifteen. At your house, then?"

"I'd like that." I let my own smile tilt my words. It was actually really easy to ask a guy out. Why had I gotten so worked up over this? I glanced at the clock on Melissa's wall. "Oh! I have to run! I'm going to be late to work!"

"Have a great day," Will said. "See you Thursday."

I hung up the phone and turned to Melissa, beaming. "See?" I said. "I can take some responsibility for my life!"

"Some," she said, shaking her head, but she smiled. She handed me a pasteboard box of baked goods. "But you really will be late, if you don't get moving."

"Thanks," I said.

"And about the other stuff? The witchcraft?" she said as she ushered me toward the door. "Have you decided what you're going to do?"

I shrugged as best I could, carrying the box. "I actually came up with an idea over the weekend. But I'll have to call David."

"So call him."

"I can't. It feels strange."

"What is it with you and phones? This is a magic thing, right? Not related to the other thing." The other thing. The bedroom thing.

"Well, they're all tied up together."

"No. *You* tie them together. To anyone else, they'd be totally separate. Think of it like working together, you know, in an office building. If you had to ask the vice president of Special Communications a question for your job, you'd just go ask him."

"Not if I'd slept with him once, and then he'd tossed me out on my ass."

Melissa frowned. I didn't know if she didn't approve of my language, or if she accepted the flaw I'd found in her analogy. "Okay. So, sexual harassment in the workplace probably doesn't apply here. But, wait! It sort of does! David is *your* employee. Your own employee can't harass you."

I suspected that the Equal Employment Opportunity Commission would have some argument to the contrary. I sighed heavily, but I didn't bother to argue. Bottom line—no pun intended—Melissa was right. I needed to call David. I wasn't going to get this whole disappearing-anima-loss-of-power-what-is-the-purpose-of-my-life-as-a-witch thing under control without him.

"I'll call him from the Peabridge. First thing."

"Brew a pot of coffee, first thing. Don't let Evelyn catch you shirking too badly."

I laughed and hurried through the morning streets of Georgetown. I wasn't actually sure *what* Evelyn would do if she caught me shirking. Both of us had come to rely on Kit more and more to answer basic reference questions. Evelyn had taken advantage of my supposed free time to give me more and more management work—analyzing our budget, preparing reports for the trustees. I appreciated the recognition of my advancement, but it wasn't what I really wanted, what I enjoyed. It wasn't what I'd signed up for when I became a reference librarian.

Even if my work at the Peabridge *was* part of the white-picket-fence-happy-happy-home-life that I imagined every time I thought about cashing in my witchcraft chips for good.

That was the problem with me. I was never happy.

At least I followed Melissa's advice when I got to work—the coffee was brewed and the Cake Walk treasures were nestled beneath their crystal domes by the time Evelyn walked in the front door. I smiled breezily and crossed to my desk, picking up my telephone like a woman on a mission.

Why was it so damned difficult to phone David?

We were working together on a problem. I had come up with a possible solution. This was all a business proposition. If he didn't answer, he didn't answer—my ability to speak to him was not a referendum on our entire relationship. I cleared my throat and punched in his number.

He answered on the first ring, snapping his name out, as if it were a two-word spell.

I stammered for a moment before telling him what I needed. At first, he was skeptical; I thought he was going to refuse. But when I explained, he listened, and then he finally agreed. "You're going to need Neko there to make this all work out," he said.

"I know."

"Good luck getting him to join us."

"I'm his witch!" I said, reciting the justification that I'd come up with while I was trying to bolster my courage.

"Good luck," David repeated, and the click as he hung up seemed to have a note of finality.

But I knew Neko better than anyone.

I dialed his cell phone, but he didn't answer. I glanced at the clock. Who was I kidding? He had to be home, still sound asleep, most likely. I punched in his home number and let it ring away. Forty-seven times.

"What!" he finally snapped.

"Hunan shrimp. My place. Tonight. Seven o'clock."

"I'm busy," he said petulantly.

"I'll order it with extra shrimp."

"I can't just drop everything—"

"And ask them to hold the vegetables."

"Jane—"

"And an order of shrimp toast, as an appetizer."

"And a side of crab shumai," he said.

What were a few dumplings between friends? I grimaced and agreed, "And a side of crab shumai."

"Seven o'clock," he said, and then he cut the connection.

Gran and Clara were easier to bring into the loop. They would have agreed to see me without the bribery of food; in fact they both sounded delighted to hear from me. Pork fried rice was just an extra benefit. I glanced at the locked drawer where my poor, suffering wallet waited, credit card unsuspecting.

If my plan worked, a Chinese feast was worth it.

David arrived first, carrying two large boxes, one in each hand.

"How much trouble did you have finding them?" I asked as I closed the door behind him.

Instead of answering, he said, "Are you sure you want to do this?"

"I don't think I have a choice."

Before I could elaborate, Neko strolled into the living room, as confident as if he still lived there. He looked sleek as ever and a little dangerous, and he held himself with a certain aloofness. "I didn't realize we were supposed to bring gifts," he said, a single eyebrow arched in inquiry at the boxes in David's hands. I wondered if he could sense the contents, even from across the room.

"I was hoping that you could help me, Neko." I'd spent part of the afternoon plotting out my peace offering. "Gran and Clara will be here in just a minute, and I want Gran to know I've been thinking about her wedding. I've chosen my jewelry, to wear with the maid of honor dress. What do you think of these?" I turned to the coffee table, where I'd laid out a pair of silver earrings. Their sharp spikes stood out like spines on a sea urchin, and they radiated a certain early-1980s' malevolence.

Neko looked as horrified as I'd expected. "What? Are you hoping to get a satellite signal in the church?"

"I just thought—"

"You just thought that you'd ruin your grandmother's one perfect day of happiness." He clicked his tongue with the disdain of a Hollywood costume designer. David actually laughed out loud at my familiar's tone of horror. "Melt those things down. Pearls," he said, as if he were teaching me a new word. "Peeearls. Drop earrings. Classic."

"Drop earrings," I repeated. And then I couldn't keep from saying, "Are you sure they'll go with orange and silver?"

Neko shuddered. "Your grandmother is one strong-willed woman."

"Tell me something I *don't* know," I said, thinking of years of teenage conflict.

"You know, it's not just the colors. She is insisting on opera music for the service. For the processional *and* the recessional."

"That's not too bad. Is it?"

"The Queen of the Night aria? For a wedding?"

I smiled. "I think she's just trying to include Uncle George. Opera has always been his thing, you know. She wants to show off a little for the guests, let everyone know how much they have in common."

He rolled his eyes. "I know." I smiled, pleased that we had gotten past our little tiff so easily. Neko, though, was not quite ready to let bygones be bygones. "While we're talking about showing off in front of assembled friends and family, you have *got* to do something about your highlights. I've seen genie lanterns with less tacky brass than you're showing these days."

Now *that* stung. Especially when I saw David fake tremendous interest in the packages that he had set down beside the couch. "You were the one who told me to color my hair in the first place!"

"But you haven't been back to Jacques for the touch-ups, have you?"

Busted. "No."

"Jane, Jane, Jane, when *are* you going to learn?" He sighed, as if we were discussing starving children in some distant corner of the world. Fine. At least he'd spewed his nastiness, and now we could move on. I'd suffered enough cosmetic and sartorial humiliation.

But, no. Neko was only warming to his job. "What *have* you been doing without me? You couldn't possibly think *that* green eyeliner would help the hazel mud you're stuck with, could you?" Before I could protest, he moved in for the kill. "And you might *think* that you'll get more dates if you dress like a boy, but I'm here to tell you, that is never, ever going to happen, girlfriend."

I glanced at my oxford cloth shirt, suddenly aware that it did nothing to bolster my less than robust figure. A distant part of my scattered mind wondered what my green eyeliner looked like now, against a face that must be flushed the tint of merlot.

I was beginning to regret that I'd added crab shumai into the bargain to lure Neko here. Surely, my complete humiliation should have been sufficient currency to bring my familiar back into the fold.

At least I was managing to entertain my warder. I was certain I heard David smother a laugh before he said, "Can I get the two of you something to drink? Before you move on to round two?"

"There won't be any more rounds," I muttered darkly. "And I'll get the drinks. What'll you have?" I turned to Neko, pasting a sweet smile on my lips.

"Do you still have the Fish Eye Chard?" Neko purred.

"No," I said, determined to keep my voice sunny. "You went through all six bottles before you left. Besides, we're going to be working tonight."

His lips moved into a taut *O*. "Soda water for me, then. With a splash of lime. And a mint leaf or two, if you've got it."

Great. We were reduced to virgin mojitos. Watery, virgin mojitos.

I escaped to the kitchen and started to play bartender. Just as I was trying to knock the last ice cubes out of their stubborn plastic tray, there was a knock at the door. David did the honors, and I heard Gran's surprised exclamation as she registered his presence. "It's always so good to see you, dear," she said, and I could picture her patting his arm, even though I could not glimpse the interaction from the kitchen.

"We ran into the deliveryman as we walked through the gate, Jeanette. Er, Jane." Clara sailed in from the living room, trying to finesse the fact that she still had trouble remembering my preferred name. "We tried to pay, but he insisted that everything was taken care of."

"The magic of credit cards," I said, taking a large brown paper sack from her and trying not to put too much emphasis on the second word. The smell of soy sauce and hot oil— or maybe a twinge of apprehension—twisted my belly.

I'd improvised, ordering for Gran, Clara and David. The good thing about building a menu for five, though, was that you could justify enough dishes that everyone was ultimately satisfied. In addition to Neko's Hunan shrimp-with-shrimp, I set out white cardboard containers of mu shu chicken, beef with broccoli, Szechuan green beans and pork fried rice, with a glorious plastic bowl of crispy sesame chicken anchoring the feast.

Locusts had nothing on us. We moved through the food like an army on the march, juggling chopsticks and serving spoons like high-grade weapons. Gran went back for thirds, and Clara devoted herself to picking out every last piece of beef from the surrounding bright green broccoli. Keeping in mind the magical feats to come, I limited myself to a couple of bites from each dish (Neko's shrimp excluded— I got none of those, given how tremendously possessive my familiar could be).

I caught David looking at me with something akin to approval.

When we'd decimated the main dishes, I passed around dessert. Clara declared the almond cookies the finest she'd ever tasted, and Neko pounced on his fortune cookie. "Here!" he called, as if we'd all only just arrived. "Take a fortune cookie! Come on! Everyone! Open them up! Hurry! Now we'll go around in a circle and read our fortunes out loud!"

He demonstrated, shattering his vanilla cookie into shards in his excitement to get to the slip of paper inside. "You will go on many journeys and have many adventures. In bed."

"What?" Gran asked.

"In bed!" Neko bounced up and down on the couch. "That's the way you read fortunes. You put 'in bed' after the words. It's much more fun! Everything's more fun in bed! Right, Jane? Read yours next."

I kept my head down, refusing to take the slightest chance that I would meet David's gaze.

I couldn't kill Neko. Executing my familiar would negate my entire magical plan. Murdering him would make the rest of my arcane redemption impossible; I would never locate Ariel. Throwing daggers at him, attacking him with boiling oil, skinning him from head to toe—each option would leave me worse off than I was now.

Now. When I was struggling to swallow, fighting to smile, trying to remember that he *wanted* me to flush with embarrassment.

Instead, I took a deep breath and sat up straight on the edge of the overstuffed green couch. "I'll read my fortune later. After we're done."

"Done, dear?" Gran was immediately attentive. "What are we doing?"

Studiously avoiding looking at David, I said, "I have a favor to ask you. Both of you—Gran, Clara." They looked curious. "It's about witchcraft."

Gran pursed her lips. When we'd had our run-in with the Coven the year before, she'd alternated between worrying about me and my desire to fit in, and worrying about herself and her disdain for a group of women who could be so divisive as to mock her witchy shortcomings.

Clara, on the other hand, looked pensive. She was far more disposed to matters arcane; she'd spent years meditating in Sedona, absorbing the powers of crystals and the vibrations of the Vortex. She had less use for the Coven than Gran had; Clara considered her basic female essence to be a greater foundation for witchcraft than any group of women who gathered together for a touch of socializing and ostracization. She responded first to my statement. "What about witchcraft? What do you want us to do, Jeanette?" She must have seen me flinch, but she didn't bother to rephrase her question with my real name.

I took a deep breath. "I haven't really told you what's been going on here. I—" I stopped as sudden tears thickened the back of my throat. I hadn't realized that I was still so emotional about the topic. I hadn't realized that I was afraid to talk to Gran and Clara. I swallowed hard and rushed ahead. "I need your help."

Gran leaned over and patted my hand. "Of course, dear. Whatever we can do to help you." She fumbled for her handbag. "Is it money? Because if it's money, I can help you, but I really have to question your planning, inviting us over and spending so much on dinner, only to ask for a loan."

"No, Gran," I said, and I actually managed to smile. "It isn't money."

"It's some type of spell, isn't it?" Damn. Clara could be perceptive. There was no reason for me to deny it, no reason to beat around any more bushes. Of course, it helped her to guess, having David and Neko standing close.

I glanced at them before I said, "Yes." And then, because I'd run out of every last delay, I said, "I've lost my powers. They faded because I didn't use them. I was distracted in the past year, with work and with—I don't know—life."

"Didn't use them!" Clara shook her head in surprise. I knew that she spent her power in dribs and drabs, casting runes every morning, stretching her magical senses to measure the aura of every person around her.

Gran pursed her lips. "Well, dear, if you lost yours through nonuse, then I can't imagine the state of *my* magic." She dusted her hands, as if she were trying to shed some dry residue. "I haven't used mine since those terrible Coven women ran us round in circles."

I stared at her, my entire plan disintegrating in my mind. "I—" I started, but I didn't know how to finish the sentence. "But—"

I threw a panicked glance at David, only to find him smiling gently. "Sarah, it all has to do with baseline powers. With raw ability. You know that your powers have always been…subtle."

Gran pursed her lips. "I'm the weakest of the three of us, when it comes to these magic things."

David permitted himself a nod. "And weaker witches don't experience the same type of drain. Oh, your power will eventually trickle away if you never use it, but the loss will be relatively slow. Even after a year of nonuse, you likely haven't lost very much at all. Not like Jane, here."

Great. Yet another so-called advantage of my amazing ability to work spells. I turned into a washed-up old husk faster than anyone else.

"So I can still help Jane?" Gran asked, and her earnest desire to assist brought fresh tears to my eyes.

David nodded. "You can still help."

Clara leaned forward. "But what exactly are we here to do? What have you tried already?"

I shrugged. "David and Neko tried to help me, when I

first realized what was going on. We thought we'd found the solution. I worked a spell to make an anima—"

"A what?" Clara turned her head to one side, curiosity on her face.

"An anima. A sort of magical robot. But she doesn't look like a robot. She looks like a woman. She— Oh, it doesn't matter. She didn't work out. She was supposed to build up my powers by getting some magical work done around here. Polishing my crystals, cleaning my books. That was supposed to bring back my own magical strength, reflect it back to me since I made her. But something went wrong, things didn't fall into place the way they should have. I got the tiniest bit of power when she spoke to me, but the rest of mine was drained away. Completely."

Gran looked at me shrewdly. "It sounds to me like you were trying to play a bit of Tom Sawyer. Get someone else to do what you should have been doing on your own."

I shrugged. "David and I thought it would work."

"Shortcuts usually don't, dear," Gran said simply.

I bit back a few words of frustration and settled for nodding my head in agreement. "You're right. And so, I've got another plan." I saw Gran's eyes dart toward David. "David's agreed, Gran. He thinks this one is a good idea."

"And what is it?" asked Clara when I steeled myself for the great reveal.

"I want you each to awaken your own familiar. I want to teach you about witchcraft, teach you like the Coven never took the time to do."

Silence.

David watched my relatives, his face impassive. Neko stared at me as if I'd suddenly sprouted fangs, wings and a trunk. Gran looked confused, and Clara seemed slightly put out. Not surprisingly, Gran recovered first. Practical, logical Gran. "I don't understand," she said. "How can teaching *us* help you regain *your* powers?"

"Magic isn't like science," I explained. "With science, when you use something up—like a battery—it wears out. Magic is exactly the opposite. Using it makes it *stronger*. My awakening Ariel should have increased the power I had at my disposal, would have, if I hadn't made a mistake. If you make familiars, and if I teach you everything *I* know, then there should be some sort of multiplication effect. I should get back to where I was. And then some, with any luck. It would be like having a coven of our very own."

Gran shook her head. "That coven was nothing but trouble."

"They were," I agreed. "But we won't be. We'll have our own rules. We'll set our own limits. We won't be like them."

Clara wasn't concerned about our social organization; she was still dwelling on having a familiar. "It's like meditation."

"What, dear?" Gran was starting to sound a bit annoyed. For the first time in ages, though, I felt a rush of love toward Clara.

"Exactly!" I said. "It's like meditation. The more you center yourself, the more energy you draw into yourself, the greater you become."

Clara picked up the figurative ball and ran. "And it's like yoga!"

"I wouldn't know about that," I said, pushing aside images of my collapsing Eagle Pose. "But, anyway, I asked David to find familiars for you. He's brought them here tonight."

Gran continued to look uncertain, but Clara's eyes swept over to the mysterious boxes. "There?" I nodded. "And they're cats? Like Neko?"

I looked at David. I didn't actually know what form the newcomers would take. He cleared his throat before he said, "No. Each witch awakens a familiar uniquely suited to her. Sometimes it reinforces her personality. Sometimes, the familiar is a complementary force." He hefted one box and brought it to Gran, then deposited the other in front of Clara.

Both women looked from the containers to David to me. "Will you do it?" I looked from Gran to Clara and back again. "I wouldn't ask if there were any other way. I need you."

Gran harrumphed. "Well, of course, dear. Of course we'll help you." Clara nodded as well.

I suddenly remembered Christmas mornings when I was a little girl, when I'd stared at Gran with all the expectation—and the barely smothered greed—that a good girl could muster. I grinned at the image and waved toward their boxes. "Go ahead, then. Take them out."

The containers weren't taped closed. Instead, they had lids that lifted off smoothly. Gran and Clara moved with an eerie synchrony, as if they'd practiced their motions in another age, another life. Both boxes were filled with mundane packing peanuts, white curls that billowed to the floor. Neko wriggled closer, and I half expected him to pounce on the cushioning material.

Gran freed her familiar first. It was a wooden statue, the length of her forearm, painted in brilliant colors—crimson and yellow and cobalt-blue. Shrewd eyes peered out above a curved black beak. A scarlet macaw.

Clara lost no time rooting around in her own box. Her familiar tumbled into her hands. It was carved from wood as well, but the artist had let the statue's natural colors shine through. A long, prehensile tail curled around four legs. A white ruff framed a fine-featured face. Clara's familiar was a capuchin monkey.

Neko had leaped to his feet as the packages were opened. He started stalking around the couch, viewing the statues from all angles. I knew him well enough that I could read his inquiry, understand the questions that he was asking as he sought to understand the magical powers unwrapped before him.

A macaw. A parrot. Long-lived and intelligent, bonding with its humans over decades. A perfect match for Gran.

And for Clara, a monkey. Inquisitive. Willing to explore anything, and capable of infinite distraction. Trouble-some—although that probably wasn't a trait that David had screened for.

But Clara was already falling in love with her familiar. Or at least with the notion of having one. She looked up at me, awe in her eyes. "What do we do?" she breathed.

I glanced at David, but he merely extended a hand, inviting me to respond. Neko came and settled by my side, warm and comfortable. Apparently, my shrimp bribe had worked completely. All was forgiven. "There's a spell," I said. I settled my fingers on Neko's shoulder, and the words came back to me, as clearly as if they were written on a page before my eyes. "For Neko, I said,

'Awaken now, hunter, dark as the night.
Bring me your power, your strong second sight.
Hear that I call you and, willing, assist;
Lend me your magic and all that you wist.'"

Gran and Clara nodded. They weren't the best-trained witches, but they could sense words of spellcraft. They could remember chants that conveyed energy. Strength. Power.

"But we'll have to change it," Clara said. "Change the first line to match our own familiars. Right?" She looked to me for guidance.

I nodded. The spell that had awakened Neko had been laid out for me by his old owner, by Hannah Osgood. The book had been waiting for me—or some other unsuspecting witch—to work the magic. The basic shape of the power remained the same for any awakening, but Gran and Clara would need to tweak the spell to their own ends.

Gran looked up from her scarlet bird. Her face was a little pinched, and I wondered what promises she was about to extract, what demands she was about to make. She surprised me, though. "Can we say it at the same time? Can we work our magic together?"

I glanced at David. "Of course," he said. "If that would make you feel better, there's no reason that you can't free your familiars simultaneously."

Clara snapped her attention back to me. "What do we do, Jean—Jane?" Her remembering my current name was a symbol of how much she wanted my instruction.

"Set the spell in your own mind. Figure out how you'll change it for your own familiar."

Gran might have been more timid about her magic, but she was a veteran crossword puzzle worker. I wasn't surprised when she nodded before Clara.

Even though I would not be doing any actual working, I settled my hand on Neko's shoulder. I'd wanted him here— needed him here—because he could center me, anchor me in a storm of magic. "Then take three deep breaths," I said. I could see Gran's tension flow away with each exhale, even as I recognized Clara's energy sharpening. "Now, offer up your thoughts." I touched my own forehead, demonstrating the motion. "And your voice." I touched my throat. "And your spirit." I settled my hand over my heart. "And recite the spell."

They started together. "Awaken now." I heard Gran's words first, her recitation as steady as a nurse reading out a patient's chart. "Winged one, soar like a kite," she said.

At the same time, Clara intoned, "Mischief, witty and bright." Then their voices joined together for the rest of the spell.

"Bring me your power, your strong second sight.

Hear that I call you and, willing, assist;

Lend me your magic and all that you wist."

I felt the familiar flash of darkness with my entire body. The world disappeared, swallowed in a wave of nothingness. Before I could register Gran's bit-off cry, Clara's gasp, everything sprang back into existence, sharper than before, clearer than ever.

A buxom woman stood beside Gran, her bright red hair contrasting sharply with the lemon-yellow of her blouse and the overdyed indigo of her jeans. Her nose was long and pronounced; her face looked as if it should be stamped on some ancient Roman coin.

And a child crouched beside Clara, a young boy with the delicate features of a child, but the snow-white hair of an ancient man. Even as I watched, he twitched in his clothes, scratching at his long-sleeved chestnut-colored T-shirt, tugging the garment out of the waistband of his matching corduroy pants.

Gran reached out to her familiar first, stroking the woman's sleeve with tentative fingertips. Distantly, as if from across a canyon, I felt energy arc between them, the magical power of witch acknowledging familiar. When Clara reached out to smooth down her boy's cowlick, I felt the magical action a little more.

Nevertheless, the magic was between my relatives and

their familiars. It had nothing to do with me. It did not begin to restore my own depleted strength.

I glanced at David, afraid to ask the questions that bubbled to the top of my brain. Had anything happened? Had we gained anything at all by awakening two familiars? He offered the faintest of shrugs, apparently unable—or unwilling—to acknowledge my concerns. My disappointment tasted like lemon juice as I swallowed hard.

Neko seemed utterly unaware of my worry as he settled one hand on his hip. "Well, girlfriend, you definitely made one huge mistake."

"What?" I said, reluctant to look away from the newcomers. My heart beat fast with the notion that I'd done something wrong, something that would endanger our magical future.

"With two more mouths to feed, you should have ordered a lot more food."

11

Clara's little boy turned out to be named Majom. The woman who perched near Gran was Nuri. Even without Neko's or David's clarification, I knew that both creatures were tied closely to their witches, bound much more tightly than Neko and I had ever been connected.

Give me credit for something—I'd checked the calendar before I decided on this desperate working. I'd made sure that Gran and Clara wouldn't duplicate the first witchcraft mistake I'd ever made. They had not awakened their familiars under the liberating gaze of a full moon.

No, Majom wasn't going to be wandering the streets of D.C., with his deceptively innocent little-boy fingers getting into trouble. We'd still have our hands full—Clara's familiar had already excused himself to use the bathroom and taken the opportunity to go through every drawer in the tiny room, dumping my makeup onto the floor. He'd been ready to add shampoo and conditioner to the mixture—just to see what would happen—when I'd walked in on him and cut short his fun.

At least Nuri, Gran's parrot familiar, was a little easier to control. She held herself aloof for the most part, perching on the arm of one of the sofas, casting her head at a curious angle as she watched us talk to each other long into the night. When asked a direct question, she would croak an answer in a voice that was curiously loud, absurdly harsh— like a lifetime smoker working out a fear of public speaking.

We soon realized that Neko had not been entirely face-tious when he'd said that the familiars needed to eat. Both were famished; I had no idea how long they had been held in their inanimate forms. I waved Neko toward the kitchen, telling him to have a ball with the cabinets and the fridge. After all, emergencies were emergencies. And I didn't have any expensive delectables stored away. Gran and Clara followed the familiars, looking like they'd never seen a kitchen before.

I turned to David, trying to keep a note of admiration out of my voice. "Where did you get them?"

"Target," he deadpanned.

"David—"

"I know people who know people." He shrugged. "I spend my days cataloging arcane collections. I'm bound to come across a few valuable tidbits."

"But what happened to their own witches?"

"They have witches. Your mother and grandmother."

"David—" I started to warn again.

"Do you really want to know?"

A shiver crept up my spine. A familiar stayed tied to a witch for as long as she was able to work her own magic, for as long as she proved her arcane value to her Coven, to herself. But if a witch lost her power? If she died? This was all skirting a little too close to my own story. I swallowed hard. "Just tell me this. Do I need to worry about anyone coming after them? Is someone going to try to take them away?"

"No."

I stared into his eyes for a moment, measuring the stark truthfulness written there. David didn't lie to me. David had never lied to me. The steadiness of his gaze made my heart pound, and I wiped my palms against my sides. "What about a warder?" I asked, as if I were changing the subject. "Are any dark, mysterious strangers going to show up pounding on the door?"

A hint of a smile crooked David's lips. "That's all taken care of. I took the liberty of entering my name into the records. As far as Hecate's Court is concerned, I'm responsible for all three of you, and your familiars."

"Can you do that?"

"I did, didn't I?"

Oh. Right. There was still that nagging thing about his knowing all the politics of this witchcraft stuff while I stumbled through, making it up as I went along. He was in-finitely better prepared for an arcane life than I would ever be.

"I didn't mean are you allowed to," I said, although I had meant that, at least in part. "I meant are you *able* to. Won't it be too difficult for you to track three rogue witches, and all the spells we cast?"

"I somehow think your mother and grandmother will be a bit easier to manage than you are. Were," he amended, as I started to protest. "You got better. A little. We'll see what happens when they come into the full bloom of their powers, but most witches don't generate quite as much chaos as you've managed. You're exceptional that way."

"Gee, thanks."

"You're welcome," he said, and his tone was so dry I could not tell if he was teasing me, or merely being excru-ciatingly polite.

Was this really what I wanted? To be enmeshed in warders and familiars and rules that I still didn't fully understand? A quiet life of mundane librarianship was sounding pretty damn good.

"Ja-ane!" Neko's singsong spared me the need to reply. "Were you going to do anything with this frozen cheesecake?"

"Aside from eat it, you mean? At a party? With a dozen other people?"

"That's what I thought," Neko purred. "I don't suppose you have enough magic to work a thawing spell, so that we can have it now?"

"Or better yet," David said quietly, "teach your mother and grandmother how to work the spell. Build their power and feed your own."

"I don't know how to teach—"

"No time like the present to learn," he said, and then he took my arm and led me into the kitchen.

I thought about protesting. I thought about saying that I'd never worked a—a what?—a thawing spell. Why would *anyone* work a thawing spell?

But then I looked at Gran and Clara, saw the excitement on their faces. And I glanced at Majom, read the mischievous curiosity in his darting almond eyes. I gazed at Nuri, saw that she was absorbing facts, sponging up information, even as she cocked her head at a critical angle. I remembered the scant droplets of power that had coalesced in my arcane well when Ariel had spoken to me. Sure, I hadn't felt anything just now, when the familiars awakened, but maybe, just possibly, I could change that.

"Okay," I said. "I have something that might work."

Majom and Nuri settled beside their witches as if they'd worked magic together for all of their lives. Neko came and stood beside me, a surprisingly comforting presence, offering up the possibility of my using my own magic in the not-so-distant future. I sensed David hovering close behind us, felt his presence like a physical thing.

Gran and Clara skated through the preparation, the deep breaths, the offering up of their good astral intentions. Still wondering if I could harness a weather charm to meet my kitchen needs, I said, "Okay. Here are the words. As you say them, lean into your familiars." I saw Gran start to shift her weight. "It's not just a physical thing, it's mental. Like you're pushing against a revolving door with your powers. The door moves, but it holds you up, as well."

Gran and Clara looked skeptical, but they nodded their willingness to try. I recited the spell for them from memory.

"Feel the winter, slowing heartbeat,
Sense the icy surface cold.
Dream of summer, think of new heat
Sunshine breaking through so gold."

As they repeated the magical incantation, I stared at the cake. I knew they had failed, though, even before they stepped away from their familiars. There had been no flash of darkness. Nevertheless, Neko poked the center of the cheesecake with a tentative finger.

"Nope," he said. "Still hard as a rock."

"That should have worked!" I was angry. Spellcraft had always come easy to me. I wasn't used to failure, used to utter ordinariness. I didn't know if the mistake had been mine or theirs; I didn't even know how to find out what had gone wrong.

"Maybe if we tried the microwave, dear?" Gran was always ready with a practical answer.

"No," Clara said, and her tone was sharp. I'd never seen her so driven, so possessed. She grasped Majom's hand, and she took a step closer to me. "We'll do this by magic. Think about the words, Jane. Make sure you had them right."

I started to protest out of habit—I didn't like Clara being the boss of me in anything. But she was right. Something had kept the spell from working, and the words were the most obvious flaw. I ran them over in my mind again.

"Bold!" I said, when I got to the end of the chant. "Sunshine breaking through so bold!"

Clara nodded tightly. "Let's try it again."

This time, she and Gran chanted together, without prompting. They didn't need me. I was dead weight. But when they got to the last word—when they got to *bold*— there was the familiar flash of darkness.

A flash of darkness and something more. A twist of wicked jealousy. A searing mental itch, reminding me that I should feel the power, that I should have the strength. I hadn't realized how much hope I had pinned on a silly thawing spell.

I opened my eyes to find David staring at me. Silent. Inscrutable.

"What?" I said.

"Nothing."

As he spoke, the few drops of power that I had gleaned from Ariel twisted sluggishly inside my mind. I caught my breath against the sensation, remembering how recently I had still been able to work magic, how recently I had been overwhelmed by sparky energy. Weeks ago, only. In David's study.

"Nothing," he said again, and neither of us believed him. But before I could figure out the right thing to say, Neko began dissecting the cheesecake, with a speed and an accuracy that would have made Martha Stewart proud.

I regretted the cheesecake three days later, convinced that I had gained a dozen pounds as I spent the entire workday fretting about what to wear for my date with Will. I needed something that said intellectual and fun, brainy and just a little bit willing to step outside the schoolgirl role.

I barely had time to be afraid of the message Neko had left on my kitchen counter some time during the day:

Everyone is coming over for dinner and a quick tour of the basement. No need for you to change plans. Leave money for takeout, and everything should be fine.

Funny, how even the most innocuous little note could sound like a threat. I dropped two twenties on the table and offered up a prayer to the joint pantheon of dating and witchcraft gods. The money should at least be enough to move the quartet of my budding witches and familiars toward their instructional goal, especially with—er, make that, even with—Neko standing by to help. I contemplated adding another twenty to the bribe but decided that wouldn't guarantee my arcane progress. And Neko certainly wasn't going to return any change at the night's end. I knew my familiar well enough to be certain of that.

My familiar… He'd managed to turn my entire life upside down when he'd come to live with me. That had been the one part of my plan that I had worried about the most—how Gran and Clara would explain their familiars. Seeing the magical companions in the flesh only heightened my concern—what would Gran say to Uncle George about Nuri? How would Clara explain to neighbors that she had a new, hyperactive little boy living with her?

I needn't have worried. Gran had shrugged with her typical aplomb. "I'll just say that she's a friend of yours, dear. I'll tell George that she needed a place to stay while she gets her own life in order. She'll stay in your bedroom, after all. I hardly think he'll mind."

I started to protest, to explain that Nuri would create absolute chaos. But then I thought about the shy awkward woman, about her relative quiet compared to Neko. Nuri would be much easier for Uncle George to become used to than Neko had been for me. And we'd worry about the long-term effect of my grandmother having a live-in familiar down the road.

As for Clara, she'd laughed when I laid out the problem. "I'll just tell people that he's my grandson. Once we're back in Sedona, I'll explain that he was the reason I came out here to D.C. in the first place."

I looked down at my belly, the belly that had never swelled for Majom or any other child, and then I swallowed away a tart reply. When Clara got back to Sedona…. That's where her mind was, already.

I shook my head and read Neko's note one more time, realizing that I didn't have any more time to debate the matter of that night's training session. Gran, Clara and the familiars were going to come over, and there was nothing I could do to protect my house. Or my witchcraft collection. Or my sanity.

Except cancel my date with Will Becker. And I wasn't going to do that.

Sighing, I ducked into my bedroom, intent on digging out some date-perfect outfit. If I couldn't be the witch I wanted to be, at least I had a fighting chance at being a decent girl-friend. Lecture attendee. Casual acquaintance. Whatever.

Neko had been hard at work in my bedroom, as well. A pair of black cropped pants were laid out on the bed; he must have excavated them from the very back of my closet. A silk T-shirt lay across them, folded as perfectly as the day that I'd brought it home from the store. Its color was halfway between blue and green; I'd been captivated by the shade when I first found it. Strappy sandals waited on the floor, perfect for both the lecture and the walking tour to follow.

I might get angry with my familiar. I might take excep-tion to his exploiting me out of food and drink. I might rage about his treating the cottage like Grand Central Station, coming and going as he pleased. I might worry that he was going to lead Majom and Nuri down paths of arcane naugh-tiness.

But I'd be a fool to argue with Neko's fashion sense. I switched my hoop skirts for the new outfit in record time.

As promised, Will was waiting for me by the garden gate. "I tried to get a parking space in front of the library, but the closest thing I could find was a couple of blocks away," he said.

"No one can ever find parking in Georgetown," I answered with a shrug. No one without magical acumen, I thought, but I had no desire to make the clarification. David somehow never had a problem locating a space directly in front of the Peabridge. If I really was serious about leaving my witchy life behind, I might as well start practicing now. It wasn't such a hardship to walk to the car.

We made our way around the corner, chatting easily about the Federalist town house across the street from the library. Will said that it had been written up in a recent issue of *Home Architecture*, but he'd been inside and thought that the magazine had missed the chance to highlight better examples of colonial splendor, elsewhere in town.

"Here we go," Will said, stopping beside a green VW Beetle. The car was plastered with the word Borrowed-car.com. "I hope you don't mind," he said. "I don't actually own a car, I just use BC when I need one."

I'd heard about the communal car rental service. They paid for cars, insurance and gas; people rented them by the hour. I liked the idea of sparing the environment, of sharing a common vehicle. After all, it wasn't everyone who had the money or desire to own a Lexus. I was just a little put off by the thought that Will was investing—literally—in our evening together. I tried to put the thought out of my mind, tried to assure myself that I didn't need to be eight dollars an hour worth of entertaining.

"Makes sense to me," I said, before the pause could become too awkward. "I don't have a car, either, but I usually borrow my grandmother's if I need to drive anywhere." Gran. Was she a conversational gambit worth eight bucks? I could surely come up with some amusing story about something she'd made me promise, something about borrowing her car. If I couldn't think of something real, I could surely make something up.

Eight dollars an hour. That wasn't *so* much, was it?

Will held the door for me like a perfect gentleman, and then we made our way across town. I fought to come up with more topics that were BC-worthy, and settled for the tried and true—asking questions about Will, rather than talking about myself.

That technique worked surprisingly well, as Will told me about his colleague, Moira Prentiss, who was delivering the night's lecture. In fact, Will was full of details about the trip that Moira had recently taken to Greece, which led to a discussion about summer vacations, which led to my sad confession that I had not traveled anywhere interesting for years.

When we arrived at the lecture hall, Will proved to have the expert eye of an urban driver; he spotted a parking space before I had even started to look for one. Parallel parking like a man born behind the wheel, he grinned up at the red stone building of the Smithsonian castle. It was the oldest part of the museum complex, hulking over the Mall like a misplaced bit of English history. I'd been to another lecture there, when Melissa had dragged me to an all-day seminar about the secrets of French baguettes. As we descended stairs to the underground lecture hall, I felt a little thrill of expectation. I enjoyed giving my own presentations at the Peabridge, but it was much more fun to sit back and let someone else do the work.

Moira Prentiss rose to the occasion. She had obviously prepared her speech well in advance. She mixed slides with entertaining stories, interspersing images from the Greek isles with shots of the nation's capital. I began to look at buildings that I saw every single day with new eyes. The Capitol suddenly looked like a museum of architectural form; the Jefferson Memorial was a perfect temple to both rational thought and a founding father.

The rest of the room obviously appreciated the lecture as much as I did; applause echoed against the celadon walls when Moira finished. Soon enough, we were trooping out into the twilight, heading down the National Mall toward the self-same Capitol that Moira had featured in her speech. "That's the thing about a good lecturer," I said. "They make you realize things you've known all along."

Will agreed. "She was great!"

I laughed at his enthusiasm. On another date, I might have been jealous. With another man, I might have questioned his complimenting another woman—an attractive, educated, well-spoken woman—while he was out with me. At another time, I might have questioned my own worthiness, wondered at my own ability to entertain, to be witty, to be enough.

Especially with the eight dollars an hour for the car factored in.

But with Will, I didn't worry about any of those things. After all, he had suggested that I join him for the lecture. He could have gone with anyone from his office, any one of his friends, but he had chosen me.

As we walked with the group, Will reached over and took my hand. His fingers folding around mine felt right. Easy. There wasn't any awkward fumbling; I didn't need to worry about my palms sweating.

I glanced at him quickly, and he smiled, squeezing my hand lightly. Even as my belly swooped, I squeezed back. This asking-guys-out-on-dates thing was great. I should have done it a long time ago.

Moira stopped the group so that we could look across the Mall at the National Gallery of Art. I could feel Will beside me, a new expectation shimmering from the long line of his arm against mine. Moira pointed out the dome atop the museum and said, "There weren't many classical Greek buildings built on a round floor plan. We don't have extensive records of Greek domes—those seem to be more from the Roman era. But the Temple of Aphrodite at Knidos definitely had a round base—it might be the inspiration for just this sort of architectural detail."

A few people asked questions, and then we continued down the Mall. The Capitol loomed above us, brightly lit in the twilight. A trio of police cars crouched against the plaza at the base of the building, their lights flashing blue and red. Will stepped closer to me, the heat from his body making me feel safe, protected.

Moira pursed her lips as we waited for a traffic light to change. "I'm not sure what's going on over there. Maybe we should just stay put."

But as I squinted across the street, I realized that I would not be able to stay where we were.

A marble terrace stretched in front of the building. Centered on the plaza, surrounded by a gathering crowd, was a woman. A tall woman. A painfully pale woman. A woman with long black hair as dark as the shadows beyond the Capitol complex. A woman clad in some sort of a filmy gown, a frothy mixture of crimson and magenta and gold.

I pulled my hand free from Will's, even as someone in our group said, "Wow! That's the Artistic Avenger!"

"The what?" Moira asked, clearly distracted, now that her plans for playing tour guide had been disrupted.

"The Artistic Avenger," the guy said. "She's been coming out here every night. She's picketing Congress, trying to get them to increase the budget for the arts. She's got a slogan and everything—Empower The Arts. Everyone's been talking about her."

Everyone. Everyone but me. Me, and every last one of my correspondents. This was the first I'd heard of the Artistic Avenger.

Will, oblivious to the turmoil in my thoughts, placed an

easy hand against the small of my back, accepting that our fingers were no longer entwined. He said to Moira, "Do you mind if we go closer?"

She shrugged and glanced at the traffic light, which was conveniently changing to green. Our little group sifted into the crowd that had already gathered around the so-called Artistic Avenger. A half-dozen policemen watched us, shifting their weight but making no move to interrupt this apparent expression of free speech.

There was no mistaking her, up close. Instinctively, I took a step away from Will, distancing myself from the human warmth, the human attraction that he offered.

Ariel, I thought, fighting the urge to close my eyes.

She turned and stared at me. *Witch*, she thought. A golden pearl dropped into the center of my powers, an immediate payback from our contact. I fought to keep from laughing out loud at the sensation, even as I struggled not to let anyone see the bond between us, the connection that pulled me forward.

Then she was moving, dancing like a professional ballerina. Absolutely conscious of the space she occupied, she spun in a tight circle, generating energy from some unseen, unimaginable point of physical perfection. I could not count how many times she rotated, could not measure the actual path of her graceful arms, her perfect legs. The crowd began to applaud, but she continued, seeming to gain strength from every person who noticed the display, who gathered around her makeshift stage.

All of us cried out as she stopped her spinning, as she transformed the glorious arcing energy into a single leap. She ended up at the base of the stairs, the shimmering marble steps that led up to the Capitol. She bent over, collecting a poster that I had not seen before, that no one had noticed before she displayed it to the crowd. I knew what it would say before I could see it.

Empower The Arts.

Silently, she worked the poster into her ballet, raising it, then letting it fall, treating it like a partner for a silent pas de deux.

I suddenly remembered a book that Gran had read to me every night when I was a little girl, when I was going through my ballerina phase. (After the flight attendant phase, before the veterinarian phase. Funny. I never had a librarian phase.) The book was *The Red Shoes*, and it retold the Hans Christian Andersen fairy tale. The story had terrified me, even as I felt compelled to hear it over and over and over again.

And when I watched Ariel dance in her fire cloud of a dress, I remembered that fairy tale. I remembered the feeling of consumption, of compulsion. I remembered the magic of a child's dreams, the magic of my own witchy abilities.

And then she stopped. She set down her poster. She stood, frozen and perfect, panting just a little in the night-time air.

People began to murmur. The policemen shifted, as if they anticipated trouble from the assembled crowd. A man held up his cell phone, taking Ariel's photograph. Another man called out, "What's your name? Who are you?"

But she did not answer. Instead, she raised her chin. Met my eyes. Quoted from *The Tempest*, from lines delivered by the play's Ariel to Prospero, to the magician who looked so distractingly like my warder. *"At last I left them i' the filthy-mantled pool beyond your cell, there dancing up to the chins, that the foul lake o'erstunk their feet."*

Ariel's speech, reporting how the spirit had tricked men with magic.

A tiny cascade of astral energy trickled back to me—nearly half a dozen drops of ripe, raw power. Even as I gasped at the sensation, my anima turned away and sprinted into the darkness beyond the Capitol Plaza. I gave chase without thinking.

"Wait!" I called. "Ariel!"

I thought that I felt her dress against my hand as I clutched at the summer night. I thought that I saw a glimpse of darkness, blacker than the midnight bushes at the base of the building. I thought that I heard a whisper as someone lighter than air glided past a copse of trees.

I clutched at a stitch in my side as I chased her—or a shadow of her—around the corner of the building. I blinked in the light of overhead lamps as we emerged on yet another marble-covered terrace. I cursed as I realized that she had disappeared.

She was gone, as if she had never been there. As if she had not revealed herself to hundreds of onlookers, to the

Capitol police. As if our encounter had been by chance, had been an accident.

I put my hands on my knees and leaned over, trying to catch my breath.

"Jane!" Will's footsteps pounded onto the terrace as he caught up to me. "What the hell was that?"

I sucked in great heaving breaths of air, trying to think of an excuse that could be remotely, conceivably, fantastically possible. Maybe the truth was a better out. "I thought she was someone I knew."

"Must have been someone important," he said.

"It was." I couldn't think how to explain. I couldn't think how to tell him that she was an anima, that I was a witch. I couldn't think how to let him know that my world was crazy and mixed up and that he'd be better off to leave me alone, if he wanted to live with even the faintest hint of normalcy.

"Are you okay?"

Well. I wasn't expecting that. Demands about Ariel, sure. Exclamations about how crazy I was acting, of course. But concern? Coupled with the pucker of a worried frown?

"Yeah," I said, pushing myself upright. "I'm fine." I planted a hand against the stitch that still felt as if it was going to sever my side. "But, Will? I'm going to need a raincheck on dinner."

Dinner, and more. Dinner, and whatever other silent bargain we had begun to strike, our fingers twined together, then his palm against the small of my back.

He set his jaw and swallowed before speaking. "I was afraid that you were going to say that."

"I'm sorry—"

"Does this have anything to do with that guy? The one who was at your house the other night?"

I couldn't blame him for asking. "Yeah," I said, regretting the answer.

Will didn't say anything. Instead, he turned around and headed back to the car. He shoved his hands in his pockets when we stopped at the traffic light, waiting like ordinary pedestrians. The lecture crowd had disappeared, moving along without us to Moira's next step on the architecture parade.

When we got back to the car, Will opened my door first, waited for me to get settled, then closed me in and walked around to his side. He put the key in the ignition before turning to me. "Can you tell me any more about it?"

I heard him trying to be reasonable. I heard him trying to make sense out of what I'd said. What I hadn't said. I shook my head and stared out the window.

Yeah, I could tell him. I could tell him I was a witch. I could tell him I had magical powers unsurpassed on the entire Eastern seaboard, when they weren't busy disintegrating from lack of attention and ill use. I could tell him I'd made an anima, that I'd somehow crossed her wires, somehow turned her into some strange activist for the arts, because of what I'd been thinking at the precise moment that I summoned her to life.

I could tell him all of it.

Because everything had gone so well whenever I'd let men know about my powers.

"I can't," I finally said, when we were halfway back to Georgetown. "Not right now. I just can't."

He didn't find anything else to say before he dropped me off in front of the Peabridge gates. I hadn't really expected one, but I still missed his kiss good night.

12

I tried to call David, but of course he didn't pick up. The man was never there when I wanted him. What sort of warder was he? I left a gibbering message and paced the living room for half an hour, waiting for him to call back.

Realizing that I could walk a marathon before I heard from my distant astral protector, I threw myself into my pajamas and climbed into bed.

I spent the night not sleeping.

I spent the night staring at my ceiling, trying to convince myself that I really could read mystical patterns in the shadows of the leaves. (With my ability to read runes apparently gone forever, I figured that I might as well try to find magical import *somewhere*.) I tossed and turned, tangling my sheets so badly that I had to get up not once, not twice, but three separate times, to straighten them into some semblance of order. I kept punching my pillow, turning it upside down, folding it double.

I spent the night worried that I had lost my anima, pinning my hopes on Gran and Clara where there was no reason to believe they could help me, tangling my relationship with David beyond repair, and now, I was losing whatever had been tentatively beginning with Will.

Shared garlic shrimp or not.

I finally gave up at four-thirty and dragged myself out of bed. I stood under my shower until the water ran cold, and then I tugged on a pair of torn jeans and a faded T-shirt. Melissa had seen me in worse.

The stroll to Cake Walk was actually a type of magic. The air was kissed with the first hint of autumn—I actually wished that I had grabbed a sweater before setting out. Occasional cars rumbled past me, jostling over the cobblestone streets and the abandoned trolley tracks. A blue jay squawked as I walked past one house, opening its mouth and releasing a sound that seemed much too large for its body. Squirrels coursed back and forth over the side-walks, occasionally stopping to nibble on the acorns they were storing away with all the industriousness that I apparently lacked.

By the time I got to the bakery, I had found my own sort of Zen. That, or sleep deprivation had finally turned off my brain, forcing me to navigate my way through the front door by willpower alone. I shuffled up to the counter, eyes closed to express my dramatic exhaustion, and I proclaimed, "Last night, I didn't get to sleep at all."

"Oh, oh, oh," finished a laughing voice melodically.

A strange voice. A man's voice.

My eyes flew open. "Oh!" I echoed, my single syllable spoken in a tone of utter astonishment.

The guy sitting at the counter was grinning. The facial expression increased his cherubic look—he had cheeks that a grandmother would love to pinch, and he carried a few extra pounds around his middle. He was beginning to lose his hair—just a bit at the top, making him look a little like an understudy for a medieval friar. The skin around his brown eyes crinkled as he registered my confusion.

I stammered, "I'm s-sorry! I didn't realize there'd be anyone else here." Frantically, I looked for Melissa behind the counter, swallowing a little flutter of panic when I couldn't find her, even crouching by the foot of the refrigerated case.

Before I could translate my confusion into a coherent sentence, I heard Melissa's feet on the back stairs. "Great," she said, as she hitched up the loose shoulder strap on her overalls. "You two have finally met!"

"Er," I muttered, suddenly conscious of my torn jeans and the ragged hem on my too-often-laundered T.

"Rob Peterson," the cherub said, extending his hand.

I shook automatically and completed the round of introductions. "Jane Madison."

"Melissa said you might be stopping by, but she figured it would be later in the morning."

This was Melissa's dream date. This was the guy she had debated asking out for over a year. This was the guy who had come into the bakery every day for forever, the guy who had a favorite coffee, a favorite pastry, a favorite type of cake.

Melissa laughed, as if she always introduced her boyfriends to me. "Iced tea or hot?"

"Hot," I said, grateful for the note of normalcy. "It actually feels like fall out there."

My best friend dug out my favorite mug from beneath the counter, filling it with water so hot it almost boiled. She waved me toward the tea selection, and I spent an inordinate amount of time selecting English Breakfast. Plain old English Breakfast. Ordinary, easy-to-choose English Breakfast.

Still ignoring the boyfriend-elephant in the center of the room, I asked brightly, "Do you have some cream? I need to brew this strong."

Melissa produced a small pitcher from the refrigerator. "Tough night last night?"

"You wouldn't believe it."

I hadn't believed it. I had thought and rethought and re-rethought about what I had seen. And the only thing that had kept me sane at three in the morning had been the belief that I could hash out the details with my best friend as soon as the sun rose. Alone.

"That sounds like my cue to head back upstairs," Rob said.

"I didn't mean—" I protested, even though that had been precisely what I'd meant.

He grinned and shrugged. "I need to take a shower before I head down to the office."

"But you were here first!" I struggled one last time to be polite. To share Melissa.

"This morning, yeah. But you've got something to talk about, and I strongly suspect it doesn't include me." He picked up his cup of coffee and walked behind the counter. He stopped to brush a quick kiss against Melissa's lips, and then he turned back to me. "It was a pleasure meeting you." His eyes twinkled, and I wondered what he'd been expecting, what Melissa had told him I was like.

"Yeah," I said, forgetting all the graceful social skills that Gran had taught me over a lifetime of meeting new people. I listened to his feet climb the stairs. And then I could just make out the faintest sound of the shower running in the upstairs apartment. Something about that noise, that slightly illicit, caught-in-the-morning sound, made me realize the import of the scene I'd walked in on. My best friend had a relationship that had progressed to spending-the-night-on-a-school-night. Not that there was anything wrong with that. "That's Rob!"

Melissa smiled. "I noticed."

"Rob Peterson!" This time, she only nodded. I couldn't help but steal a glance at the calendar, at its smooth, unblemished page of blank squares, nary a red X in sight. "But he seems like a really nice guy!"

Melissa harrumphed a little. "You don't have to sound so surprised."

"Well—" There wasn't any graceful way to finish that sentence. Instead, I settled for a new direction. "No! It's just that I was surprised to finally meet him. Surprised to find him here so early!"

"Or so late," Melissa said, utterly unconcerned.

I knew that I was supposed to say something ribald, something encouraging, something utterly in keeping with our feminist-charged friendship. I knew that I was supposed to give her a high five, or some complicated handshake, or exclaim, "You go, girl!"

Instead, I passed my cup back for a refill of hot water.

She obliged, and then she said, "So? What's up?"

"It's probably nothing major…"

"Of course. You make it over here by six o'clock every morning, when there's nothing major going on."

I made a face. "Will and I went to a lecture last night, down at the Smithsonian."

"Oh, no! Not a lecture!" Her mocking tone made it sound as if we had done something worse than tour every last nightclub in D.C.

"That's not the problem," I said, and my voice was serious enough that she stopped her joking. She leaned in, intent now on what I had to tell her. "Have you heard about the Artistic Avenger?"

"The what?"

At least I wasn't the last person in town to know about the newest crackpot sensation. "The Artistic Avenger. Apparently, she's been camping out on the Capitol steps. Campaigning for better funding for creative enterprise. Her slogan is Empower The Arts."

"Your anima!"

I nodded grimly. "Ariel."

Melissa sucked in her breath and said, "What happened?"

So I told her about all of it, ending with Will driving me home, about our awkward parting. "I don't know what to do, Melissa. I really like this guy."

"Then tell him."

"I can't do that!"

"Why not?"

I sighed in exasperation. "What am I supposed to do? Put on my favorite apron, invite him over for a cup of coffee and say, 'By the way, I forgot to mention that I'm a witch.'"

"Sounds about right. Personally, I wouldn't bother with the apron, but to each her own. And you might want to take a couple of Belly Laughs, so that you have something to feed him when he starts to ask you questions." She gestured toward the caramel nut clusters on the counter between us, rounded into high domes of salted sweetness.

"I'm not joking!"

Melissa shook her head. "Neither am I! Listen to yourself, Jane. You sound different when you talk about this guy. You're relaxed around him. You're comfortable talking to him. You aren't twisting yourself into a pretzel to be his idea of the perfect girlfriend. *You already trust him.* Now you just have to share this one little thing with him."

I started to protest out of habit, but then I cut off my own words.

Melissa was right. Things *were* different with Will. I didn't sit at my desk, hoping against all breathless hope that he was going to set foot inside the Peabridge. I didn't stare at my phone with laser vision, trying to make him call. I didn't worry about every word that I said to him, didn't weigh each and every syllable before I dared to set it into a conversation.

I was comfortable with him.

Even though I'd only known him for a few weeks, I was comfortable with him.

And if—*if* was a huge word, but it was one I was going to have to swallow at some point—*if* there was really something there, really the basis of a true relationship, then Will was going to have to find out about my powers. I wasn't exactly going to settle down in the suburbs with an SUV, a Jack Russell terrier, two-point-four children, and a husband who knew nothing of my magic—*Bewitched*'s Samantha Stephens all neatly packaged for the twenty-first century.

Unless, of course, I abandoned my witchcraft forever.

That had seemed like such an attractive option, only a few days before. But now, I wasn't so sure. I had seen Gran and Clara working with their familiars, but their thawing spell had not helped bolster my powers in the least. I had been so disappointed when I'd realized that they weren't pouring astral energy back into me, weren't returning it like the grudging Ariel. I didn't have the faintest idea of what I actually wanted.

"You really think I have to tell him?" My voice dropped to a whisper.

Melissa answered by nodding as she passed me a fortifying Bunny Bite. I put the entire morsel of carrot cake in my mouth at once, letting the cream cheese frosting melt across my tongue while I contemplated taking the proverbial witchcraft bull by the horns. I chewed and swallowed and then thought of my next line of argument. "What if he totally freaks out? What if he never wants to see me again?"

"Better to know now, right? Now, rather than later, when you're in this thing even deeper?"

I stared at her. "You still rip off your Band-Aids without even a moment's hesitation, don't you?"

She grinned and offered me another Bite. "But I always have something good waiting, to distract me from the pain."

Before I could agree, before I could say that I would tell Will everything about my bizarre magical self, there were more footsteps on the back stairs. Rob poked his head in from the hallway. "Coast is clear? The distaff debate can pause long enough for a man to walk through?"

"Absolutely." Melissa beamed.

As Rob seized a having-come-downstairs kiss, the front door of the bakery opened. I turned, grateful for the distraction, only to see Neko glide inside.

"I thought you'd be here," he said to me.

"Why did you think that?"

"Hot date last night? I stopped by your house this morning? The bed was tossed like burglars had a field day, but you were nowhere in sight? No manly shoes shoved beneath your bed?"

I glared at Neko and then braved a look in Rob's general direction. Melissa's beau was staring at my familiar, a look of bemusement on his plump-cheeked face.

"Hell-o there," Neko said, emphasizing the first syllable of his greeting and darting a glance at Rob's arm around Melissa's waist. "I don't believe we've met."

If Melissa hadn't been my best friend, I might have missed her gritting her teeth. No, that was a lie. All three of us heard the sound. And if ground molars weren't enough warning, any innocent onlooker could have heard Melissa's exasperated sigh, her frustration as haunting as a barely remembered tune. "Neko," she said. "This is Rob Peterson." She turned to Rob. "Neko is one of Jane's closest friends."

My familiar offered a hand, shaking Rob's as if he were absorbing some secret message from the touch of flesh on flesh. I glanced nervously from his face to Melissa's. My best friend stretched a smile over her teeth. I knew that she was thinking about the last time she had introduced one of her boyfriends to Neko. I was pretty sure that Jacques had not even looked over his shoulder as he followed my familiar out of Melissa's shop, out of her heart, out of her love life forever.

"Pleased to meet you," said Rob. He turned back to Melissa. "I've got to get down to the office. That deposition is still scheduled for this morning, and it may actually stretch into the afternoon. But you're up for dinner?"

"Of course." She grinned, and I suspected that a smile that

broad was meant to be a comment on something a bit more than the cementing of evening plans. "Give me a call when you know what time you'll be free."

Rob kissed her and then hurried to the door. He turned back on the threshold. "It was really nice to meet both of you. We'll have dinner soon, Jane?"

"Absolutely," I said, and he sauntered away.

Neko barely waited until the door had closed behind Rob before he whirled back toward Melissa. "Don't I get a cup of hot chocolate? Hold the chocolate and double the milk?"

Melissa was shaking her head, a rueful smile quirking her lips. "Just a sec."

"What?" Neko said to me as I stepped up to the counter. "Why are you both looking at me that way?"

"No way," I said. "It's just that we're both pleased you didn't decide to steal Rob away from Melissa."

"Steal Rob—" He took a step back in indignant protest, fluttering his right hand above his heart as if we were slaying him with our criticism.

"You have to admit," Melissa said, "there's precedent." Precedent. She *had* been spending a lot of time listening to legal mumbo jumbo.

"Girlfriend, I might be an absolutely irresistible man, but there are some limits to my powers of persuasion! Did you think I'd make him gay just by shaking his hand?"

"Of course not!" Melissa protested.

Neko eyed her archly. "I've told you before, and I'll

remind you as often as you need to hear it. Jacques leaned my way before he ever asked you out on a date. It's not you, it's me, girlfriend."

Melissa clanked his mug of heated milk onto the counter. "Let's just forget about Jacques, okay? I mean, about Jacques and me. Truce?"

"Truce." Neko buried his face in the cup, emerging almost a minute later with a white mustache thick enough to get him headlined in the Got Milk? campaign. He turned to me. "But I'm here for a real reason, Jane. You have got to get your grandmother under control."

I immediately pictured Nuri, wondered what sort of problems my grandmother was having with her familiar. Magic had always come hard to Gran; even more than Clara, my grandmother had been ostracized by the Coven because her powers were weak. Maybe I had pushed her too hard. Maybe she shouldn't have awakened her own familiar. Maybe she was so miserably unhappy that she'd never work a magic spell again.

"What's wrong, Neko?"

"Small countries have mobilized armies with less planning than your grandmother is investing in this wedding."

I snorted, letting relief blow away my astral worries. If we were only talking about wedding details, then everything would be fine.

"What do you mean?" Melissa asked, turning to me with a look that was almost accusing. "I can't believe that *your* grandmother is the type to be worried about the trappings of a wedding!"

Neko sighed dramatically. "To the rest of the world, she's a sweet, quiet old woman. But to those of us helping get ready for the big day…"

I glared at him. "You volunteered!"

"I thought I'd be able to offer an opinion or two and then be done! I didn't realize that staging a wedding for a couple in their eighties was going to take more effort than putting a man on the moon!"

"What's the problem now?" I asked.

"The string quartet has been tossed out. She's looking for a full band. Nine people. Plus a DJ for the band's breaks. George loves saxophone, so we need two."

"She just wants people to have fun," I said weakly.

"And she's obsessing about party favors."

"Come on, Neko. Most brides give their guests some type of gift."

"Your grandmother wants to hand out a CD."

"So? They shouldn't be too expensive to burn. What's she thinking of? Their first dance?"

"Opera." He shuddered. "She wants to include opera, Jane. A different aria for each guest. A personalized CD for every single person who attends. The guest list is up to two hundred!"

"That's ridiculous!"

"My point exactly." He set his mug on the counter with a finality that said we had reached a deal. "You'll tell her that she's going too far."

"I don't know…." I tried to picture me lecturing Gran

about wedding etiquette. I couldn't really imagine how the conversation would go. She was the one who had spent a lifetime telling *me* what was right and wrong. I wasn't sure that either of us would survive having the tables turned. "Maybe I can get Clara on board. We can tell her together."

"I don't care how you do it. Just make her see reason."

"You sound desperate."

He looked at me slyly. "I'm not the one who's desperate. But you will be, once you see the dress she's planning for you."

My throat dried in sudden panic. "What?"

"You'll see," he sang.

"Neko, I already know about the color."

"What about the color?" Melissa asked.

"Orange," Neko said with a distinctly evil pleasure. "And silver."

Horror spread on Melissa's face. "You've got to be kidding."

Neko shook his head. "Orange, because it's George's favorite color. And silver, because they've dated for twenty-five years." Well, at least there was some reasoning behind it. My grandmother had not *completely* taken leave of her senses. Neko sighed in exasperation. "You cannot believe how many times I've told the matchbook people that the colors aren't a mistake."

"Matchbooks?" I said. "No one gives out matchbooks at a wedding anymore."

"Someone does," Neko said, his mouth twitching into a cruel smile. "Along with embossed cocktail napkins, Jordan almonds and four hundred votive candles."

"She's eighty-five years old!" I said.

"But she's determined to have the wedding she never had as a girl." Neko sparked the words with a dramatic twist of his neck, a hand cast to his forehead.

I shook my head. "My own grandmother. Bridezilla. Who would have believed it?"

"I haven't even started to tell you about her plans for tossing the bouquet." He looked toward the front door wickedly, and I watched Melissa blush.

"Enough," I said. "Torture us by telling us about my dress. Just how horrible is it?"

"I wouldn't dream of ruining the surprise. You'll see a swatch when we get together after work today."

"We?" This was the first I'd heard of plans involving any group.

"Nuri and Majom are getting restless."

Melissa looked up from the tray of Blond Brunettes that she was slicing. "Who are Nuri and Majom?"

Oh. Between Rob and Will and animas and life in general, I hadn't even had a chance to tell Melissa about my own little attempt at managing a coven. "Familiars. For Gran and Clara. We awakened them the other night. They're going to help with the…situation in the basement."

"Of course," Melissa said, shrugging like she heard that sort of thing every day. "Who *wouldn't* want more familiars running around D.C.?" She smiled sweetly at Neko. "No offense intended."

"Of course," he agreed, pushing his mug closer to her in silent request for another peacemaking refill. "None taken."

"We can't get together tonight, Neko," I said.

"Why not?"

"I have other plans." Well, I *would* have other plans. If I followed Melissa's advice and contacted Will.

"Plans more important than rebuilding your magic?" He actually sounded serious, for the first time since setting foot in the bakery.

"If you must know, I'm going to call Will Becker. I'm asking him out. Again." Because the first time had gone so well. Because every time we got together, my witchcraft got in the way, and I was determined to have one single, solitary date that was normal. Normal. Like any other woman in the world. Like a librarian. Not like a witch.

"Will's the one you had dinner with the other night?" I could see the little wheels spinning inside my familiar's skull. He was smart enough not to mention garlic shrimp. Or breath mints.

"That's the one. I owe him an explanation or two. We saw Ariel last night, at the Capitol."

"You what?"

I filled him in quickly, ending with, "I could hardly explain what was really going on. Not after you and David frightened him off the other night with your Men In Black routine."

"*We* didn't frighten him off!" Neko sounded shocked and appalled at the notion. I glared at him. "Well, maybe, we were a little…intimidating. Have you stopped to think that he might just be easily scared?"

"Neko!" I said. Even though I knew my familiar was just clowning around, the question bit deep. I really wanted things to work with Will. I really wanted to be able to tell him about my witchcraft, to get that deep, dark secret behind us.

"Wait a second," Neko said, drawing out the words. "You really like this guy!"

Frantically, I looked at Melissa for help, but she just shrugged and turned around to start a fresh pot of coffee. "He's a nice guy," I said helplessly. "I just don't know how to tell him about…well, you know."

"Just say the words, girlfriend."

"It's not that easy."

"Pick up the phone. Make the date. Say the words. Tell him you're a witch. If he's not man enough to handle it, he's not the right man for you."

"Yeah, right."

"I'm serious. *Tell him.*"

I glanced at Melissa. She was staring at Neko, apparently amazed that they had offered identical advice.

"I will," I said reluctantly.

"Promise?"

"What?" I asked, suddenly out of patience. "Have you turned into my grandmother now? I said I'll call, and I'll call." I fumbled for a chance to get away from talking about my life and loves. "Let's do witchcraft training Sunday afternoon."

Neko shook his head. "Gran and I are going to pick up your dress on Sunday. Your dress and her veil. Do you know that she's determined to wear her old gown?"

"From when she was seventeen?"

"She can still fit into it."

I thought of my grandmother's ability to pack away food and muttered something wholly uncharitable.

Neko raised an eyebrow, then wisely retreated into scheduling. "I'll work with Nuri and Majom tonight, keep them from climbing the walls. I can teach them some tricks all familiars should know these days."

"Spare us," I said.

He ignored me, barreling on. "Sunday, Sarah and I will get the gown. We can all train on Monday. And you can come by your grandmother's on Friday for a fitting. I promised to do the alterations myself. Someone else might think the fabric was a mistake. Or the design."

I read the glee on his face, and my heart plummeted. It couldn't be that bad. There was no way for *any* dress to be that bad.

It was orange-and-silver.

It was going to be that bad.

I shuddered and passed my mug across the counter for a refill. "Mojito therapy," I croaked to Melissa.

She grinned. "When?"

"Next Friday. At Gran's place. It's the only thing to get me through that fitting."

Neko shook his head mournfully. "I'm telling you, girlfriend, there isn't enough rum in all the world to get you past that dress."

And the scary thing was, Neko had never been wrong before when it came to me and fashion.

13

All afternoon, I wrote conversations.

It really wasn't very difficult. I knew exactly what I would say. I could roll my words around and around, tasting them like one of Melissa's delectable treats. I'd practiced the phrases for a long time, after all. I'd come out of my witchcraft closet before, so to speak. I'd told any number of people that I had magical abilities: Melissa, Gran, Clara. The Inexcusable Beast. The Coven Eunuch.

Okay. Those last two confessions hadn't gone so smoothly.

But I refused to believe that my problems in those two instances were because my confidants were male. Those problems had come about because my male confidants were two-faced, scum-sucking liars. With other women in their lives.

But Will wasn't like that. I had to believe that Will wasn't like that. I had to believe that I had learned something through the days, weeks, months of torture, from the self-doubt and the questioning that had followed my time with the Irreparable Bum and the Coven Eunuch.

It scared me a little to realize how much I wanted Will to be different from the others. How much I wanted the thing that I felt between us to be real, to be true. A gnawing corner of my mind kept saying that I'd never had a decent relationship with a guy, that I'd never had a real, truthful, healthy romance (even with the man I'd been engaged to, well before all the witchcraft stuff came into the picture). I did my best, though, to give myself the answers that I knew Melissa would give me, if she'd been sitting in the Peabridge, if she'd been close enough to shake some sense into me—literally or figuratively.

Just because I hadn't met my true match yet didn't mean that he wasn't out there for me. Just because I had managed to screw up every other romance in my life didn't mean that I was doomed to ruin this one. Just because every other guy that I'd dated with even a scintilla of hope had turned out to be a loser didn't mean that Will would be.

Will was different.

That became my mantra for the afternoon. Will was different. Therefore, he and I could talk. Will was different. Therefore, I could tell him the truth about myself. Will was different. Therefore, I could be honest with him. Will was different. Therefore, he would accept my being a witch.

Well, Will was going to *have* to be different for that last bit to fly.

When I hit the self-reassurance wall, I decided to spend the afternoon working on one of our most boring, most needed long-term projects at the Peabridge—the dreaded shelf-read. Armed with a listing of every single item that we owned, I strode back to the farthest part of the library, to the most distant shelves. I flipped to the appropriate page in my printout and began comparing the list of what we *should* have on the shelf to the reality of what was there. For each missing book, I made a notation in the margin—I'd have to see if it was checked out. If not, we'd try to track it down from wherever it had been lost or misplaced, working to keep our collection whole and healthy.

It was mind-numbing work. I needed to be careful to match numbers exactly. But at the same time, the task was mechanical. I could do it with one part of my mind, freeing the rest of my thoughts to write and rewrite, and re-rewrite conversations.

Me: "Will, I have something to tell you. It's serious."
Him: "How serious?"
Me: "I'm a witch."
Him, shrugging: "Wow. That's cool. Want to order Chinese?"

Yeah. Like that was really the way things were going to go. Try again.

Me: "Will, there's something I need to tell you. It's serious."

Him, horrified: "Oh my God. You're pregnant."

Me, grateful for the heads-up: "Um, we haven't done anything. And now, I know we won't."

Nope. Still not there. Another try.

Me: "Will, I have something to tell you. It's serious."

Him: "I'm listening."

Me: "I'm a witch."

Him: "A witch. Like you've got magical powers and everything?"

Me: "Just like. I can cast spells. I can create charms. I can read runes."

Him: "Wow. I always thought that a witch would be different. Frightening. Like something from another world. But you're totally normal."

Me, smiling a little: "Well, not totally."

Him, reassuring: "You are in every way that matters. Thank you for trusting me enough to tell me this, Jane. I can only imagine how difficult it was for you."

There. That was the perfect conversation. A little bit of humor, a healthy dose of honesty. We'd end by understanding each other perfectly.

Conversations were really so much easier, when you just had a chance to practice them in advance. I contemplated calling him that afternoon, asking to meet for dinner that night. But that might give him the wrong idea. After all, I'd come off sounding pretty desperate if I asked him out that day for that night. Wasn't that against the rules? I'd wait and call him on Monday. Give him the weekend to realize how much he missed talking to me. Even if things had been strained the night before. Especially because things had been strained the night before.

I tossed my shoulders back and lifted up my ballpoint pen, feeling better than I had since the moment I'd seen Ariel in front of the Capitol. This would actually work out fine. Everything would be perfect.

I completed an unheard-of six pages of shelf-reading. I might not have my romantic house in order, but my boss was going to love me.

I held on to that glow of positive determination as I shut down my computer at the end of the day. I held on to it as I said goodbye to Kit, as I waved across the lobby to Evelyn. I held on to it as I stepped into the garden, as I breathed the crisp air that told me autumn was truly, finally arriving in D.C. I held on to it as I walked to my front door, imagining my quiet evening at home, now that I had cleared away the need to call Will.

But I totally lost it when I saw Will sitting on my front porch. He stood as soon as he saw me.

"What are you doing here?" I squeaked.

"Your assistant called me."

Kit? Why had Kit called Will? *How* had Kit called Will?

She didn't have his number. She didn't know anything about him. I mean, she'd seen him in the library, the day I spilled my coffee, and maybe that other time, the day he met Mr. Potter. But to phone him? I tried to convert my surprise into an English-language sentence. "When did she do that?"

"She?"

"Kit."

"Kit?"

Okay. Now I was getting annoyed. "My assistant. Who called you?"

"The person who called me was a man."

And then I began to realize what had happened.

Neko.

Neko, who had stood in Melissa's bakery and told me that I needed to "just say the words." Neko, who had practically made me promise that I'd get in touch with Will. Neko, who knew me well enough not to trust me when I said that I would call Will of my own volition.

"Oh," I said, increasingly aware of the silence that was spinning out between us. Time for a halfhearted save of face. "That would be my other assistant. My confusion." So much for telling Will all the truth about my secret life. I swallowed a grimace.

Will shoved his hands in his pockets, looking for all the world like a high-school senior trying to decide what to say to the girl with the locker next to his. His eyeglasses were a little askew on his nose, and my fingers twitched with the desire to reach out, to straighten them, to make everything right. At last, Will said, "You wanted to see me? He said that you have something you want to talk about?"

"I guess," I said, forgetting to sound like I had assistants make appointments for me all the time. "Of course. I mean, he's right. That is, I do want to talk." I gritted my teeth. It had been easier trying to kiss a boy good-night when I was on a high-school date, worried that Gran was listening behind her front door. I sighed, knowing that my rehearsed conversation would work better in the comfort of my own living room. "Would you like to come inside?"

"Thanks."

I took my time fitting my key into the lock. I needed to run through my lines one last time. I struggled to reassure myself. I had worked it all out. Right there, in the back of the library. I'd finally come up with the phrasing that worked. How did it begin? What was I supposed to say?

I finally had to turn the key, open the door.

Will looked around as he stepped inside. "At last," he said. "I see the inner sanctum."

"Not so interesting," I extemporized, shrugging. The movement made the lace across my bodice itch, and I resisted the urge to scratch. There was only so much awkwardness one man could be expected to tolerate in a single evening visit. I settled for reaching up to my head, unpinning my mobcap and pulling my hair free from its haphazard chignon. I clenched the beribboned muslin cap, folding my fingers into a tight fist.

"A drink!" I said, as if I'd discovered an exquisite new species of butterfly. "Can I get you a drink?"

"Sure," Will said, and the awkward shift of his shoulders told me that he was just as uncomfortable as I was. Once my powers were fully restored, I was going to have to devise a special punishment for Neko.

I hurriedly led the way into the kitchen.

A bottle of red wine stood on the counter—Fish Eye Merlot. The corkscrew was laid out neatly beside it, flanked by two spotless glasses. Paper cocktail napkins fanned out in a neat array. A plain white bowl sat nearby, filled to the brim with bright orange goldfish crackers.

A note curled from beneath the bowl, and I recognized Neko's scrawl from across the kitchen. "Sorry," the page said. "This is for your own good." I grabbed at the paper and crumpled it into a tight ball, before Will could see my "assistant's" confession. Admonition. Whatever.

"Care to do the honors?" I asked, passing the bottle and corkscrew to Will. He took them reflexively, and I shoved an emergency handful of Pepperidge Farm's most popular snack food into my mouth. As Will pulled the cork and poured, I busied myself toting napkins and crackers to the table. The glug of wine seemed loud in the room.

Will passed me a glass. "You've got a whole fish theme going here, don't you?"

"Yeah," I said weakly. "It's sort of a favorite with me."

Will raised his glass, touching his rim to mine. We both sipped mechanically.

I remembered my opening line. "Will, I have—"

Unfortunately, Will chose that precise moment to fill the silence himself. "It sounded like—"

We both stopped, waiting for the other to go on. Will popped a few goldfish into his mouth, but I shook my head firmly. "Please," I said. "You go first."

He chewed and swallowed. "I was just going to say that your assistant said this was urgent. I told him at first that I couldn't make it, but he said you really needed to see me."

"Oh! I'm sorry. I mean, if there's someplace else you need to be…."

He shook his head and gulped some wine. He *was* as nervous as I was. And I had to admit that I found his discomfort really cute. "No," he went on, endearing himself more to me with every syllable. "To be perfectly honest, I didn't have anything else planned. It's just that things got so weird after that lecture…. I thought that you might need some space. Some distance."

"I know I acted really strange." I looked around my own kitchen, hoping for some wild distraction. It was too bad that my powers were on the fritz. I could have done with one hell of a spell-working session right then. I could have erased Will's memory altogether, taken us back to a time before Ariel, before he'd seen me running around the United States Capitol like a madwoman.

Not enough powers for that, though. No memory spells. Nothing but the truth.

I took a deep breath and recited the sentence that I'd

crafted so carefully at work, just that afternoon, "Will, I have something to tell you. It's serious."

Like a star performer, he recited his line perfectly. "I'm listening."

A little bit surprised at how easily this was going, I went on to my next line. "I'm a witch."

He stared at me. "That's not funny."

I couldn't keep from saying, "What?" He'd dropped a line. He was supposed to say, "A witch. Like you've got magical powers and everything?"

Instead, he put down his wineglass and pushed his chair back from the table. "Come on, Jane. That's not funny. You have your assistant call me. You have all of this laid out, wine and food, like you're looking forward to seeing me. You make me sit down, and you start in on this totally serious conversation, and then you turn it into a joke?"

"It's not a joke!" I was stung. This had all been going so perfectly. Where had my carefully constructed conversation gone astray?

"Yeah, right. You're a witch. Worked any spells lately?"

"As a matter of fact, my spell-working isn't going so well right now. That's what I'm trying to tell you. That's what this is all about. I was trying to get my powers back, and I made that woman, um, the Artistic Avenger, to help me out."

"Made that woman… Are you nuts? Or do you just think that I'm some kind of idiot?" There was anger in his voice, but something else. Something that I recognized. Something that I'd felt myself, more than once.

Before I could identify what I heard, though, I had to respond, "Of course not!"

"Do I really look that gullible to you? Is this some sort of game? Some scam that you work on people who come to do legitimate research at the Peabridge?" He blinked, and I could read shock behind the lenses of his eyeglasses. Shock, and defensiveness, and that something else, that all-too-familiar emotion that I couldn't quite put my finger on.

"It's not like that!" I let a little of my own self-protectiveness transform into anger. "I really *am* a witch!"

"I suppose you've got a broomstick, then? A black cat?"

"I do!" I said desperately. "Not a broomstick, no, that's ridiculous. But I've got a black cat. You spoke to him! He told you he was my assistant. Neko."

Will clambered to his feet. He glanced around my kitchen, his eyes wild. I could see his gaze focusing on the corners of the room, on the shiny black front of the stove. "I suppose this is where I should say, 'Where are the hidden cameras?' because I'm starting to feel like a fool."

I shook my head, misery rising like a lump in the back of my throat. This entire conversation had gone so much better when I had been allowed to write all the lines. "It's not like that!"

"What's it like, then?"

And that's when I recognized the emotion. That's when I knew precisely how Will felt. I knew, because I'd felt that way myself, before.

Embarrassed.

Will thought that I'd been mocking him. Like I'd been leading him on. Like I'd lured him here to make him feel bad, to feel like an idiot, all for my own cruel pleasure.

And I couldn't think of my lines, I couldn't think of my words, I couldn't think of anything I could say to make it better. To make him understand. To make him know that I hadn't tried to hurt him, that I wasn't trying to make a fool out of him in any way, shape or form.

Tears pricking at the back of my eyes, I shrugged and walked away.

I crossed the living room. I opened the door to the basement. I palmed on the light.

I held my breath as I walked down the stairs, hoping— fearing—that I'd hear his footsteps behind me. I waited, desperate for the sound of him crossing the living room, as well.

And then I heard him.

I heard him on the stairs. I felt him brush behind me. I saw him walk into the center of my basement.

I crossed to the far side of the bookstand, so that I could watch him as he took in everything in the room. Like any good intellectual, he noticed the shelves first, the volumes and volumes of leather-clad books. But then his gaze was pulled to the intricate box that stored my crystals, the wooden container of handcrafted layers, carefully hinged and folded.

Of course. He was an architect. The construction drew him.

He studied everything—the small wrought-iron cauldron

on the bottom shelf, the bags of dried herbs beside it. He started to read the titles on the books, swallowing audibly as he processed some of the phrasing, some of the archaic words.

"I can't believe these are real," he said, and I could barely make out his whisper above the pounding of my heart. I could hear his surprise, though. Surprise, and something else. He *wanted* it to be real. He wanted to believe.

"They are."

"But you could just collect this stuff, right? You wouldn't have to work any real magic with it. You could be one of those fans, like the people who have every *Star Wars* doll ever made."

I had to prove myself to him. However sparse my powers might be, I had to show him the truth.

I glanced at the crystals that Ariel had cleansed for me. I couldn't imagine scraping together enough energy to use their stony strength, to work their intensive brand of magic.

Of course, the runes were a lost cause, as well. Their bags still sagged in shapeless masses; I hadn't bothered to replace them, since I still wasn't able to muster my powers into anything resembling full witch status. I was afraid to take a book down, terrified that I would open it to reveal blank parchment, empty pages that would make my magic seem even more a sham. Or worse yet, pages where the ink drained away before our very anxious eyes.

I was on my own. Without my familiar, without my warder, without any of the familiar tools of my trade, I was on my own.

And yet, I could feel the faintest curl of magic, deep inside myself. It was the core of my remaining power, the precious drops hoarded from Ariel's mind-speech. It flickered, faint, nearly invisible to my astral sight.

If I used it all, trying to convince Will that I was a witch, would anything magic remain to me? Would I turn myself into an ordinary woman, trying to prove that I was something more? Did it matter?

I had to prove that I was not lying.

Nothing ventured, nothing gained.

I raised my left arm in front of me, cupping my hand at waist level. I took three deep breaths, trying to calm myself, trying to center myself, as I offered up my mind and my voice and my heart.

I closed my eyes and I whispered a spell inside my mind, one of the simplest I had ever read. I would have mastered it as a child, if I'd started down this witchcraft path in the normal way, like an ordinary magical girl with an ordinary magical life.

Dark shies;
Light vies.
Clear eyes,
Fire rise.

And when I dared to look, I could see faint blue flames glowing inside my cupped palm.

I couldn't use them for anything. A moonlit night would

provide more light. A soft breath would provide more warmth. As a symbol of my witchcraft, they were pretty sorry, utterly failing to leap high against my basement shadows, to crackle with the core of my supposedly awesome power and strength.

But they were real. They were there. They were a physical manifestation of my power, perhaps the last that I would ever show, if I couldn't track down Ariel, couldn't work things out with Gran and Nuri, Clara and Majom. If I couldn't find out what had gone wrong and why.

Will looked from my palm to my face. His own features were slack with surprise, and he took a step back, as if he were afraid of me. "It's not a trick, is it?" he whispered.

I shook my head. "Not a trick."

"But this is incredible! Who else knows?"

The blue light flickered as I thought of everyone who knew I was a witch. "Some of my family. Other witches, their attendants." Two ex-boyfriends, I thought, but I didn't say. "A handful of others."

"Handful?" he said, nodding toward my own cupped fingers. That's when I knew everything was going to be all right. That's when I knew that he was laughing, that he was accepting, that he was understanding everything I was telling him. He reached toward the blue fire dancing on my palm, and he repeated, "Handful?"

"In a manner of speaking," I said, and I shrugged, letting the magical power dissipate. The fire had consumed all the droplets of power that had lurked deep in my thoughts. I felt the vaguest sense of possibility, of potential, but I had absolutely no magic left to call on. Nothing.

In the end, some might have called the working frivolous. But I had needed to do it. I had needed to make my point.

"You're amazing," Will said.

I flushed. "You must say that to all the girls."

"No, seriously! I can't imagine what it must be like! To have magical powers! To figure out who you can trust and who you can't, with a secret like that!"

Yeah, I thought about saying. I haven't always made such good choices there. Instead, I said, "It just seemed like something I needed to do."

I didn't bother to tell him that I was empty now. That I might not work another spell ever again. I didn't want him to feel any sense of guilt.

He swallowed, and his eyes were wide. His glasses made him look vulnerable, like an orphaned schoolboy struggling to be accepted as a man. "Thank you," he said.

"For what?"

"For trusting me. For trusting me enough to tell me. To share the truth with me."

I tried to think of the right answer. I tried to remember my next line. I tried to discover the perfect thing to say, the flawless response.

I remembered that writing conversations in advance was an absolute waste of time.

I shrugged and said, "I thought that this was something you should know. Something you needed to know, if we were going to spend any more time together. That is, if you still want to see me. If you're not put off by all of this…."

I waved a hand around the room, taking in all the strangeness, all the differentness, all the arcane substance that had been my life for the past two years. I couldn't figure out what else I could say, what else I could do.

But Will knew.

He'd known since he'd asked me out for dinner. He'd known since we'd walked through Georgetown's quiet nighttime streets. He'd known since that horrible car ride home, since the silence that Ariel had shoved between us, a silence all the more terrible because we had both wanted to move beyond it, both wanted to share our words, our thoughts. More.

He closed the distance between us. He pulled me close to his shirt, crushing my lacy bodice against his plain broadcloth shirt. He ran his fingers through my hair, nestled his hands against my scalp, pulling me close for a kiss.

I laughed against his lips, tasting Neko's well-placed merlot, and my amusement raised a chuckle from him, like a funny question, asked and answered. We had meant to have that conversation the night of our first date, the night that David had waited for me like an overactive chaperone. We had moved toward it again in the days of left messages, the fumbling conversation where I asked him out. We had planned on arriving here the night that we saw Ariel, the night that she ruined everything at the Capitol.

His fingers traveled down; I felt them scrabble at the back

of my neck, where an ordinary woman wearing ordinary clothes would have sported a zipper. He fumbled a little lower, then to the side, obviously perplexed by my costume.

I caught his hand and guided it to the line of perfect, miniature silk-covered buttons. "You have got to be kidding," he breathed, and his rueful frustration forced a full-fledged laugh from my lungs.

"Wait until you see the whalebone," I said.

"Whalebone?" he whispered, and I heard a hint of comic despair.

For just a moment, I considered showing him the costume's remaining secrets, right then, right there, in the middle of my basement, surrounded by the instruments of my wayward astral power. Glancing around, though, I realized that the only convenient horizontal surface was the cracked black leather couch.

We could do better than that, surely.

I clutched Will's fingers with my right hand and gathered up my skirts in my left. "Come on, modern man. I'll show you what strong stuff our colonial foremothers were made of."

Upstairs, Will tumbled beside me on my bed. I wished that I had enough magical stock to charm my clothes off my body, to undo the buttons and the clasps, to spirit my hoops and silk and lace across the room. I wanted to tweak my body, to work the contraceptive spell that I had mastered once before.

I twinged as I thought of that other magical working,

though. I didn't want to remember that mistake. I didn't want to think about David. I didn't want to think about magic, or the arcane world, or Hecate's Court, or warders or familiars. I didn't want to think about everything that might be lost to me forever.

Instead, I wanted to think about a real, human man—not just think, but I wanted to act. I fumbled in my nightstand drawer, digging out a tiny foil packet. The technology of man would work, where the magic of woman faltered.

For the record, Will figured out the mechanics of the costume in very short order.

14

I woke up early.

I squinted at the clock and saw that it was not yet seven o'clock. I lay in bed with my comforter pulled up around my shoulders, lulled by the warm pocket between my sheets, by the perfect softness of my pillows. I could hear myself breathing—deep, quiet breaths that sent me back toward the grassy hill of sleep.

Until I remembered.

I froze, listening, double-checking that someone was breathing beside me. That *Will* was breathing beside me.

Nothing.

Already starting to swear inside my head, I rolled over, not even bothering to take the comforter with me, in a coy, seductive fashion.

Nothing. Zippo. Nada.

Oh, sure, the sheets were kicked around. The pillow bore an imprint; a head had clearly rested there during the night. My bedroom door was open, giving me a clear shot of the bathroom door—also open—and the basement door—closed, just the way I'd left it when Will and I returned from my little downstairs peep show into the wonders of witch-craft.

I could also see half the living room. Half the empty living room. Half the deserted, abandoned, dried-up, useless, stupidly trusting living room.

Wait. The living room wasn't any of those things. I must have been thinking about something else.

I threw myself out of bed, barely bothering to tug on a pair of ratty sweatpants and a worn T-shirt. I slammed into the kitchen, fighting not to throw dishes onto the floor when I saw the remnants of our late-night supper, eaten between giggles and gossip, between secrets and sex. We'd devoured every last strand of spaghetti, but the kitchen still smelled of olive oil and the garlic that I had gleefully crushed into the single bowl that we'd shared. A green canister of Kraft parmesan cheese stood on the counter, a proud soldier saluting a simple, laid-back life that my familiar would never have embraced when he'd lived downstairs. Neko would have had fine hand-shaved parmesan, or gone without.

Gone without.

Now there was an idea I could have embraced. *Should* have embraced. What the hell had I been thinking? How had I believed that I could trust Will? How could I believe that he would be waiting for me in the morning, smiling and eager, ready to continue where we'd left off the night before? Why did I waste the last of my failing powers on proving something to him?

I'd made this mistake before. Made it more times than I cared to remember. Made it often enough that I should just cash in all my chips and move into a convent. Yeah, the praying and the singing and the worshiping stuff might get old, but at least I wouldn't have anyone tempt me into making an absolute, aching idiot out of myself.

I realized that my head was pounding. Somewhere in the course of the evening, we'd finished off Neko's wine, and we'd opened another bottle that I'd somehow kept secret beneath the sink. The alcohol, combined with the carb overload, made me feel sick to my stomach.

Coldly, mechanically, I salvaged a glass from a cabinet. I didn't bother with ice cubes. Warm tap water was good enough for me. All that I deserved.

I glanced at the clock on the stove. I could call Melissa. She'd have the bakery open by now.

But I realized that I didn't want to call my best friend. I didn't want to talk to anyone. I didn't want to repeat tales of my hopeful, naive stupidity. Besides, Melissa's boyfriend, the cherubic Rob Peterson, was likely sitting right beside her. She'd have to counsel me in front of him, or code her answers into something that would make me feel even more ridiculous than I already did.

I collapsed onto one of my ladder-back chairs and crossed my arms on the kitchen table. There was a time when I would have cried. There was a time when I would have taken weeks out of my life, mourning the relationship that I'd thought I had, teasing myself by dissecting and resecting what I thought had been a romance.

Now, though, I was more mature. More restrained. More accustomed to my own fallibility, and the certain disaster of the men I chose to bring into my life.

I was resigned. I could take a shower. I could head over to the Peabridge, even though it was a Saturday. There was plenty of work to be done, however boring it might be. Shelf-reads. Filing. Updating the catalog. I could pull on my colonial costume, dash some blush across my cheekbones, slap some lipstick on my smile and pretend as if nothing had happened, as if nothing was wrong.

And if that weasel dared set foot inside the library, if he dared come into the Peabridge with his requests for feder-alist gardens or mock wooden paneling…I'd sic Evelyn on him. That's what I'd do. I'd tell him that he was on his own, as far as our collection was concerned, but that he was welcome to talk to my boss about his research needs. I wouldn't even offer up Kit. Kit was too good for a traitor like Will.

I pushed away from the table and threw my shoulders back. I actually dusted my palms against each other, like I was casting off physical detritus from the destruction of my so-called love life.

I needed to do something to prove to myself that I was serious, to pound into my poor little brain the truth—the absolute truth—that I was done with Will, done with men, done with the notion of romance altogether. I needed cleansing, a spiritual release that would let my mind, and body, too, know that everything was going to be different now, everything was going to be new.

Yoga.

That's what had gotten me into this mess in the first place. Melissa and her stupid special class. The smooth-talking instructor and her ridiculous Eagle Pose.

But I wasn't a total loser. I'd accomplished other yoga poses before. I could do them again.

In fact, it was morning. The sun had risen. I could do a sun salutation with the best of them. I could prove—to myself and to anyone else I chose to tell—that I greeted the day with a perfect balance of peace and harmony, of joyous acceptance of my place in the universe. *Namaste*, and all that crap.

I hurried into the living room, the only space in my little cottage large enough for a full-fledged announcement of my yogic freedom. I pushed one of the hunter-green couches toward the wall, and then I hefted the coffee table on top, freeing up the entire oval rag rug in the center of the room. My yoga mat was buried somewhere in my closet. No reason to dig for it, when I was on such a roll.

I started out on all fours, arching my back into Cat Pose, then sinking it toward the floor in Cow. I concentrated on my breathing, turning my anger and frustration into smooth, measured inhales and exhales.

From Cow, I stood and centered myself for sun salutations. I was pretty sure that I could remember the sequence—the instructor had coached me through it often enough at that torture chamber of a yoga studio.

Mountain, standing straight and tall, hands in prayer position as I took three deep breaths. Hands up, sweeping over my head as I arched my back, then folded down to put my head against my knees. Well, as close to my knees as I could get, after a late night and too much wine. Lunge and another inhale as I stepped back with one foot, and Plank as I settled into the new pose. A trembling push-up as I launched into Stick, then released the pose into Upward-Facing Dog.

And then, my old friend, Downward-Facing Dog. The yoga instructor insisted, every time I struggled with the pose, that it was relaxing. Rejuvenating. Refreshing.

I knew better. It was uncomfortable. Ungraceful. Unsustainable.

I forced myself into the triangle form, pushing my butt into the air as I stretched forward with my palms and fought to lengthen my calves so that my heels could touch the rug. Relaxing, my ass.

Which would really, rather comically, have been the point, if my front door had not swung open at just that moment.

I toppled sideways onto the rug, bending at the knees to break my fall. I could already feel my cheeks flushing as I scrambled around to face the doorway. There were a limited number of people who would just enter the cottage without knocking—David, and Neko, maybe Melissa in a pinch.

And Will. Apparently.

Will, who glanced at the shifted couch and the coffee table, and my very un-Zen rag rug. "So, let me guess. You were the ringer in that yoga class we took."

"You came back!"

He displayed a grocery bag. "I went to get breakfast."

"Breakfast?" I sounded like I was learning a new language from Berlitz.

"I wasn't sure what you'd want, so I got a lot more than I should have. I thought I couldn't go wrong with bagels— sesame, pumpernickel, egg and everything. Which is your favorite?"

"Sesame," I said weakly.

"I didn't know if you were a cream cheese person or butter."

"Butter," I whispered, and then I found my true voice. "Why didn't you leave me a note?"

"A note?"

"Saying that you'd gone. Saying that you'd be back."

"I didn't think—" He cut himself off. Understanding washed over his face, as visible as the tide rising on a dry and sandy beach. "I didn't think," he repeated, sounding miserable as he shrugged his shoulders. "I thought I'd be back before you got up. I didn't realize that I'd have to go to a different place to get jelly. And to get anything other than orange juice."

"Orange juice?" I asked, trying to keep from shaking my head, to keep from physically acknowledging the wall of relief that soared in front of me. I scrambled to my feet.

He still sounded like his favorite puppy had run away from home. "I didn't know if you liked orange juice. I stopped to get apple, too. And grapefruit."

A smile played at the corner of my lips. "Apple's the best."

"And I got dessert-from-breakfast, too. A cinnamon pull-apart."

It wouldn't be as good as anything that Melissa made, but I certainly wasn't going to disillusion him now. "Dessert-from-breakfast is the best meal of the day." I led him into the kitchen, started reaching for plates and silverware as he unpacked his bounty onto the kitchen table.

"You really thought I'd left?" He sounded wounded.

"I just—"

"And the first thing you did was yoga?"

Well, when he said it that way, it sounded totally and completely absurd to me, too. I tried to explain once, twice and a third time, but then I gave up and settled into our breakfast feast. After we finished eating, he helped me move the coffee table and the couch back into place in the living room. His kiss tasted like orange juice when he offered to help me make the bed. We didn't get very far in that enterprise.

Saturday bled into Sunday, which shifted into Monday morning. When Will left for his own apartment and work,

I found myself suddenly lonely, wandering from bedroom to living room to kitchen and back again, without any mission, without any conscious thought.

I was more tired than I cared to admit to myself, and my fatigue only increased as the day wore on with its routine, mundane library details. I spent the better part of the afternoon reaching toward the aching gap in my powers. I kept nudging them, like a child testing a loose tooth, hopeful that they'd somehow start to regenerate. I was thrilled that I'd managed to get through to Will, that I'd managed to share my witchy history with him, but I was terrified that my kindling those blue flames would be the last spell I'd ever work.

By evening, I was a nervous wreck.

When Clara stepped over the threshold, Majom immediately scampered into the kitchen. I could hear him opening and closing drawers, as if he were searching for the secret to the universe, and I almost called out to ask him to save some for me, if he found it. Nuri swooped into the room behind everyone else. She perched on the arm of one of the sofas, watching all of us with tight, nervous turns of her head.

"Well, dear," my grandmother said, kissing my cheek. "You look lovely this evening."

"Thanks, Gran," I said, adding a faint blush to however I was looking. I'd gotten home from work and changed into my favorite pair of comfortable jeans. I had pulled on a lightweight black mock turtleneck; the evening was actually cool enough outside that my breath had been visible as I came home from the library. My hair was pulled back into an easy ponytail.

There was a certain desperation in my practical work clothes, but I wasn't ready to admit that to Gran and Clara. No reason to put more pressure on them. So what if helping to create Nuri and Majom had not added to my stock of power? Who cared if the thawing spell had been a bust? No one had said that the effect of creating my own witchy community would be immediate. Bringing Gran, Clara and their familiars into my makeshift plan might still work; there just might be a delay to the effect. My relatives might just need to cement their powers a little more, to grow as witches in my loosely structured commune.

Commune, not coven. This was something new to all of us, and we were just going to have to feel our way through our arrangements. David had never led me astray before, when we'd plotted my place in the world of witchcraft. He had to be right this time. He had to be right, or I was truly, completely screwed.

A crash from the kitchen punctuated that thought, and Clara called out. "Majom, come out here and sit with us."

The boy appeared in the doorway. One hand was hidden behind his back. "I want to stay in here."

Clara answered with an indulgent tone I'd never heard before. "You can go back there later. For now, come sit beside me on the couch."

A tiny braid of jealousy frayed inside my belly. Would

Clara have spoken to me like that if she'd been around while I was growing up? Would she have patted the cushion beside her and settled an easy hand on my hair, tousling it with a smile as she extricated a pewter napkin ring from my grimy, closed fist? Fat chance that we'd get to that point now, with her chomping at the bit to move back to Sedona.

I glanced at the clock. "I don't know where David is. He should have been here by now."

Gran shrugged. "Traffic was terrible. That Artistic Avenger blocked all of Constitution Avenue with her display."

I felt like I'd been punched in the stomach. "Artistic Avenger? What Artistic Avenger?" I faked the question.

Gran clucked her tongue. "I know you're busy at work, dear, but you really should make time to read the paper. Your anima is famous. There was an article about her in the Style section on Monday."

Clara chimed in, as if we were presenting Current Events in homeroom. "And there was another one in the Metro section today."

"Oh," I said weakly. "I just hadn't heard her called that. Artistic Avenger?"

Gran laughed, a tinkling silvery sound that I hadn't heard in ages. "That's the name she's chosen. George actually suggested inviting her to the wedding, if we can figure out how to reach her. Such a celebrity! She would make our little get-together memorable."

Yeah. She'd do that all right. This wedding stuff was now officially out of hand.

Before I could discourage Gran from inviting my greatest arcane failure into the orange-and-silver chaos that was shaping up to be the Public Embarrassment of the Year, my front door swung open. Neko and David ducked inside, bringing with them a whiff of autumn freshness.

As Neko launched into a tale of blocked traffic and magically induced chaos, I met my warder's eyes. He offered a tight nod of a greeting, then I saw his gaze dart around the room, flicking against the closed doors to the basement, the bathroom, my bedroom.

Surely, he could not tell what had happened over the weekend. Surely, he had no way of knowing about the midnight dinner I had shared, the easy breakfast I had enjoyed, the two stolen days of playing. Surely, he did not know about Will.

Clara spoke first, breaking a silence that didn't have time to become uncomfortable. "I hope that you're going to show us more about potions, Jeanette. I'd love to brew something that will strengthen my perception of auras, with Majom's assistance, of course. We'll be able to do so much together, once we're back in Sedona. Once we're home." She cast another fond smile at the boy.

Right. Auras. Like those really existed.

Maybe she'd remember my real name when she was back in Sedona. Back where she belonged.

But we'd better get started, if we were going to find out anything about regenerating my own powers. It might take ages to get Gran and Clara up to speed. And with the

Artistic Avenger making herself the talk of the town, it seemed as if I was going to need my power even more than I'd expected.

"I have to warn you—I've never been a real expert on potions."

"Maybe that's for the best," David said. His voice was calm, courteous, steady with the perfect dispassion someone might show in a grocery store as they decided whether the Granny Smith apples looked better than the Winesaps. "You never really focused on developing your powers with potions, so they probably haven't been as deteriorated by the recent…lapse."

Lapse. Yeah. That was a good term for it. Better than "the recent unpleasantness," which is what I'd thought he was going to say. He fixed me with a pointed stare and said, "Why don't you and I bring up some supplies from downstairs? Everyone will be much more comfortable if we work here in the living room."

That sounded perfectly reasonable. But I had no desire to go down to the basement with David. No desire to be alone with him at all. Not if he was going to lecture me about Ariel. Not if he had some way to sense what had happened with Will.

"Neko!" I said, as if my familiar were my favorite person on the face of the earth. "Why don't you help me! David can…David can explain to Gran and Clara more of the basic theory behind potions!"

Neko, traitor that he was, looked to David for approval. I

actually felt a little weak with gratitude that my warder consented. Neko followed me into the basement.

"So," he said, as I knelt beside the bookcases to excavate some muslin bags of dried herbs. "What were you doing with the light spell Friday night?"

"You felt it?"

"Of course." He sniffed. "I always feel it when you work magic."

"What? You never told me that before!"

"You never asked." He glided away, with all the aplomb of a tabby seeking out a stripe of sunlight.

I couldn't keep from asking even though I dreaded the answer, "And David? Can he feel me, too?"

Neko snorted. "Of course. How do you think he tracked you down the first night you ever worked a spell?" I remembered that night, as clearly as if it had happened yesterday. Then, thinking of what *had* happened yesterday, I blushed.

Neko whirled on me as if he'd heard my capillaries flood. "Do tell, girlfriend!"

"It's nothing!" I said, and I grunted as I got to my feet. With the Grand Inquisitor here, I might have done better to try my luck with David.

"Nothing, like showing off your powers for an unsuspecting beau? Or nothing, like luring a man completely into your bed?"

"That's none of your business!"

"Was he good?"

"Neko!"

"Oh." He pursed his lips into a pout. "I'm so sorry, girl-friend."

"Neko, you are just saying that so I'll give you details! I am not going to tell you one word about what happened Friday night. It is absolutely none of your business who I see when I'm not busy with witchcraft things."

"Not much busy-ness with witchcraft things these days, is there?"

His matter-of-fact barb made my belly turn. Chagrined, I loaded my familiar down with bags of herbs, adding a silver wand for good measure. I turned on my heel to storm up the stairs in front of him.

Neko smiled archly as he set my arcane treasures down on the coffee table. While my love life had been clinically dissected under my familiar's microscope, David had wrestled Clara, Gran and their familiars into order. Each woman was sitting on an end of the couch, her assistant nestled close to her side.

Majom was picking idly at some spangles that dripped from Clara's sleeve. I wouldn't have been surprised to see him place one of the sequins on his tongue, experimenting with the taste. Nuri nestled close to Gran, as if the couch were too crowded for four to sit comfortably. She kept a wary eye on all of us, tilting her head to a precise angle that always kept Gran in her sight. Her fingers clenched and unclenched in her lap, and I wondered if she was even aware of the gesture.

"Okay," I said, scowling at Neko as he sniffed the air. What was he going to accuse me of next? Committing Downward-Facing Dog in my own living room? "Potions." I sat down on the rug, across from the couch. Neko obediently settled beside me, resting against my knee with a comforting, familiar pressure.

Gran and Clara both leaned closer to me. While my grandmother's face was etched with a solemn politeness, Clara's eyes were narrowed. I recognized her expression as one of intense concentration. For one moment, I glanced at David, wondering if I could live up to Clara's expectations. If I could live up to my warder's. I caught his chin dip in the most minute of nods.

It wasn't much. It certainly wasn't a vote of confidence. It would never substitute for the dozens of conversations that we probably needed to have, somewhere, someway.

But it was permission to proceed. It was a statement that I was in charge, at least for now. That I knew what I was talking about, that I could lead the women in my family deeper into the ways of witchcraft, into the magic that I had once studied and mastered. That I could begin searching for a path out of the dark forest where my magic was lost.

"Potions," I said again. "Potions can generate some of the strongest magic, because they distill arcane essences, refine them and combine them in new and powerful ways. For example, we can cleanse our…auras…by creating a purifying potion, a draft that will wash away negativity and evil. We can start with three separate elements—galangal root and fennel and water collected under the light of a full moon—

and combine them into one." I dug in one of the muslin sacks to produce the necessary dried ingredients.

When David set a silver flask in the center of the table, I tried not to flinch. I'd seen the flask for the first time almost a year before, when I'd prepared for my magical workings with the Washington Coven. "Thank you," I said, taking care to keep my voice even. He merely nodded an acknowledgment, stepping back out of the range of my vision.

His presence wasn't even required here. We weren't going to do anything dangerous. We weren't going to summon any substantial power (maybe none at all, on my part). But I knew better than to suggest that he leave, even if I was desperate to avoid talk of the Avenger, of Will. I smothered my restlessness with a sigh and said to Gran and Clara, "Take a sniff. The galangal is Chinese ginger. You should recognize the aroma of the fennel."

Gran exclaimed, "They have fennel seeds at the Indian restaurant that Uncle George likes so much!"

I nodded. "Because they purify. They freshen the breath, but they also purify the space around them."

Clara jumped in eagerly. "We used to have galangal at the co-op, in Sedona, but I haven't been able to find it anywhere out here. The tea centers me in my fourth chakra." She fluttered dramatic fingers over her heart.

I bit back a typical exasperated response, even swallowing the suggestion that she return to her precious Arizona co-op now, rather than after the wedding. I needed to keep her here for a while yet. I needed her help; she and Gran appeared to be my last hope of ever practicing witchcraft again.

I made my voice steady and said, "Exactly. Now, we can take a silver vessel and add the rainwater." I didn't even bother to be surprised when David produced a trio of silver cups from somewhere. I recognized their design from a display we had at the Peabridge; they were classic examples of colonial simplicity, memorialized by Thomas Jefferson and other founding fathers. Yet another warder's trick, having them on hand, I supposed.

I poured some rainwater into one and felt the faintest thrum, like a piano note that had been struck once and left to fade in a concert hall. I could sense the potential in the pure liquid, the teasing sense that I'd known its power long ago, that once I could work magic.

Neko must have felt the magic, as well. He leaned in even closer, matching his entire body to mine, from hip to shoulder. With another person, it might have been awkward to move with that pressure; it might have felt unbalanced. Here, though, in the comfort of my living room, it felt destined. It felt *right*.

Setting my hopeful apprehension aside, I brewed the potion. I showed Gran and Clara how to add the ginger-root, how to swirl in the fennel seed with a careful application of the silver wand. I reminded them of the proper hand gestures, the ritual offering of thought and voice and spirit as they touched their foreheads, their throats, their hearts. I encouraged them to reach out to their familiars, to bring

Majom and Nuri into the magical working as mirrors, as reflections of magical strength. I told them the words to use, the formula that had been passed down from one witch to another through the ages.

And I sat back to watch the magic unfold.

My potion was an utter failure. No matter how much I trusted Neko to reflect my powers back to me, nothing ventured led to nothing gained. The combination in my silver cup remained ordinary dried roots and seeds, floating in a splash of clear, mundane water.

Clara caught on first. Her open mind worked to her advantage as she fiddled with magical things. I might criticize her for believing in the Vortex, for sensing harmonies in the earth, for babbling on about people's auras. But she was able to harness her magic far better than most first-time witches, and I could only assume that some of her mumbo jumbo was actually real.

Gran struggled, though. At first, she couldn't remember the words. Then she added the fennel seeds before the galangal. The third time, she was so nervous that she knocked over her cup, spilling water across the coffee table and sending Majom scrambling into the kitchen for a towel.

When she hunched forward on the couch for her fourth try, Nuri edged up beside her. The red-haired woman stretched her arms wide, making Gran and Majom lean backward, but then she clasped the silver cup in curled, confident fingers. "Try again," she said, and her smoky voice was softened by a secret urgency that made her whisper.

And with Nuri's help, Gran brewed the potion. She added each ingredient in order. She swirled the resulting mixture precisely in its cup, counting out loud to make sure she did not wait too long before decanting it.

As she worked, I felt her magic rising. I sensed it across the table, like the electric tingle of a storm in the distance. The instant that the potion clarified, the precise second that it crested its magical potential, I felt a charge leap out, a power that I could see, that I could feel, that I could actually *taste*, even though it was not my own. That force, without any sort of personal arcane buffer, was enough to knock me backward. I caught myself with my hands behind me, suddenly aware that David was keeping me from falling farther. His legs were warm against my shoulders until I leaped to my feet.

"Excellent!" I said, my voice so falsely hearty that even Gran gave me an odd look. "No! Really! You created the potion perfectly!" I forced myself to stop exclaiming, ordered myself to gaze reassuringly at my four preening students. From the corner of my eye, I could see Neko's frankly curious look. I babbled on, trying to smooth over my aching lack of powers with idiotic words. "I could definitely feel it, feel the force that you created. It didn't add to my power, but I could sense what was happening. I'll be back to full strength in no time, if we keep training like this."

Gran beamed at me as she patted Nuri's arm. "We're certainly glad to hear that, dear." Her words, though, were almost lost in a yawn. "Excuse me! I didn't realize how tired that would make me!"

David glided forward, settling a steady hand over Gran's. I knew the look on his face; he was reading her status, measuring her fitness. He'd touched me often enough with the same dispassionate care. I wasn't surprised to hear him pronounce, "You should eat something. We all should."

"Pizza's on me!" I said, masking my concern with false good cheer. My pocketbook might not approve of the lessons I was teaching Gran and Clara, but I had to soldier on. I couldn't think of any alternatives, at this point.

"Double anchovies!" Neko announced immediately.

"Green peppers and black olives," Clara said. Apparently, she was back to dabbling with vegetarianism, at least for the night. Must be preparing for life near the Vortex.

"Pepperoni, sausage and hamburger," Gran said contentedly.

I headed into the kitchen for a pad of paper, using the errand to compose myself. I hadn't expected my magical loss to hurt quite so badly. I hadn't expected to miss my powers nearly as much as I did.

It took almost a quarter of an hour to work out our order, dividing three medium pies in halves to capture everyone's preferences. Nuri called dibs on any extra crusts. Between cleaning up from our training session and converting the kitchen counter into a buffet, the rest of the evening flew by. I had one shaky moment when Neko questioned the broad variety of Will-provided fruit juices in my refrigerator, but I managed to convince him that I had bought them for Majom and Nuri, not knowing the other familiars' tastes in food and beverage.

It was after ten o'clock when Clara finally rattled her keys. "We should get out of here, Jeanette. Let you get your rest. Besides, I have some packing to do."

I stifled a yawn against the back of my teeth. I had been fading for the past hour, but I wasn't about to get into a conversation about *why* I was so tired, especially since I couldn't blame my fatigue on actually working any magic. I pasted on a smile and said, "We'll have to find another time to work together soon."

"Yes, dear," Gran agreed, as she got to her feet with Nuri's assistance.

By then, Majom was plucking at Clara's sleeve, pulling her close to whisper some secret in her ear. Nuri yawned, stretching her arms so wide I was afraid that she was going to knock Gran over. Neko cast an appraising eye at his fellow familiars. "Can I squeeze in with the four of you for a ride home?"

"Neko," I said. "Stay and help clean up."

"Love to, but I can't. Jacques is waiting for me." He paused, as if giving me a chance to say something, but I was stuck coming up with an argument. "At home," he elaborated. I still couldn't figure out a proper justification. "In bed." He favored me with an enormous wink. "I'm sure you understand."

"Get out of here, you!" I shoved at him before he could say something even more inappropriate in front of my octogenarian grandmother.

Only after the door closed did I realize that I'd left myself with another, more substantial problem. David was picking up plates and carrying them into the kitchen. "Oh, leave those," I said. "I'll take care of them." He shrugged and ignored me.

I turned on the faucet in the sink, increasing the flow as high as it would go. I tried to tell myself that I needed it to heat up quickly, so that I could wash the dishes properly. I wouldn't waste water just to drown out a possibly uncomfortable conversation.

Idiot me, I hadn't counted on David's patience. He let us wash the dishes in silence. He let us rinse the glasses. He let us dry everything and return every one of my possessions to its proper cupboard. He closed pizza boxes and stacked them neatly beside the trash can, an unspoken promise to carry them out to the Dumpster behind the library later.

He only spoke when I was folding the terry hand towel into perfect thirds over the drying rack. "The light spell worked on Friday night, even if the potion didn't tonight?"

"I'm allowed to work a light spell. Any witch can!"

"I didn't say otherwise, Jane."

"But you thought it. You thought it very loudly." I flounced into the living room, moving with all the exasperation of an insulted teenaged girl. I threw myself onto one of the couches.

David sat beside me, leaving a full cushion between us. "I'm worried that you've spent the last of your powers. That's dangerous. Someone could claim Neko. Could claim me. Mabon is eight days away."

"I don't think we're getting Ariel back on Mabon," I said.

"And you don't have to be so noble and subtle. I know that you're telling me we wouldn't have to worry about any of this, if I'd just been more responsible in the first place. I know what you're thinking."

"Actually," he said, and his voice was so even that I actually hated him for a moment. "You don't."

I stared at him. I wanted to tell him that he was wrong. I wanted to tell him that I knew every thought that had ever crossed his mind, that I could tell him exactly what he'd meant to say. But I couldn't do that. I couldn't lie to him outright. Unbidden, tears pricked at the back of my eyes. A sob caught in my throat.

"What's wrong?" he asked.

I started to count out the answers. I was going to be dressed in hideous orange and silver at my grandmother's wedding. The mother I'd only found two years before was getting ready to abandon me, again. My job was going nowhere in a hurry. I wasn't sure where my boyfriend was, or even if I could call him a boyfriend. The ridiculously self-named Artistic Avenger was still at large, while I was not a single step closer to raising enough power to bring her in, to salvaging a spell that I had screwed up because I'd been thinking about my warder, thinking about a relationship that was obviously never, ever going to happen. Mabon was eight days away.

David sat on the far side of my living-room couch, holding every muscle still, as if I had miraculously worked some spell to cast him in stone.

I pulled my knees up to my chest, tucking my fingers into

the sleeves of my turtleneck sweater. "I don't know," I said, and my voice was very small.

"Start at the beginning," David said reasonably.

I only shook my head. I wasn't even sure where the beginning was anymore.

"You're tired, Jane." There was no judgment in the words, only a statement. "You need some sleep."

I swiped at my eyes and nodded. "It's been a long day," I said, but that only made me want to laugh crazily. I sniffed, instead.

Another night, David would have walked me to my bedroom. (The room that Will had entered for the first time Friday night.) He would have tucked me into my bed. (The bed that Will had pounced on Friday night.) He would have lain beside me, head on my extra pillow. (The pillow that Will had slept on Friday night.)

He would have left before dawn.

I clambered to my feet and crossed to the front door. "Good night," I said.

David was no fool. He knew when he was being dismissed. He'd done the dismissing well enough in his own right. "Good night," he said, matching my even tone perfectly. "Lock the door behind me."

"Of course," I said, not even bothering to roll my eyes.

And I did.

I locked the door so that I was safe in my living room. Alone. And I went into my bedroom. Alone. And I climbed into my bed. Alone. And I fell asleep.

Alone.

15

I was trapped on a kitchen step stool, penned in by a madman with a pincushion and a measuring tape.

"Girlfriend, if you're not going to stand up straight, I can't be responsible for how you look at the wedding." Neko clicked his tongue in exasperation.

I sighed and leaned toward the counter, snagging another one of Melissa's Honey Moons, specially baked for my fitting. Nuri had already eaten half a dozen, retreating to a chair in the corner of Gran's small kitchen after seizing each golden cookie. Deciding not to press the shy redheaded woman into doing my dirty work, I begged Melissa, "Please, please, *please* will you give me one of those mojitos?"

Mojito therapy had taken over Gran's kitchen—lime, mint, rum and seltzer were arrayed across the counter. So far, our strategy was a success, even if my dress was still hideous.

Gran lifted her own glass, where mint leaves floated amid the light-green alcohol-infused soda. "These are really quite good, dear. You should have told me about them a long time ago. We should serve them at the reception."

"Absolutely, Gran," I grumbled, scarcely managing to banish leftover teenaged angst from my reply. Mojitos at my grandmother's reception. What would she come up with next? Why didn't we just invite Paris Hilton, Lindsay Lohan and any other unemployed starlets who happened to be free on Halloween, to guarantee that we had the jet-set party of the century? What had happened to my grandmother, to the totally normal woman who had raised me, to her endless reams of common sense and good taste?

I looked down at the orange-and-silver taffeta of my dress, thinking that I'd be willing to let common sense go forever, if I could only get back a hint of good taste.

"Stand straight!" Neko hissed.

Melissa passed a glass to me as I attempted to oblige. I could just catch a glimpse of myself in the foyer mirror. The dress sagged across my front, clearly cut for a woman with more cleavage than I had to brag about. The waist nipped in dangerously, gathered together with an attached sash that sparkled in silver lamé. As Neko muttered through his mouthful of straight pins, I took miniature steps in a circle, turning on the step stool so that he could perfect the hem. I winced when I glimpsed the back of the dress over my shoulder. Its halter neckline left a huge expanse of flesh bare, a stretch of skin that was only broadened by the gigantic silver bow that emphasized what the designer would certainly have called my "derriere."

I could not believe that any designer had ever made such a horrific creation, much less that my grandmother had seen it in a magazine. It was just my luck that Neko's Jacques knew someone in the design house, someone who'd been able to finagle an orange one on such short notice.

Orange. Gran had not been kidding. The dress rivaled Gatorade in its coloring. I sighed. I only drank Gatorade when I was suffering from a deadly flu.

I swallowed half of my mojito in a single swig.

"There," Melissa said, clearly smothering a laugh. "It looks much better, with those darts taken in."

"Much better," Neko agreed. He was getting his revenge for all the arcane study I'd forced him to complete in the past two years, for all the times I'd awakened him to help me with a spell. "You're lucky I can handle the sewing."

Gran beamed.

Well, that was really the most important thing, wasn't it? That Gran was beaming? I might think that she had turned into a monster planning this wedding. I might think that I was caught in the midst of a campy sitcom from hell. I might think that Gran had gone wholly and completely around the bend. But my grandmother—the woman who had raised me, the woman who had nurtured me through my own tempestuous teens—was happy.

"What do you think, Neko dear? The shoes will be dyed to match the dress, of course, but maybe we could attach some silver bows to them? You know, to pull it all together?"

"Absolutely, Gran," my traitorous familiar said. "Silver bows for the shoes would be perfect."

I hated both of them.

Melissa lifted the mojito pitcher even before I asked for a refill. Then she turned back to my grandmother. "So, Mrs. Smythe? What have you decided about the cake?" Melissa had brought along a dozen samples.

"I can't make up my mind. White cake seems so…plain, even though yours tastes divine, dear. But we really don't want to step too far away from tradition, do we?"

I almost choked as Melissa rotated her serving plate. Orange and silver was hardly the headline color combination in *Letitia Baldrige's Guide to Weddings*. Melissa merely said, "Why don't you try the lemon again? We could do it in three layers, with a coat of marzipan over everything. That way, we could color the outside orange. And decorate it with silver dragées."

If looks could kill, Cake Walk's doors would never open again. I was surprised to realize that even Neko's considerably distant limits had been reached. "Buttercream would be better," he insisted, intent enough on conveying his message that he extracted the pins from his mouth.

"I'm just not sure," Gran fretted.

"Not marzipan," I said firmly. "The almond would taste terrible with lemon cake."

"Now, dear, you've never liked almond. It's all a matter of taste."

I stared down at my hideous dress and bit back a reply.

I liked almonds just fine—Melissa's Almond Lust and Lust After Dark were two of my favorite confections. But marzipan was disgusting.

Melissa laughed and said, "We have a little time left. I'll leave these samples here. You can try them again in the morning, when you're drinking a cup of coffee. They'll seem different, with the bitter, instead of with mojito."

"Thank you, dear. I don't mind if I do have a bit more of that drink. Jane, why haven't you made these for me before?"

As Melissa topped off my grandmother's glass I just shook my head. She was going to be totally plastered by the time we were done. I glared at Neko. "Aren't you through yet?"

"Temper, temper," he said, placing one last pin. "There. Now go take it off and be very careful that you don't jostle the pins."

"Or what?" I muttered as I stepped down from the step stool. "Will you come help me with this?" I said to Melissa.

She followed me down the hallway to my childhood bedroom. Nuri had been staying there, but I still found the light switch on the wall with a reflexive pass of my palm. I barely managed to get the door closed before Melissa burst into laughter. "What is so funny?" I grumbled.

"I'm just looking at these walls and that dress. If I don't laugh, I might cry." The bedroom hadn't been repainted since my high-school days, and the Barbie-pink was even more intense than I remembered. It did absolutely nothing to tame the wedding orange.

"Just help me get this thing off," I said. Thankfully, Melissa obliged without further commentary. I settled the horrible gown across the foot of my old bed and shuddered. I couldn't pull my slacks on quickly enough, even as I fumbled for the side zip with nervous fingers. It was as if I believed the dress could control me with hideous powers of its own, as if it could sail through the air and attack me, guaranteeing that I would wear it forever and ever and ever. Hans Christian Andersen's red shoes would be a preferable form of torture. I glared at the sartorial disaster and quoted bitterly, "Belike you mean to make a puppet of me."

"*Taming of the Shrew*," Melissa responded immediately. "Just remember what happened to fair Katharina. She wore her gown gladly in the end."

"She was an idiot," I said, but I was cut off from further Shakespearean discourse by the ringing of my cell phone. "That'll be Will. I told him we could meet for a late dinner when I was through here."

I snapped open my phone, but it wasn't Will calling after all. It was David.

"Lincoln Memorial. Now."

"What?" It may have been the mojitos, or the hellish swirl of orange and pink before my eyes, but my warder's snapped order made no sense.

"Ariel. She's at the Lincoln Memorial."

"What is she doing?" I waved at Melissa to hand me my shoes.

"She's got banners stretched across the entire monument. And posters that denounce the administration as a culture-hating horde of congressional groupies."

"You have got to be kidding."

"Does this sound like a joke?"

I could picture the pulse beating in his throat, the hard line of his jaw as he bit off his words. David definitely wasn't joking.

"Where are you now?" I asked.

"In my car. Fifteen minutes away from the memorial. This is on the radio. There's going to be press."

"I've got Neko with me. We'll meet you there."

"Hurry."

And then he hung up, just like some action hero in the movies—no goodbye, no sign off. I had never thought that ordinary human beings would gain anything by sparing themselves a couple of simple syllables. I had never thought that I'd be trying to stop an activist anima from taking a federal landmark by storm, either.

"It's Ariel on the loose," I said to Melissa. "I've got to go."

"I'll come with you," she said immediately. "Maybe I can help."

"Seriously? If you want to help, stay here with Gran. It'll take forever to explain to her why I'm in such a hurry." I gave my best friend a sideways glance. "Besides, you can backtrack on that whole marzipan thing. Steer her back to something sane. Something white. Something normal. What the hell were you thinking?"

"Jane, let her be happy. This is the biggest party she's thrown in her life. She's never going to do anything like this ever again."

I glared one last time at the dress. "We can only hope so, anyway."

I grabbed my purse and hurried down the hallway. "Come on, Neko. We've got to go." I'd interrupted him midstory; his hands were still fluttering around his face as he told Gran about some amusing exploit. She was laughing and clutching a mojito glass that was far too empty for a woman of her weight. Amazingly, though, Neko heard the urgency in my voice and responded by crossing immediately to the front door. I rushed to join him. "Gran, I'm sorry to be fitted and run, but I've got to get downtown."

"What?" Nuri squawked, as if she were upset by all the commotion.

Gran protested. "I thought we'd have a chance to work on wedding plans a bit more! I want to talk to you about balloon sculptures. George and I were thinking about having the triumphal arch from *Aida*."

"Melissa's much better at that sort of thing than I am," I said truthfully. Of course, anyone in the entire metropolitan area would be better than I was. "I'll call you tomorrow, Gran." I saw her start to formulate her usual request. "I promise. Neko!"

Miraculously, I hailed the first cab that drove by. As we

climbed into the backseat, I fished out my cell phone again. My familiar was clearly bursting with questions; I could see them popping from his smirking lips, but I held up a finger for a moment of private conversation.

One ring. Two. Three. Four. Damn, I was getting voice mail. I took a deep breath and tried to keep my voice as light and steady as possible. "Will, hey there. Look, I hope you get this before you get to the restaurant. An emergency has come up, something about—" I glanced at the back of the cab driver's head "—something about the stuff in my basement and that woman we saw at the Capitol. I have to go to the Lincoln Memorial. I'll call you as soon as I know what's going on. Bye!"

"Stuff in your basement," Neko repeated guardedly as I flipped my phone closed.

"Hush," I said, nodding toward the driver. "David didn't give me any details. I don't know what he wants us to do."

I thought it would be easy to find him at the memorial. It was almost eight o'clock on a late September evening, when the tourists were long dispersed back to their home-towns.

I hadn't counted on Ariel's ability to generate her own publicity.

Three camera trucks were lined up along Constitution Avenue, their satellite aerials pointing toward the sky. A flock of reporters roosted on the memorial steps, weighed down with shoulder-held cameras and microphones and endless coils of cable. As I stumbled out of the cab, I tossed a twenty to the driver. "Keep the change," I said, unwilling to wait for whatever I was supposed to get back.

Neko shook his head as he took in the crowd. "David is not going to be happy."

That was the understatement of the year.

Ariel stood at the top of the historic steps. A velvet rope was draped across stanchions, blocking off a long rectangle of space, as if she had all the right in the world to be there. She had somehow managed to string a banner across the four columns at the center of the memorial. I knew from the lecture that I had attended with Will that those columns were reminiscent of the trees that had once served as the centerpiece of Greek worship, the forest that had been the ancestral home of religion. And I knew from my prior experience with my anima that the columns were now a backdrop for a powerful statement, for a political declaration that was likely to be broadcast on the front page of the Saturday *Washington Post*.

Empower The Arts! roared the banner. Lincoln Freed The Slaves! We Must Free The Arts!

She had a way with rhetoric, my anima. If only she would use her powers for good, instead of for evil.

Well, it wasn't evil to get funding for the arts. But I had never, ever intended for her to take on that mission. I had only meant to get a little help rebuilding my own astral strength. I had only wanted an anima to help out around the house. I was still stunned at how far my little magical experiment had gone astray.

Even as I gaped at the banners, I wondered how she had gotten them up there. Why hadn't the police stopped her? Why hadn't anyone prohibited her from turning the entire Lincoln Memorial into her personal stage?

"How did she—" I breathed.

Neko answered exasperatedly. "Magic."

Well, duh. After all, I had poured all of my power into Ariel when I made her. I had created her with the last remnants of my ability. I had given her all of my spells and charms, trusted her with every ounce of witchcraft that had still been at my disposal.

She hadn't returned the favor, but she'd sure invested the capital wisely.

Now that I squinted at the banners, I could see that they weren't real. They were figments of the collective imagination, strung across the columns on a hope and a dream. The letters wavered in the memorial's floodlights, flickering like a movie projection. I remembered similar spells that I had woven, magic that I had worked where I had stolen the heat of the Potomac River, the glint of silver moonlight.

My anima was a damned good hand at magic.

And now, with the unbroken attention of several hundred people, she began to plead her case. She was dancing again, weaving the same ballet that had captivated the crowd outside of the Capitol. This time, she spread her arms wide, conjuring up signs from the darkness. People gasped as they worked out the words, but no one seemed to realize that she was crafting her posters out of nothingness.

Empower The Arts, said the first one, her old standby.

All Our Life Is Drama, said another.

Museums Are Not Dead, said a third.

Each sign raised a scatter of applause. She pirouetted with her handiwork, swirling in the floodlights. Dance Is Life. She ran from one end of the vast memorial platform to the other, raising cheers with her words.

"We've got to do something. Now." I felt David's words against my back more than heard him. He grasped my arm and pulled me closer, relying on Neko to follow with a familiar's ingrained bond.

"What?" I said, reluctant to turn away from Ariel's spectacle. "I can't control her. I can't even feel her. Not with magic. Not now."

"Do you see what she's doing with the signs?" We were jostled by the crowd behind us. Everyone was pushing closer, forcing us up against the velvet rope.

"They're not real, are they?" I squinted to make out the precise magic, to understand what she'd done to weave her arcane messages.

"No." I knew David well enough to comprehend that his anger was boosted by his inability to control what was happening.

The crowd behind us started to chant. "A-ven-ger! A-ven-ger! A-ven-ger!" I felt as if I was at a pep rally for the emo crowd.

Ariel kicked her dance into high gear. She was moving faster now, more smoothly. I felt Neko twitch beside me, almost as if he was going to pounce on her. The posterboard messages changed faster, flashing forward with a speed fed by magic. Each one transformed, until they all said the same thing: Empower The Arts.

The crowd behind was enraptured, spun into my anima's production like audience members at a hypnotist's stage show. Everyone was eager to reach Ariel, desperate for her attention. Someone planted a hand between my shoulder blades and shoved me hard so that he could get closer to the magical creature on the limestone stage.

Even as David grabbed at my arm to steady me, I staggered forward, my head breaking the plane of the velvet rope. I blinked, and everything changed.

Ariel was still there. She was still dancing. But her frantic energy was absent. Her terrible power was gone. She raised her hands above her head, and they were empty. Her arms were spread, without any poster, without any words.

The velvet rope held back her power. It delineated the force that mesmerized the crowd. If I could get past the rope, I could get to her. I would have a chance at regaining control over my anima, at taking back the magic that was rightfully mine.

David pulled me back to safety so abruptly that my teeth rattled. I tugged at his arm. "The rope! We have to take down the rope!" I had to shout to make myself heard above the crowd.

Somehow, he understood me. Somehow, he knew what had to be done. He bellowed at Neko, ordered him to stand

ready to catch Ariel. He put his hands on the nearest stan-
chion, spread his fingers around the polished brass.

One, I could hear him count. Two. Three.

He tugged with the strength of a man who spent his after-
noons splitting wood. The velvet swayed wildly, and three
of the stanchions tumbled down the steps. The crowd went
wild, leaping forward, frantic to breach the barrier, desperate to get to Ariel, to her magic, to her message.

Neko and I, blessed with a split-second warning, were the
first people to hit the top step. I scrambled up to my anima,
skidded to a stop in front of her, Neko slipping to my side.

Come, I thought, holding out my hand.

Witch. Her voice was as flat as it had been in my basement.
Her eyes were dull. But a single drop of power fell onto the
parched landscape of my mind.

I order you to return to me, I thought. *Come home. Now.*

She raised a hand, as if she were intent on cutting me off.
There was a brutal barrier between us. I knew that Neko
felt it, too; he was forced to step back, shoved away by the
tremendous power she projected. I felt heavy, smothered by
a force, a gravity that I had never known before.

And suddenly I understood just how much my initial
spell had failed. Not only had I freed my anima. Not only
had I released her upon the city. Not only had I invested her
with a bizarre mission, a freakish obsession based on a single
wayward thought. But I had somehow blocked the natural
channel between us. I had somehow locked up all of the
power that she was generating, all of the magic that spun out

of her own spellcraft, all of the strength that should have flowed back to me. It was there, growing, pulsing, generating more and more pure arcane ability.

But I could not reach it. I could not free it. I could not take back what should have been mine.

"Jane!" David's bellow cut through my revelation.

I turned in reflex. The crowd had caught up with Neko and me. They were no longer held back by the velvet rope; they weren't restrained by any sense of justice or rightness or reserve.

Without another thought, Ariel turned and ran, darting around the side of the building. Neko scampered after her, leading the pack that clamored for more information, for more dancing, for more, more, more.

I fell to my knees at the top of the suddenly desolate steps.

David's hand on my arm was demanding, irresistible. "Are you hurt?" His voice was so harsh I almost failed to recognize it.

I shook my head. After a few deep breaths, I managed to say, "It's working. My magic is building. She has it all, within her. It's locked up, so that I can't get at it."

David pulled me to my feet. "They'll be back in a minute. Let's get out of the spotlight." He marched me down the endless steps, holding me upright when my knees decided to imitate Jell-O. Only when we were on the ground level, half-enrobed in shadows beside the Reflecting Pool, did he let us stop. "I don't understand," he said. "The night that you created her, you said that everything worked exactly as we planned."

I stared into the darkness, toward the accusing finger of

the Washington Monument. George Washington. The man who could not tell a lie. "About that spell," I said, unable to meet his eyes.

"What happened, Jane?" His words were frozen.

How could I tell him? How could I admit that he had distracted me? That I had been thinking of his arms, of his chest, of his bed, of that entire glorious, mistaken afternoon, when all the time I should have been focused on creating my anima? How could I admit that I had let a stupid promotional *poster* sway my concentration?

"My God, Jane, are you all right?"

I whirled at the new voice, recognizing it even before I found the speaker. Will.

He skidded to a stop beside us. "What's going on? I grabbed a cab when I got your message. The driver had on WTOP. They said there was some sort of disturbance at the memorial." He glanced up the stairs. "Some sort of riot?"

David stepped forward before I could speak. "It's over now. Everything is under control."

Will ignored him. "Jane, are you all right?" he repeated.

"I'm fine."

David put a hand on my arm. "I said, it's over now."

I slipped away from his touch, crossing my arms over my chest. Will looked from me to my warder. "It's David, right?"

"That's right." I could hear the abrupt authority in his voice, the animalistic boundary that he was drawing. I didn't want to be part of that argument, though. I didn't want to be his possession.

"Well, thanks for making sure that Jane was safe." Will planted his feet more firmly. In a different age, he would have been summoning his second and setting a place for dueling pistols at dawn. He turned to me and offered a soothing hand. "Let's get out of here. Are you ready for dinner?"

"Dinner?" David sounded like an adult laughing at a child's knock-knock joke.

"We had plans." Will managed to swallow some of his defensiveness.

"Jane doesn't like to eat dinner this late." David was tossing down his own gauntlet.

"She didn't have any problem accepting my invitation this afternoon," Will said.

"Where are you going?" David asked, eyes narrowing. It sounded as if he thought that Will was lying, that he was making up our late-night dinner plans.

"If you really have to know, Paparazzi. In Georgetown," Will said. That was news to me, and I winced, but only because David and I had once shared a midnight meal there. "A little alfredo for two."

My warder apparently had not forgotten. He raised a provoking eyebrow. "She prefers baked ravioli. For dinner."

"But sesame bagels for breakfast."

I couldn't believe it. David was actually knocked silent; Will had deflated him with one simple line. A line that made me blush as David absorbed its full import, but one line all the same.

My warder turned to me stiffly. "We have to finish this conversation. Tomorrow. Phone me after you wake up."

He strode into the darkness. Before I could even look at Will, my familiar came loping out of the shadows. "Neko," I said, cutting off whatever was going to pass as a smart comment from him. "Go after David. Tell him everything you learned."

"But—"

"Now," I said. "Go."

For once, he listened to me.

I was shaking by the time I turned to Will.

"I'm sorry," he said. "That was ugly. That was possessive and stupid and...rude."

"It was," I agreed. I could see his face fall in the darkness, read the disappointment in his expression. I said, "David can have that effect on people."

"Really?" Will said. I knew that he was asking about more than my warder's behavior. I knew that he was asking about me. I knew that he was asking if I forgave him, if I was willing to have dinner with him, if I was willing to do more.

My heart was still pounding. I looked up at the floodlit stairs, realized that people were wandering up and down, as if it were any other night at the tourist spot.

Ariel must have gotten away, slipped from the crowd. She was out there, somewhere, burgeoning with power that was rightly mine. I needed to find her, needed to tame her, needed to control her like the anima she was supposed to be.

But for now, I needed time away from the chaos. I needed

a human companion and a night without witchcraft and worry, without spells and deception. I slipped my hand into Will's. "I'll share alfredo with you any time," I said. I managed not to look back at the memorial steps as we walked away. And for the rest of the night, I managed not to think about Neko and Ariel. And David. I didn't think about David at all. Not even when the couple next to us shared an order of baked ravioli.

16

September ended, and Mabon, the Autumn Equinox, passed without any change in the magical environment. Ariel, the Artistic Avenger, the anima that was holding all of my power hostage, had apparently gone underground.

I heard about her often enough. *The Washington Post* set up Avenger's Watch, running a hotline by phone and a blog on their Web site. People sent in their sightings—dozens each week. I knew that some of them could not possibly be true. Ariel would not cut her hair, would not—could not— even bleach it. She was bound to wear her gauzy dress, no matter how cool the autumn air became. She was not going to take a trip to Rio, to the Bahamas, to Australia, to perfect a tan, no matter where the rumormongers placed her on the globe.

I knew that she wasn't a real, human woman. She was bound by the way that I had created her; her body was set, even if her mind had somehow gotten away from me. Those surface features could never change.

Still, she remained perfectly elusive. She'd apparently lost her taste for dance concerts. She modified her tactics, leaving giant signs sprawled across places no real person could access. Empower The Arts was splayed across the reading room of the Library of Congress, the letters shaped out of books that had been pulled from the shelves, stacked on the floor. The slogan found its way onto the columns at the World War II Memorial, in bold, black letters that took some poor custodian days to scrub away. It was stenciled onto the doors of the National Archives.

Ariel had a taste for vandalism that frightened me. But she certainly had a way of making her message heard.

I was booting up my computer on the Tuesday after Columbus Day when my phone rang. A quick glance at caller ID said it was Will, calling from his cell.

"Hey there," I said. "Why aren't you sleeping?" The busy life of an architect was catching up with my boyfriend—let me say that again, my *boyfriend*. He was finding it difficult to juggle nights at my place, days at his office, and the huge Harrison project that was swooping toward deadline—the housing plans for his dot-com billionaire with a colonial mansion fixation. I'd left him in my bed, curtains drawn, pillow over his head, groaning that he was going to take a personal day.

"I'm heading back to my place. At least it'll be quiet there."

Oh. That didn't sound good. "What's going on?"

"David phoned. Apparently, he thinks that you're screening your calls, because he called three times back-to-back. I picked up the fourth time."

I winced. David and I had been seeing each other twice a week, working with Gran and Clara on building up their powers. The witchcraft instruction was going only slightly better than our verbal correspondence. We nodded hello and actually verbalized goodbye. Otherwise, we spoke only to Gran, Clara and the familiars, pretending that we were too busy, too driven, to have anything else to say.

Even Neko had given up making snarky comments, trying to reconcile us by way of his wit. There was a certain grim determination about every training session. The mood was made darker by the fact that I still had not succeeded in teaching Gran or Clara anything substantial. Sure, they could thaw a cheesecake. They could even, on a good day, summon their familiars, silently, from across the room.

But manipulate crystals? Brew a potion with any truly useful qualities whatsoever? Empower even the smallest charm?

They could not harness their magic, and I was absolutely unable to find a key to unlock that barrier.

I was just about ready to call a stop to the charade altogether. So what if the Artistic Avenger kept up her campaign? So what if she successfully lobbied Congress to increase funding for the arts? She wasn't doing any harm on the magical front.

And I was more and more certain that I was willing to let the magical bit of me slip away. What good had it done me, in the past two years, anyway? It had gotten me romantically involved with two real losers. It had dragged me into a snake pit of female jealousy that made high school look like fun. It had burdened me with a familiar who thought it was a game to pick apart every single thing I wore, ate or touched. It had left me with a brooding, possessive warder who apparently thought that I was more a thing for him to own than a person for him to respect.

Life would be simpler without witchcraft. Life would be sane. Life would be normal. Life would be the perfect slice of pie I'd been feasting on with Will for nearly a month, minus the drag of failed training sessions. I was so, so tempted.

I sighed and said, "What did he want?"

"He said to call him. As soon as possible."

Great. I still hadn't really told Will about David—at least not about sleeping with him. As far as Will knew, David was just my overprotective, overbearing warder. I kept telling myself that Will didn't need to know anything else. After all, I was never going to end up in bed with David again. Not a chance of that.

David was just a Number—a guy I'd slept with in the past—and Will and I weren't sharing Numbers. I had no interest in the women he'd slept with before me; there was no reason to count them up. (Okay. I had a little interest. A lot of interest. But I cared more about keeping my own list secret, than about learning the specifics of Will's.)

"I'll get back to him," I said, trying to sound brisk and businesslike. And I would—when I was good and ready. I relished the opportunity to pay him back for all of *my* phone calls that he had ignored. Besides, I really resented his triple-calling. As *if* I would be the sort of person to screen my calls. Oh. That's right. He actually knew me pretty well.

I glared at the red "message-waiting" light on my desk phone. Now, I was virtually certain that at least one call from David had triggered the signal. Well, that was fine. I could ignore him at work as well as I could ignore him at home. I glanced at the drawer where I kept my purse locked away. It was a good thing that Evelyn insisted that we keep the library a cell-free zone. David couldn't reach me there, either. I'd talk to him when I was good and ready. And his hounding me at home made me that much more inclined to wait another day or two.

I softened my voice and said to Will, "I'm sorry that he bothered you."

"I'm not," Will said, and I could hear his grin over the phone line. "He sounded really surprised when I picked up the phone."

There was that gorilla behavior again. Why didn't they just agree to a cage match and be done with it? I rolled my eyes and grunted, "You Tarzan. Me Jane." Will responded by roaring like a lion. I started hooting like a chimpanzee, because I'd always had a soft spot for Cheeta.

I looked up to find Evelyn standing over my desk. "Whoops! I've gotta run." I hung up the phone and hastily spread a professional smile across my face.

My boss tried to erase her startled expression, but she wasn't quite fast enough. Not for the first time, I wondered what she really thought of me. I knew that she despaired of my ever gaining the level of professionalism that she hoped for. She pursed her lips and said, "Jane, I have a special project for you."

Oh, goody. "Sure. What do you want me to do?"

"The fire marshal came by yesterday. He's concerned about the papers on top of the bookshelves, down in the basement. If the sprinklers ever came on, they couldn't flow freely with everything stacked up there."

If I recalled, Evelyn was the one who had decided to use the bookshelves as auxiliary file space. She'd argued that there was never enough storage in a special collection like ours. "Did you want me to move them?" I asked, trying to cut to the chase.

"I think you should read through them. See if there's anything worth keeping. They should be duplicates of our vendor records from the eighties. That'll give you a good idea of the management issues the library has faced over time."

Great. Paper records of purchases made decades ago. And Evelyn wondered why we ran out of space. "I'll get right on it."

So, this was the glory of management. Kit got to spend her day working with patrons, answering questions, and I ended up with dust-reddened eyes, with vision blurred by peering at endless invoices. I would have loved the chance to brew a cup of coffee or two, even the old-fashioned coffees I used to make, with time-consuming foamed milk and patron-confusing choices like macchiatos and cappuccinos. How nostalgic I could become for the words *con panna*.

If I was going to waste an afternoon sorting meaningless material, I'd rather be doing it in my own basement, at home. Maybe I could find the courage to open my books, try to read from them before the writing faded away, attempt to force my way back to magic or destroy every last volume trying. At least then I'd know where I stood. Then, I'd know that the books would never trouble me again.

Once again, I was going to meet with Gran and Clara after work. I was going to try—once again—to lead them through a bout of spellcasting. Try—once again—to figure out a way to bolster their powers. Try—once again—to shape our little witchy community into something that could support me, that could feed my powers back to me. My frustration made a headache pound to life behind my eyes.

I sighed. Life as Will's mundane girlfriend, even a girlfriend surrounded by dusty decades-old invoices, was sounding better and better.

Around four o'clock, Kit appeared in the doorway of the

storeroom, bearing a cup of coffee and a trio of Bunny Bites like a peace offering. Or some upscale prison meal. "I saved the last three Bites for you."

"Thanks," I said, smiling wanly.

Kit waited while I fortified myself with one. She declined my offer of another. Settling on the edge of my work-table, she took off her tricorn hat and began turning it from corner to corner to corner. "What's up?" I asked.

"I've made a decision."

"About?" I took a sip of coffee and leaned back in my chair, rubbing at my neck to ease a kink.

"Grad school."

"Wonderful!" I said. I managed to sound enthusiastic, even though my first thought was a wail of despair. My intern was going to abandon me now? She was going to leave me to the tender mercies of Evelyn and a pack of pre-schoolers? "Who's the lucky winner? Brown or Harvard?"

"Maryland."

I blinked. "Excuse me?" Not that there was anything wrong with the University of Maryland. It was just a mile or two outside of D.C.; it sprawled across a huge campus. But with 35,000 students, it dwarfed Harvard or Brown. And I certainly hadn't heard anything phenomenal about its public policy programs, certainly not anything special enough to lead a full scholarship Ivy League student to change her mind.

"Maryland. Library school. I can apply by February and start classes over the summer."

"But you're going into public policy! You're going to build the schools of tomorrow! You're going to save children from themselves, and create the communities of our future."

Kit smiled wryly. "I know that's what I said I wanted to do. But I really like what I'm doing here—the programs we run, knowing our individual patrons. I don't want to discuss policy, in big, broad terms. I'd rather implement a specific reading program for teenage boys, something that will bring them in and keep them here."

"Kit…" I wasn't sure how to respond. I understood exactly what she was saying. I, too, had chosen to be a librarian because I liked to work with people. I liked solving problems on a human scale. But Kit could go *anywhere*. She could do anything. "Are you sure?"

"I'm obviously not thrilled about the whole public policy thing, right? I mean, what sort of enthusiastic grad student puts two Ivy League schools on hold for months while she decides what she wants to be when she grows up? I've decided. I know what I'm going to be. A librarian."

I grinned. "I'm happy for you."

"I need your help, though." She leaned in close, as if Evelyn had surveillance equipment in the now-bared sprinkler heads. "I need to figure out a way to keep working here. I know that the library doesn't have any money to pay me full-time, long-term. But maybe I could write a grant or something? Something that I wouldn't even have to tell Evelyn about, until after it's a done deal."

I remembered my own attempts at grant writing and how

poorly they'd been received by our boss. "I wouldn't recommend that."

"What should I do, then? I probably won't get a scholarship if I go to library school. I'm going to need to work full-time."

I sighed. "Let me think about it. Maybe Mr. Potter can help us come up with something."

Kit grinned. "Thanks. For now, though, we'll keep it a secret?"

"Mum's the word."

She turned to leave, but then stopped. "Have you picked up your messages this afternoon?"

"No." I gestured to the stacks of paper around me. "I didn't want to give myself any excuse not to finish this."

"Well, your phone rang all morning. And that David guy started leaving messages at the circulation desk, right around noon. He's been calling back every hour on the hour."

I sighed, even as my heart skipped toward concern. "Thanks. I'll call him back."

A phone hung on the wall of the storage room. I punched 9 to get an outside line and then added David's number. He answered halfway through the first ring. "Montrose."

"It's me. Look, I've got a job here, and you can't just treat the circulation desk like they're your private answering service."

"Neko's gone."

"What?" My knees melted. My body sagged against the wall, and I would have fallen without its support.

"She took him. She claimed him."

"Who?"

"Ariel."

No. It wasn't possible. Sure, David had told me weeks ago that Neko was vulnerable, that he was up for grabs, since my own powers had virtually disappeared. But Ariel? Neko? I couldn't breathe. I couldn't think.

"There are rules!" I heard the shout behind my words. "She's not even a witch! She can't do this! You've got to stop her!"

"You're not listening to me, Jane. She already has. She registered her bond to him with Hecate's Court. It was just a matter of time. Anyone with power could bind him."

"But she doesn't have power! Everything she has belongs to me!"

Everything. Including Neko. Including my familiar, the creature who had guided me along all of my witchy stumblings, who had taken my force and reflected it back to me hundreds of times over the past two years.

Neko, who was accustomed to roaming the city streets, to traveling wherever he wanted, whenever he wanted. *Our* bond had been created under the light of the full moon; he had been entitled to that roaming. But his ties to Ariel would be different. He would be restrained. He would be restricted, like an ordinary familiar, bound to an ordinary witch. He would be miserable.

"What can we do, David?"

"I don't know."

Those were the most frightening words in the world. David always knew. David always told *me*. He always had a plan and a path, a way for us to get through anything that happened.

"I'm leaving work now," I said. Evelyn's management exercise be damned. Neko's disappearance was more important.

"I'll meet you at the cottage."

Gran and Clara were already in the living room when I burst through the front door. The entire contents of my jewelry box were spilled across the coffee table, and Majom was picking through the detritus, separating my necklaces and earrings and bracelets with the dedicated intensity of a heart surgeon making his final stitches. Nuri sat on one of the couches, cocking her head as the mid-October light glinted off my treasures.

"Hello, dear. We decided to make ourselves at home." Gran saluted me with a mug of tea.

"You need more honey," Clara announced. "You really shouldn't get the stuff from the grocery store, though. Those little plastic bears are cute, but fresh lavender blossom honey from free-range bees will enhance your dream recollection."

I wanted to point out that all bees were free range; that was the entire idea of having insect pollinators flying around. It wasn't worth the battle, though. I didn't have the time.

"David will be here in a moment," I announced. "Neko is gone. Ariel has him."

It took a moment for them to register what I'd said, but then Nuri cried out, a horrible, grating shriek of loss. Majom scurried across the living room and buried his face in Clara's skirts. Gran was the first to recover. "What can we do?"

I had never seen her look so stricken.

Sure, I'd seen her sick. I'd seen her fight off walking pneumonia for weeks. I'd seen her in a hospital bed, with oxygen, scaring the life out of me as she drew each rattling breath as if it might be her last.

But I'd never seen her afraid. I'd never seen her totally at a loss for direction.

Before I could try to figure out an answer, David walked through the front door. I whirled to face him. "What else can you tell us? What else have you found out?"

He shook his head. "There isn't much to say. Familiars are registered with Hecate's Court. It happens automatically, when a witch bonds with them." He cast a quick look toward Nuri and Majom, clinging to their witches. I crossed my arms over my chest and tried not to feel like the odd woman out. I longed to feel Neko by my side.

"The connection was registered some time during the night. There isn't any background information, there's no enforcement body. The Court just receives notice of the binding, so that they can hold a witch accountable if anything goes wrong down the line."

"And if I want to say that Neko is still bound to me?"

"Then you contact the Court. Using your powers."

My nonexistent powers. Or at least the ones I had no access to. His words felt like a slap in the face. Automatically, I reached out to gauge the current depth of my arcane ability. The same handful of precious drops sat there, the last gift that Ariel had given me when I confronted her on the steps of the Lincoln Memorial. Nothing else that we had done, nothing else that I had taught Gran and Clara, had made the slightest bit of difference.

Clara spoke. "Maybe *we* could do something, instead. Maybe I could reach out on Jeanette's behalf?" I was ready to scream at her, to remind her for the thousandth time that I had changed my name after she'd abandoned me.

David's voice cut through my rage, though, freezing it with his simple denial. "It doesn't work that way, Clara. You can't argue for anyone else."

"It's not fair!" I protested, because I couldn't think of anything else to say. I felt sick, as if I had swallowed a frozen, greasy stone.

David was silent for a moment, and then he gestured toward Gran and Clara. "Why don't you four go downstairs. Keep working on the summoning spell you tried on Sunday—you can practice it together. Jane and I have to talk." Obediently, they all trooped to the basement.

I wanted to call out to them. I wanted to make them come back.

But that was ridiculous. I knew what David was going to ask me. I knew what he was going to make me say. I knew that he was going to force me to answer the question he'd asked at the Lincoln Memorial; he wanted to know what had happened when I'd made Ariel, what had gone wrong. While I didn't want to tell *him*, I couldn't imagine admitting the inner workings of my smutty little mind in front of my own mother and grandmother.

I sank onto the couch and clutched my brocade skirts in my fists. I was so accustomed to my Peabridge attire that I automatically shifted the hoops out of my way.

David sat on the other couch, but he leaned forward, every line of his body expressing the urgency of his question. "I've let you avoid talking about this. But we're out of time. What happened when you created Ariel?"

My palms were suddenly slick with sweat. I closed my eyes, as if that would make it easier for me to recite what I'd done. I could picture the three of us, huddled in my basement. I could remember Neko—Neko!—leaning close to my side. I took a deep breath past a pang of loss so sharp that I thought I would cry.

"I had all the elements at hand," I said, remembering how the magic had felt. "I'd already mixed the earth and water, breathed the air." I could remember the tension, the awkward sexual energy that had arced between David and me. Now, sitting in my living room, he nodded, as if he remembered it, too. "I said the spell. I said the words out loud."

I struggled for a way to explain. I fought for a way to tell him what had happened. I longed for my old powers, for my witchy abilities, because I was certain that I could have reached out to his mind, transmitted my utter mortification without needing to reduce it to words. But I had no powers. I had no familiar. I was no longer a witch. "I thought about you," I whispered. "About us."

He caught his breath, but I held up a hand, begging him not to interrupt me, because I'd never find the courage to go on if I stopped there. "I thought about you, and a stupid poster that Melissa had in the bakery. An actor, who looked like you, who was playing Prospero. The poster had a slogan, Empower The Arts. It all got tangled in the power of naming. I didn't understand what I was doing. I broke the connection to the anima. I twisted it. I did something wrong, because I couldn't stay focused. I got lost, thinking about you. About…what happened."

I dashed tears off my cheeks as I wrapped up lamely. "I didn't know how broken she was, in those first few hours. I didn't understand just how far I'd let her slip, just how far my concentration had strayed. I was supposed to give her the mission to rebuild my strength, but it got all mixed up. She ended up with Ariel's mission, Prospero's goals, from the play. From the actor *in* the play. I don't know how to make any of it right. I don't know how to change any of it. I don't know how to get Neko back!"

I was crying honestly, then, ripping sobs that gasped out my confusion and frustration of the past two months, my terror of what I'd done to my familiar. David started to move toward me, reached a hand across the chasm between our seats, but then he pulled back. I wanted him to touch me, I wanted him to soothe me with his voice, with his fingers.

But at the same time I knew that his decision was right, that I had made another choice. I wanted Will *and* him; I wanted to be a woman and a witch. I wanted the world I'd known forever, and the magic I'd known for two short years. I wanted everything, and nothing at all.

"I'm sorry," I whispered, hiding my face in my hands.

"It's my fault as much as yours."

"No," I said. "I was the witch. I was the one who was supposed to hold the magic."

"And I was the one who was supposed to keep you safe."

It didn't matter. We could both be wrong. We weren't any closer to a way out of the mess.

"So when you work with your grandmother, with your mother?" he asked at last. "Is it the same problem? Am I blocking your thoughts there?"

"It's not you," I protested automatically. I thought for a moment, and then I answered his question more thoroughly. "No. The problem there is something different. I only know how to teach them the way that I was taught, the way that you taught me. I know how to push them, how to drive them, how to force them to take on more power. But they don't have enough power on their own—even if they used every scrap that's there."

For the first time, I thought about what that meant. I was using the only model for witchcraft that I'd seen. David himself had learned through conventional means; he taught me the only way he'd seen witches taught, by the Coven. By a group of women who struggled and snapped like a pack of feral dogs, fighting to be the strongest witch in the gathering.

Sure, I had risen naturally in their ranks because of my

own late, lamented, ingrained power. But Gran would never have that raw strength. Clara neither.

"If I could just get the two of them to work together…" I fought for words, trying to picture what I was describing, how it would feel. "If they shared their energy with each other… If they used their familiars to focus their own force outward, *toward* each other, rather than inward…"

The more I rambled, the more sense it made. When Nuri helped Gran, the pair was able to do precisely as much as Gran could handle. My grandmother was the limit; she was the cap. When her fragile body reached its full potential, the partnership was done. The same with Clara, actually—her cap was higher, but the limitation was the same.

If they worked together, though, if they reflected power off of each other… They each excelled in different ways. They each had different strengths. If Clara harvested some of Gran's success, grew it on her own, bolstered it through Majom…

Magic wasn't science, I had told them. Our arcane powers weren't subject to the laws of physics. Two plus two could be greater than four, if we could only figure out the way to shatter addition.

"Gran!" I called. "Clara!" I took the steps to the basement so rapidly that I skipped half of them, relying on the handrail to keep from falling.

They looked up at me from the cracked leather couch. From Neko's cracked leather couch. I tried not to think of how often I had seen him perched on the sofa, eager to help with a magical working. Nuri and Majom huddled on the floor, clearly disconsolate.

"Let's try something new!" I said.

"Jane, dear, are you all right?"

"I'm fine, Gran. I think that I have an answer, though. I think that I've finally figured out what we've been doing wrong."

"Dear, I don't know that we're doing anything *wrong*. I just think that I'm not strong enough to help out as much as you'd like. Even the Coven wasn't able to do anything with me last year." My heart twisted to see her disappointment, the grim lines beside her mouth.

"Hush," I said. "We're not the Coven." I looked at Clara, made sure that I had her attention. "Both of you, separately—I want you to try the light spell."

Light. The easiest spell I knew. The one that had cost me the last of my power. The one that I had used to show Will who I was, what I was. The one I had used to convert myself from a witch into a woman.

Gran and Clara had worked it a dozen times over the past month, trying to harness its simple formula, trying to convert its basic order into something new. Now, they thinned their lips, nearly identical expressions reminding me that they, too, were tired, that they, too, wanted a way out of this mess.

They chanted together:

"Dark shies;
Light vies.

Clear eyes,
Fire rise."

A tiny flame spread on Gran's palm, ruby light so fragile that I might have imagined it. Nuri nestled closer to my grandmother, leaning her entire body against Gran's frail form, and the light flickered brighter for a heartbeat, only to fade again.

Clara was only doing a little better. Her flame was emerald, filling her palm briefly when Majom leaned in to assist.

Reflexively, I reached out for their powers, tried to gather them close to myself. Nothing. I had no way to grasp what they had done.

"Okay," I said. "Let it fade. Now, we're going to do something different." I gestured toward Clara's familiar. "Go over there, Majom," I said. "Sit beside Gran." The boy looked at me quizzically, checking back with Clara to make sure that it was all right to move.

"Go ahead," she said. "I'm not going anywhere."

He cuddled next to Gran, who reflexively dropped a hand to his shock of white hair. I nodded and then said to Nuri, "And you, sit next to Clara." The woman complied, although she twisted her head at an odd angle, as if she did not trust Gran to stay seated on the couch. Clara settled a commanding hand on Nuri's shoulder, keeping a steady eye on me.

"All right," I said, taking a deep breath. "Now, Gran and

Clara, put your free hands together. Cup them, there, between you." They matched actions to my words. "We're going to try it again. But this time, the familiars are going to reflect power *across* your grouping. You're going to share. You're going to build the flame together."

I looked at David, silently asking him if he thought this would work. He tilted his head to one side, but he wasn't predicting failure. Instead, he was admitting ignorance. He was saying that he had no idea what would come of my attempts.

I forced a shaky smile. They would try it. They would try it because they loved me. They would try it because they believed in me. They would try it because they wanted me to be happy, they wanted me to find my powers once again. My powers. And Neko.

"Together," I said.

And they recited the simple spell once more.

"Dark shies;
Light vies.
Clear eyes,
Fire rise."

Two lights blossomed on their palms, red and green, the visible symbol of their strength, however limited that might be. This time, though, the familiars shifted, vaguely uneasy with the new arrangement, utterly unaccustomed to the different balance I was forcing on them. I smiled encouragement, and Gran reflexively pulled Majom closer. Clara leaned against Nuri, as if she were sharing a secret with the woman.

And the light grew.

Crimson swirled into evergreen, like stars sprinkling across a miniature galaxy. The ball of combined fire pulsed like a double heartbeat, filling first Gran's palm, then Clara's. As the witches realized what they were doing, as they recognized their joined strength, the light grew brighter. The ball swelled, expanded, filling the space above their forearms. Hazel eyes met hazel eyes above the light, and something silent, something secret passed between the woman who had raised me and the woman who had given me birth.

Gran looked at me, astonishment stretching her mouth into an O. "It's so bright!"

Clara laughed. My mother, the woman who lost herself in New Age frippery, distanced herself from true emotion, from all honest feelings, laughed.

Majom fed on their excitement, starting to bounce up and down on the couch. Nuri craned her neck, shrugging her shoulders in a way that released tension none of us had known she'd held.

David stepped forward, serious and dark against the brilliant play of light. "That's enough," he said. "Don't tax yourself too much. Not this first time."

Carefully, supporting each other, balancing their strength through each other's familiars, Gran and Clara let the light die down. As the flames folded in on themselves, ruby chased emerald, swirling like a star fighting to be born.

Just before the light popped out of existence, I heard a chime, deep inside my own psyche. A solitary drop of crimson power slipped into the well of my abilities, followed almost immediately by a precious sliver of green. My strange commune of witches and familiars, of relatives and friends, was feeding my damaged power at last.

Reflexively, I reached out to share the good news with Neko, only to be reminded brutally of his absence. Watching my mother and grandmother, watching their familiars, watching my warder all celebrating the new vision of witch-craft that we had used, that we had *created*, I felt nothing but the chill of loss.

We still needed to find Ariel. We still needed to fight to get Neko back.

17

We spent two weeks looking for Neko. Two weeks of combing the city, tracking down reports—no matter how vague—of the Artistic Avenger. Two weeks of driving by landmarks, looking for the next public display of Ariel's fanaticism.

David even took it upon himself to check with the Washington Coven. I volunteered to go with him, to see if I could extract any information from that bitchy sisterhood, but he shook his head ruefully, saying that he'd probably get further without my tagging along. Given the way I'd thrown their invitation back in their collective face the year before, he was probably right.

The loss of Neko cut deep; I ached every time I thought of him stranded, alone, tied to whatever calculating magic

Ariel had accumulated since I'd last seen her. I forced myself to call Jacques every morning, to let him know that nothing had changed, that we were still looking, still trying, still hoping.

I came to hate my anima.

Nearly every night, I worked with Gran and Clara, attempting to bolster my own powers. Our new technique, the communal sharing of powers, wasn't perfect. Gran needed to adjust to Majom's childishness, to his inability to sit still and his constant exploration of anything new around him. Clara needed to accept Nuri's oddness, her awkwardness as she provided her familiar services. Gran tired quickly, requiring everyone to shift the way they shared energies, the way they exchanged information.

As I watched the four of them learn to work together, though, I was proud. Every night, I saw my little community grow stronger, learn to trust each other more on the magical frontier. Each successful working dripped additional power into my depleted well.

One night, a week after Gran and Clara first worked the light spell together, I dared to open up one of my books—the old classic, *On Awakyning and Bynding a Familiarus*. I selected it in a fit of hopeless nostalgia, remembering how I had read my first spell from its pages, awakening Neko to my service.

Sure enough, the parchment stayed stable. No words ran off the page. No ink faded as my eyes pored over the words. I read until after midnight, hoping to find something I could use, something that would draw Neko back to me. For the first time since Ariel had fled, I was able to use my collection, to research everything I could find about animas.

But there was nothing.

From that night onward, though, I tried to find Neko with the limited powers I had regained. I would touch the link between us, send a thought down the well-worn channel that had bound us together for so many months. Each night, after Gran and Clara left, taking their familiars with them, I would light a taper and settle down on the cracked leather couch. I stared into the flame, trying to remember how I had felt when Neko was beside me every day.

Annoyed.

Okay, I tried not to remember that. I tried to remember how he had bolstered my powers, how he had bettered my witchcraft.

Occasionally, I'd get a tantalizing hint of him. I'd see him— or something that my astral senses insisted *could* be him— huddling in an enclosed space. Try as I might, I couldn't break through, though, couldn't get to the core of my vision.

I wondered if Neko even knew where he was, if he could tell me, if I ever did manage to reach him directly. He was accustomed to roaming so freely; I had controlled him the way that I would have wanted to be controlled if our relationship had been reversed.

Ariel wasn't likely to be such a fan of the Golden Rule. Her binding Neko would surely have brought him under new restraints. She could keep him in a literal closet. She could even return him to his statue form when she was not actively working magic. She could do whatever she saw fit to do. She was his witch.

And I was *her* witch. The irony did not escape me. I was supposed to be able to manage her, restrict her, use her to my own best advantage.

And I would, if I could only find her again.

Of course, I couldn't work on witchcraft every waking moment. Will came by the cottage every night, even though he was busy with his own projects, his architectural plans. Sometimes we were too exhausted to talk; we settled for spooning underneath the comforter in my bedroom, falling asleep in companionable silence. We shared quick breakfasts, snatches of daytime conversation over the phone. I got used to e-mailing him three or four times a day. The little time we had together was easy, comfortable.

One night, when Gran had declared herself too tired to attempt any magical workings at all, Will and I went on a double date with Melissa and Rob. We ended up at a wood oven pizzeria, gorging on individual pies. Melissa and I gave Rob an inordinately hard time for putting pineapple on his pizza. Will and I traded slices—one of my pepperoni and goat cheese for one of his black olive and pesto.

Melissa and I went to the bathroom together, and I started crying while I was making lipstick fish mouths at myself in the mirror.

"What's wrong?" She ran a paper towel under the faucet and passed it to me. I tried to dab underneath my eyes.

"It's perfect."

"And you always cry when things are perfect."

I sniffed inelegantly—snorted actually—grateful that Will was nowhere close enough to hear. "I always thought that we'd do this. That we'd get together with our boyfriends. That we'd just have fun."

"And?"

"And I never realized how much I would love it."

"I don't understand you at all, Jane Madison."

"I should be working with Gran and Clara. I should be trying to find Neko and Ariel. Instead, I'm here with you and the guys."

There. I'd said it out loud.

"You're doing all that you can do." I started to protest, and she shook her head. "Jane, listen to me. You're not a bad person, if you decide to walk away from the witchcraft. You're allowed to give it back. It's not like someone has a gun to your head."

"Ariel—"

"You'll find her. I know you will. And you'll restore Neko. And then you'll make the biggest decision of your life. But I'll be there for you, no matter what you do decide."

I managed a wavery smile. "Even if we never double date again?"

"Even if. But I've got to tell you—Will's a lot of fun. He's a good man, Jane."

"I know."

And he was. The best I'd ever dated. Even if he would

never, ever understand the secret part of me, the inner part of me, the witch.

My growing bond with Gran and Clara stressed the importance of community, the importance of sharing. Half a dozen times, I caught myself starting to tell Will about a spell that they had worked, about a moment when the familiars mirrored something so precisely, so perfectly, that it seemed as if all of us had created something entirely new. Entirely fresh. Entirely different.

Entirely beyond his realm of understanding.

He always listened. He always expressed enthusiasm or concern or quiet, steady support—whatever I needed most at the moment. But I knew that he did not truly get it. He couldn't. He'd never felt magic sparking through him, never known the heady thrum of that energy, the steady *being* of magic filling him, carrying him away.

But Melissa was right. I could make the decision later.

As if running a witches' commune and balancing the first true reciprocated love of my life wasn't enough, I had Gran to worry about. She had decided to scuttle all of her wedding plans.

Clara argued with her. I argued with her. Even Nuri squawked a rebuke.

Gran insisted that it was unseemly. That we couldn't throw the party of the century if Neko had—God forbid— died. And we wouldn't throw the party with him missing.

"Gran," I argued in the fifteenth round of our debate. "He *isn't* dead. I'd know it. Or David would."

"We'll wait till he comes back, then."

I forced myself to keep a gentle tone. "He might never come back, Gran. You can't put your life on hold for him." Words of wisdom I'd do well to listen to myself. I hurried on to the one true weapon I had in my arsenal. "What will Uncle George think? This is his wedding, too."

In the end, we compromised. Gran's long years of service with Concert Opera let her cancel her reservation at the performance hall without any penalty. We decided that the Peabridge auditorium would do just as well for the ceremony; the reference room—already equipped with substantial tables and plenty of chairs—would be fine for the reception.

We canceled the band and the caterers. A taped collection of Pavarotti arias would do as well as the dozen live performers Gran had contemplated. We'd make do with deli trays from the local grocery store. In a moment of Neko-worthy inspiration, we realized that we could sell off the pounds and pounds of orange Jordan almonds during the weeks leading up to Halloween, marketing them to library patrons from the Peabridge's coffee bar as "Halloween Treats." They went like hotcakes—I liked to think that we were providing the hot autumn hostess gift in Georgetown that year.

In her newly abstemious mood, Gran decided that a floor-length veil was overkill; in fact, she ditched her entire white wedding gown completely. She had a lovely gabardine suit, its graceful evergreen skirt and jacket perfect for presiding over Concert Opera board meetings—or an autumn evening wedding. The hairdressers, with their sweeping updos, were deemed unnecessary, as well. Besides, Clara had never agreed to wear anything other than a gauze skirt and a peasant blouse, her hair neatly brushed for the occasion.

Melissa was still on board with the wedding cake, but plans for the marzipan monstrosity were set aside. In Neko's honor, we went with plain white cake, covered in lots and lots of buttercream. We laid in a couple of cases of champagne, for toasts.

Even the matchbooks weren't a total loss. We decided to hand them out with the votive candles, little gifts for everyone who attended. Individualized opera CDs mercifully became a thing of the past.

The funny thing was, no one really noticed how much the plans were scaled back. Gran was disappointed at first, giving up the party of her dreams, but she truly believed that she was doing the right thing, in support of Neko, wherever he was. Uncle George was actually relieved—I could see smiles take over from the vague air of puzzlement that he'd been sporting for the past several weeks.

The only thing that survived the wedding purge wholly intact was my dress. Orange and silver, now in commemoration of Neko. As I pulled it on over my head, I had to admit that he'd done a stunning job with the alterations. The neckline still plunged, but it no longer gapped in an embarrassing way. The butt-bow would always be a bit much, but what sort of maid of honor would I be, in a dress that I could conceive of wearing anywhere else?

The sash and bow glittered in the moonlight as I walked from my cottage to the Peabridge. It was Halloween night. Samhain. The importance of the Witches' Sabbath seemed emphasized by the full moon that sat heavy in the sky overhead. Once in a blue moon…

I knew from my colonial research that a blue moon was a farmer's term, a reference to a second full moon in a month. They only coincided rarely with Halloween—five or six times a century—and the night of Gran's wedding, in a streak of witchy luck. Not that any of the guests would know or care.

Will and Rob had agreed to serve as ushers, helping the guests to their seats in the Peabridge auditorium. The notion of "friend of the bride" and "friend of the groom" was meaningless when the bride and groom had been dating for two and a half decades. People ended up sitting with friends and enjoying themselves. We'd planned on starting at eight o'clock, a quiet evening wedding, but people arrived late, victims of Halloween and the riotous street celebration that took over the core of Georgetown's commercial streets.

My library assistant, Kit, served as wedding coordinator for the evening. She made sure that the key participants were ready on time, that all the men's suits were tugged into alignment, that all the women had rubbed traces of lipstick off their teeth. Relying on the Peabridge's new sound system (a recent gift from Mr. Potter—fitting, even though he had not known how it would be used when he made the donation), Kit played Handel's "Ombra mai fu" for the processional.

With Mr. Potter serving as best man and as my escort, I walked down the auditorium aisle, holding a nosegay of sweetheart roses that matched Gran's own simple bouquet. Mr. Potter whispered a kiss against my cheek at the foot of the aisle, and then we both turned to watch Gran enter.

David walked beside her, offering his arm with all the formal gravity of a warder. He shortened his stride to match her own, managing to balance concern for her welfare with the recognition that this was her evening, her moment to be the center of attention for all the assembled guests. When he brought her to my side, he completed a short, formal bow. Unplanned, Gran raised her fingers to his cheek, thanking him as if he were a Boy Scout who had helped her across a particularly busy street. Flaunting custom, he whispered back up the aisle, taking a seat near the back of the auditorium.

I could feel Gran trembling beside me—nearly overwhelmed by excitement and the exhaustion of our nightly magical study. I leaned close and whispered, "Are you all right?"

"Oh, yes, dear." She actually patted my arm, as if *I* were the one who needed comfort. "I'm perfectly fine." She looked across the aisle and found Uncle George's eyes. He was standing, straight and proud, a single sweetheart rose tucked into his buttonhole. The phrase "he only had eyes for her" was created for that moment. I somehow suspected that Uncle George would have dragged Gran down to City Hall just about any time in the past two and a half decades, if she would have agreed.

Judge Anderson, a member of the Concert Opera board, did the formal honors. The civil ceremony was simple and straightforward, delivered with all the solemnity a wedding deserved. Nevertheless, the judge started by taking a few minutes to deliver some personal words to Gran and Uncle George.

"Sarah, George, I've known you now for nearly twenty years. Together, we've seen pearl fishers and bohemians, emperors and queens. But rarely have we seen two people who love each other with the steady, simple love the two of you share."

As the judge went on, I looked out over the assembled guests. Most were nodding at the various operatic references. A few were leaning over to whisper to friends, obviously noting some remembered detail from productions past.

Clara sat in the front row, Majom beside her. My mother had stepped up to the plate in a major way; she had given her familiar a Rubik's Cube to keep him occupied and relatively quiet. He was twisting the block methodically, a frown puckering his forehead. I figured we'd have at least five minutes before he realized he could peel off the stickers and reattach them to any face of the cube, completing the puzzle in an unconventional flash.

As I watched Clara, I tried not to be frustrated by her attire. The gauze skirt, I'd been expecting. The peasant blouse was a given. But she had insisted on wearing her pink kunzite jewelry. She had long advocated that the crystal meant unconditional mother love; I could still remember her lecturing me on the stone while poor Gran was collapsing on a bench at the Natural History Museum, victim of undiagnosed pneumonia. Clara wore a silver pendant, with a faceted trillion cut stone reflecting the auditorium's subdued light.

Unconditional mother love. From the mother who was leaving for Arizona in a week.

Clara had not wavered from her plan to return to Sedona. She had mentioned it endlessly during the past several weeks, taking every opportunity to tell Gran and me that she was tired during our training sessions, that she had stayed up late packing, that she had gotten up early to take some books to the library for their annual sale. She mentioned Goodwill, Salvation Army and a dozen other charities, all of which seemed were reaping a healthy benefit from my mother's decision to run away. She even told Majom that he would love the red rock box canyon just outside of town. She was definitely leaving, definitely abandoning me. Again.

I'd asked myself why a dozen times. I'd tried to decide if she was leaving because she really missed Sedona, or if she was leaving because she couldn't stand being around me. I thought that maybe—just maybe—she was staging this whole thing so that Gran and I would beg her to stay.

But I took my cues from Gran. Gran, who simply smiled and nodded as Clara talked about packing. Gran, who merely agreed that Majom would love playing outdoors in the Southwest. Gran, who had made her peace with Clara's broken family bonds decades before.

I tried, anyway. More often than not, I found myself bitter, angry, more resentful than I'd been at any time since Clara decided to turn my life upside down by returning.

More to the immediate point, I couldn't imagine how we could find Neko, once Clara had skipped town. Gran and I would work together, of course. Under ordinary circumstances—whatever *those* were where magic was concerned—my power had been jump-started enough that I could work with Gran, that we could bolster each other's astral force. But with Nuri as our only familiar… I wasn't sure that we could do anything without Clara and Majom tied into our community.

Of course Clara hadn't considered our needs in the slightest. She'd made up her mind to leave back in August, and nothing that happened had changed her thinking. I didn't know why I was surprised. She hadn't thought of me twenty-three years ago, when she ran away the first time. Why would anything be different now?

I shifted from foot to foot, trying to ignore my orange-dyed slippers, which didn't quite fit. I could feel a pinch across my toes, where the silver bows attached. I'd worn them as a silent salute to Neko, but I already regretted the nostalgic urge. Black ballet slippers would have been a better memorial. Commemoration. He wasn't dead. Missing, but not dead.

Judge Anderson was saying, "So many of our operas use images of food, of feasts, to explain the richness of love."

I looked out over the rest of the crowd, determined not to dwell on Clara, not to let my bitterness taint this evening for Gran and Uncle George. Melissa was sitting in the front row, as well, on the opposite side from Clara. I couldn't remember the last time I'd seen her in a dress, but she had donned a navy velvet jumper for the occasion. Her cheeks were flushed, as if she were still warming up from her walk from the bakery.

Rob sat beside her. The guy was clearly smitten. He listened to the judge, laughing at the appropriate times, nodding judiciously. But his every motion was attuned to my best friend. He seemed *aware* of where she was, what she was doing. Even sitting in the auditorium chairs, he seemed to be waiting for her.

I thought about all those years of horrible first dates, all the stories that Melissa had shared. She had kept Gran in stitches so many times, relating disaster after disaster. It would be patronizing for me to say that I was proud of her. I was happy for her. Pleased for her. She deserved the guy she finally got.

Thinking of guys, I had to look at Will. His glasses were tilted on his nose, and his curly hair was doing its best to impersonate a rat's nest. He'd put on a dark suit for the occasion. He'd teased me all afternoon, saying that with his black and my orange, we made the perfect Halloween couple. He'd sweetened the teasing with a couple of fun-size Snickers bars, so I didn't complain too loudly.

I couldn't help but think what I had been doing a year ago, how I had stood against the Washington Coven.

I had to look at David.

He had taken a seat toward the back of the room. He was clearly trying to step back from this family event, trying to remove himself from his role as warder for all three of us witchy women. Even from the podium, I could see the glint of his flawless white shirt, and I knew that his charcoal suit would be perfect.

I could see—could feel—his eyes meet mine across the room.

I wasn't certain, though, what he was saying, what he was thinking. Was he also remembering that other Halloween night, a year ago? Was he thinking of the magic I had worked, strong and powerful, with my now-missing familiar at my side? Was he remembering my humiliation in front of a group of women who had never had my best interests at heart, even when they had pretended to reach out to me?

Reflexively, I stretched for the bond between David and me, the magical one. I had tested the connection obsessively since power started to trickle back into my storehouse. I knew precisely how much weight I needed to place on the link, how much I needed to apply to pull him toward me. I could measure out my energy precisely, count it like a miser's coins. I could control it, without sparks and confusion, without whipsaw unpredictability.

Will shifted in the front row, and I backed off from the bond, as if the touch had burned me. David didn't move.

Judge Anderson was finally intoning the wedding vows. Gran and Uncle George repeated their lines carefully, proudly. At the judge's instruction, the couple exchanged rings. They kissed.

They were married.

After twenty-five years of dating, after whatever tempests had brewed in their respective teapots, after decades of saying that there was no need for change, for formality, Gran and Uncle George were one couple, united in the eyes of the law.

Kit pressed a button and Andrea Bocelli's voice rang out, filling the auditorium with Fauré's "Chanson D'Amour."

Gran and Uncle George led the way down the aisle. I followed, taking Mr. Potter's arm and reminding myself to walk slowly, to ignore all the eyes that had to be drawn to the silver lamé bow across my ass.

When we passed David's chair, he was gone.

The guests gathered in the upstairs reference room, eager to congratulate Gran and Uncle George, to compliment Judge Anderson on a job well done. Melissa swiftly took on the job of cake-cutter, and Will volunteered to open a bottle or six of champagne. Everyone chatted and laughed, and I knew that the simple ceremony had been better than anything Gran had hoped for.

Still, I sought her out after a few minutes, to make sure that she wasn't too wistful about the party that hadn't been.

Uncle George was clapping his hand on Mr. Potter's shoulder, regaling a group of opera friends with a story about some ancient production. Gran had taken the opportunity to snag a chair, slipping off her sensible black pumps.

"It was beautiful, Gran." I sat beside her, using my years of Peabridge costume expertise to shift the lamé bow toward the side.

"Thank you, dear. It's wonderful to be surrounded by friends. I'm just so sorry that Neko couldn't be here."

"We're doing everything we can," I said.

She sighed, and then she looked around the room. "There, dear. Why don't you bring David a nice slice of cake, and a glass of champagne? He looks so lonely standing by himself."

Our warder was, indeed, lurking by himself, staking out a corner by my not-so-beloved coffee bar. I didn't want to be rude, but I also didn't want to be the one to bring him into the crowd. I was still more than a little unnerved by how easily I had reached out to him, by how routinely I had touched the connection between us during the service. I tried to tell myself that it was the memories, it was the calendar. It was the power of Samhain that had set my nerves a-jangle.

"Some cake?" Will said, appearing from nowhere, balancing three plates. He settled one in front of me and one in front of Gran, taking the third for himself. Gran looked pointedly at mine before glancing toward David, but I managed not to understand her instruction. I was spared a direct command by Mr. Potter's jovial voice as he stepped to the center of the room.

"Ladies!" he exclaimed. "Gentlemen! Friends!" It took a

moment for the mutter of side conversations to die down. "Now is the time for the best man to give his toast!"

"Hear, hear!" some hearty soul called. I smiled. Gran's friends were formal in a quaint, old-fashioned way that I had loved ever since I was a little girl. Before Mr. Potter could begin his speech, I snuck a bite of wedding cake. The buttercream was flawless—rich, smooth vanilla, the perfect complement to the delicate cake beneath. Neko would have been in heaven.

"It's the custom," Mr. Potter said, "for the best man to tell about his longtime friendship with the groom. I'm supposed to tell an amusing little anecdote about a time we shared, a time before the groom met the bride, a time before the happy wedding at hand." He paused dramatically. "Well, no one here has known George that long! After twenty-five years of George and Sarah dating, any story I might tell would be so old and so outdated that you would boo me out of this fine room."

On cue, someone booed, and the rest of the crowd laughed. I snared another bite of cake.

Mr. Potter continued. "When George first told me that he was going to propose to Sarah, we had a good, long laugh. We joked about wedding registries, and how George and Sarah could finally afford to get a decent set of pots and pans. But when we stopped joking, George told me that he knew they didn't need any gifts. They didn't need any markers from friends. They had all the worldly riches they could ever use."

I looked at Gran. Her eyes were clear, and she held her head high. She obviously knew what Mr. Potter was about to say, and she was excited by it. She reached out and squeezed my hand.

Mr. Potter looked toward me, as well. "In fact, George and Sarah wanted to *give* gifts, rather than to receive. Your invitations all said, 'No presents, please.' What they didn't say is that Sarah and George are the ones distributing presents tonight."

Mr. Potter gestured, and Gran climbed to her feet after sliding her shoes back on, twitching her deep-green jacket into place with a single efficient tug. Mr. Potter held out his other hand, and Uncle George took it; the three of them stood in the center of the reference room, holding the perfect attention of every single guest.

Mr. Potter cleared his throat, and then he said, "George and Sarah decided to take my advice. They decided to donate to a favorite charity, a different charity than the one that most of us know so well, to the Concert Opera. In honor of their wedding, George and Sarah have made a very generous donation to Human Rights Watch."

There was a rush of pleased surprise from the assembled guests. I wondered how many people in the crowd were familiar with the watchdog group, how many realized that Gran and Uncle George were supporting gay rights. Listening to the hubbub, I twitched my lips into a smile. Neko would have been snarkily amused.

Mr. Potter raised his glass. "To Sarah and George," he said. "Long may their generosity guide us all! Cheers!"

"Cheers!" sang the crowd, and glasses clinked against glasses.

A swirl of well-wishers came between Gran and me. I turned to Will, caught him laughing at the surprise on a couple of guests' faces. "Did you know about this?"

"Rob mentioned it earlier. He helped them find a lawyer to draw up the appropriate papers." Will leaned in and kissed my cheek. He knew that I was worried about Neko. He whispered, "I'm going to get us more champagne." I nodded and watched him cross the room. I shuddered involuntarily, suddenly chilled without him standing right beside me.

When I turned back toward Gran, Clara had approached. "What a wonderful gesture!"

"It was just something that we wanted to do, dear," Gran said.

Realizing that the three of us were alone for a moment, I couldn't keep from asking, "But why the change? Why not something to do with opera?"

Gran looked around at all the guests. She dropped her voice enough that Clara and I both had to take a step closer. "I had to do it. For Neko." She cleared her throat, and then she shrugged. "Besides, do you remember that night, two years ago?" I narrowed my eyes. Two years ago, my powers had just awoken. Two years ago, I had just been learning what it meant to be a witch. Gran helped to narrow her meaning. "You had spent those days down in the basement, organizing your collection, after that horrid man lied to you. And we finally lured you up to the kitchen with fresh-baked chocolate chip cookies."

Oh. That night. "I remember."

"Do you remember the secret that I told you then?"

Of course I did. Gran hated opera. She had gone along with Concert Opera for years because Uncle George loved it, because it was important to him. I nodded.

"Well, I told him."

"You what?" My voice was louder than I meant it to be. My exclamation attracted a little attention. Majom came dashing across the room from where he had been studiously pushing buttons on the terminal for our online catalog. Nuri sailed behind him, as if the familiar had accepted the responsibility to watch over her colleague for the night.

"What?" Majom asked, launching himself against Clara's hip. Gran clicked her tongue, patting him on the head in a hopeless attempt to get him to settle down.

"It was time," she said to Clara and me.

"I would say so, Mother."

"But why? Why now?"

"I couldn't get *married* with that sort of secret between us. It wouldn't be right. It wouldn't be fair to George." She could date the man for twenty-five years, but marriage changed everything. It was sweet, in an old-fashioned way.

"But what did he say?" I was fascinated, awed.

"He said I should have told him twenty-five years before. And he said that his hearing's going, so he's not able to appreciate the performances the way he used to. We've decided to keep working on the board, to continue socializing with all our friends, but I think we'll probably miss a few performances next year. And, with any luck, a few more after that!"

I shook my head. All those years. All those lies. A facade maintained in the name of love, torn down almost overnight.

Before I could say anything, Majom perked up. He cast his eyes toward the ceiling and stood up straight, dropping the fork that he was using to spear the remnants of my slice of wedding cake. Nuri followed his gaze by reflex, and then she also jumped to her feet.

It took me a moment longer to hear the noise. It sounded like a train, barreling down on the library. No, not a train. A plane. A dozen planes. Flying lower than any planes had any right to fly.

"Those are fighting planes!" Clara said. "Scrambling fighters—we used to hear them at the Sedona airshow every year."

The other guests had heard them now. Chairs were pushed back. Plates and glasses were dropped on tables. Everyone hurried to the doors, dashed into the garden, looked up into the moonlit sky.

I turned around in the midst of the chaos, wondering what was happening. Adrenaline fired my blood. Reflexively, I reached my powers toward David, skating toward his protection. As I triggered the bond between us, I felt another touch, another astral tug.

Faint.

Distant.

So vague that I had to sit to concentrate. I closed my eyes, ducked my head into my hands, trying, trying to find that contact once again.

And there it was. So far away that I could barely feel it.

Neko.

Jane. We're at the White House. Come now.

18

Before I had fully registered the faint words, David stood before me. "Let's go."

Clearly, his warder's knowledge had brought him into the link; he had heard Neko's message. But had he heard the faint tinge of desperation? The outright fear? Did he know what we were traveling to meet?

Clara spoke up first. "What? Where are you going?"

David was looking over his shoulder. The reference room had emptied out; all of the wedding guests had run outside to see if there were still fighter planes in the sky. I said, "We found Neko."

"Where?" asked Gran. Understandably, she looked around the library, as if she expected my mischievous familiar to be hiding behind a table.

"He's at the White House. And he needs us."

The words sounded absurd, like the summons of a comic book hero. And yet, they made perfect sense. Ariel had been playing all around the nation's capital; she had acted out her mission on the steps of Congress, on the thresholds of federal landmarks. Stepping up to the president's own home wasn't really much of a change for her.

"Are you ready?" David asked. "I can take all of us there."

Clearly, he wasn't talking about driving. However impressive, his Lexus wasn't going to cut through traffic at this hour. Between Halloween revelers in Georgetown and Secret Service officers responding to whatever had summoned the jets, it would take hours to get across town.

I looked around the room. I had to tell Will what was happening. I had to let him know where I was going.

"There isn't time," David said.

"But—"

"There isn't time." I knew that tone. I knew the iron behind those words. I'd seen David carve out ultimatums before, mandate my training, my safety. There would be no arguing the point.

Will would have to understand.

David was already orchestrating everything, taking it out of my control. "Sarah, put your arms around Majom's shoulders. Good. Nuri, hold on to Clara. I'll take you first."

He put both his hands on Clara's right arm, pulling her close as if they were going to practice some somber ballroom dance. Nuri flew into the embrace, and then all three blinked out of sight.

"Clara!" Gran exclaimed, and Majom scrambled out of her grasp, pouncing on the spot that his witch had occupied only moments before. I seized the boy just as David flashed back into sight, mere inches from where he had started.

"Sarah, now," he said, reaching out to clutch Majom's hand at the same time that he settled his right palm on Gran's shoulder. I started to speak, but they were gone before I could finish drawing a breath.

Just—gone. Not a shimmer of air, not a glint of light. One moment, they were standing in front of me, and the next I was staring at empty space.

Magic shouldn't be that easy, I thought. There should be a visible transition, like the old transporter on *Star Trek*, shining with dancing lights as people came and went. I didn't understand. I'd never truly appreciated what my warder was capable of doing.

David reappeared. Silently, he held out his hand to me.

"I—" I started to say. But I didn't know how I intended to end that sentence. I didn't know if I meant to protest. I didn't know if I meant to thank him. I didn't know if I meant to say that we were back to where we had stood a year ago, on Samhain, as our future rode on my ability to master powers I wasn't sure I had.

I set my fingers onto his palm, and then there was nothingness.

Not darkness.

Nothing.

I had no body. I had no mind. I had no way of seeing, knowing, being. It was as if I were a blind woman and someone stood behind me, asking, "How many fingers am I holding up?" I had no tools to say.

I wasn't.

And then, I was.

I was standing in the middle of a green lawn. A tall iron fence stood behind me. Lush grass was underfoot, chilled with evening dew. The full moon sat serenely overhead, impossibly close, impossibly low in the sky. Incongruously, I could still taste buttercream and champagne at the back of my throat.

Fighter planes screamed overhead.

I blinked, and everything around me started to move again. David was dropping my hand, stepping forward to see if Gran was all right, if Clara and Nuri had found their footing. Majom was frozen, staring up at the sky, his little jaw dropped in shock.

White lights flooded the lawn around us, as brilliant as if we were being invaded by an alien mothership. I squinted, and I could just make out that the spotlights were on the roof of the iconic building behind me, the White House. The massive instruments picked out the six of us—Gran and Clara, the familiars, David and me.

Beyond the lights, I heard the machinery of war. Jets shrieked by again, joined by the whupping sound of helicopters beating to hold their place in the sky. Men shouted orders to each other, anger merging with brutal military urgency. A siren rose and fell and rose again, like an endless ocean breaking waves against us.

I stumbled forward on the grass, trying to get my balance, trying to figure out what was happening, why I was here. If I squinted, I could make out shapes on the lawn in front of me, curves and straight lines that had been seared into the ground, baring moist black earth. I shook my head, blinked hard, and then the shapes coalesced into letters, into words.

Empower The Arts.

The slogan was emblazoned in the White House lawn, etched there by some unknown force. Stunned, I looked up, and then I finally realized that we did not number six, there in the center of the maelstrom.

We were eight.

One more figure, known so well to me—slight, jaunty, standing out like a stain of ink in his midnight clothes against the noon-bright lawn. Neko.

The last presence, the object of my dreams from the past two months. Impossibly tall. Impossibly thin. So pale that she almost disappeared in the floodlights, except for her midnight hair. A cloud of a gown swirled around her, bleached of its crimson and orange and yellow in the bright, white light. Ariel.

Witch, she thought, raising her hands above her head.

As she spoke the word inside my head, a rain of golden pearls fell inside my thoughts. The force of her power was so great, the energy of her magic so strong, that her single thought sent a cascade of astral wealth tumbling into my storehouse. It swirled into the green and red accumulated from Gran and Clara, tempting, tantalizing, never enough.

But her word was more than a greeting. When she lifted her fingers above her wind-whipped hair, she cast a spell. Her magic was wild, different from anything that I had read and mastered in my books. She did not use words; she did not speak rhymes.

She *thought* her magic into being. One flick of her wrists sent a golden dome above us. I could not see what she did, but I could read the effect. As I looked around, shocked, I saw Neko stagger a step closer to the anima. He moved like a zombie, like a creature possessed. Every line of his body was set against Ariel, fighting against her power. And yet she used him. She bounced her magic off of him. She used his essential nature to magnify her own beneath the golden dome.

"Neko!" I cried out.

I was astonished that I could hear my voice. The dome had changed everything. It had cut out the real world, sealed out the military might assembled above the White House lawn. It tempered the floodlights, turned them from blinding white to a warm gold, a shade that reminded me of sunshine and sand and warmth on a beach. When I peered at the insane world outside of Ariel's dome, I could see that everything was moving much more slowly than we were moving inside; the people seemed almost frozen in their own time.

I called out again, "Neko!"

He turned to me carefully, as if he needed to give conscious thought to managing each separate muscular contraction. He might have thought about smiling; I saw the beginning of a twitch in his lips, but he came nowhere near completing the motion. Nevertheless, I could hear the words that he slipped between his gritted teeth. "Nice dress, girlfriend."

Shocked, I looked down at my orange and silver nightmare. Ariel's golden light had tempered the Gatorade; it seemed more like a mai tai now. The silver lamé, though, glittered with a vengeance.

"Are you all right?" I exclaimed, taking a step toward my familiar.

Ariel did not let him answer, though. Instead, she sealed his lips, pulling his gaze toward her, so that he could no longer look at me. I could read the resistance in every stiffened muscle of his body; I could see him fight her control. But still, he took a step away from me. Another. Another. And then my anima draped herself against him like an obscene parody of seduction.

He's my familiar now, Witch.

Again, I felt her words raise a power in me, like the jangle of a miniature slot machine paying out. I was grateful for the strength—a weakness that she caught immediately.

And you are mine, as well.

Another coin. Another link in the chain that she was building, the chain that already bound Neko, that she was stretching toward me. She was giving me strength. But she could take it all back, take it all away from me. She could gather me to her, in the same way that she had gathered Neko. She could bind me. Bind me, and Gran, and Clara, their familiars, David. She could control every one of us. If I did not find a way to stop her.

"What's going on here, Jeanette?" Clara's voice was angry, frightened. Majom stood in front of her; she had pulled the boy close so that his head rested against her belly. The golden light made his white hair look blond.

Nuri repeated, "What?" for good measure. The solid woman had not abandoned Clara, but she had reached out for Gran, bringing her into their frozen still life. All four members of my commune stared at me as if I had the answers, as if I knew all the facts. I wanted to tell them that I didn't have the least idea what was happening, that I couldn't control, couldn't predict what was going on.

I wasn't about to admit that, though, to my creature. I wasn't going to add to my anima's arsenal in any way that I could prevent. I could only hope that my thoughts were blocked from hers, that she could only read my conscious mental speech, not the ideas that flickered in my mind before I voiced them.

Instead, I looked to my warder. Our warder. David. I forced my voice to sound even, testing it once inside my head before daring to speak aloud. "The circle is cast, then? Our workings here can't harm anyone outside?"

David nodded tersely. "The circle is cast."

Sometime after this was over, I'd have to talk to him about that. I'd have to find out how Ariel had managed her arcane protection without invoking the elements, without laboriously tracing out the cardinal points on a compass. It might come in handy to be able to act so quickly. You know, if I ever needed to act on my plan to take over the world, starting on the White House lawn.

I had no idea if that's what Ariel actually wanted, if that's what she had planned. But there was no time like the present to find out. I turned to her, keeping my arms loose at my sides. "Empower The Arts, Ariel? Isn't that a little over the top? A little too much of a good thing?"

At first, I thought that she wasn't going to answer, she wasn't going to give me the benefit of her strength from a mental reply. But then, I realized she was merely parsing my words, trying to figure out what they meant. I remembered her, crouching in my basement, in the confusing minutes after I had made her. Neither of us had known the truth then, the way that the magical world apparently worked. Neither of us had known the consequences.

When she spoke, it sounded as if she was weaving the words to make unfamiliar fabric, harnessing a known warp and weft to create an unexpected design. *You ordered me. You set my mission.*

Again, that damned distracting payoff, the clamor of new power hitting my body, my mind, like a drug. All of a sudden, I understood women who let themselves be kept. I understood women who let men control them with trinkets, who let jobs bind them with bonuses. I wanted to do anything that Ariel required, anything that she demanded, just so that she would speak to me again. Instead, I summoned strength I didn't know I had to announce, "I created you to serve me. I ordered you to do my bidding."

Yes, Witch.

Ah! She answered me. Even when I challenged her, she fed me. The words felt so good. I took a step closer, as if that would strengthen the bond between us, as if I could eke out a fractionally higher payoff by forcing out another mental reply from her. The motion brought me nearer to Neko.

On the surface, he looked perfectly calm. His right foot rested slightly in front of his left. His weight was evenly distributed. Ariel curved against him, her flowing gown obscuring the precise line between their forms.

But when I looked at Neko's face, I could see the strain that he was under. I could see the eyes of a prisoner. His jaw was set so hard that I feared his teeth might crack. He was a bound man, a tempered man, a constrained and emasculated man.

He was a familiar, wholly bound to a witch. Not even a witch—an anima, who had taken on a role that was not hers, who had taken on power she could not be permitted to keep.

"No!" I said. "You are not doing what I commanded! I only meant for you to bolster my powers. I only meant for you to feed me back my strength."

I am doing that.

And she was. Oh, yes, she was, and the shimmer of her words almost made me beg for further confirmation. One stern glance at Neko, though, was enough to make me bite my tongue. Hard. Hard enough to draw tears to my eyes.

"But the rest of it," I said. "It was a mistake. It was confused. You were new-made, and I was not clear. I never intended you to embrace the role of Ariel, from the play." I waved at the etched grass beneath our feet, at the slogan burned there. "I never intended you to spread these words. I'm a librarian, not an activist!"

You intended it all. I know. I remember.

This time, my mind was not flooded with power alone. This time, I was not treated solely to a fraction of my squandered strength, rationed out and returned to me as I had once requested. This time, I was shown what Ariel herself had seen. I was given her mission.

It was all there, wrapped inside a golden cloud. I sensed her newness, her confusion, as she gathered together her consciousness from raw earth and water, from the air and fire that I had poured into her making. I felt her uncertainty as she heard my commanding spell of awakening, as she recognized me as her witch, as her creator.

I felt the solidity of her first thought, the strength of her resolve. I felt the fierce certainty as she absorbed my thoughts, my memories, turned them into herself.

Empower The Arts, I had thought. I had flashed upon the afternoon I'd spent with David, the incredible sparking power that we had shared in his office, in his bed. Empower The Arts, I had thought. I had shied away from that recollection, desperate to separate myself from what I had done, what we had done. Empower The Arts, I had thought. I had reached out for the poster, for the image of Prospero, the actor David, the safe David. Empower The Arts, I had thought. Save me from what I had done. Empower The Arts. Strengthen me. Empower The Arts. Move me past my own resolve.

And so she had.

My anima had done precisely what I had commanded. She had skipped over what I had meant; she had plunged into what—precisely—I had *said*. She had let me flee my own thoughts, my own desires. She had mastered her mission early, breeding power, collecting strength. But she had hoarded that energy, keeping the magic that went beyond my own. She had stockpiled it so that she could complete the mission I had given her, the mission I had never intended, the mission that I had made explicit.

And now she was beyond me. Outside me. Greater than I could ever hope to control.

Every droplet of power that Ariel spared for me was born out of the swirling pool of her abilities—my abilities, multiplied by her dumb working. She had absorbed all of my commands; she had regenerated my powers. But she had kept the surplus for herself—was going to continue to keep it for herself—because that was what I'd asked of her. That was what I had commanded.

For the first time, I was fully conscious of what I had done, of just how badly I had betrayed myself. My familiar. My warder.

I looked at David.

He saw what I saw. He knew what I knew. He remembered what I remembered—the afternoon in his house, the evening in my basement. Even as I understood all that had happened, and how, and why, my warder understood it all, as well.

I was standing in front of him, more exposed than I had ever been before. I wasn't the witch who had overextended herself and needed to be tucked into bed. I wasn't the student who had stretched her powers thin, mastering a new spell and needing to be fed a restorative dinner. I wasn't the protégé who had lulled him into relaxing, who had stolen a kiss one night long ago. I wasn't the woman who had come to him in curiosity, in longing, who had drawn him to his bed.

I was Jane Madison.

I was the sum of all my roles, the combination of witch and woman. I was more naked before him than I'd ever been before, than I could ever have imagined being. This wasn't about a ridiculous orange dress. It wasn't about silver bows on my shoes. It wasn't about the memory of a green cotton sundress, torn off my body and tangled on his floor.

It was about me.

"Help me," I said.

Or I thought. Or I breathed. I don't know how I spoke to him. I don't know how I reached out for him. I just knew that he was the only thing that could guide me through this knowing, he was the only person who had the power to bring me back to where I'd been before, to what I'd been, before I'd given so much away to Ariel.

And he stepped toward me.

He locked eyes with me. He waited for me to acknowledge his presence, to tell him that I understood that everything was changing, everything had changed. He was my warder. He was my protector. He was the man who was sworn to keep me safe, sworn to protect me as a witch, as a woman.

I nodded once, filling the tiny physical movement with a thousand thoughts, a million words.

And then he raised his hands to either side. He stepped back toward the edge of the golden dome. He turned his head to his right, turned toward Gran and Clara, reminding me that my community waited to serve.

They were staring at me. I could tell that they did not have the faintest idea what had passed between us, not between Ariel and me, between David and me. They were dazed and confused. Gran looked tiny in her dark green suit, as if she'd stumbled into someone's closet and decided to try on their grown-up clothes. Clara looked angry, defiant, as if she resented being kept out of the astral loop.

David was right. My mother and my grandmother were my strength. They were my hope. They were my answer.

Looking at each other, moving as one, we touched our fingers to our foreheads. We breathed, in, out, centering. We touched our fingers to our throats. Another breath. We touched our hearts. We hovered on a perfect edge for spellcraft.

With Gran and Clara watching, waiting, I kicked off my orange and silver shoes, letting them arc away into the golden light. The ground beneath my feet was freezing, but I set my jaw, stepping squarely into the middle of the patch of bare earth in front of me, the *A* from *Empower The Arts*. I felt the dirt through my stockings; I arched my toes and dug deeper into the scarred ground, glorying in the essence of Earth.

"Out of earth I did call thee!" I proclaimed. I parceled out a quarter of the power that had accumulated in my mind, one fourth of the green and red and gold energy that spun and arced through my thoughts. Easily, gently, I lobbed it toward Gran and Clara, watching as they caught it.

Gran stumbled forward to keep the light from touching the ground. Majom jumped beside her, suddenly eager to move, to leap, to be free from the ridiculous stasis that we adults had imposed on him for far too long. Nuri swooped in opposite him, lending her strength to the mixture, bringing Clara into the loop. Together, they kneaded the energy I sent them, stretching it, growing it into something more.

For the first time since her creation, Ariel moved awkwardly, staggering toward the other witches and dragging Neko beside her. *You cannot bind me with Earth.*

For answer, I reached around and grasped my silver lamé bow, the folds of fabric that had driven me to despise my dress, despise my grandmother's taste, despise Neko's delight in making me look like a fool. I clutched the cloth and pulled sharply, liberating the idiotic bow from the gown. I swooped down as if I were dancing, rolling the glinting lamé over the grass, harvesting the chill dew that had collected after sunset.

"Out of water I did call thee!"

I raised the cloth above my head, felt the tiniest sprinkle of droplets cascade into my hair, onto the dress, onto my bare arms. I gathered up another parcel of my power and cast it toward Gran and Clara. Clara caught it this time, working it into their communal creation, weaving it into their whole.

For the first time ever, Ariel spoke with emotion, or maybe it was only with speed. *You cannot bind me with Water, Witch.*

I laughed at her words, laughed at the sparkling power that she shared with me. I brought my hands to my lips, cupped them to capture my own exhaled breath. "Out of air I did call thee!"

I flung half of all my remaining power at Gran and Clara. They caught it together, weaving it into their light, crafting together green and red and gold like a tapestry. Majom laughed at the game, and Nuri squawked; all of them shifted farther apart to accommodate the light that grew between them.

I joined them in their circle. I joined them in their dance. I wove between Majom and Gran, between Nuri and Clara, feeling the power of our working expand and grow. The four of them moved with me, joining hands until we were spinning like children, laughing in a breathless game of ring-around-the-rosy.

We were not done yet, though. We had not completed the working. Fire. We needed fire.

Ariel knew the same. She stared at me, unmoving. *I am your creation, Witch. I exist to serve you. You cannot cast me out when I have done no wrong.*

But she was mistaken. She had never intended any wrong, but she had worked it nonetheless. She had kept power that was rightfully mine. She had led me on a fruitless chase across the city, skirting legal authorities from a world that would never comprehend the magical bonds between us.

She had taken Neko.

More than anything else, that was what drowned my pity. She had taken Neko. She had drawn my familiar away, stolen him against his will. She had locked him into servitude in a way that I had never contemplated, could never countenance.

"Clara," I said, drawing us all to a breathless stop. "Mother."

I held out my hand, and she reached for her pink kunzite pendant. The stone glinted in Ariel's golden light; it captured the dome and the wind-whipped storm of our working. It blazed with the strength of unconditional love, of mother love; it sparked with pure power.

Clara lifted the crystal over her head. She passed it to me in silence, with tears in her eyes. I raised it high, let it turn freely in the light, sending out its magical flame.

"Out of fire I did call thee!"

I offered up the last of my strength, the last of the power that I had gleaned from Ariel, from Gran, from Clara. Crimson and gold and evergreen poured forth from the center of my astral being, spinning into the light, spinning into the working of our community. Majom leaped higher and higher, stretching our crafting, and Nuri waved her arms to magnify the force that Gran and Clara were feeding.

They were my family. They were my school. They were my community, my more-than-Coven. They took what I gave them, and they made it more, endlessly more than I could ever have made on my own. They spun my magic into a blanket, cast it into a cloud. Our strength billowed up, billowed out, spread against the dome that represented Ariel's strength, her stubbornness, her stone-hard misunderstanding.

But it wasn't enough. They couldn't completely obscure the golden limit of Ariel's power. They couldn't completely take the ground.

I dug deep inside, excavating the last glimmer of magic that was mine, that was solely, specifically mine to give. There was nothing, though, nothing left to pour into our cause.

I looked at Ariel. I looked at her icy beauty. I looked at her distant strength. I saw how I had created something out of fear, out of misunderstanding, and I saw how I could never hope to regain control over her.

And then Neko moved. As if the gesture cost him his last ounce of strength, he rolled his eyes heavenward, managing to convey a cross between a prayer and exasperation.

I hurtled forward to bring him into our communal working.

My body crashed against his, and I felt him crushed between Ariel and me. I opened my mind to him, let him see the balance of what I had worked with Gran and Clara. I showed him the magic that we had discovered without him, the community that we had built while he had been away.

He stumbled.

Physically and astrally, he stumbled.

He had no frame of reference for what he was seeing. He had no way of understanding what we had done. He had no way of realizing that Gran was feeding off of Majom, that Nuri was reflecting power back to Clara, that the familiars were paired in ways that witches had never tried before.

And yet, trusting me, he figured it out. He leaned in to me with whatever fractional strength he was able to summon. He pressed his black silk shirt into the taffeta of my orange dress, letting the colors flow together like the Samhain garb, the Halloween games, that had captured the imagination of all the mundane world around us.

That movement, that tiniest act of rebellion, gnawed at Ariel's cruel bonds. Neko snagged a bit of our magic and spun it around. He flung it back to Clara with all the awkwardness of a kitten scrambling over a ball of yarn. She laughed and tossed the skein to Nuri. Neko understood what was happening. He collected more of the communal magic and spun it out to Majom. He laughed as the strands expanded, gusting out to the very limits of Ariel's dome.

For the first time since creating our arcane community, I felt the full, unadulterated power of what we did. With my familiar involved, I could receive the complete reflected magic of our working, I could be a part of the whole, the unlimited, unrestricted sharing with Gran and Clara. I reveled in the balance, gloried in the strength.

I turned to Ariel.

She stood alone beneath the brilliant, jewel-bright blanket. Her hair hung slack beside her face. Her gown swung from her shoulders like a shroud. I raised my hands above my head, pointed my fingers directly at her heart.

"Go to darkness, let light flee.
Return to nothing, nothing be.
Return all power, give away
All that made thee. Go your way."

The flash of darkness was the strongest I had ever seen. All the golden dome, all the red-green-gold blanket, all the klieg lights and the starlight and the world simply disappeared.

And then they were back. The starlight, anyway. And the swollen moon. And the spotlights. And the sound of helicopters and jets and a dozen men shouting angry, urgent orders.

Ariel was gone.

I met David's gaze across the scarred and trampled grass. My powers were back, restored and more. I felt more complete, more alive than I had ever felt before. I could measure every blade of grass beneath my naked feet. I could see light glinting off of every weapon arrayed against us.

The tapestry of energy swirled close around the seven of us. In my mind, witch to warder, I handed the strands over to David, giving him permission, letting him do his job.

He took the power seamlessly, as if he'd never doubted that I could act, that I *would* act in precisely the manner I had. He nodded once, verifying that all of us were covered, that all of us stood together, and then he pulled us into a perfect lack of being.

19

We returned to the Peabridge mere moments after we had left. No one had time to miss us. The wedding guests were still outside, staring up at the sky, searching for more signs of the scrambling jets everyone had heard. Moonlight flooded through the glass panels in the Peabridge doors, streaking across the library lobby.

David said, "Are you all right?"

I nodded, not yet trusting myself to answer. He glided over to the doors, carefully turning the locking mechanism. Our guests would think that the doors had closed behind them accidentally, that they were inadvertently locked outside. We'd steal a few extra minutes of privacy.

He turned to Clara and Gran. "Sit down," he said. "You need to ground yourselves with food." He picked up a plate and gestured toward one of the deli trays. "Majom, help them with that."

The boy scampered around the table, full of energy and excitement, as if he'd just witnessed some Fairy-tale Fireworks Fiesta at the end of a long day in an amusement park. He selected meat and cheese and thin slices of bread, pausing to put almost as much in his own mouth as he guided to the plate. His white hair bobbed up and down as he delivered the bounty to his witches.

David nodded, watching until he saw Gran accept a bunch of grapes, until she started to chew, steadily, methodically. Even across the library, I could hear that her breath was coming easier, that she was returning to whatever passed for normal in the annals of an eighty-five-year-old bride. Clara scavenged a cup of water from the coffee bar, administered it to Gran as if it were some prescription medicine, even as she fed herself a handful of almonds. Nuri fluttered back for a refill on the water.

Majom took advantage of everyone's distraction to dart back over to the serving table. There was a crash and a clatter, and then the boy turned to Clara, his hands covered in buttercream. His eyes were wide with surprise, as if he had not meant to work any mischief. Gran laughed—actually laughed—and called him to her side, reaching for a napkin to clean off his fingers.

A weight I hadn't known I carried lifted from my chest. I sank back against the corner of my desk, suddenly unsure that I could stand a moment longer. I was laughing along with Gran, but the sound was silent, and my vision was sharpened by tears I had not shed.

I clutched the wooden edge of the desk to steady myself, turning away so that I did not frighten Gran or Clara, did not disturb them with my quiet nervous breakdown. My fingers were tingling, sparking with an energy I had not known in months. Without being consciously aware of the fact, I knew that David had turned from my witches, from our familiars, that he had glided across the room to me.

I folded my arms around my belly, trying to seal in the tumult of my emotions. I had met my anima. I had laid her to rest. I had regained my power—every last drop that I had forfeited to my creation so many weeks ago—and more. Much, much more. I had bared myself completely to my warder. I had let David see me—all of me—in a way that I never had before. There was nothing left between us, no wall. No barrier. I breathed as deeply as I could, trying to settle the roiling forces that filled my mind.

I sensed David standing above me, felt his presence sparkling, vibrating. I could not turn to face him, though. I could not look as he settled his charcoal jacket over my shoulders.

There was nothing sexual in the motion. Nothing seductive. He was a warder caring for his witch. He was a doctor treating a patient. He did not ask for more; he did not look to see if anything else was offered, wanted, needed.

"You have to sleep," he said.

"Soon." The one syllable cost me more than I had expected. I was exhausted in my bones. Dully, I wondered where Neko was, whether my familiar would help in any way, could banish even the slightest bit of my exhaustion.

Before I could summon the energy to say anything, to think anything, there was a rattling sound from the front of the library. Someone had discovered that the doors were locked. I knew that I should tell David to open the door, to let them in, but I couldn't remember the words. A note of good-natured dismay rolled over the crowd outside, and I heard someone suggest circling the building, searching for another door.

Then, sooner than I expected, there was laughter and the smooth sound of a key fitting into the lock. Kit led the way back into the Peabridge, brandishing the ring of keys that Evelyn had entrusted to her for the evening. "Didn't you hear us knocking?" she said. "We got locked out!"

"How did that happen?" Clara interceded and I took another deep breath, trying desperately to regroup. David placed a plate in my hands, guiding my fingers to a slice of cheese. I put the food in my mouth. I moved my jaws. I swallowed.

Happy wedding guests surged back into the library. The break had reminded everyone that the hour was late, that they needed to return home, that they were going to have a terrible time fighting the Georgetown Halloween traffic.

Will tumbled in with the rest of the guests. I saw him register David's jacket around my shoulders, acknowledge the plate that shook in my hands. I barely had enough presence of mind to lean forward on my desk, to drop the hem of my dress, to camouflage my naked feet. I forced myself to smile as he crossed the room to brush a kiss against my cheek.

"Halloween, and they scare the neighborhood half to death with scrambling jets. Can you believe it?" He didn't really need an answer, though. He shook his head in disgust before fishing a key ring from his pocket.

From a distance, I remembered that he had agreed to play chauffeur to the newlyweds, to drive them across town to their honeymoon suite at The Hay-Adams hotel. Across the street from the White House. I swallowed hard. Borrowedcar.com had come through with a luxury town car for the night, the best eight dollars an hour I ever could have spent.

Concern creased Will's face. "You look exhausted! Do you want me to stay here? I can help clean up."

"I'm okay," I said. I needed Will to leave. I needed to get him away from here, away from me, so that I could think about what had happened. So that I could sleep. Sleep and recover from everything that had taken place in the space of a few heartbeats, beneath a magical golden dome.

"I can call a cab to take Gran and Uncle George," he said.

"No!" Calm down, I told myself. That was too sharp. "I can't do that to them," I explained. "Not a regular cab on their wedding night. Besides, it'll take forever for one to get here, through the Halloween parade."

He still wasn't convinced. "I'll come back afterward, then, and help clean up."

I stifled a yawn. "Kit will do it. Really. There isn't very much to do. By the time you get back, I'll be sound asleep."

I put my hand on top of his, squeezed my fingers gently around the keys. I could work a spell. I could make him leave. Instead, I forced myself to meet his eyes with a wan smile.

He said, "I'll see you tomorrow, then?"

"Tomorrow. That would be perfect."

It wouldn't be. It would be far from perfect. But I didn't know what else to say.

"You did a wonderful job tonight." He gestured toward the decimated deli trays, the scattering of champagne flutes. He had no idea what other job I'd worked tonight. He never would. Even if I told him, he'd never understand.

"Thanks," I said.

His kiss was quick, chaste. He frowned at the charcoal jacket, though, as he drew back. His hand cupped my jaw, spreading a familiar warmth down my spine. I felt as if he was reminding me of a secret I had forgotten. "Sleep well," he said. "I'll bring the car around to the front." And then he left.

In moments, Uncle George had collected Gran, placing an arm around her waist as they posed in front of the Peabridge doors. They took their leave like a couple at a classic 1950s' wedding; Gran standing straight and proud in her suit. She clutched her sweetheart roses to her chest, raised the blossoms to her face to breathe deeply of them one last time.

I managed to climb to my feet, then, catching her eye just

as she turned her back on her guests. I shook my head once, a tiny, mute denial, and then the flowers arced through the air, flying on a precise path that might have been boosted by a little communal magic.

Melissa laughed as she clutched the roses against her velvet jumper. Rob was standing beside her. His eyebrows shot up in surprise, but then he leaned in and kissed her, and they both nodded their heads before the affectionate applause of all the guests.

Gran and Uncle George's departure primed the pump. Guests flowed away quickly, waving farewells, stopping by to plant fond kisses on my cheeks. Everyone had had a wonderful time. Everyone was so thrilled to see such a happy couple. Everyone so appreciated everything I had done.

Clara collected Nuri and Majom, telling the familiars that they could both stay with her for the night. For all her sangfroid, I could see that my mother was exhausted; her hands were shaking as she pulled Majom close to her side.

I scrambled at my throat, lifting the delicate chain of silver that I'd barely remembered was there. Clara's pink kunzite glinted in the overhead light, capturing just a sliver of the blue-white moonlight that streamed through the library door. "This is yours," I said, holding it out to her.

"I want you to have it."

Our fingers met as I tried to put it in her palm, as she handed it back to me.

"Don't go," I said, before I had a chance to think about the words. "Don't go back to Sedona."

"Ah, Jane," she sighed, and I almost forgot to be pleased that she used the correct name. "I'm no good here. I'm not meant to be in the big city. I belong somewhere where I can talk about crystals and auras without people thinking I'm crazy. Where I can mention the Vortex, without people rolling their eyes."

"I don't—"

"Jane, your grandmother taught you not to lie."

Clara was shrewd. Shrewder than I'd given her credit for. I spoke without thinking about the words. "But Gran and I need you. We—" I barely hesitated "—we love you. *I* love you."

She raised a hand to my cheek, and for the first time ever, I saw Gran's tenderness in my mother's eyes. Gran's tenderness, and her steel. "Jane, I love you, too. But this is something that I have to do. It's not about you. It's about me."

My tears had to be from my exhaustion. That was it. Exhaustion. I closed my fingers around the kunzite crystal, let the pendant sink into my lap. "Thank you," I whispered.

Clara was every bit as tired as I was; I could read her fatigue in every line of her sagging body. "David," I said, calling him to my side with the softest of words. "Can you make sure that they get home safely?"

"I'm here for you."

"You're here for all of us. You're their warder, too. I'm fine. I just need to walk across the garden."

He wanted to argue with me. He wanted to tell me I was wrong. He wanted to tell me that I was a stubborn witch, a difficult witch, the most challenging witch he'd ever heard of. I could understand all that. I could read it through the energy that sparked between us, crackling along the taut links of our recharged astral bond.

But he had to concede. He *was* bound to Clara. And to my command. Stiffly, he walked across the room, gathered together all three of our companions and herded them out the door.

I smiled. Majom would have a field day with the buttons on the sleek Lexus dashboard.

Kit came back from a trip that she'd taken to the Dumpster, already making short work of the cleanup. "I'm just going to make sure everything's taken care of downstairs," she said.

"Good idea."

"The last thing we need is a piece of cake left down there, bringing in mice."

"Always thinking like a librarian," I said, and she laughed.

Then I was alone in the reference room. I closed my eyes and took a steadying breath. For the first time since unmaking Ariel, I became aware of a shadow at the edge of my vision, a blank spot in my astral perception. I shook my head, trying to clear the defect, but the disturbance remained.

I looked around the room. There was a crumpled napkin that Kit had missed. A serving plate with the remains of the wedding cake. A champagne flute on the coffee bar, half-full. Nothing out of the ordinary.

But there, in the shadows by the stacks. Black on black. And one very pale face.

"Neko," I whispered.

He slinked across the room, a curious sideway walk, as if he wanted to come to me but was afraid to do so. Despite everything that had happened that night, his leather pants were immaculate. His silk T-shirt looked as if he had just taken it from a dresser drawer. His hair was perfectly arranged, each short strand gelled to its proper place. He looked exactly as he had the night I first transformed him from a statue of a cat.

I reached out for the bond between us, the magic bond, our link. Nothing.

That was impossible, though. I had worked with him. I had brought him into the circle, joined him with Majom and Nuri, with Gran and Clara.

But then I realized the true power of the working that we had completed that night. Neko had belonged to Ariel. He was not rightfully a part of our commune, and yet we had brought him in, included him in our working. We'd been powerful enough to work with anyone, even with a familiar who was foreign to us, separate from us, apart.

I extended my powers around him. I could sense his astral strength, measure that strange, reflective power that no witch could ever master on her own, that every witch desired. He was unbound. He was available. He was a familiar without a witch.

"What do I do to bring you back?" I asked.

He shook his head, feinting a look at the library doors. Moonlight still streamed in, cold silver spilled across the floor. "It's a full moon. You should wait until tomorrow. Wait until you can bind me to you fully."

I shook my head. I couldn't do that to him. To us. "How do I set the bond?"

His expression was flat. "You know the spell. Nothing's changed." He trembled like a feral cat, tempted to snatch food from my palm, but ready to run at my first misstep.

Without ceremony, I took my three deep breaths. I offered up my thoughts, my voice, my heart. I could have recited the words in my sleep.

"Awaken now, hunter, dark as the night.
Bring me your power, your strong second sight.
Hear that I call you and, willing, assist;
Lend me your magic and all that you wist."

The flash of darkness was more stunning than usual, maybe because of my exhaustion, maybe because of the depth of longing I dripped into every word. I shuddered as the working slipped into place, as some subtle balance changed between us.

And then I reached out with my mind. The familiar bond was there, filling the channel, filling the gap. The mental linkage was smooth and supple. I ran a mental touch along it, watched Neko stand straighter, taller. Prouder.

"Go to Jacques," I said.

"You bound me. I'm here to work with you."

"Do I look like I'm in any condition to play with more magic tonight?"

He smirked, snapping back to his old self. "You look like someone who needs some help with your makeup, girlfriend. Honestly, did you think that bronze eyeshadow would *complement* that dress?"

"The dress is your fault. You're the one who let Gran go with orange." I smiled.

"And you still haven't done anything with your hair. You need to see Jacques more than I do."

"I doubt that," I said. "I really, truly doubt that. Go."

Neko rubbed a hand across his face, looking like he was washing away fatigue, or the memory of a nightmare. He paused by the library door, settling a hand on his hip and casting one more critical glance my way. "That dress does look better without the bow. There's hope for you yet, girlfriend."

"Get out of here!"

Before he ducked out the door, he grabbed the serving plate from the reference table, collecting the last generous wedge of wedding cake. He dipped his finger into the buttercream and sampled it before disappearing into the night.

I staggered toward the stairs that led to the auditorium. "Kit!" I called. "I'm ready to head home."

She came to the foot of the stairs. "Go on. I'll close up. I just found a box of papers down here. I think they're extra invoices. There's some great stuff here—I'm just going to finish going through them."

"Don't work too late," I said, shaking my head at the enthusiasm in her voice.

"I won't. Sleep well."

"You, too."

I pulled David's jacket closer and ducked out of the library, making myself ignore the chill of the garden path on my bare feet. I barely bothered to strip off the horrible orange dress before I tumbled into bed. The comforter was heavy on my shoulders as I pulled my pillow over my head, determined to block out the slightest sliver of the moon's cool light.

20

I turned the brilliant orange matchbook around, corner to corner to corner, tapping it against the table on each rotation. Four orange votive candles sat on my kitchen table. Three wicks stood at attention; the fourth was tilted over, leaning against the wax. With a flicker of thought, I made it stand as straight as its companions.

Twenty-four hours later, I was still marveling at the power that filled me.

I couldn't say, precisely, how Ariel had grown my magic. She'd deepened it, broadened it. When I reached inside myself, there was *more* there, more than I had ever invested in her. It felt as if someone had ripened my powers, turned them from grape juice into wine, from simple cow's milk into heady brie.

I longed to ask her what she had done. Half a dozen times, I reached out to her, gathered my thoughts to question her, to learn. But then I would remember that my spell had worked, that my anima had been reduced to rune dust on the White House lawn.

Not that anyone would ever find evidence of her there.

The Washington Post was screaming headlines about the prankster who had broken into the White House grounds for Halloween. Details weren't being released; there was a lot of talk about mission secrecy and national security. Rumors were already flying that the entire thing had been a training exercise, that the jets had been scrambled to test their ability to respond in a real emergency.

Of course, Ariel's handiwork remained behind—the Empower The Arts slogan was etched deep in the grass (at least until an official White House gardener could tear up the lawn and replace the damaged part with sod.) The Artistic Avenger was front page and center again; experts were calling her a terrorist, comparing her to PETA, to the Environmental Liberation Front, to worse.

In other words, official Washington was stumbling on, as if nothing much had happened.

By the time I'd gathered all the news, it was well past noon. I'd stumbled back to my bedroom, oddly hungover from the night before. I'd taken my time hanging up my bright orange dress. It seemed wasteful to leave it bunched on the floor, even if I'd never wear it again. I hung it next to David's jacket in my closet, taking time to twitch the skirt into place.

I stood beneath a stinging shower, chasing away a myriad of aches and pains that had blossomed while I slept. I scrubbed at my feet, making sure that no remnant of presidential earth remained between my toes.

I knew that I should eat. I knew that I should complete the process of grounding myself, of returning my awareness to the mundane plane. The thought of food, though, turned my belly.

I needed to talk to Will.

Every time I pictured myself standing on the White House lawn, every time I remembered David stepping toward me, gaze bound to mine, arms lifting from his sides, every time I replayed everything that had happened the night before, I knew that I needed to talk to Will.

I'd reverted to my old self, phoning him at his office when I knew he would be home. I'd left him a message, certain that he checked his voice mail several times a day. I'd asked him to come by in the evening. After dinner. So that we could talk.

I tried not to imagine the unease I knew those words would bring.

I spent the rest of the day in the basement. All of my books were normal; I could read them without destroying their pages. My crystals hummed with energy, drawing me into an hour of dazed contemplation as I basked in their vibrating concert. Alas, the runes remained a lost cause; I'd need to procure new ones. I made a little ceremony out of dumping the dust from the ruined tiles, scattering them around the dead flower beds outside my front door.

At eight o'clock, I put the kettle on, telling myself that

I'd have a cup of tea, even if I couldn't eat. I was waiting for the water to boil, sitting at the table, fiddling with match-books and candles, when there was finally a knock at the door.

Will had his own key, but he'd chosen not to use it.

"Hey there," he said, ducking past me to enter the living room. The moonlight was bright behind him—only my magic told me that we were actually one day past full.

"I was just making a cup of tea," I said. "Want one?"

"Sure."

I led the way into the kitchen, painfully aware that I hadn't waited for him to kiss me. I stood in front of my cupboard as if it held all the secrets of the universe. "Is mint okay?"

"Yeah."

There were things I was supposed to say. I was supposed to ask him how his day had been. I was supposed to tell him what I'd done with mine. I was supposed to chat, lightly, easily, the way we'd talked for months.

I couldn't think of a single complete sentence.

I didn't bother with a teapot; I just poured water directly into our mugs, dropping in separate, lonely tea bags. Will was sitting at the table when I turned around. Silent. Waiting.

He picked up his mug obediently, raised it to his lips. The steam immediately fogged his glasses, and he sat back as if he'd been slapped. "I'm sorry!" I said, jumping up for a hand towel.

He waved me off, pushing away the traitorous mug of tea.

He wiped his lenses clean with a handkerchief, then settled them back on his face, crooked as always. "I'm not going to like this conversation very much, am I?"

"Will…" I'd had all afternoon to think, and I still didn't know what to say.

"Something happened last night, didn't it? Something magic?"

I nodded. He deserved more than that, though. He deserved the truth.

"I've got my power back," I said. "All of it. And then some."

Swallowing hard, he said, "Tell me what happened."

And so I did. At least, I tried to. I told him about David spiriting us away. I told him about appearing on the White House lawn. I told him about fighting with Ariel, about working with Gran and Clara, about finding a new balance for power, a new way of being in the magical world.

I could tell that he didn't really get it. He didn't really understand. Each individual word made sense, but he would never grasp the wonder in my voice, never understand my longing, my aching amazement as I spoke of the power that had flowed through me.

He tried. He asked questions. He expressed concern about Gran, about Clara. He said that he was happy that Neko was back, that my familiar was safe and sound and appeared not to have suffered any lasting harm.

"And?" he said when I was finished.

"And what?"

"And what are you not telling me?"

I shrugged. There wasn't any easy way. There weren't any easy words. "It's not enough for me to tell you about all this after it happens. I need someone who can share it with me. Be there with me."

"Be with you in the middle of the White House lawn?" he said wryly.

I shook my head, recognizing the question for what it was, a delicate deflection of pain. "I'm sorry, Will. I need more. I need someone who can be there in the magic, who can work with me, weaving power with power."

"I love you, Jane!" That was the first time he'd said the words. They lay in the room between us, stark. Raw. Edges all the sharper because they were true.

"And I love you, too," I said. That was true, as well. "But, Will, I can't share my magic with you. Having it separate, having it apart, makes me feel like I'm lying. Like I'm cheating."

"Are you?" I couldn't blame him for the anger inside his question. I couldn't be surprised when he asked what I'd been bracing for all along. "Have you slept with David since we met?"

I closed my eyes, then forced myself to open them, to meet his challenge. "No. Not since we met."

He heard the full accounting. He heard the truth. He heard what I didn't tell him, what I hadn't thought he needed to know.

He stared at me, and I watched the rigid anger slowly crumble in his jaw. I watched his shoulders slump. I watched him recognize reality. Absorb it. Accept it. He even managed a cracked half laugh. "It's really *not* me. It's you."

My heart swelled with love for him. "I'm sorry," I whispered. And then I reached across the table with both hands. I touched his eyeglass frames, adjusted them to sit evenly on his face. "I'm really, truly sorry."

He pulled away, as I had known he would. He pushed his chair back from the table. He jumped to his feet, shoved his hands into his pockets. "I've got to go," he said.

"Call me," I said.

"Yeah, I will."

"I mean it," I said. "When you're ready. When you want to talk."

"Right."

I didn't follow him to the door. It would have felt too much as if I was chasing him out of my cottage, out of my life. He didn't slam the door. He shut it gently, carefully. I waited until I was certain that he wasn't coming back and then I stalked into the living room. I put my back against the oaken door and slid down slowly, letting it catch me as I started to cry.

It took a long time to get all of the tears out. These weren't mojito therapy tears that could be laughed away with a best friend. These weren't child tears that could be wiped dry by a caring mother, a dedicated grandmother.

These were tears of frustration, of anger, of failure. I hadn't lied to Will. I did love him. I wanted to be with him. I wanted to bring him into my crazy, magic, mixed-up life.

But I couldn't. And I wanted something else, something more, something I still wasn't certain I could ever really have.

I stood up. I made myself walk into my bathroom. I washed my face, combed my hair. I stopped in my bedroom and collected David's jacket. I snagged my key chain from the bowl beside the phone.

There was no need to tell Gran that I was taking her Lincoln. If she needed to drive anywhere, she could always rely on her husband.

As soon as I left the city behind, the night time roads were dark. The interstate had overhead lights, but the county roads were lit only by moonlight. Only by moonlight and the Lincoln's high beams as I sped toward the Pennsylvania border.

This time, I found the final turnoff on the first try. A little bit of magic, a little bit of memory—the side road glinted in the night like a beacon. The grass was still high, waving in a midnight breeze.

The house sat quietly in its clearing. No lights were on. The porch looked deserted, its glider abandoned. I listened to the Lincoln's engine, ticking its way to coolness. I forced myself to open my door, to climb out of the car.

I hugged David's jacket to me as I took a deep breath of the cold country air. The smell of wood smoke was heavy; I could see a faint stream curling from the chimney. I smiled, wondering how much exertion had gone into the split wood that fed the fire.

A shadow whispered toward me from the porch. I'd been wrong. The glider had not been abandoned. It had held Spot, the black lab whose sleek body almost disappeared in the night. The dog shoved his head against my arm, levering his nose against my side until I reached down to pet him. His tail moved like a scythe, and a faint whine rose in the back of his throat. I said, "Okay, then. Let's go."

My voice was a lot shakier than I expected it to be.

The dog led me around the back of the house, to the kitchen door. He butted his head against my arm again, clearly telling me to knock. I wanted to resist. I wanted to run back to Gran's car. I wanted to flee back to the known and the safe, to my cottage, to the Peabridge, to everything I understood.

I raised my hand and knocked.

David was waiting for me.

Of course, he was waiting for me. I'd driven a full-sized automobile down his driveway, headlights blazing. I'd crunched on the walkway from the front of the house to the back.

I was his witch.

"Hello," he said, and the greeting was so ordinary, so common, it stole my breath away.

"Hello," I said. I held out his jacket. "I wanted to bring this back to you."

He took it and stepped aside so that I could move into the kitchen. The only lights gleamed from under the cabinets; the entire room looked as if it had been sleeping peacefully until I'd arrived. Two goblets glinted on the center island, flanking a tall green bottle. David had already poured. He passed one of the glasses to me, asking unnecessarily, "Wine?"

I nodded. The crimson liquid smelled spicy, rich.

Spot whined, and David pointed toward the dog-bed in the corner of the room. He backed up the gesture with an authoritative flash of his hand, a silent command. The dog's nails clicked on the tile floor as he complied, and the lab sighed as if he'd completed one of Hercules's labors when he sank onto the plaid padding.

I followed David into the picture-perfect living room. He draped his jacket over the back of one chair. I forced myself to sit on the couch and was relieved—terrified—when he sat beside me. I swallowed wine noisily. Flames crackled in the fireplace in front of us.

He watched me over the rim of his own goblet, matched my motion as I set my glass on the wooden coffee table in front of us. I looked around the room, studying its perfect precision, its spartan, designer-certified shelves. "There's a problem," I said.

"Yes?" I could smell his shampoo on his hair. I remembered the sight of him, still wet from his shower, wrapped in the gray towel that had revealed far more than it had hidden.

I forced myself to take a steadying breath. "I don't think there's enough space on the shelves."

He looked over his shoulder, studying the shelves in question. When he turned back to me, he settled closer. I wanted to push away, to restore the distance between us, but there was nowhere else to go. I felt like I had risked everything on that single sentence; I had dealt every card in my deck, and I had nothing left to play. I couldn't breathe while I waited for him to reply.

"Enough space?" he asked.

"For all the books in my basement." My answer quivered.

"And why would we need to fit all of your books on these shelves?" He sounded amused. Tolerant. Patient.

I forced myself to deliver my answer, forced my words past the distraction of his body so close to mine. "I'll have to take them with me when I move out of the cottage. When Kit takes my job. She'll need the place to live, since I'm sure Evelyn won't be any more generous with her salary than she was with mine."

"You can't move out here." My heart stuttered. David went on. "What about your grandmother? She needs you nearby."

That answer was easy. "She's got Uncle George. Besides, Nuri can summon us if anything happens."

"And Clara?" There was a clear smile behind his words now.

"She's going back to Sedona. Anyway, I think she and I just might get along better with some space between us. A lot of space."

"And Melissa?" He shrugged like he was trying to solve one of the central problems of the universe. "It'll be a lot harder to have mojito therapy all the way out here."

I thought of my best friend, sweetheart roses clutched to her chest. "Somehow, I think mojito therapy is going to be a lot rarer from here on out."

David was enjoying this. "I thought you *liked* being a librarian?"

"I do!" My nerves made me sound as if I was arguing. A log on the fire spat as it settled lower, sending up a little geyser of sparks. I tried again. "I do. But I've pretty much done what I can do at the Peabridge. It's time to try something else."

"Something else?" He stretched, as if he were disinterested, and then he settled back on the couch, closer yet. His arm trailed along the back of my sofa cushion. "There aren't too many jobs out here in the country."

"I could run a school."

"A school?" He actually laughed out loud. I felt his fingertips on my shoulder, inching along to trace the neckline of my blouse.

"A school for witches," I said defiantly. "A training ground for women like me. Like Gran and Clara. Witches who don't want to work the Coven way."

"The Coven way," he repeated, and I felt the pulse of his fingertips against the hollow of my throat.

The magic flared between us just before he kissed me. I'd felt it building, gathering, coalescing even as my body responded to his touch. But I think that both of us were surprised when it snapped along the witch-warder bond like an electric shock. Like an electric shock—startling and brilliant, but without the pain.

"I'm sure you can work out something," he whispered against the corner of my mouth. "Some sort of school."

"With you," I said, pulling him closer. My fingers tingled where they met his flesh. "With your help."

And then he was pulling me to my feet. He was settling his palm against the flat of my back. He was steering me toward the stairs with an urgency that made me want to laugh. He was answering the way that I had wanted him to answer, that I had *yearned* for him to answer, during my long, nighttime drive.

But I stopped at the foot of the steps.

I wanted to go with him. I wanted to return to his bed. I wanted to erase the past three months of doubt and regret.

But I was still afraid. I was still afraid that I would wake up alone in that perfectly orderly bedroom. That I would come downstairs to find David silent and withdrawn. That I would find Warder-David in his place, grim and protective.

"Jane," he whispered, and he swept aside my hair to kiss the back of my neck.

The shock went through us again, the electric power, the promise of our magic. This time, though, he did not pull away. He folded his arms around me, pulled me back until I could feel his heart pounding in his chest.

My pulse raced to match his. Power pounded through my body, carried by every cojoined heartbeat. Our bond was a physical thing, enfolding us like golden robes. My power was melded to his; my strength was meshed with his. We were two astral beings, each drawing on the power of the ancients, separate, but inalterably together.

This was the man who had seen me—who had seen to the magical core of me and beyond—in Ariel's magic circle on the White House lawn. This was the man who had stepped toward me, who had locked his gaze to mine, who had raised his arms to protect me, to join with me, against all the power arrayed against us.

His warder's magic beat around us, through us, his strong and driving energy mixing with the swirling force of my own witchy powers, giving, taking, until I could no longer be sure which magic was mine, which was his.

This was why I could never have stayed with Will. This feeling, this force. Will could love me, always. He could honor me. He could respect me. But he could never share this feeling, this magical awareness, this perfect, golden perception of all the world around me, within me. No matter what he did, Will would never share this witchy part of me.

But David could. He did. He felt it, too.

I heard his breath catch in his throat. I forced myself to pull away from him just a little, just enough that I could turn to face him. I made myself look into his eyes, recognize the expression there. The love. The chance that he was taking with me, the vulnerability that he had never shown to another person, to another witch.

"David—" I started to say, and his name wove into our power.

"Jane," he said, closing the conversation, wrapping it back

around us, binding us together more completely, more honestly, than I'd ever been bound to any man—Will, or the Coven Eunuch, or the Imaginary Boyfriend, or all the other missteps I'd taken to arrive here, now.

Now I knew that, despite his playful seduction in front of the fireplace, David proposed more than a magic-charged romp. He was offering more than a warder's required service. He was making a broader statement, announcing a deeper plan. We'd reached a new place, a different place, a place far scarier than any I had seen with him in two long years of attraction and respect, of flirtation and regret.

I turned away, suddenly overwhelmed by the gravity of it all. David was changing the rules. David was breaking down walls. My warder, who had always done what was right. My warder, who had always pulled back, always pulled away, even when I had not wanted him to do so. My warder, who had always been gone in the morning.

Terrified to accept what he was offering, I let myself be distracted by Spot, who was shifting noisily in his plaid bed. I scanned the kitchen through the doorway, glancing at the back door, looking for an escape, for a separation I was not at all sure I wanted.

I spied a brown paper bag that I had missed on the kitchen counter. A knife sat beside it, serrated edge barely visible in the dim light. "What's that?" I asked.

David answered with a kiss that left me clutching at his arms for balance, a physical answer to an emotional question that I had not even known I still wanted to, needed to, ask.

Sheets of magic tumbled around us, so completely inter-twining our powers that I could no longer say where my witchy abilities ended, where his warder's tricks began. The bond between us expanded in my consciousness, the rope that had pulled him to me across time and space, the tie that had forged between us when I first stumbled on the magical books in my basement.

This was what I needed. This was the rapport I craved. This was the balance, the nature, the meaning—this was the most that witchcraft and love combined could be.

"Sesame bagels," he whispered against my throat, turning me back toward the stairs. "For breakfast."

★ ★ ★ ★ ★

Jane and David seem settled for a while, but there's
still some magic being discovered in this world!
Don't miss Mindy Klasky's new book coming next year.
THERE'S THE RUB

Melissa Senate

A *New York Times* article lists fifteen questions couples should ask before marrying. Ruby Miller and her fiancé, Tom Truby, have questions one to fourteen *almost* covered. It's question fifteen that has the Maine schoolteacher stumped: *Is their relationship strong enough to withstand challenges?*

Challenges like…Ruby's twin sister, Stella. The professional muse, flirt and face reader thinks Ruby is playing it safe. And that the future Mrs. Ruby Truby will die of boredom before her first anniversary or thirtieth birthday, whichever comes first.

Challenges like…sexy maverick teacher Nick McDermott, Ruby's secret longtime crush, who confesses his feelings for her at her own engagement party.

Questions to Ask Before Marrying

"Senate's prose is fresh and lively." —*Boston Globe*

Available wherever trade paperbacks are sold!

RDIMS89560TR